THE HOURGLASS
THRONE

Praise for *The Hanged Man*

"Edwards skillfully blends rigorous characterization with political intrigue, action, and haunting worldbuilding in the exciting follow-up to 2018's *The Last Sun*. Edwards conjures a believably dangerous setting filled with tarot imagery and supernatural menaces. Series fans and new readers alike will be hooked."

—*Publishers Weekly*

A thrilling and satisfying follow-up to *The Last Sun*, *The Hanged Man* proves that K.D. Edwards is the real deal. The story shines with unique and complex world-building, stellar writing, and a fast-paced plot that is rounded out with humor and heart-felt emotional moments. I didn't want the book to end!"

—Tammy Sparks, BOOKS, BONES & BUFFY

"Much like *The Last Sun*, *The Hanged Man* is a quest story, and yet it is much more than that. It is theater of the mind. It is the finest form of escapism I have ever read. There are no proper terms to express how powerfully this book affected me . . . *The Hanged Man* receives 5 out of 5 Sigils!!!"

—Ben Ragunton, TG Geeks podcast

Praise for *The Last Sun*

"Edwards's gorgeous debut presents an alternate modern world that is at once unusual and familiar, with a grand interplay of powers formed by family and the supernatural. Intriguing characters, a fast-paced mystery, and an original magical hierarchy will immediately hook readers, who will eagerly await the next volume in this urban fantasy series."

—*Library Journal* STARRED review

"Edwards's debut combines swashbuckling action, political intrigue, and romance into a fast-paced and enjoyable adventure . . . Intriguing worldbuilding and appealing characters set the stage and pique the reader's interest for sequels."

—*Publishers Weekly*

"Jaw-dropping worldbuilding, fluent prose, and an equal blend of noir and snark make for that most delicious of fantasy adventures, an out-of-this-world tale that feels pressingly real. A smart and savvy joy."

—A. J. Hartley, *New York Times*–bestselling author of the Steeplejack series and the Cathedrals of Glass series

"A fast, fun, urban fantasy in a wonderfully original world, full of slam-bang magic and interesting characters."

—Django Wexler, author of *The Thousand Names*

THE HOURGLASS THRONE

THE TAROT SEQUENCE | BOOK THREE

K. D. EDWARDS

Published 2022 by Pyr®

Cover illustration © Micah Epstein
Cover design by Jennifer Do
Cover design © Start Science Fiction

Inquiries should be addressed to
Start Science Fiction
221 River Street
9th Floor
Hoboken, NJ 07030
PHONE: 212-431-5455
WWW.PYRSF.COM

10 9 8 7 6 5 4 3 2 1

ISBN: 978-1-64506-055-0 (paperback) | ISBN: 978-1-64506-071-0 (eBook)

Printed in the United States of America

This novel, nay series, would not exist without my writing group.
A massive thank you to Scott Reintgen and CS Cheely, in particular, for getting
me across the finish line, along with all group members past and present:
Blakely (our Founder), CS, Scott, Paige, Ali, Jen, York, Caitlin, Tyler,
Kwame, Emmalea, Taylor, Susan, Rhett, Jodi, Ben, Sara, Dan, Debbie,
Del, Glenn, and honorary member Mac.

For content warnings on my books, as well as access to a series glossary and free
between-the-novels stories and novellas, please visit my website at:
http://kd-edwards.com/extra-content/

CONTENTS

THE REJUVENATION CENTER

"—ucking cut you!"

I slapped Brand's hand away from the radio dial and swerved back into my lane. "Why do you always jump to cutting?" I demanded. "Use your words if you don't like the radio station I picked."

Since the pop rock song was off and he'd got his way, Brand settled into the passenger seat with a smirk.

I was driving our beat-up old Saturn toward a corner of the city almost exactly due south of Sun Estate. While summer brought the earliest sunrises of the year to New Atlantis, we were still a half-hour shy of one. The air around us was the gray-tinged black of pre-dawn.

Nothing short of an emergency would have normally got me out of bed before sunrise, let alone two hours before it, which is when Lady Priestess had called with an urgent request. All I knew was that an unknown barrier had appeared around the rejuvenation center, and they couldn't reach anyone inside by phone or text.

I'd given myself thirty minutes to add a few stealth and infiltration spells to my sigils—at her vague recommendation—while an even-grumpier Brand went from room to room assembling his leathers and chest harness.

"It takes so much longer to get out the door now," he yawned. "I miss Half House."

"No, you don't. You've got dozens of people to boss around now."

"I've got dozens of people who need to be bossed around because their heads haven't grown out their ass yet, which is the state they'd need to be in to do what they should be doing without being told. Why didn't Lady Priestess tell us any more about what to expect? Were there any background noises?"

"What sort of noises did you expect me to hear?"

"I don't know," he said. "Scions-clutching-their-pearls angst? Man-being-eaten-by-crocodile screams? We usually know more before we take a job."

"Good thing it's not a job then. Can you hand me my coffee?"

I waited a beat, but no coffee edged into my peripheral. As streetlamps sliced blades of yellow across the windshield, I gave him a quick look. "What?"

"This isn't a job?" he asked.

"No. It's a favor. I guess that's the sort of thing Arcana do for each other."

"So we're not getting paid?" he asked, louder now. "Is this the sort of thing we can look forward to now that you're a part of the Arcanum?"

Okay, maybe he wasn't grumpier than me, because my temper flared. "How should I know? Did you see me leave the last Arcana meeting with an orientation manual, Brand? There was no orientation."

"Jesus fucking Christ," he said, but handed me my coffee.

I sighed into the plastic lid. "Thank you."

He waited until I'd taken a long, caffeinated sip. "But she emphasized stealth spells? That's all you have stored in your sigils—stealth spells?"

"Hell no. Most of my sigils were already topped up. Oh! Addam lent me a sigil with Telekinesis in it. Well, I stepped on his head by accident first, but then he woke up and lent it to me." I predicted the turn of Brand's face. "Air conditioning is out in our room, so we slept on the floor. But, hey, Telekinesis. That'll be fun if I get to use it."

He flicked a look my way that had us both almost smiling, because let's be honest: we'd been cooped up on the estate for a while, and the truth was that we really, really hoped we'd get to use more than stealth skills.

We'd relocated to Sun Estate months ago. New Atlantis had been no different from the rest of the world: we struggled with the birth of a novel coronavirus. A heavy investment in magical remedies had allowed us to contain our outbreak so we no longer needed masks or social distancing.

But we'd also had to close our borders and cut off contact with the human world until they found their own vaccine solution.

Personally, I'd spent the quarantine months focusing on little except the rehabilitation of Sun Estate. I'd picked up my father's mantle and was the Arcana of the Sun Throne, and I needed a base of operations. I needed a compound. I needed, eventually and pointedly, a heavily *fortified* compound.

Kicking out all the ghosts and ghouls that had taken up residence in the ruins of Sun Estate was an expensive and tedious process. Every literal square foot of safe ground we gained was measured in hundreds of dollars and hours of spell-work, largely using an incredibly difficult and special magic taught to me by Lady Priestess—which explained why I was on her radar. But we'd finally reached the point where a sizable percentage of the estate was safe behind wards and other protection.

We'd moved the Dawncreeks onto the estate as well—Anna, Corbie, Layne, and a newly rejuvenated Corinne. Anna, Max, and Quinn spent half a week with us, and half a week at Magnus Academy learning how not to stab someone with the wrong fork during a formal dinner. I had just started holding regular court sessions, which meant I had homework of my bloody own. Things, in all, had been very domestic lately.

"So you and Addam are dressing in each other's sigils now?" Brand asked.

"I'm not going to be baited."

"Just making conversation. Take a left up there."

"It's easier if we—"

"*Left,*" he barked. "Look at the windows on that building. There are green and amber lights around the corner."

His instincts were always quicker than mine. I turned left, and sure enough, there was commotion around the bend in the block ahead of us.

"Does that mean you don't like Addam being around so much?" I asked him after a pause.

"Don't you dare fucking use me for cold feet."

"I don't have cold feet! I was just worried it might feel weird. I'm *checking in* with you. Addam's practically moved into the estate."

"Yeah, and it was weird the first time he wandered into the kitchen in his boxer briefs. Now it's called morning."

"He still hasn't *officially* joined the Sun Throne. He's still technically a member of Lady Justice's court."

Brand turned in his seat so hard that the seatbelt groaned. "Why do you sound worried?"

"I didn't say—"

Brand tapped his head, indicating it hadn't been anything I'd said out loud.

But amber and emerald lights were now dancing across the hood of our car. Ahead of us, just around a corner, was a line of wooden sawhorses blocking off the mouth of an alley.

Immortality was a myth. Sort of.

Through closely guarded rejuvenation magics perfected by Lady Priestess's court, Atlanteans could make their bodies go on forever. The mind was another matter entirely, though, which is what made immortality a myth in practice. After half a millennium, most people, one way or another, found ways to die.

I always suspected that those who lasted longer, like the Tower or (reputedly) the Empress, were just smarter at knowing how to reinvent themselves. I suspected the trick was building a mental firebreak between shitty life experiences in order to find the desire or motivation to attempt another hundred years on the same rickety roller coaster.

That said, nearly all Atlanteans of even modest means took advantage of Lady Priestess's magic. She practiced rejuvenation at two centers on the island, and the particular center before us was the premier facility, where heavily funded courts sent their people for complete life-cycle rejuvenation. It was a process that involved several stages and weeks of residence.

Put together, this created a number of uncomfortable scenarios and a dozen times as many questions. The building treated a clientele of powerful people. The idea that someone had created an uncrossable barrier around the facility wasn't nearly as worrisome as the question of *how* and *why*.

The guarda official who appeared at the driver's window went from bored to formal in a finger snap when I told him my name. I saw him give the Saturn the side-eye, but he ordered one of his people to valet park the car.

"Crowd forming," Brand murmured when we were on the sidewalk. He nodded in the direction of people in clean uniforms by a nearby sawhorse.

The officer heard that and said, "Morning bakery crew. They were the ones who discovered the barrier and called it in."

"Still no contact with anyone inside?" Brand asked.

"Nothing. No reply to texts or calls—we're not even sure the messages are passing through. Lady Priestess herself is on the scene. I can—"

"I am," Lady Priestess said from behind him. "Here, that is. I'll speak with Lord Sun now."

The officer bowed his way out of the conversation as Lady Priestess stepped forward. She was a short woman edging into middle age, with straight brown hair and cat-eye eyeglasses that pulsed with the power of a sigil. Her voice was as wispy as her wandering attention, which begged to be underestimated.

"The barrier is around the corner. Just down there. I've tried all the tricksy magics I had on me, but nothing seems to work." She said this while staring intently at Brand, who tensed a bit and shifted his weight to the balls of his feet.

"Has the guarda ascertained how far the barrier goes beneath the ground?" I asked. "Or whether it's a dome or wall?"

"Details," she said, waving a hand airily, and still staring at Brand. She said, with something like pride, "I have had over three dozen children. None of them have ever had a Companion."

And then she turned and walked away.

Brand and I waited a good ten seconds before exchanging glances.

"Did she just brag that she's never bought or stolen a human baby?" Brand whispered.

"That would mean she just called me a kidnapper," I said.

"I wish. Kidnappers usually have plans. You can't even match your fucking socks. Not to press a button on that whole kidnapping thing, I mean."

"Not to," I agreed, but added the weight of the comment to everything else piled on my shoulders.

"Lord Sun, Lord Saint John," a young woman called. She rolled over in an electric wheelchair from the direction Lady Priestess had vanished. Her hair was short and bleached platinum, and she wore an expensive business suit. She craned her head up at me and said, "My name is Bethan. I'm Lady Priestess' second oldest. She asked me to answer any questions you might have."

The Papess Throne was renowned for its fertility. I'd heard somewhere that Lady Priestess staffed her senior roles with direct descendants only, to keep attempted coups within the family.

"What do you know, Bethan? And call me Rune."

"Brand," Brand said.

"My lords. I'm afraid we have more questions than answers at this point. When the morning staff tried to enter through the back, they encountered the barrier. My mother and I were on-site within the hour, and we've tried what techniques we had on hand to break through. We were unsuccessful. We tried all the elements. We tried to phase through it, and to establish a portal to the other side. Nothing has worked."

"How far up or down does it go?" Brand asked. "Do you have drone footage?"

"It's a dome on top. The drones didn't spot movement in the windows, or anyone in the interior courtyard. We can see that there is electricity inside, though, which is something. As for underground, we sent people into tunnels that extend below the facility and join several buildings in the area. The barrier walls are present there as well, albeit curved. We suspect the totality of the barrier is less a dome than a sphere."

"Has it injured anyone?" I asked.

"No. Touching it causes no effect. It's simply . . . there."

"And you want me to try breaking through?"

Bethan smiled. "My mother appears to think you or Lord Tower may be able to help, yes."

"You called the Tower?" Brand said before he could help himself. Then he gritted his teeth. "He's behind me. He's behind me right now, isn't he?"

I looked over my shoulder. "Nope."

"Thank fucking God," he said under his breath. "It's too early."

"What do we know of the people who are supposed to be inside the building?" I asked.

"We have eighteen clients on record from multiple courts. An evening staff of twenty-one, and an overnight staff of thirteen. We haven't been able to pinpoint our last point of contact, but I have people trying to contact the evening staff, who would have departed by eight o'clock last night. If we can account for them, it helps narrow the incident window."

Eighteen clients across multiple courts. High-value individuals from different houses. This had the making of a diplomatic incident. I understood now why the Tower had been contacted. If something had happened to the clients, it wouldn't send ripples through the city so much as fracture lines.

"Show me the barrier," I said.

Bethan dipped her head and escorted us away from the guarda activity. Her chair made almost no sound at all as it moved. She saw Brand's glance at the crowd and said, "We're keeping the employees and guarda out of the building's sight-lines."

"Then you'll want the guarda to turn off their patrol lights. The colors are reflecting everywhere."

"Not that you're going to keep this quiet much longer," I added. "Morning commute is starting. In a half hour, we'll be swamped with foot traffic."

"Still, I'll have the lights turned off for now," she murmured, and began typing a message on her phone. She wore mesh, half-finger gloves that left her thumbs exposed.

As we headed down an alley that connected with the side of the rejuvenation facility, Brand pulled a set of compact binoculars from one of his pockets. Layne had bought them as a gift with their first hospital paycheck, now that they'd been moved from unpaid hospital volunteer to part-time aide. Their necromantic abilities had allowed them complete immunity to the coronavirus, making them a critical asset in the early days of the hospital's pandemic response.

While the binoculars made sense now, Brand found a lot of other occasions to whip them out and brag—coffee shops, imminent postal carrier deliveries, teenager acne watch. I suppose that's why I didn't mention he was about to bump into the invisible magic barrier.

"Fucking hell!" he said, and recoiled.

"So we can confirm it causes no physical trauma," I said.

"Did you see that there?" he accused.

"Absolutely not," I said. I made a show of squinting hard at what was, to me, a wall of flaxen air, not unlike the dimness of sunlight on a cloudy day. "Ah. There. There it is."

Beyond the barrier was the edge of a tree-lined plot of grass that led to the front entrance. The building was like a block letter O, with an open area in the middle. It was not a translocation, oddly enough. The center was custom built over the last ten years, using bricks baked from the healing mud of Italy's Bormio region.

"Give me a minute, please," I murmured, and stepped right to the edge of the barrier. I closed my eyes and tilted my head, pushing my face into the morning's dampness. The magic in front of me was strong. Wickedly strong—maybe stronger than anything I'd seen outside the Convocation's own protections when the Arcanum was in session.

I'd seen Lord Tower crack barriers before. I was not sure I could. Then again, Lady Priestess and her people hadn't had luck either. I could live with failure in numbers.

I looked back down the alley as two people turned into sight. One strode forward with definitive, advancing footsteps; the other made no noise.

"Rune," Lord Tower said. "Brand."

"Where's Corinne?" Mayan, Lord Tower's Companion, asked.

Brand froze—he knew Mayan was aiming at a target, he just didn't know where the target was placed.

"Corinne is home with the kids," I said slowly.

"The trained Companion who spent over eight weeks in this facility is home," Mayan summarized. "With the children."

I gave Brand a look that said, *Fuck?* Brand gave me a look back that said, *Fuck!*

"We picked a small party for the infiltration," I explained.

Mayan gave Brand a good hard stare. "I'm establishing a command center. One of my people will be on comms. The link will be magic—light-based—which we think will work better than wireless tech. Excuse me while I make arrangements."

"You bring out such a playful side in my Companion," Lord Tower said to Brand, as both Mayan and Bethan excused themselves.

"Can you see that barrier right there?" Brand asked, pointing behind him.

"You'll need to call on deep magic first," I said quickly.

The Tower flicked a look at me, flicked his eyes upwards in what may or may not have been an eye roll, and said, "Oh. Yes. There it is."

"Can you tell who made it? Or how it was made?" I asked.

He walked forward until the tip of his shiny black shoe touched the point where the barrier curved into the earth. He reached out and placed a fingertip along the dim glow. "Arcana-level work," he finally said. "Maybe a principality?"

"Not an Arcana?" I asked.

"No Arcana I know did this. There are very few other options beyond principalities, and of those most are so remote as to be implausible."

Principalities were simply Arcana without formal courts. The lack of thrones kept them from being true power centers in the city, but also afforded them a certain ability to operate under the radar.

"Do you have a suspicion about who or what created it?" I asked.

The Tower continued to run his eyes along the barrier—high and low. "You'd be surprised how many truly dangerous hypotheticals I monitor on a daily basis. Whether this is related to any of them? That's why I am here." He began to calmly remove the links from the cuff of his bespoke shirt.

"Would you mind, sir, if we discuss a practical matter," Brand said. The *sir* was like a road flare. "In the spirit of Arcana courts working together, it would be gauche to discuss compensation. But, being that we're a very young court, perhaps you may be able to share some equipment or field tech with us."

Brand didn't often make the Tower smile—or genuinely smile—but he got within shooting distance this time. "I thought you and Rune had already upgraded. Purchased . . . drones and earbuds?"

I sighed. "Corbie borrowed the earbuds without asking. He wanted to tell us what the bottom of the pool looked like."

"Then I must make a gift of the light-based technology Mayan is bringing. It's a new spell—I have hopes it'll outpace modern jamming technology. Although, Brandon, you should remember that Lady Priestess is now in your debt. In a way, that is compensation. A favor is a powerful thing."

"Of course, Lord Tower," I said, before Brand could share his views on favors between courts. (*"Fucking Monopoly money."*) I had a much better appreciation for favor banks than he did.

As he began to meticulously fold the sleeves of his shirt, the Tower asked, "Are you excited for your gala?"

He was referring to my formal, ridiculously public, and upcoming coronation. "I spend a good portion of every day thinking about it," I said honestly.

"I'm excited," Brand volunteered. Which would have been odd, if you didn't know that he'd been allowed to choose half of our gift registry.

"It's a necessity," the Tower said. "Formal exchanges of power like yours are public gestures, yes, but they're also one of the few times Arcana gather in a show of force. Ah. Mayan."

Mayan handed me two headsets while also extending his hand to Brand, saying, "Phone."

Brand hesitated a second, then passed his phone to Mayan.

"I'm downloading an app owned by the rejuvenation center. Lady Priestess has provided the both of you with full user permissions. The app has blueprints, client information, and also monitors patient vitals. Check those first, if the app works inside the barrier. I'll also have a field agent online with you. Her name is Julia."

"No," Brand said immediately. "No thank you. I have experience with her. She's not a team player."

The Tower said, "She annoys you."

"Yes," he said.

The Tower simply smiled and waited for Mayan to proceed. Brand hid his sulk behind his binoculars, staring at the facility.

"Julia can link you with any of us for private talk," Mayan said. "The public channel is restricted to people authorized by the Arcanum. For now that includes Julia, the two of you, Lord Tower, myself, and Bethan Saint Brigid."

"We'll try to establish contact as soon as we're inside," I said. "But we need to get through the barrier first. Since we've just got the two headsets here, I'm guessing that means you don't think we'll be able to bring the entire barrier down."

"I'm not sure yet, but at the very least, I can get the both of you inside," Lord Tower said. "You should—"

"Rune," Brand snapped. "Use Addam's searchlight trick. Third floor, three windows from my left."

Addam had invented a mix of cantrips—lens and light—that, when combined, created a piercingly strong beam. I didn't ask any questions because I felt Brand's urgency. I whispered the words and aligned the cantrips, and aimed the beam at my feet. When the magic stabilized and I had control of it, I swept it along the bricks of the rejuvenation center until Brand grunted and I hit the window he'd referenced.

Brand stared through his binoculars as Mayan pulled out a set of his own. The two studied whatever they saw quietly.

Brand said, "Looks like blood."

"Nice spot," Mayan said after a pause.

Brand held the binoculars to my eyes so I didn't need to drop my light. It took a second, but eventually my depth vision adjusted, and I saw it. Half a handprint on the lower edge of the glass pane. My light brought out the liquid red sheen.

Brand snapped the binoculars shut. "They have electricity inside. Even if they don't have outside communication, someone could be flicking the lights on and off, fucking Morse-coding us. But instead we have blood and barriers."

"Hostages?" Mayan murmured. His lips settled into a grimace. "Or bodies. Let's get you in there."

"I'll hold the barrier for you and Brand," Lord Tower said to me. "Find out what you can. I'll work on bringing the barrier down for larger forces. Brace yourselves."

The period for small talk was over, and I felt adrenaline washing through me. Lord Tower stalked up to the barrier. He undid the first button of his shirt, revealing a leather strap tied around a bundle of old, bent nails. He touched them, and the release of mass sigil magic nearly blew us off our feet.

Car alarms went off three seconds later, and an alley cat screeched. The magic gloving the Tower's hands was so hot I could see a mirage haze around his fingers. He lifted both hands, tensed, and then slammed them into the barrier.

For a second—for barely the inhale of a single breath—nothing happened. Then his fingers began to blister and burn. A bubble of blood appeared below one nostril, quickly turning into a thick red stream.

"Gods' teeth," he swore, and as he did, I began to smell cooked flesh. A low groan escaped his lips, and his eyes widened in surprise. It barely lasted a second until it firmed into resolve. His wrist muscles bunched as he increased the force of his push against the barrier.

"Can I help?" I said loudly.

"Be ready," he gasped. "Be . . . NOW!"

I saw a portion of the barrier thin to the palest of yellow. Since Brand couldn't see, I grabbed his nondominant hand and shouted, "In my tracks!"

I ran through the split in the barrier, Brand my shadow. As I passed the Tower, I saw his hands up close. The tips of two fingers were already gone.

"Clear!" I yelled the moment we were on the other side.

The Tower dropped the spell. He may have sagged back, but it was hard to tell, because Mayan was already behind him for support.

"Headsets," Brand said in a clipped voice. We divvied the sets up and adjusted them. He tapped the on button of his own pair and said, "Are you online Julie?"

"Oh, don't be an asshole," I whispered, because I knew enough of Julia from the Lovers raid to know she hated the name Julie.

"Julia here," she said, as unflappable as I remember.

"Julia, this is Lord Sun," I said. "I need a private link with Lord Tower. Right now."

"Understood. Hold."

Brand gave me a curious look, but let me have a moment. He stepped off to the side.

"Rune," I heard in my head.

There was a level of strain in the Tower's voice that made my heart skip. I said, "Don't be a hero. Get medical now."

He either breathed hard or chuckled. "That took . . . effort. I admit to having misgivings, now, about sending you in on your own."

"I'm never on my own," I said, and gave Brand's back a quick smile.

"I was speaking in the plural, and I am still concerned."

"Do you think this is one of your daily world-ending hypotheticals?"

A pause. Then, "I do not know. I'm calling for backup. Buy me time, Rune, but do not engage. Please."

My heart skips became drumbeats. I hadn't ever needed a level of backup *beyond* the Tower. He was the city's backup.

I switched back to the public channel, confirmed Julia was there, and joined Brand under a chestnut tree, where he was likely scoping our best point of entry.

We decided on the staff entrance. The path to it had less cover than the tree-filled acreage by the front doors, but also the least number of windows to be spotted from.

"So that's our plan?" Brand asked, tapping the mute button on his headset. "To buy Lord Tower time?"

I tapped my own mute button. "When the barrier comes down, they'll rush the building. If whoever created that barrier is still on-site, things will get loud fast."

"So we'll stay quiet, poke around, and try to figure out what we're going to end up fighting."

"Piece of cake," I overstated.

"Cake doesn't give the Tower a nosebleed," Brand said. He saw that I made a face. "What?"

"Did you see the Tower's hands?"

"What about the Tower's hands?"

"He lost some of his . . . er, fingers. The tips of them. They burned away."

Brand didn't even attempt a joke. All it took was a half-inhaled breath for him to understand the magnitude of that statement. He exhaled the word, *Fuck.*

We started moving toward the door. "Maybe we should try to get Corinne on the line, too," Brand said uncertainly as we crouched behind a hedge and duck walked. "Should we have woken her up?"

"Yes?"

"I'm just not used to having other people to think about when we go in the field," he said quietly in a rush.

"*Me too*," I hissed back in total agreement. "I was just getting used to having Addam to call on when the shit really hit the fan, and now we have people we're supposed to assign on a daily basis. Either management is good or it's fucking terrifying."

Brand unmuted his mic. "Jul . . . *Julia*, we're in sight of the door. There's a keypad."

"Obtaining code from Lady Saint Brigid. One moment."

Brand pulled out his phone while we waited and booted up the application that Mayan had downloaded. "They've got thumbnail photos of staff and guests. And . . . I see the vitals menu. Shit. This better not be working."

"Brand," Mayan said through the mic. Just that one word. Not unlike how Brand often just says my name as if it were an entire soliloquy.

"Yes, I know I'm live," Brand said testily. "And this app better be broken, or else you've got seventeen flat lines."

"This is Bethan Saint Brigid. I helped create the app. Are you looking at a menu that shows nine squares per screen? And are the squares blank, or truly showing a flat line?"

"Nine squares, and I can swipe up to see more. Eighteen squares total, seventeen flat lines and one blank. What does that mean?"

"It likely means seventeen deaths." Her voice sounded like chalk—dry and rasping. "If a square is blank, it means that person has either been removed from the premises, or the armband tracking their vitals has been disabled or removed. I . . . must speak with my mother. In the meantime, you can use bypass code 115599 to open almost any door except the center's vault."

"Can we track where the bodies are?" I asked, and Brand shot me a quick glance of approval.

"Not normally. There are privacy concerns. Our IT people could configure something, but as data is not passing through the barrier you'll likely find . . . what you're looking for before then."

Brand muted his mic and said, "Worst scavenger hunt ever."

We kept low and made for the door. Brand typed the bypass code into the keypad, and the light below the number zero flashed from red to green.

We each took a side. I shook my hand and sent a burst of willpower into my sabre, now curled into its wristguard form. The metal softened and stretched, then scraped over my calloused knuckles. It solidified into a sword hilt that could shoot firebolts on command.

I scanned high and far, Brand scanned low and near, and we went through the door.

"Clear," we both whispered in unison, and stepped into a cheerily painted employee area with hard floors and yellow walls. There were banks of lockers and coat hooks, and the air conditioning was set to arctic levels.

Moving low and slow, we advanced into a long, tiled corridor that headed into the public areas of the building, and also branched off to a large administrative office suite. We sifted into the suite first, at the headset advice of Bethan. She said the night manager shared an office with the daytime director.

The carpet and walls were teal with white trim. The main room had two desks. One was nearly buried under potted plants; the other was lined with bedazzled, framed pictures of a smiling girl in pigtails.

Brand tapped my shoulder and nodded toward a glass-walled office to our left. As he moved toward it, he nudged the mouse on each desk, checking to see if the computer was locked or open. All of them were locked—except for the monitor in the boss's office.

Brand sat at the desk and alt-tabbed between open applications. There were only two: email, and some sort of security interface.

"Purse on the chair," I said. "And there are sneakers under the desk. Maybe she changes into them when she leaves work?"

Brand looked over his shoulder, where I was hovering. He muted his mic. "So we're both going to do this? We can absolutely both do this, instead of having you stand guard at the door to watch for killers."

"We're also in danger the entire time you're making a long, sarcastic point, you know," I whispered, but went to stand guard at the door.

"Lady Saint Brigid," Brand said into his mic. "The night manager was looking at camera feeds in the building. The one in front of me is outside a room with a green door."

There was a quick, surprised intake of breath on the line. Bethan said, "That is extremely unusual. It sounds like a residence. To access that camera without good reason would be an unforgivable invasion of privacy."

"Do we have permission to scan recent emails?" Brand asked.

"Yes," Bethan said after a noticeable pause, maybe to consult her mother. "We trust your discretion."

It was good she did, because Brand had already started scrolling through emails.

"Check the sent box," I suggested, which got a grunt from Brand. I sneaked back over to the desk but kept my sabre pointed at the doorway. Brand had pulled up an email the night manager had sent.

"Who is Jane Bludrick?" I asked over the headset.

"The senior director," Bethan said. "She uses that office in the daytime."

"Your night manager sent a message to Bludrick. It says: *J, please pull the records on Jade. There's some tension around her. I'm concerned.*"

"Amongst each other, the staff refer to guests by their suite names," Bethan said. "The video, the door—that would be the jade suite. I'm going to step off the line for a moment and have my people pull up client records."

Brand tabbed back to the security interface. It took some trial and error, but he figured out how to tile the screen with all the building's cameras. There were over twenty-five squares, and over half of them showed blue error screens.

"We'll have to ask her if these cameras were always broken or offline," Brand murmured.

"If what is broken?" a new voice asked.

It took me a second to realize Lady Priestess was on the line. Brand clamped his lips shut and refused to speak, because he hated talking to Arcana he didn't know. So I said, "Most of the security cameras are offline."

"We do not operate with broken equipment," she said.

"Then we'll assume it's intentional," I said. I pointed to a series of images on the bottom. "That's downstairs, Brand. The building's physical plant is in the basement. All the cameras are working."

"If they'd infiltrated or extracted from there, why not destroy those cameras first? And I think those images are the attic—look how the roof slopes."

"So maybe not a basement or rooftop entry," I said.

"Or they were already here." Brand shook his head, frustrated. Too many variables. He expanded some of the screens at random, probably looking for bodies or signs of violence. We saw none.

Just as we decided to head further into the first floor, there were three clicks on our headsets. Julia said, "I've opened a private channel for the three of us. Just tap the bud three times. I thought you might need the privacy—the main channel is crowded."

"Oh," I said. "Thank you. That's a good idea."

"You're welcome, Lord Sun."

Brand was trying to give me a meaningful eye roll about Julia's efficiency, but I pretended I couldn't see. We both triple-clicked back to the main line.

"There's a cafeteria and spa on this floor," Brand told our audience. "We're moving there now."

We backtracked to the main corridor.

"Should we go check that jade room?" I asked.

"Let's clear floors as we go. Residences are on three; the medical units are on two. We could see if there are records on this person creating *tension.*"

I started to agree with him, but Brand's hand shot up. He stiffened, turned his hand into a knife blade, and slashed it to my left.

"Holy *shit,*" I whispered as I saw what he did.

Sabre aimed, I stepped into a small room with thick cement walls. There was a built-in series of locked slots, not unlike safety deposit boxes. And dominating the room was a massive vault door. The door was open and hung at an angle. The hinges on the upper right had popped loose, and, at about chest-height, the metal near the opposite edge was ragged and torn.

"Those are finger marks," Brand whispered. He fit his hand into the indentations. "Not weapon marks. Not claws. Just hand strength."

"Lady Saint Brigid, your vault is compromised," I said.

"Please, call me Bethan. Did you say finger marks?"

"The door was torn clear. What sorts of things did you keep in the vault? Could that be the reason for whatever is happening?"

"There would be a small supply of currency, for daily needs. But the vault is mainly used to store client sigils. We do not allow sigil spells on the premises—we don't want anything to interfere with the rejuvenation magics on the second floor. But . . . Why take them? You can't steal sigils."

That was close to the truth, but not precise. Sigil ownership was a complicated bond, affected by ancient magics not dissimilar to that which enforced our vows and oaths. Sigils could be bought and sold. They could be inherited. And they could even be won through the death or defeat of anyone who had a claim on the sigil, so long as that claim wasn't first shared with others.

I muted my microphone. Brand did the same. We looked at each other for a long moment, but it turned out no words were necessary. We both knew that absolute conquest and flat vital signs opened the door to an entirely plausible theory. They'd figure it out themselves soon enough. We unmuted our mics and walked into the vault.

There was enough room inside for both of us, with space to spare. Everything was in disarray. Bins had been overturned, their contents scattered. Objects—*sigils*—littered the ground. I crouched and lightly ran my fingers across a corncob pipe, a tortoise shell monocle, some plain metal discs.

"Interesting," I said.

"All of these baskets are empty," Brand said. "Those are sigils on the ground?"

"They are, and they're really . . . specific. They look like junk, actually. Not very fashionable."

"Says the man with a cock ring on his thigh," Brand said, and the fact that he hit his mute button first was the only reason I didn't punch him in the kidney.

"They're random," I continued in a firm voice. "It's like . . ."

"Like someone picked what they wanted. Like they were shopping. If I was robbing sigils I'd take them all. A corncob pipe can still be used to light people on fire."

"Are you muting, Brand?" Mayan asked.

Brand scowled, but unmuted. "The vault was rifled, and plenty of sigils were left behind. Whatever happened, it feels . . . personal? Amateurish."

"We'll run an inventory," Bethan said. "It'll be easy enough to find out what's missing."

"We're going to head toward the—"

An intercom system gently pinged overhead. Lady Priestess said, "Good morning, guests. I hope you had an enjoyable night's sleep. The facilities are officially open, and your experience is our most singular purpose. I'll now ask LaShawna to read today's news."

The programmed message ended in silent news-lessness.

Over the com, Lady Priestess said, "I was told a recording of my voice would make people feel welcome."

The vault didn't have any more to tell us—though I did pause to slip fingers into the indentations on the door, which were smaller than mine.

Back in the corridor, we slowly advanced through the first floor, passing closed spa, boutique, and retail suites. The only space that was open and accessible was a cafeteria that was much too upscale to be called a cafeteria. Inlaid coral lettering above the door called it the *Commissary*.

"There," Brand whispered, pointing to a table with a glass of wine on it. "Awkward seating, there's a better view by the window, but someone wanted walls at their back. And . . . blood."

I stepped around him and looked at the bottle of red wine on the table, along with the crystal wineglass with wide hips. There were spatters and smears of blood along the tabletop.

"Someone sat here for a late-night glass of wine? They were hurt and then bled?" I guessed. "Not much blood though."

"Rune," Brand said, in the tone he used when he wanted me to look more closely. I noticed that he'd also muted his mic.

I bent close to the wineglass. It wasn't just spattered with droplets of blood. There were bloody fingerprints on it. I touched a finger against one of the larger droplets on the tabletop and saw that it was gelatinous—old enough to still be liquid, but not fresh. And . . .

Ahh. And there were smears under the glass.

"Someone sits down and gets hurt," Brand said. "How does blood get *under* the glass? Play it back again, but imagine someone already covered in blood sitting down and casually drinking a glass of wine. Imagine that someone being our killer—what does it take to sit still and relax after something like that?"

"Are you muting again?" Mayan said. "Explain what you're seeing."

Brand took a quick breath through his nostrils, unmuted his mic, and said, "Julia, private channel with Mayan Saint Joshua, please."

"Connected," Julia said.

"You're leaving it on mute," Mayan immediately criticized.

"I am," Brand agreed. "And maybe fucking remember that I know how a fucking headset works, and maybe fucking think we're maybe fucking saying something or seeing something the Tower wouldn't appreciate us saying on a public line. Or maybe we're trying to minimize dialogue while we're trapped in a barrier with a killer."

"Julia, please return us to an open line," Mayan said. Then, brittle, "Brandon Saint John will update us as it becomes convenient."

Brand gave the glass another squint, then angled his gaze upwards. "I don't like this. We're not going upstairs with a target on our fu—on our backs. We're maintaining radio silence and moving to a private channel with Julia. She can pass you the running commentary."

No one had time to protest, because the Tower immediately said, "Proceed."

"There is more information first," Bethan said quickly. "We have the guest log. I can identify the families—" She stopped, a pause so slick it may not have even happened. "And names of those involved."

This was Atlantis. We were not human. I didn't blame Bethan—the living were always a far greater threat than the dead. I'd be more worried about which families had lost loved ones today, too, as opposed to the currently theoretical survival of the actual kin.

"How many guests are throne affiliated?" I asked.

"Is that relevant right now?" Lady Priestess asked.

"Only to see if it affects me," I said bluntly. "Lord Tower?"

"There's a male scion from a lesser house of the Crusader Throne. A female scion from a greater house in the Bone Hollows. And there's a member of a . . ." A half-second pause. "A family that once pledged to your father. The Ambersons."

"I know them," I said, surprised, and that sounded so naïve and stupid that I almost broke skin when I bit my lip.

"Who is staying in that green room?" Brand asked. "The jade room."

"That's the interesting thing," Bethan said. "It's what we call an Alan Smithee package. It's our highest degree of anonymity. It happens, sometimes, especially with Atlanteans who are technically under exile orders—

it's very expensive, and very secure. We maintain few personal identifiers beyond what we need to provide treatment."

And payment, I thought. They'd certainly maintain the method of payment for someone who could afford such complete privacy.

"We need to go upstairs," I said. "And Brand is right—we need to run silent. Lord Tower, I know you'll look into the court affiliations to see if what's happening is some sort of . . . I don't know, unsanctioned raid? Or politically related? But I've got to be honest, I'm seeing a lot of personality in the violence so far. I think we may be looking for one person."

"Understood," Lord Tower said. "Brand, you're positive that email you read said *her?* The troublesome client was called a *her?"*

"I'm positive," Brand said. He mouthed, *Because I can spell.*

"Very good. Rune, we'll hold contact unless imperative. Continue to buy me time."

Brand and I both triple-clicked our earbuds. "Julia?" I said.

"Yes, Lord Sun."

"Anyone else other than Julia?" I asked. *Silence.* I let out a gusty sigh. "That was annoying."

"It so fucking *was,*" Brand said in an aggrieved voice. "Is this what it's going to be like? Having all these voices in our head whenever we're on a mission?"

"You keep asking me if *this* is what it's going to be like," I said. "I have literally shared every moment of my existence with you. When did you see me sneak away and have different life experiences?"

He went over and checked the lobby through a big archway. An elaborate, double-headed stairway snaked along the walls for two levels above our heads. Shaking his head, he knifed his hand back in the direction we came. "There's a staff stairwell back that way. Let's take that. I want a look at the medical facilities."

So we began backtracking, clearing as we went all over again, because Brand insisted on stuff like that. The stairwell in the administrative section was eggshell-painted concrete and linoleum tiling, clean and functional.

We moved to the second floor. The medical units there looked like hotel hallways that had been accidentally decorated in healer equipment. The walls were freshly painted; heavy crystal vases held cut flowers barely a day away from their stems; and the magazines were all current.

"I smell smoke," I whispered, "and there's a crackling sound?"

"Electrical fire," Brand said, breathing through his nose. "There's burning plastic too. Julia, what's our twenty?"

"You're in the intake lobby. Ahead are the triage areas. Past that you'll start getting into the actual rejuvenation suites. I'm trying to patch into their system to see if any fire alarms have been triggered."

"We'll find out soon enough. We're running silent."

"Acknowledged," she said, and the headset went quiet.

Brand already had his knives out. I began touching my sigils. Angular facets of light appeared around my body, and a fever-flush raised the gooseflesh on my arms. I pulled Shield inside me, and sent Fire into my sabre hilt to strengthen its already powerful enchantments.

Balancing our body weight in a low crouch, we stepped around the nursing station and into a hallway. Examination areas were on each side, doors open, rooms empty. Ahead of us, the smell of smoke grew stronger, and a twitching gray flicker filled the nearby archway.

He swung left, I swung right, and I began tracking the corners of the room with my sabre to see if anything was prepared to jump out at us.

"Clear," Brand breathed. "And holy shit."

This room was filled with medical equipment and a row of reclining chairs. Under the electric hum of technology was something stronger and older, a type of magic unique to the Papess Throne.

At least three banks of hardware had been destroyed. Most of the monitors were dead, but one was flickering and sparking, filling the air with the toxic smell of burning plastic. Brand went over to one of the control boards. Torn wires trailed to a data port on the wall. A massive hard drive stuck out of the drywall about twenty feet away.

I spotted the blood first, spreading in a pool from behind a half-closed cloth curtain. We went over to it together, Brand four steps ahead to keep an eye on anything that may enter from the other side of the room. I lagged, thinking I'd be the one to check a pulse.

Then I saw the bodies.

"Jesus fucking wept," I swore, and stomach acid churned up my throat.

My brain tried to piece the body parts together in my head. I wasn't even sure how many bodies were actually piled there, because they were not *whole.*

And worse, so much worse, my brain decided to hijack this moment by making me remember *other* horrible and recent moments. Through memory's eyes, I saw a young man crawling into a safe. I saw a floor littered with gleaming white skeletons. Saw waves of power coming off a noose, ripping metal insects into existence.

Brand muted his mic and whispered, "Stay with me, Rune."

"Okay," I said, swallowing. I breathed through my nose—and now I could smell the copper and shit under the acridity of burning equipment. I dug my nails into the palms of my hand until the pain sent the memories scurrying. "Okay. Okay. Julia, confirm for the others that there are fatalities. Details to follow once we clear the floor."

"Confirmed," she said, and clicked off the line to make her report.

"Torn vault," Brand said. "That computer equipment must weigh at least two hundred pounds, and it's been chucked through the wall."

"The . . . torn bodies," I added. "Strength. Sigil magic could do this—but you'd need overlapping spells to protect your joints and bones." It was easier, treating this like a case. Like an investigation. "It's excessive. That glass of wine downstairs? That's dismissive. The sigils that were picked through? That's dismissive. I'm reading this as temperamental noble."

"Angry," Brand added. "Someone is angry. Destroying equipment sends a message, even if it's just a tantrum." He nodded back to the pile of bodies. "They're all in scrubs. I think they're staff."

"Blood trail leads from there," I said, seeing the drag smears leading into another room.

Brand edged far enough toward that doorway until he could see what was beyond. "Capsules," he said. "Like big tubes?"

"The rejuvenation chambers," I said.

I joined him, and I did not look at the bodies again as I passed.

The destruction in the next room was even more pronounced. The huge machines—which kept scions in stasis for days or weeks while their bodies rejuvenated—were destroyed. Ripped out of their moorings; kicked across the room; flipped over.

There was a body on the ground by one of the machines. A young man with hair to his waist. His neck had been flattened or crushed. It was as thin as the width of my hand.

Someone coughed.

Brand and I both turned in fast circles, trying to pinpoint the source. I kept my sabre pointed, primed to fire.

Brand cut his hand toward a half-open door, and we moved toward it. He stopped with his hand on the knob and gave me a look. I nodded. He pushed the door slowly to quickly silence any squeal or creak.

Through the widening slice I saw rows of shelving units filled with pill bottles and elixir vials. A pharmacy?

We slid into the room, clearing the corners. Two people were hogtied on the ground with torn computer cords. Brand gestured for me to approach while he continued to walk around the shelving units, making sure we were alone.

A man and a woman. The woman was dead; she had no pulse. The man must have been the one who coughed, but he wasn't conscious now. I put my hand on his wrist and felt a racing, irregular heartbeat. His face was raw and swollen from a beating. One of his eyes was blackened, its red bruise just beginning to show the faintest sign of purple.

First I sent a spark of willpower into my sabre. A garnet dirk boiled up from the hilt, which I used to cut the man's ropes. Then I touched the emerald ring on my finger and released a Healing spell. I didn't know where the worst injuries were, so I feathered my fingers along his jaw and sent the energy into him. The skin under my touch warmed and reddened like a sunburn.

Brand came back to my side. He crouched with a knee on the ground and studied the area around us. His eye caught an overturned tripod. He dropped to a push-up position, and from that angle saw something I couldn't.

He reached under a desk and fished out a digital video camera.

"I can't even tell what's wrong with him," I whispered. "I don't even know if this is enough to stabilize him. What's that?"

"Not sure. Battery is dead. But it's not part of the security system, so maybe there's some footage on here that's relevant. Julia?"

"I'm here."

"Tell Mayan there's at least one survivor. Condition critical. Rune's used a Healing on him, but he's not conscious."

"Acknowledged."

We both had pockets, but Brand's were usually filled with weapons of mass destruction, while mine usually had snacks. Or at least they did before I had a six-year-old running around my life; now I was just as likely to have acorns, which Corbie insisted our dinosaur liked. The digital camera was small but bulky, so I stuck it in my front jacket pocket.

We couldn't do anything else for the injured pharmacist, so we back-tracked to the main medical suite. There was another collection of offices along the north side of the floor. A plaque on the wall announced the area as *Counseling.*

"Weird," Brand murmured, pointing to a richly carpeted spiral stairway inside one of the individual counseling offices.

"They all have a stairway in them," I added, looking at the room on the other side of the hall.

There was a click on our headset. Brand said, "Something to add, Julia?" And then, grudging, "Thanks for maintaining radio silence."

"You're welcome," she said crisply. "You're right under the Playrooms.

Staircases on the blueprints correspond with individual rooms above each counseling office."

Brand spotted a blood trail, nudged my arm, and went into the office it led from. By a clear footprint, he knelt and peered. "Bare feet. Walking toward the medical area. It looks like someone came downstairs this way."

"So they'd be below us? Unless they doubled back to the main staircase?"

"Unless they've left the building altogether," Brand said. "Maybe the barrier is supposed to slow down the discovery of the bodies? Should we check upstairs? Or stay with the wounded?"

"I can't do anything else for this man right now. I say we go upstairs— I want to see the jade suite."

We went up the carpeted stairway to the third floor. At the landing was another room, nearly identical in size to the counseling office below us.

And that was where the similarities ended.

The third-floor room was decorated like the American 1970s, complete with an open closet filled with bellbottoms and polyester, and random kitsch like Chia Pets, a waterbed, and bottles of Campari on a sideboard. On a bamboo nightstand were red-glass vases filled with condoms, lubricant, and dildos.

And there was a body. A young man wearing a tie-dye T-shirt and nothing else was sprawled in a pool of wet carpet, a jagged slice of broken coatrack sticking out of his chest. The point of the coatrack had gone clean through his sternum so that the body appeared to be floating an inch above the ground.

"I know I should be looking at the body," Brand said, "but what the fuck am I looking at?" He poked the corner of the waterbed.

"They do call it the playroom," I said.

Brand shook it off and went over to the dead man. "Is this poor shit staff or guest?"

"Not sure. But he wasn't torn apart. I'm thinking that this room wasn't a destination, it was just a path downstairs. Or the killer was in a hurry?"

"Julia, what's ahead of us?" Brand asked. "Where is the jade suite?"

"The guest residences are on the other side of the floor. Between you and the suites is a bar, an infinity pool, a gym, and more privacy chambers like the one you're in."

"Can you find us a roundabout route to the residences?" I said. "Something direct?"

"Yes, my lord. There should be two doors in this room. One of them leads to the staff area. That'll avoid the public areas."

"That one," Brand said, pointing to a door painted the same color as the wall. He went over and laid a palm on the door, applying enough pressure to control the motion of opening it. When it was ajar enough for perspective, he raised his hand in a *this way* gesture.

The cement corridor outside was lined with doors to other playrooms. The corridor funneled into a square antechamber, which opened up into a massive room filled with racks and racks of clothing and accessories. Not much of it was modern—there was a huge selection of male and female clothing from centuries past.

On one table I saw a basket of pamphlets. The cover read: *Revisit the decade of your youth in our certified privacy chambers, with our internationally renowned staff of intimacy therapists.*

Rejuvenating bodies came with consequences. The stable hormones of adulthood were slowly peeled back, layer by layer, leaving you with the energy and adrenaline of youth. The rooms on this floor were where those hormones were . . . released.

We crossed an open space lined with mirrored vanity stations. There were two partially open doors in this area. Brand approached one, sniffed, and said, "Chlorine. Maybe the infinity pool." I went to the other door and saw an uncarpeted hallway. It seemed to continue in a straight line to the other side of the third floor.

"Julia," I said. "I think I see which way to go. How do we find the jade suite?"

"Lady Saint Brigid reports that each room is marked with a colored door. Once you're in the resident wing, the jade suite will be the last door on the left."

Since it didn't look like the killer had come this way, we moved at a fast walk down the hall. The door at the end was closed, which Brand opened with more caution than I'd seen from him yet. He even had us slide low to the ground, to contain and misdirect our body space.

There was no killer on the other side. Just a kill zone.

There were bodies everywhere. We walked into the hallway, and even Brand took a second to remember to sweep his eyes in a professional three-sixty.

The violence was both efficient and graphic. I saw it clearly in my head: a strong spell-caster moving through a crowd of people without sigils or spells of their own. The killer had barely treated them as human, just as punching bags for their rage. *Less* than punching bags. Punching bags remained whole after you hit them.

"We're going to need to walk through the crime scene," Brand said. And since we'd been doing that since we set foot inside the building, I knew he meant that we were literally going to need to step *on* the crime scene. The blood spatter and viscera was everywhere. At least I wasn't about to throw up this time.

"It's not as bad," I said slowly. "It's bad, but not like the staff we saw in the medical area. Whoever did this wanted those people to suffer."

I continued to speak as I followed Brand's footsteps. "So imagine this happens in the middle of the night. Most guests are asleep. Maybe some are in the social areas. The killer is angry. People come to their doors to investigate shouts or screams. And . . . this happens."

"I don't think the killer is still here," Brand said.

"No. I don't either. Green door—up there."

"We probably should just step aside and wait for the Tower to bring the barrier down," Brand said.

"We probably should," I agreed, as neither of us stopped walking.

In a way, the worst violence we'd seen yet was inside the jade suite, a plush set of rooms decorated in light green accents. There was a body there. She hadn't been ripped apart—she'd been beaten to death. She wore a black apron over tan pants and a white blouse now soaked a deep claret.

There was a floor-length mirror by a chaise lounge in the corner. Medical gauze littered the floor. Brand poked through the pile with his dagger, showing how the ends were stretched and torn, not cut.

Though an open doorway was a smaller bedroom dominated by a king-sized mattress. The sheets were unmade and covered in items that radiated power. *Sigils.* None of them looked like they'd been placed there—they looked like they'd been discarded or tossed away. I peeked around the edge of the bed and saw where some had bounced and landed on the floor.

"Why throw away sigils?" Brand asked. "These are pretty generic—discs, pocket watches, hair pins . . ."

"They'll be tied to bloodlines," I guessed. "Some sigils aren't tied to a single user, they're tied to a family. Like Addam's platinum discs. If you defeated Addam, you couldn't take his sigils by conquest, since they belong to the Crusader Throne."

Brand wandered back into the living area. I went over to a closed wardrobe and opened it. On the other side was a lot of unusually basic clothing, not quite what you'd expect from a wealthy customer. Simple sandals sat at the bottom of the wardrobe, covered in a flaking greenish clay. I filed that away—it was specific enough to be unusual.

I followed Brand back into the living room. I was half a second away from telling Julia that we'd cleared the room when Brand said, "Holy shit," and knelt by the battered young woman.

"This was recording," he said, holding up a cell phone that had been hidden under the woman's arm. He showed me the lock screen. "She may have been recording what happened."

He gently picked up the woman's hand, wiped off her thumb, and rolled it along the phone's button until it unlocked. He navigated to the camera functionality, and sure enough, the last item in the album was a nineteen-second video.

He tapped the play button.

Tinny sound. A crooked camera angle showing only carpet. The camera jumped as the person recording backed up jerkily.

Shouts. A woman's deep, scratchy voice. A younger woman's hysterical voice.

WOMAN ONE: *You water-blooded fools! You incompetent perversions!*

WOMAN TWO: *My lady, the bandages, it's early, you shouldn't—*

WOMAN ONE: *What is this failure? Where is my youth!*

WOMAN TWO: *My lady, please! Please! Let me call the night manager, she'll—*

WOMAN ONE: *{Screams in fury}*

WOMAN TWO: *{Screams in surprise}*

The screams only continued from there, moving from shock to genuine pain, and finally to terror. There was no video of the people involved, just the shifting scenes of carpet at a distance, and then up close as the beaten woman fell. The video stopped suddenly after that.

"Gods," I whispered, as a piece fell into place. And then something else occurred to me, and I repeated, though in a different tone entirely, "Oh, gods. Julia, confirm who is on this line."

"My lord? It's a private line. Just the three of us."

"I need you to be sure."

"I am. As sure as I can be. Should I—"

"Are we being recorded?"

"No, my lord. You're a member of the Arcanum. I would never record you without your explicit permission. Is anything—"

"You will speak to no one of this. Not a supervisor, not a friend, not a lover. No one."

The line went dead for a second before she replied, somewhat haughtily, "My discretion is absolute, my lord."

"Julia," I said, raising my own voice. "Tell me you understood what I've said."

"Of course I understand. But I would never—"

Brand had been looking at me with a puzzled expression. He didn't know why I was upset. But he understood what I was upset about. "He's protecting you," he interrupted. "Shut up and do what he fucking says."

"I will speak of this to no one," she said.

"Thank you. Vacate the line. Set up a direct communication with Lord Tower immediately. Ensure our absolute privacy."

"At once."

Brand didn't even have time to raise an eyebrow. The Tower was there a beat later with a single, "Rune."

"We found a short video. A woman I believe to be the killer was in a rage because rejuvenation hadn't worked."

"Hadn't worked," he said, with slight emphasis on the second word.

"It failed to make her young," I said.

Lord Tower went silent. He understood what I was saying, and the potential implications of it. "Stand by. I have the assistance I need. We're about to bring the barrier down."

I went over to a draped window and parted a curtain. My willpower pulsed into my vision, bringing the barrier into soft definition. I felt Brand at my shoulder, his breath on my neck. Ten seconds later, the faint sheen of the yellow barrier turned pale blue. Then the blue deepened until delicate traceries of frost spread along the curve, thickening into a glacial shimmer. I felt the release of multiple mass sigil spells, and the barrier detonated into whorls of colorlessness not unlike snow.

I knew someone on the island who was a master of Frost magic, and who the Tower wouldn't mind calling for backup.

"I think our big sister is here," I said.

Everything became a mess of activity after that.

The Tower's elite staff spread through the building. The wounded pharmacist was stabilized and taken to the hospital under armed escort. For a while, I heard the shocked sounds of Lady Priestess in the hallway, along with the throatier calmness of Lady Death. But the Tower sequestered me in the jade suite, asking Brand for a private moment with me.

He closed the door and spent a good two minutes just studying the violent diorama before him. And then he watched and re-watched the video clip three times.

"A woman. Mature, from the sound of the voice," he said. "You saw no other signs of unusual magic activity?"

"Such as?"

"You would know. The forbidden sort."

"No. Nothing that couldn't be explained by sigil use in the hands of a very good spell-caster. You think I'm right, don't you? That this was either an Arcana or principality?"

"I believe I do." He went over to the mirror and stared at the bandages on the ground.

I'd learned recently that all powerful Atlanteans—the ones who topped the scales as either freelance powers known as principalities or as the Arcana who led courts—were marked by a unique, secret power called the Arcana Majeure. I'd used it before by accident, not knowing what it was or, most importantly, what the *cost* was. It wasn't unlike using an imaginary sigil that was powered by your own life force. You never got back the life you expended. It ate away at your ability to rejuvenate. Lord Tower had told me the reason he always appears as a man in his early forties was that centuries of periodic Arcana Majeure use had made it impossible for him to rejuvenate younger.

What sort of life would an Arcana or principality have lived to prevent any sort of rejuvenation?

"Could this be the Empress?" I asked.

"I don't believe so. I could have broken through any barrier she raised, at least."

There was another matter I'd been waiting to bring up. I looked at Lord Tower's back and said, "One other thing. Please don't kill Julia."

Lord Tower turned and gave me a beautifully blank face.

"This isn't a fishing expedition," I said. "You know exactly what I mean. There's no reason Julia will ever link what happened to the Arcana

Majeure. Why would she, if we've done as good a job as you think keeping it secret? And if we haven't, shame on us."

The Tower said nothing, so I did something I'd never done before, not ever.

"Anton," I said. "Please. As a favor to me. I've got enough blood on my hands already; the only thing I can hold onto is that nearly all of them deserved it. She does not."

He buried a sigh in the motion of pulling out his phone. He swiped open a text, read it, put the phone away. "Let's join Lady Death outside. She and Brandon have moved to the courtyard."

"Is that my answer?"

"Julia will be under constant surveillance for the next three months. If I hear so much as a word of this breathed through her lips, she will be handled. That is the best I can do."

"Fair," I agreed, and let it go. I had enough responsibilities in my life; I had no time to navigate this issue further beyond Lord Tower's word.

Because he was the Tower, he didn't bother with anything as mundane as an elevator or stairway. He brushed a manicured nail—from his unbandaged hand—over a ruby ring, held out his arm, and manifested a Door. The short-range teleportation spell looked like a miniature tornado until it anchored to the ground and stabilized. A circular portal now hovered in the air.

Lord Tower held out his arm, which I stared at. He shook the arm. I rolled my eyes and put my hand on his wrist. I felt the surge of his willpower as he guided us into the portal. Whatever he did seemed to affect the unstable nature of teleportation. Usually, I wound up on my ass, with gravity spinning around me like a snapped tether. This time I simply emerged from the other side standing on thick, springy grass.

Lady Death and Lady Priestess sat around a glass patio set, with Brand and Mayan at attention behind them. Everyone here knew what the Arcana Majeure was, which was not accidental. No one else—not even

Lord Tower's guards or Lady Priestess's daughter—were in eyesight or earshot for this discussion.

Lady Death, a woman appearing near my age with the help of at least one rejuvenation treatment of her own, had dark skin; thick, shiny hair; and favored the color red. Her braids were gathered atop one shoulder, and nearly all of her jewelry invisibly sparked with the power of sigils.

"A grim morning, little brother," she said. She nudged a chair with her foot, angling it toward me.

I sat down with the gusty sound of not-being-as-young-as-I-once-was. It bothered me that Brand was standing, but when I flashed a look at him, he gave me a small shake of his head.

"Those were hard sights inside," she said. "You and Brand continue to take me to the nicest places. I still haven't washed the battleship from my eyes."

"We're unlikely to have much time to speak alone like this," Lady Priestess said in a distracted voice, fiddling with the corner of her cat-eye glasses. "Bethan will be suspicious. I have a lot of clever children, but she's the most stubborn about it. She doesn't know about the Arcana Majeure, of course. And I'm assuming we'll mention that—because that's a very likely culprit for failure to rejuvenate."

"First—are we agreed that this is officially an Arcanum matter, and will be afforded our highest levels of confidentiality?" Lord Tower asked. "No one is to view evidence, or participate in the investigation, without Mayan's explicit approval."

Mayan dipped his chin at Lord Tower. Everyone else voiced their agreement.

"I have some thoughts about what Brand and I can do next," I said. "We need to bag the shoes in the jade suite—the mud on them looked distinct."

"It will be done," Lord Tower said. "As for you? You have a court to run. Mayan will reach out if he needs assistance."

I didn't say anything right away. With only a little throat clearing, I said, "I would like to remain involved."

"You are Arcana. You will remain *informed*," the Tower corrected. "Your days of running down suspects are over, Lord Sun."

"Oh," I said. And I didn't know what to do with that. My brain told me to get angry, but this was probably one of those times that my brain was getting me in trouble. So I did the throat-clearing thing again. "Given my experience, it seems like I should at least advise. I may have good insight."

Lady Death threw back her head and laughed. "Oh, little brother, I will so enjoy becoming friends with you." Then, more seriously. "Don't be too eager for a seat at this table. It will come soon enough."

I gave her a tight and not entirely ungrateful smile.

"Very well. While we're together and the matter is fresh, let's review what we know," Lord Tower said.

SUN ESTATE

I woke up before Addam again, which rarely happened. I was so surprised I almost woke him up to talk about it.

But because it was rare, I kept my thoughts bottled up, and just enjoyed the way that the sunlight fell on his turned face. And half of his chest. And one leg. I'd pulled most of the bedsheets over me again, it seemed.

I may have appreciated his beauty for all of two minutes before realizing his ass cheek had a dimple too. Weren't the two on his face enough? Did nature really feel he needed an encore? It seemed unfair.

"Hero," he sighed. "You appear to have claimed ownership of my sheet again."

I started laughing as he rolled around, grabbed the top sheet, and fluffed it in the air. As it began to settle like a parachute, he moved on top of me and kissed my neck *good morning*.

When he was done, he pushed up with his elbow so that he could look at me. I got lost in his burgundy eyes for a moment—they really were lovely—until he said, "You are awake."

"It happens."

I felt the coolness of his metal hand against one cheek. "Are you still upset about yesterday?"

Yes, I was still a little frustrated about yesterday. Most of the time Brand and I went into the field, we followed the job to its messy end. It felt odd to be sidelined. But the investigation of the rejuvenation center aside, there had been related fallout to handle. A family once associated with my court, as well as the Dawncreeks, had lost a member; as had Addam's court. Many families across the city had spent yesterday in the sorts of discussions that follow a murder: grief, shock, planning, plotting.

"No," I said, and touched one of his few tan lines, tracing it around a V of chest. "Just a busy day ahead."

"But since you woke up early, it's as if it's still *yesterday*," he argued. "We have so much time until today becomes today."

"Do you have any specific ideas for using that time?"

"There are several ideas in my locked nightstand drawer."

"You're a freakish and beautiful car crash, Saint Nicholas," I said. "But Brand knows I'm awake and I can feel him approaching like a homing missile." That wasn't a lie, either. Through my bond, I could feel the *he's-finally-fucking-awake* energy of my Companion as he headed toward my suite.

Addam sighed, but nodded against me. "I need to run to my condo this morning anyway. Perhaps we can have lunch?"

If I had an immediate reply, I fumbled it, because he mentioned his condo. My brain decided to freeze time and dissect the statement for any possible meaning. He didn't say *I need to run home.* But he also called it *my condo.*

Months ago, he'd hit me with a truth bomb. *I know I will never be the love of your life.* At the time, I'd been lost in the wonder of his vulnerability. But as the weeks went by, I became more and more ill at ease with the way he saw his role in my life and court.

Addam saw something on my face. He settled back on his haunches, pulling the sheet into his lap. "Is everything well, Rune?"

Addam put a lot of energy into trying to understand me. This, I knew. He excavated for clues like an archeologist—a painstakingly slow and precise process. And what's stranger is that he actually enjoyed that. The problem was that I didn't necessarily understand *him* as well as I needed, because I had no clear idea what we were becoming to each other. How would I even ask? *Hey, Addam, just checking: have you given up your entire life to join my court forever, even though you think I can't love you as much as I do?*

There were three quick bangs on the door before it swung open. Brand poked his head in. He saw Addam half-naked, scrunched his eyes shut, then slammed the door so loud that a picture frame on the nearby wall tilted crazily.

Almost immediately, the door reopened. Brand leaned back in sheepishly. "That really makes a sound when the doors aren't cheap hollow cores. Fucking mansions. And sorry, it didn't sound like you were doing any cozy shit through the bond. My bad."

The door shut more quietly.

Addam turned to look at me, which made his abdomen do all sorts of interesting things. His serious look lightened into a faint smile. "You are unaccustomed to long conversations. I have a sense, though, that there is a long conversation before us. Are you ready to have it?"

"I was until you said it would be a long conversation. I thought I'd just shout some bullet points and run."

"If not now, then soon. I will bathe now." He leaned in and kissed me on the lips. "Good morning, Rune." Then he kissed the top of my head. "Good morning, Rune's-mysterious-behavior. We'll all talk later."

He didn't seem to be eating the acorns.

I threw the last one from my pocket. It bounced off a rock inside the elasmotherium's enclosure and hit him in the horn. He made a lowing sound and shuffled around so that his ass was facing me.

I'd stopped by to visit Flynn during my morning patrol. I'd been in the habit of doing that every day, just to make sure nothing nasty from the haunted era had decided to move back in after our latest round of evictions.

Lady Death, in administering the division of the Gallows estate, had given me the prehistoric rhinoceros as a gift. Corbie was in love with the creature, which was partly why all of the wardstones penning Flynn into a half acre were designed to also withstand a nosy six-year-old boy.

"What are we going to do with you?" I sighed. "You have arthritis, you know."

The creature's tail swished.

"Fine. I'll store some healing sigils tomorrow and visit with the vet. Corbie thinks your back leg is hurting you. I don't know why."

The creature shuffled back around to look at me, as if I'd said something to interest him.

It wouldn't be the first strange thing about the Siberian unicorn. Something about Flynn's tenure as an ifrit's familiar had given him an . . . aura? I didn't know how to explain it, which was saying something, because I was generally smart about this sort of thing.

On the plus side, undead and ghosts gave Flynn a wide berth. That was a help—though I'd also paid heavily to relocate undead and haunts rather than kill them outright. It wasn't their fault the prodigal son had returned.

Across the entire estate, only two troubling areas remained. My father's old tower, which was separate from the main house, was untouched. He'd used it as his residence, study, laboratory, vault . . . Insanely powerful wards had surrounded the tower at the moment of his death, and I hadn't yet worked up the guts to break them. One day, I'd work with Lord Tower on it.

And then there was the carriage house. I'd surrounded the entire thing in wards and was, for now, content to let it rot within its fortified oasis. That was where I'd spent the night, the day that Sun Estate fell. That was where I'd been held and tortured.

I brushed my hands on my pants, turned, and headed in the direction of the beach.

Sun Estate had been one of the first translocations to Nantucket, back when Nantucket was still Nantucket. My father had always been good at hiding his acquisitions from public eyes—such as stealing a nearly bull-dozed mansion from Long Island's gold coast and dropping it onto his private island property. I waffled between whether the mansion was technically beautiful or not, with its flat surfaces and sudden angles—but it was breathtaking, which sometimes felt like beautiful.

Our chief contractor—the woman responsible for the complete rehabilitation of the estate until our money ran out—told me I was lucky the mansion had rotted in place. All of the pieces lay where they'd fallen, protected from looting by the dangerous haunts. That meant that magical restoration was possible. Renew a rotted railing? You'd have to do it the hard way if you didn't have all the original debris sitting right below it.

Not that it made much difference in the price. We'd begun the renovation with a four million-dollar check and now, nine months later, we'd lost a zero in our bank account balance. Every single square foot of recovered ground came with a steep cost: a mix of physical labor, magic, and raw materials.

The grass under me got sparser and sandier until it was all beach dune. I heard the pound of little footsteps behind me, and a tiny hand tugged on my sleeve. I looked down to see Corbie. The moment he knew I was looking, his face transformed into an expression of poorly acted discomfort. He made a show of tenderly shifting from one foot to the other while staring at the sandy slope in front of us.

"You just crossed an entire lawn in point-two seconds," I said. "But hot sand is too much?"

He pretended he didn't understand what I was saying, and took a wincing step. "Really hot," he whispered, but soldiered forward another step in his bare feet.

I picked him up and headed to the beach.

Thirty minutes later, Anna painted my last fingernail with a clear layer of polish. We were in a set of beach chairs near the tide line, where the sand was damp and cooler. She'd asked to practice on me, which was odd, but sure.

"Blow on them," she said.

I waved my hand in the air. "I didn't think you wore makeup."

"I don't," she said.

"Then why practice?"

"I'm not," she said. "I lied. Brand paid me."

My gaze snapped to Brand, who was throwing a football around with Max and Quinn. Well, really, he was throwing a football, and Max and

Quinn were running and picking it up. Then I looked down at the bottle of nail polish in Anna's hands. I snatched it and saw it said, *Apple Bitter.*

"I told you to blow on them first," she complained, and snatched the bottle back.

"Why did Brand pay you to put this on my nails?" I demanded.

"Because you bite them, and it looks stupid when you're sitting on a throne."

"I do *not*—" I breathed through my nose. "I do not have a throne."

"Magic is metaphor," she intoned, a clear mimic of me. "And it's a big chair you sit in while deciding who to punish or help. What would you call it? I'm going to play football. I can throw better than Max."

She ran off. I pulled my phone out and texted Brand a quick *fuck you.* He made a show of checking his phone lazily, then ambling toward me without urgency.

"Any problems on patrol?" he asked.

I held my middle nail up for him to see.

"Leaders don't have hangnails," he said. "Get over it."

I got over it. It was still early enough to be hot as opposed to baking hot, so I tilted my face into the heat and enjoyed it. "Patrol was fine," I said. "I think the only problems we have left have to do with construction, not hauntings."

"Our funds are running low."

"We have almost a million dollars in the account."

"And we blew through three million dollars in nine months," he said. "Half of that was in marble slabs. We need to prioritize the rest of the repairs, Rune."

If it was just a matter of infrastructure, I wouldn't be getting wrinkles around my eyes. But infrastructure meant safety. It meant a solid line of defense. It was the difference between a compound and a *fortified* compound. I opened my eyes and let my head roll left, staring down the stretch of rocky, natural shore. "I really hoped we'd be able to renovate the beach," I said unhappily. "All the other Arcana with beachside compounds have pretty beaches, with bathhouses and piers and floating docks. But that's the last thing we need to spend money on."

"Then maybe we don't spend money on it. Ever. Maybe we'll leave it exactly like it is. Do Anna and the boys look like they're missing out on anything?" He gestured to where the kids were sprawled on the wet sand to see who got nibbled by the tide first.

"Maybe not," I breathed, and relaxed a little. I was tenser than normal, which lasted for three whole seconds before I got even *more* tense because I remembered that I was sort-of having a weird moment.

"Fucking hell," Brand said. "What is going on in your brain today? You're making me nervous."

"It's nothing," I said. I nodded toward the kids and changed the subject. "Do you ever think what it would be like to rejuvenate to that age? Look how much *energy* they have."

There was a moment of deep, suspicious silence. I glanced over my shoulder and saw Brand glaring at me. He said, "You told me we wouldn't go further back than twenty-five."

"I know. No one does. I was just asking."

"Rune, hear me now. If you ever rejuvenate me to a skinny teenager with acne, and undo everything I've put my body through to get in this shape—"

"I didn't say—"

"No, I need to finish the threat, because you need to understand I would make your life a living hell."

"You can't rejuvenate that young, they won't let you," Corinne said, coming up behind us. She'd brought her own chair with her, and snapped it open with a twist of her wrists.

It was still a revelation: her young, unlined face. We'd met during a period when she was rapidly aging following the death of her Atlantean scion, Kevan, whom she'd been bonded to as a Companion. Now she was younger than both Brand and I. She looked like Anna's older sister, not foster mother.

Since the two were bonded as new Companions, Corinne would age naturally until Anna turned twenty-five, at which point Corinne would rejuvenate again to bring their ages in line.

"Are you doing okay?" I asked, seeing the bags under her eyes.

"I'm still furious with you."

"I know. We should have woken you up and brought you with us yesterday. But that's not what I mean."

Corinne had known the Amberson family—the family who'd lost a member in the rejuvenation center attack. Lord Amberson had made Kevan Dawncreek a peer and involved him in their magical studies work. The last I knew of the Ambersons had come from Corinne—she'd said that they'd lost their status as a greater house when Sun Court fell. Apparently, the last few years had seen them recover somewhat, at least financially.

"I never really knew Elicia. The woman who—died. She was Lord Amberson's maiden sister. After he died, I lost touch with them."

"Are you still okay with making contact?" I asked. "If it's too much, I can—"

"No. No, I'll invite them to your gala, if they're interested in attending. It's a nice gesture, and will allow us to pay respects."

In the back of my head, I also had to admit to myself that it was tactical. In much the same way that I'd brought the Dawncreeks back into the Sun Court, maybe there were other old Sun Court families who'd be interested in an alliance? I needed people. I needed funding. I needed spell-casters and fighters.

Corinne added, "Shouldn't you be getting changed, by the way? Don't you hold court hours after lunch?"

"Yes," I grumbled.

"We've got interviews after that. I'll find you then—I just want to go catch Layne before he runs off for the day."

I didn't say anything, just held my breath and waited.

She closed her eyes and grimaced. "Fuck me. *They.* Before they run off for the day."

"Tell them I said hello, and if they have a hospital shift, to bring me back some of the passion fruit Jello. We can—*FUCKER!*" I made a face and wiped my lips on the back on my hand.

"You weren't even aware you were biting your nail, were you?" Brand said. "See? I'm brilliant."

I got ready for office hours.

I was doing my best to subvert the image of what "office hours" meant, unbitten nails aside. I picked jeans and sneakers for court, thinking my black leather jacket added enough gravity to keep me from seeming sloppy. Plus, it was covered with handmade wards that made it passably useful as body armor.

I walked from the room I shared with Addam to the first floor—well, trekked, really. Everything was a trek in Sun Estate. Something as simple as moving from bed to bathroom to coffee maker to back veranda edged into the territory of a commute.

When the virus had been at its height and every house was quarantined, Lord Tower had helped my new, larger family relocate to Sun Estate, where at least we could be together. There was more than enough space for Brand, myself, Queenie, and Max; along with Addam and Quinn; and then the Dawncreeks, complete once Corinne finished her rejuvenation treatments. The kids were back on a school schedule: four days a week on campus, three days a week at home.

Even *thinking* about all of these people exploded into a list of domestic tasks.

Had we found money to hire more kitchen staff for Queenie yet? She was resisting the idea of sharing her kitchen, but her kitchen was no longer nine-feet wide. What was Corinne's role going to be, now that she was Anna's Companion, and strong enough to be counted on in field actions? Was everything okay between her and Layne—who'd been spending a lot of time with the principality known as Ciaran, which was its own unique domino chain.

Max and Brand were waiting for me outside a doorway. I'd turned the old glass-walled solarium into my meeting space. My father had held concerts there, once, taking advantage of the northwestern sunsets.

Max picked a piece of sunburned skin off his nose. He still had his slender fae build, but was also growing tall and broad-shouldered. His button-down shirt had scorch marks from our nearly busted dryer.

The three of us entered the solarium and passed a small contingent of Arcanum guards who were double-checking the room for . . . I don't know. Bombs? Protester signs? Rotten fruit? All Arcana received a dozen highly trained protectors, which was good, because we couldn't afford hiring our own security force yet, though we were in negotiations to contract one of Addam's former security teams from his mother's court.

Putting together a security force was one aspect of ruling. Another was listening to your people when they had problems. And I did have people now, beyond those I called my family. We'd hired custodial staff and groundskeepers. And they all had issues that were important to them—like direct deposit, and healthcare, and visiting sick aunts, and on and on and on.

That would be the first half of my afternoon. The second would be interviewing potential seneschals: someone who could handle the day-to-day operations of the court. Brand had absorbed that role while the repairs were in progress, but we needed to start specializing. He had enough on his hands with security and grounds reconstruction; handling the politics wasn't a fair use of his time.

I took a slow, deep breath, and said, "Good afternoon, everyone." I went straight to the chair at the end of a massive cherrywood table with matching chairs. It seated thirty and had been donated by Addam, who said he'd found it unused in a storage room of the Crusader Throne. He'd forgotten to pull off the outrageously expensive price tag that had been dangling from one of the struts.

I sat at the head of the table, with Max at my left hand, and Brand retreating to a defensible corner.

The solarium was ringed with folding chairs that Queenie had found at a flea market. They were nice, and matched, which was enough for now. In the chairs, I spotted a young woman, a red-faced older man, and a man with a cane. More people were starting to shuffle into the room.

I asked the young woman to go first—she was house staff, and handled the residences on the upper floors. I saw that she cradled her arm as she came toward me, and when she was close enough, I spotted the reddened skin of an injury.

"Oh, no, no," I said, and immediately shot out of my chair. "Here, take that seat right there." As she settled into the chair, I took the one next to her. "Burn?"

"Chemicals, my lord. Some got under my rubber gloves. It's not that bad."

I touched my emerald ring and released a Healing spell. I'd have to start thinking about storing more than one a day at this rate, at least until we could afford a healer. "The thing is?" I told her. I gently applied pressure to her wound and sent the magic into the injury. "It kills me to know that people wouldn't find me immediately when they're hurt. That makes me think I'm not approachable."

"Oh, but you are, my lord."

"Then next time, as soon as you're hurt, or as soon as you see *anyone* hurt, you'll find me or the Lords Saint Nicholas immediately. The three of us always have a healing spell available. Deal?"

"Yes, my lord. That feels much better, thank you."

When I was done, I headed back to my chair. Brand was flashing a hand signal at Max, and Max was hiding a page in the little notebook he carried with him everywhere.

"Okay, that wasn't so bad," I said, and decided I didn't want to waste time being suspicious of them. "What's next?"

I saw six more people over the next half hour.

Someone needed to work second shift instead of first shift, but their supervisor was telling them no. (I approved it. Having more custodial support in the evening would be good.) Two of the groundskeepers were fighting over the one riding lawn mower we had. (I assigned them to different parts of the estate, and gave them each two days a week to use the lawn mower as they pleased, while making a note to check our budget for more equipment.) One by one I whittled the room down until the last supplicant was shuffling out.

I turned around in my chair just as Brand flashed Max a V. That stopped whatever I was going to say. "What are you doing?"

"Nothing. Security stuff."

I turned around in the other direction and peered at Max, who had his finger place-held in his notebook. I snatched up the notebook, quicker than his startled reflexes. On one of the middle pages he'd written, in big black letters, "9," "7," "8," "8," "7," "8," and then he was halfway through a "4."

"Are you . . . Are you *judging* me?" I asked. I stabbed a finger at a nine. "Was that the first one? I *healed her!*"

"I got the sense that you didn't remember her name," Max admitted. "Brand gave you a ten though."

"Do you have no sympathy for me at all? Do you know what I've been doing? This? My entire morning? Leading *a court?*" I ticked the items off on my fingers. "Workers comp, workplace grievance, a request for reasonable accommodation . . . I am HR. I am our human resources department, Brand. I am an HR manager."

"Then decide on a goddamn seneschal," he said. "You've been through fifteen applicants. Pick one. There's a whole bunch waiting in the library."

"It needs to be someone we both trust, so don't act like I'm being unreasonable. Are you telling me you have a best candidate so far? Was it the one who picked his nose and wiped it under the table? Or the person who spelled Temperance wrong while describing the job they lied about? Or, hey, what about the person who is part of a movement to free Companions and send them back to the country of their birth. That didn't stir up horrifying episodes of guilt and anger at all, right?"

I stopped, picked up my water glass, and breathed loudly into it. Eventually I opened my eyes and saw that Brand and Max were waiting quietly for me to recover.

"Am I doing okay?" I asked them quietly.

"Yes," Brand said.

"Yes," Max said, only he smiled.

"All right then. Let's go interview those seneschals."

To get to the library on the upper floor, we needed to go through the main hall. Corinne was there, waiting.

"Are you going to join us for the seneschal interview?" I asked her.

"Actually," she said. "I was coming to find you about that. I was told to send you and Brand in alone."

"Excuse me?" Brand demanded.

"It's fine. The room is cleared, and there are two guards outside."

"Who told you to send us in alone?" I asked.

"The . . . candidate," Corinne said.

"There are supposed to be half a dozen candidates in there," I said.

"Not any longer."

Now that was interesting and foreboding. I gave Max a look, shrugged, and finished the trek to the study with just Brand at my side.

The library wasn't quite repaired yet, but we'd put more attention into it than other parts of the house, mainly because cleaning it was one of the easiest slices on the chore wheel, and there were comfy sofas to be lazy on. People were known to trade the privilege for cash.

All of the random strangers I'd expected to see had been dismissed. Only one person remained, and that person was Diana Saint Nicholas, Addam's severe aunt, the sister of the sitting Lady Justice.

She was a woman who appeared to be in her late forties or early fifties, with long dark hair and burgundy eyes. She sat in a chair facing the door.

While I stood there and stared, surprised, she raked her eyes from my head to my feet.

"No," she said. "First lesson. You should wear slacks and formal footwear for our interview. I must insist."

"I'm interviewing you?" I said.

"No," she replied, and left it at that. She folded her arms and waited until I realized she was serious. I exchanged a look with Brand, so she added, "He can stay. I'll speak with him first."

Interested in seeing this play out—and seeing no advantage to throwing a fit—I left, went back to my room, and rooted through the dirty laundry for slacks. My boots would have to be formal enough. I lost myself in the mechanics of changing, because I wasn't sure how the larger situation was sitting in my brain.

By the time I got back to the library, Brand was in a big puffy chair opposite Diana. His hands were folded in his lap, and he was nodding seriously. When he saw me, he looked almost guilty, and sagged into a fake, insolent slouch.

"Okay, let me get my arms around this," I said, and took a seat on a sofa. "You're interested in being my seneschal?"

"Are my reasons important?" she asked.

"Well . . . yes? Isn't that one of the usual interview questions?"

"Tell me, Lord Sun. How many centennials serve you?"

"I don't call my people servants. They're my staff, friends, and family. And . . . we have . . . some." One? Maybe? Corinne was a centennial—she and Kevan had come from old Atlantis. And the dinosaur was technically over forty thousand years old, though it had spent most of that time in stasis as a summoned familiar.

"The fact that your pupils are darting back and forth suggests you don't know the answer," she said. "Do you have any idea what a disadvantage you'll be at, negotiating with courts with millennia of combined experience? You need my knowledge, and I miss my nephews."

"Lady Justice is irked enough I've co-opted her sons. She's not going to be happy if I steal you, too."

Diana crossed her legs and leaned back in the chair. The lines on her face were hard and faint, and they didn't fold seamlessly into her smiles so much as her frowns. "My sister never made me her seneschal. She made me the caretaker of her children. This is where I find the greatest need—with these children, here. And I would also point out that you're being overly generous in her concern for her sons."

She hit the S on sons, and I felt my own frown settle into place. Lady Justice's dismissiveness of Quinn had always rankled Addam, and didn't impress me either. Quinn had been a sickly child, raised by Addam. The rare prophetic gifts he'd developed later in life had been overshadowed by his infirmity—a mark of shame for traditional Atlantean houses.

"So you think I need you because of your experience," I said.

She made a frustrated sound. "Lord Sun. That is only the start of what you need. I've spent the last hour walking the estate with your Cook. Your oldest ward, Matthias, is having a growth spurt. His ankles are showing. The girl with the burn mark has brambles in her hair—Annawan. You appear to have a giant rhinoceros living behind wardstones with a singular flaw—they're vulnerable to physical movement. You've devoted resources to repairing your kitchen and living areas—but you are *Arcana.* Your first priority should have been on the public-facing spaces."

"If you think I'm going to be the type of Arcana to care about the impression he leaves on others, I'm going to disappoint you," I said.

"I don't think that at all. I think you need *people around you* who care about the impression you leave on others. You? You I expect to be something new. Something we need on *this* island, at *this* time, at *this* point in our history. I am very interested to see what you become, Rune Sun."

"I still think Lady Justice would kill me."

"I thought you didn't care about the impression you left on others?"

she asked. Her hands were knitted together so tightly that the tips were white. "Lord Sun—"

"This won't work if you can't call me Rune."

"Rune," she said. "I . . . miss Quinn. I've become very fond of him. This situation would benefit us both."

I caught Brand rubbing his thumb across his index finger knuckle. When he rubbed it over the nail, it meant he was playing a violin for me. When he rubbed his knuckle, it meant someone was playing me like a fiddle. He smirked and shrugged when he saw I noticed him.

"I'm not going to change clothes every time you ask," I sighed.

"I would hope you never do it again. That was a bit of a test. Though . . . perhaps you'll take my advice on courtwear."

I buried my eyes in my hands and itched my eyelids.

I heard movement, and Lady Diana settled into the sofa next to me. "Rune, listen to me. These first few months are critical. Your coronation approaches. As soon as that happens, it will be the firing of a starter pistol. Some of the old Sun Court houses will immediately approach you, as will other unaffiliated houses. Turn them all down. Anyone who comes forward so quickly will be curious, needy, or greedy. You will want to wait for the second wave—the people with something big enough to offer that they're slow to make a decision; or so much to lose that their trust must be secured."

I lowered my hands and looked at her. It was good advice.

"I'd like a room with a view of the elasmotherium," she said. "It is rather . . . marvelous. And Lord—Brandon. Brandon, I know that you've been serving much the same role as Rune's seneschal. I would imagine it may be difficult for you to share some of those responsibilities. I understand that."

Brand pulled out his phone. Two seconds later, Lady Diana's phone began to ping. And ping. And then it was like electric popcorn.

"Those are all the emails I've been ignoring," he said. "Have at it."

There was a knock at the door. On the other side, Quinn said, rather loudly, "Is my aunt here? Or are you in school—though I'm not sure what that means? It's one or the other, this close to it actually happening."

Lady Diana was the first person to smile, and it was genuine, which made me feel better about the decision I hadn't quite made.

"Brand," I said. "Would you excuse us? I'd like to talk with Lady Diana."

"Sure thing." He went to the door, cracked it open just enough so he could put his arm through and shove Quinn back, and slipped out.

I looked at Diana and said, "I have enemies."

"You do."

"And they're only getting stronger."

"Your point?"

"Diana," I said. "I am not always a safe person to be around."

She said absolutely nothing. She just watched me.

So I said, "I don't need a seneschal who will protect me. I need one who is strong enough to protect the people around me, from dangers without and within. Against my will, I seem to be getting drawn into matters I'm not sure I'm ready to face. I need people who can be just as scary as I can be when it really counts."

Slowly, the edge of her mouth turned upwards.

Another day of this weird new life I now led was over. The kids were sleeping in the ballroom, which is where a lot of us tended to wind up for some reason. We actually kept a trunk of blankets and yoga mats in the corner of the room because of it. I was thinking I might join them because Addam was spending the evening at the Crusader Throne, helping his Aunt Diana speak to his mother about becoming seneschal.

Brand and I meandered there after doing a final perimeter walk, which may have been the only reason we caught Anna in the hallway with a bag of weed.

"Annawan Fucking Dawncreek," Brand nearly shouted.

She jumped and spun around.

"Explain yourself," I said.

"I—"

"Because there is no way you think I'm okay with this. You are twelve—"

"*Thirteen,*" she said.

"—thirteen years old," I finished. "Do you know what that'll do to your development? At this age?"

She glared at me. "Will it kill my brain cells?"

"Yes," Brand said. "And it'll slow your reaction time, dull your reflexes, and undermine your training."

"So I might wind up stupid? And unable to care for myself and make responsible decisions when I grow older?" she said.

"I'm wondering if you'll be so flippant once your aunt finds out," I said.

"She'll make me tell her where I got it."

"So will I."

"Uh-huh," she said. "Did you know that the room that Aunt Corinne and I share used to belong to Brand? And that there's a loose floorboard in the closet?"

Brand's eyes went wide. I saw this through my own widened eyes as I exchanged looks with him. Brand snatched the bag out of Anna's hands and shook it. An old freshness ward had preserved it, but the buds inside were still so ancient they nearly made a clacking sound.

"Twenty bucks," I said. "And you never mention this again."

"Fifty," she said. "Snacks are expensive at school."

"I've got two twenties in my pocket," I said, and pulled out all the cash I had on me.

"Deal," she said, and plucked the American bills from my hand. She went into the ballroom without a second look at the pot.

Brand and I stared at the old Ziploc bag. There was even a pack of rolling papers inside it. "I think I remember this," Brand mumbled. "Didn't we used to get it through the guy who tended the orchard?"

"It . . . I mean, it can't be good anymore. Can it?"

"Probably not," Brand said, which wasn't a no.

"We could make sure it's inert. Then we could dispose of it properly."

"That would be very responsible of us," he agreed.

"Roof," I said.

Sun Estate had a lot of random towers and balconies. The northwest wing, in particular, had a steep ladder-like stairway to a turret roof that faced the ocean, invisible to all nearby windows. We made sure Layne and Corinne were keeping an eye on things, and made an escape.

While Brand rolled a joint, I kicked at the leaves, dirt, and branches that had blown across the round space, which was as wide as ten big footsteps.

I took the first hit. It was as abrasive as a sandstorm. I didn't cough, though. After a second, smaller hit, I passed it back to Brand. "You remembered how to roll those," I said on a dragon-plume exhale.

"Only because you lick the paper shut like you're giving it a messy French kiss." He took a hit and immediately started hacking.

"So much for those nice pink lungs," I said. "Maybe we should have baked your share into a little brownie."

"Fuck off," he coughed, and tried again. He managed to keep the second inhale inside for a full two seconds.

While he got his lungs sorted, I went over to the crenellated roofline, which was as tall as a normal railing.

I was already getting high, because the world was *just there.* Huge and beautiful and full of loud, dark waves. The black ocean was topped by a sparse starscape, smelling like salt and seafood. I forgot how powerful it was, to face a nighttime ocean from such a height. It made me feel small and grateful.

"This is *ours,*" I said, turning in a slow circle. My eyes began to sting. "Again. It's ours again, Brand. We're *back.*"

He came over and handed me the joint. He didn't pull back after; I felt a line of warmth remain along the side of my body.

My eyes blurred. I always got a little weepy when I was high. But how couldn't I? We were back. This was *Sun Estate*. And while I'd been playing Arcana, Brand had rebuilt it. Torn it from the grasp of entropy, reversed its slow slide into ruin.

"What a gift you gave me," I murmured. "Taking over the renovations. Thank you, Brand. You took on so much. Thanks for holding out until we got more help."

"Dolphins," he said, and shrugged.

He meant the time we'd smoked pot and drank beer and caught sight of a pod of dolphins playing offshore. A pretty memory, and I think he was just saying that he was happy to be home, too. "You're already high," I said.

"No," Brand said quickly. Then he said, "No." And then he decided to say it one more time. "No."

I burst into laughter. Then Brand started laughing. And then we both ended up sagging against the parapet.

"Oh, gods, that wasn't funny at all," I said, giggling. "I'm worried we may not be able to safely throw this pot away. It might, you know, contaminate the groundwater."

Brand made vague motions with his hands, like he was trying to sketch out actual word bubbles. He managed two. "Half House."

"Yeah. We've come a long way in a pretty quick time, haven't we?" Another wave of intoxication hit, a massive, flannel-covered wave. I laughed and took another hit.

"I like being a Companion," Brand said. "It always made so much sense to me. Like, when we were kids? And Nanny Patience used to tell us that please was the magic word? Even then, I remember thinking, I can't wait to be a Companion, because having a lot of knives on you would make conversations go so much quicker than using a weak-ass magic word. Breathe. *Breathe!*" He pounded me on the back.

I wasn't sure what he meant until black dots danced in my vision. Oh, yeah. I exhaled smoke and coughed.

"Remember when the Hanged Man made me stop breathing?" I said. "That sucked."

"You want to get high and talk about the Hanged Man?"

"You're right. Bad choice. Why didn't we bring food?"

"What if we flip a coin to see who does a kitchen run?" he said.

"Can I toss the coin?" I asked.

He grumbled about it but said yes. We had a single Canadian quarter between us. I flipped it in the air, and it vanished over the edge of the tower.

"Just what, exactly, were you unclear about?" he said.

We looked over the edge of the tower and only saw a giant black spot where an ocean was. Then we got lost in that for a long, long time, because the world was *right there*. Sun Estate was *right there*.

Brand started poking his lips after what felt like hours and hours. "Are these moving? They don't feel like they're moving. Am I making a sound right now?"

"I'm not sure. Try barking. Or mooing."

"You fuck," he said. He closed his eyes. "I mean fuck you."

"If this pot robs you of your ability to swear . . . I mean, the *possibilities*," I marveled. "It's like kryptonite."

"It's not robbing me of any of my abilities," he said angrily.

"Did you hear the trapdoor opening?" Addam asked.

"Of course I did," Brand said, then just about jumped out of his skin.

"Addam's here!" I shouted happily. And he had a wrinkled plastic bag from the kitchen dangling from one finger, which was so unexpected that it felt like a hallucination. "Addam are you really here?"

"I am," he said, and brushed his lips against my head. "Did you just say the words *this pot?*"

"Anna found our old stash. It's making Brand cough a lot and forget how to swear. Do you want some?"

Addam's lips curled into a small smile. "I shall observe, for now."

We all decided to sit down on the ground. Addam had somehow

decided to bring snacks, beer, and a blanket with him. He got between me and Brand, and flapped the blanket out so that it covered all three of us. We each got an arm around our shoulders, though I got the cool metal hand.

Brand said, "Remember that time we both got high? And your father came in?"

"I do," I said.

"So tell the story," he said.

"You already know it."

"But Addam doesn't," Brand said. He made an exasperated sound. "I'm giving you permission to blather. Seize the fucking day."

"Your swear function is returning. So. Okay. We were watching this TV show. And my father walks in. We're both incredibly stoned and freaked out. So we just sat there watching the TV, really quiet and intently, like it was some school project and not a supremely weird reaction to an authority figure coming into your room. And droplets of Lysol are still literally floating through the air. So I get nervous and start saying, wow, look at this actress. Her gaze is so intense. I can't believe she can hold that look so long, it's a really good show, Dad, want to watch? And after another long moment, my father says, *The video is on pause, Rune.*"

Laughter was startled out of Addam.

"And he turned around and walked out," I said.

Addam kissed the top of my head, kissed the top of Brand's head, and said, "My guys."

And we got silent after that again.

Because the world was right there.

THE PRINCIPALITY CIARAN

"What's that? What's with the arms?" Brand demanded.

I stopped in the middle of a staff exercise, gasping for breath. "I'm keeping my balance, asshole."

"That's not balance, that's the fucking dance chorus for a 1950s musical. You're supposed to be a fighter, not a sailor on shore leave."

I waited until he moved down the line to criticize one of the kids, and glared daggers at his back.

It was Sunday, two full weeks after the events in the rejuvenation center. It was a day we usually reserved for family training sessions before the kids went back to Magnus for a four-day session.

Max was practicing staff work. Quinn and Addam sparred, trying to retrain Addam's weapon grip now that he was fighting with the weight of a metal hand. Corbie was dancing around Corinne, trying to snag an extra graham cracker out of her hand. And Anna was sulking by herself. She'd been punished since yesterday, after she'd made Corbie eat a teaspoon of popcorn kernels, locked him outside in the afternoon heat, and told him the popcorn was going to pop in his stomach. By the time an adult got involved, he was reciting a tear-filled litany of who needed to adopt each of his stuffed animals.

"Look at where your hands are," Brand barked at Max after a quick exchange of staff blows. "You've exposed them. I'm not even trying to hit you—I'm trying to hit *them*—and when I hurt them enough that they're not doing their job, you're finished."

"Anything else?" Max asked through gritted teeth.

"Yes. Sweep your feet along the ground when you move, don't pick your foot up and put it down like that. If something is behind you, you want to bump into it, not put your foot on it and lose balance."

Max stopped swinging his staff, bent over, and took a few lungfuls of air. I watched the look on his face fade from irritation to determination, and he launched into another series of horizontal strikes.

Brand eventually came back to stand next to me, watching Max. "He's good," he whispered.

"He has a good teacher."

"Don't butter me up. You're not done yet."

"You know," I said, "I'd like a little credit. I'm here, aren't I? Have you seen my stomach? You can actually see which muscles might be a six-pack."

"A six pack of what? Plush stuffed animals?" When I opened my mouth to argue, he waved his hand in the air. "No. No. You keep saying you're *getting your six-pack back*. What does that mean to you? It's not like they're a leaf blower you lent to a neighbor. This is a daily commitment."

"I—"

"Dad bod," Brand enunciated.

"What?"

"You want me to be okay with your dad bod."

"I . . . I . . ." Each I started with a different outraged inflection, which simmered into a baleful what-are-you-saying gesture with my arms.

"You want a dad bod," Brand repeated. "And that's fine. I get it. You're an administrator now. Fine. I'll be the only one who keeps in shape. You're the Arcana—it's your decision if you want to leave me behind and do something different."

My anger doused. "Guilt trip? You're pulling out a guilt trip?"

"Quinn!" Brand yelled. "Leave the butterfly alone! Go hit your brother with the sword!"

"Do you think we need to get Max more training?" I asked.

Brand gave me the look he usually gave me when I was changing the subject. He let it happen with an eye roll. "So you're actually saying I'm *not* good enough?"

"You are, but I'm wondering if we need a fae fighter."

"You think he should be using his shapeshifting?"

"We know he can manipulate his nails and skin color. I keep wondering what if he could do more than just grow his nails. What if he could sharpen or thicken them?"

"That almost sounds like Beast Throne stuff," Brand said, and damned if he didn't shudder a little. Lord Devil's court was the home of the island Weres, where he was as well known for his shapeshifting magic as he was his brutal reign.

"The fae used to have ranks of fighters, long ago. Maybe some of the training still exists? Nothing to do with the Beast Throne."

Brand stared at Max another long moment, then said, "Let's think about it."

He was about to head back over to Max when Corbie tugged on his sleeve. He had cracker crumbs on his upper lip, and Quinn's old 3CUPS T-shirt hung to his knees. "I want to train," he said in his hoarse voice.

"You want to train," Brand repeated.

Corbie nodded.

"Okay," Brand said. "Show me what to do when a strange man comes up and offers you a bag of candy."

Corbie's eyes went wide. Then he squinted in concentration, and stood straight with his hands folded politely behind his back.

Brand sighed. "Okay, a strange man who looks like a really bad guy comes up to you and offers you a bag of candy. What do you do then?"

Corbie mimicked chopping at the air with a series of martial arts moves while deftly swiping an invisible bag out of the bad guy's hands.

"I appreciate your honest priorities," Brand said. "You're in. I'll train you."

"Oh, boy!" Corbie shouted, dancing from foot to foot. Then he shouted, "I need to pee!" and ran for the edge of the field.

That, apparently, was too much for Anna. She stomped over to us, taking special care to raise clouds of dust. She planted herself in front of us and said, "If you won't let me train with staves, let me practice my magic. I need to practice my magic."

"You told Corbie his stomach would explode," I said.

She continued as if I hadn't spoken. "My magic is getting *worse,* not better. It's *harder* to use it since you started training me."

"That's because you had no skill or discipline. Your use of magic was tied to your emotion. I'm giving you control, Anna. Do you want to be reliant on temper tantrums to cast spells?"

Her face shut down. Gods, she reminded me of Brand. That same neutral fury when challenged. "Anna," I said, but calmer. "I need you to trust me."

"And why do you think magic is more important than staff work?" Brand demanded.

"Can you smash a bottle with the power of your mind?" Anna said.

Brand looked around him and spotted an empty glass iced tea bottle on the arm of a lawn chair. He went over, picked it up, and smashed it against the pavement. He said, "Mind move hand. Hand move bottle. Bottle smash. And by the way, Anna, that's the sort of reasoning that keeps scions from fighting their way out of a paper bag. But I'll tell you what—we'll flip for it. Heads, you go tell Queenie we're ready for breakfast, then sweep up that glass. Tails, we have a one-on-one training session, however you want."

"Fine," she said, and the two of them squared off for a coin toss.

After Brand won, she hopped a nearby railing onto a patio, and vanished into the house without complaint. I watched her go with a worried expression, and turned to Corinne. Corinne beat me to the conversation by saying, "Would you let Brand run the coin toss?"

"Hell no. He cheats. And that's not like Anna," I said. "She's never rude. She's got opinions, sure, but she's not usually angry like this. What's going on?"

Corinne gave me a troubled look. "I don't know. I used to know every thought in her head, but now... Have you talked with her about being your heir? Does she understand what that means?"

"It doesn't mean anything right now. I just want her to be a kid."

"Perhaps that is what you should talk about," Addam suggested. He settled onto the ground and tugged me to a sitting position beside him. When we were level, he grinned at the sweat on my forehead and drew a smiley face in it.

Not long after that, we all gathered our things and headed to breakfast. Sunday brunch had become a Thing. Everyone was welcome—family, friends, staff. We didn't have a big budget, so it was mostly a large spread of cereal, huge jars of yogurt, and juice from concentrate. Queenie splurged on one item, usually, and today was eggs and seasoned hash browns.

She even kept separate plates of shredded hash browns for me, Brand, and Max. We gave her a Sunday peck on the cheek and retreated to a corner of the western veranda. In good weather, we sat there. It was the largest outdoor space facing the ocean.

I'd barely shoveled one plastic forkful into my mouth when Mayan walked through the French doors. His braids were knotted into a bun at the back of his head, and he had an accordion folder in his hands.

A year ago, I would have pretended not to perk up. Now, I perked up.

Mayan went over to Corinne first, kissed her on the cheek, and said something that made her smile. Brand and I, plates in hand, casually edged closer. We were in earshot when Corbie ran up to Mayan and said, "Did you give me a pony ride when I was a baby?"

"Was this photographed?" Brand said. "Corbie, ask him to do it again."

Corinne put a gentle but firm hand over Corbie's mouth, whispered the words chocolate chips, and pointed to some pancakes that Queenie had made special for him. He ran off.

Mayan glanced around at the crowd milling about the banquet table. "Sorry to come calling unannounced. I'd like to borrow the three of you." His gaze took in me, Corinne, and Brand.

"Rejuvenation Center?" I guessed.

"Rejuvenation Center," he agreed.

* * *

We climbed into a minivan, which may have led to many jokes, except it was armored to its grille with tech and spells. It even had a built-in desk and laptop. Mayan instructed the driver to circle the neighborhood, then raised the partition.

"It's been two weeks since the incident," he began. "The Arcanum has kept a lid on public reaction and is in direct communication with the affected families. For all that, we're hitting dead ends. I'd like to review what we know."

"Thanks for including me," Corinne said, which was slightly edged, but quickly lost in a frown. She looked at me hesitantly. "That's all right with you?"

"Of course," I said, and meant it.

"I'll start by letting you know that the pharmacist died. He never regained consciousness in the hospital."

"Damn," Brand whispered. "What about the video I found near him?"

"I'll play it in a moment. Other new info includes the sigil audit, and a debriefing with the center's daytime manager." Mayan opened the accordion folder and shuffled through the contents. He laid some paperwork on the built-in desk's surface. "Much of our follow-up confirms on-site speculation. The only sigils that were ultimately taken were tied to individual guests who died in the massacre. Seventeen in total. None of the sigils had a legacy bond to the individual's family, which means they could be claimed in conquest. There's also a psychological profile here based on the usable sigils that were discarded. It seems to align with what Rune suggested: if the individual in question needed sigils, then dismissing usable ones due to personal preference indicates a . . . mindset we traditionally associate with the nobility."

"Then why wear simple clothes? With mud on her shoes?" I murmured.

Mayan pulled out another report. "The mud is a type of clay found in the deepest parts of the Warrens. You know as well as I do that infiltrating the Warrens for information is not an easy mission. And we've turned up little. Lord Fool's court has representation there, so we're trying to locate him for discussion."

There were two known subterranean areas of the city. The Warrens were a mishmash of translocations gone horribly wrong. And beneath the Warrens were the Lowlands, an area as much cave as translocation. Neither was a safe place, and no maps of them existed.

"Trying to locate him?" Brand asked. "Is he missing?"

"Lord Fool is unpredictable. And highly mobile. Being unable to reach him is not so unusual as to suggest a critical concern at this juncture."

"You mentioned the daytime manager," Corinne said. "That would be Jane Bludrick. She and I had coffee every morning I wasn't in the machine. Honest sort."

"She's been cleared, and her debriefing did provide a few interesting items. We've created a composite sketch of the woman we'll call Subject Jade." He put a finger on one piece of paper and slid it from the rest, angling it toward Brand.

Brand picked it up and showed us. A pencil sketch depicted an old woman—a genuinely old, heavily wrinkled woman. I'm not sure I'd seen an Atlantean so ravaged by mortality, and certainly not a noble. None would risk letting their body age to such a state before seeking rejuvenation treatment.

"Any pictures of post-rejuvenation?" I asked. "I know it didn't work, but did it change her face at all?"

"Yes. But I have no composite of that. Anyone who saw it is dead. I only have an email from the tech saying that rejuvenation yielded minimal results, and was deemed a failure. The matter was flagged for Lady Priestess's personal review given the extremely unusual results."

"What else did the daytime manager say?" Brand asked.

"Trying to backtrack the identity of Subject Jade through payment was a dead end. She used an extremely expensive and private package."

"Jane mentioned that some guests check in under anonymity," Corinne said. "But it doesn't make sense, in this context. The package costs as much as . . . what, a sigil? Six figures, at least. If this Subject Jade is hard up for sigils, how can she afford the treatment?"

"Maybe she had to spend money to make money," Brand said. "Maybe someone else paid for it."

"I suspect that," Mayan said. "But, again, the nature of the transaction precludes tracking the source of money. There was one other interesting detail. Apparently, at the time of the murders, the center had a low client list, and follow-up research shows that none of those clients were particularly strong spell-casters."

"That's too neat a coincidence," Corinne said. "She picked this time deliberately."

"If she did, it means Subject Jade could have always intended to kill witnesses," Brand said.

I shook my head. "Maybe. But that certainly wasn't in her head when she snapped. That was rage. That was a tantrum. That woman is a noble, I think we're right about that."

"I agree," Mayan said. "And we also suspect, based on other details, that she's a principality-level power. Corinne, that is highly privileged information, and please don't ask questions on how we know that." He looked at Brand and I as he said it, though very subtly. The message was received: Arcana Majeure was not to be discussed.

"But this is where it gets interesting," he said. He opened a heavy panel in the desk to reveal a video screen and keyboard. A video app was already queued up to play. He pressed a button, then leaned back so we had an unobstructed view of the screen.

It was not long.

A man's arm blocks the screen. It snakes back, showing a freshly damaged face. There is a woman's body in the edge of the frame.

In audio only, a voice—a woman's raspy voice. "You wretched dogs! You foul, useless dogs!"

The man opens his mouth and says something as his fingers spasm against the ground, then he reaches out again and pushes the camera away. The vid spins—man, desk, wall, darkness.

I reached past Mayan and rewound the footage four more times before I felt I'd seen it enough. No one stopped me.

Finally, Brand said, "Our guest."

"That's what I heard him say too," Corinne said.

"He's telling us it was a guest," I said. "Did you hear the woman's accent?"

Mayan smiled at me. "Wretched. She said it in one syllable—*retched.*"

Old Atlantean was a strange language. It heavily adopted English and Latin words, yet truncated some, and expanded others. People still pull the word *wrecked* into two syllables; but in this case, *wretched* was crammed into one.

"Old Atlantean," I said to Brand. "So she's likely a centennial." I leaned back in the soft minivan seats, resting my brain against the headrest. "I understand *why.* Anger over lack of rejuvenation? That sense of superiority thwarted? What I don't understand is *how.* How the hell does a principality who is also a centennial—who may have been alive *hundreds* of years if she uses an Old Atlantean accent like that—stay off the radar this long? And how do they suddenly wind up *on* the radar?"

"Exactly," Mayan said. "I need you to talk with Ciaran, Rune. He's the friendliest principality we have available to us. He refuses to talk to the Tower about this directly, but is willing to discuss it with you alone. I know it's rude to ask you to go anywhere without Brand, but Lord Tower will lend this to you." He tapped a hand on the roof of the minivan. "It's one of his personal rides. You'd survive a tornado hit in it."

I looked at Brand, who shrugged uncomfortably and said, "The driver will wait and bring Rune back too, right?"

"My word," Mayan said,

Brand looked at me, and opened his mouth, but I beat him by saying, "I'll look up and down. Total three-sixty."

He gave me a quick, one-side-only smile. It was a bit of an Addam gesture, but it looked good on Brand, too.

Then the smile dropped off my face. "Wait. Ciaran is inviting me to his home? I get to see where he *lives?*"

Ciaran's home. Holy shit.

The outside was a half dome, with no windows, on the southeastern end of the city. It was set back in a small, wooded area off Nazaca Road, a powerful global ley line. My skin itched as I walked through my friend's dense, protective wards, toward the ornate front doors. Inside, I stared at a tiny marble mudroom, until a quiet fae staff member ushered me down a short hallway, up a flight of stairs, and into an explosion of colorful gaudiness.

"What the fu . . ." I whispered, turning in a slow circle once I was left alone.

It was some sort of bathhouse from an earlier century. Turkish, I think? There were shiny green and blue tiles, polished teak wood beams, bronzed lanterns. The ceiling was glorious: arched and painted a rich red. There were no windows, but small, circular panels of wall had been painted in bright colors and covered in gauzy muslin.

I went to a wall, where a plaque said the baths were available to women until noon, and men until six o'clock. Below, on a smaller plaque, were rates for admission in shillings.

"It's beautiful, isn't it?" Layne said behind me.

I turned in surprise. Layne was wearing calf-length boots and a yellow sundress. Their light brown hair, fresh with pumpkin-colored highlights, was pinned back away from their face.

Ciaran and Layne had formed a tight, unconventional friendship. I had no idea how old Ciaran was, but I strongly suspected he was as old, if not older, than Lord Tower—and I'd seen memories inside Lord Tower's head that were centuries old. Layne, on the other hand, was a teenage trauma survivor. I'd learned recently that Ciaran had used his dreamwalking ability to help Layne navigate their night terrors.

I refused to be alarmed by their friendship: the evidence of Ciaran's good intentions was too manifest, and I trusted him. Corinne was another story. She was coming to accept Ciaran's role as a mentor, but the amount of time Layne spent away from Sun Estate bothered her.

"Hey you," I said. "Does Corinne know you're here?"

It was both the right and wrong thing to say. I watched their face close down.

"Layne," I said.

"What?"

"Do you really need me to put this into words? You are fifteen. I give you a tremendous amount of freedom, but there are limits."

"You don't trust Ciaran to keep me safe?"

"I trust you to tell your aunt where you are at all times."

"And if she has a problem with me being here?"

"Then you need to do a better job convincing her," I said, which was harsh but true. I softened my tone and said, "Deal?"

Layne nodded. "Ciaran is on his way. We were making a snack. I'll bring some to you."

They turned and left too quickly for goodbyes. I barely had time to sigh before Ciaran slid in the room through a different doorway, timed too closely for an accident.

"Darling," Ciaran whispered. "I am so hungover today that even my thumb hurts from the number of times I flicked my lighter. You must bring Layne home so I can stop pretending to be a role model."

I gestured around me. "This? This is a translocation. Right?"

"Mmm," he said, and went over to one of the chaise lounges. I'm not sure I'd ever seen a chaise lounge that Ciaran declined to drape himself over.

I took one of the brightly painted seats near him. "Is Layne inviting themself over too much?"

"Ach, no. Not to worry about that. They're lovely. I just happened to have a bit of an all-night soirée since last Thursday."

I smiled and shook my head. "Thanks for inviting me. I'm guessing you don't like having people here?"

He looked around him. What he saw wasn't what I saw; the emotion in his eyes was guarded and very real. "You are discreet."

I decided to change the subject. "You know why I'm here?"

"Oh, yes. Lord Tower was somewhat vexed I refused to run to the Pac Bell at his bidding. Bless his scratched little heart."

He sank back into the lounge and folded his hands on his stomach. Ciaran was a thin, tall, handsome man of indeterminate age. He always looked as if he'd just bit his tongue and licked his lips. His hair was green today, not the normal blue, which nevertheless matched the room and chair fabric.

"Are you excited about your gala next week?" he asked.

"People keep asking me that. What's to be excited about? It's like a zoo benefit to show off the new exhibit. Brand is excited because he got to pick half of the gift registry."

Ciaran pulled out a pack of cigarettes and field stripped one. He handed me the filtered end, and took the unfiltered half between his lips. He lit the end with a rhinestone-covered Zippo.

Passed the lighter, I lit the cigarette and enjoyed a highly forbidden treat.

"Very well," Ciaran said. "No more small talk. Tell me what happened. All of it. From the very start. I want to know what color *boxers* you chose when they woke you up in the wee hours. Details, Sun."

So I told him. It took the better part of forty minutes, because I respected Ciaran enough to make it a thorough debrief.

Mayan had sent copies of both videos to my phone using a secure app. Ciaran appeared to play both videos several times, until I realized he'd only watched them once and then swiped into my photos, where he was thumbing through recent pics.

"Godsdamnit," I said, grabbing it back.

"Addam has quite a toned backside," he remarked. He blew smoke on the tip of his latest cigarette to make the ember flare. "You caught that Old Atlantean accent?"

"One of the reasons I'm here. Plus the suspicion that she's a principality. Do you know of any other reason rejuvenation magic would have failed?"

"Why would I? I have little to do with Lady Priestess and her niche economy."

"But you know more about magic than anyone else on this island," I said, which made his eyes flick to me. "Can you think of any other reason rejuvenation magic would fail so spectacularly?"

"Yes," he said after a pause. "Someone could be actively working against it. Sabotage, in other words. But in such a circumstance there would be signs, and Lord Tower's team would not miss them. You've arrived at a rather secure assumption—it's likely related to Majeure use."

I leaned forward in my chair, careful not to ash my cigarette on the beautiful tile. "How is this possible, Ciaran? An unknown principality who is potentially centuries old?"

"Perhaps she didn't come into her abilities until late in life. There are stories, old stories, about trauma triggering latent abilities. Perhaps she's been abroad. Perhaps . . ." He trailed off, and narrowed his eyes. "But that barrier. That barrier. If it really took both Lord Tower and Lady Death to break it? Strength like that has faded from fact to rumor to history to myth. We're simply not the people we were in our own legends."

"Do you have any thoughts?"

"I do, actually. You came to me because I'm an old principality."

"But beautifully maintained."

He managed to curtsy from his sprawled position. "You should widen your circle, if you're asking for information. There are people not in power who are as old as Lord Tower and I."

"The Empress?"

"Well, certainly. But I'm thinking more local. She is not on this island. I believe I would know if it were otherwise."

I didn't ask how, but that was interesting, if not entirely surprising given what I suspected about Ciaran's true origins.

"Lady Death took over from her mother, the Dowager Lady Death, during the Atlantean War," Ciaran reminded me. "Her mother was never a great power, but she was a massive gossip. And she is *old*. Very, very old. Perhaps we can all share a vodka gimlet at your gala."

"Sounds like a plan. Unless the Tower wants to talk with her sooner. Can I ask you something else?"

"Of course."

"Have you spent much time in the Warrens? I heard you have."

Ciaran made a face I didn't quite understand—a bit reluctant, a bit acknowledgement. "Those of us with power have a responsibility to those without. There are people who need and deserve help there. There is so much *life* there. So much *potential*. Such a great need for help and hope. I would hate to think anything I say to you results in Lord Tower deploying phalanxes of armed guards into the Warrens."

"If this Subject Jade is there, I'm not sure we have a choice. She's dangerous and powerful, and she nearly set off a house war."

"It's hypocritical, Rune Sun. Do you know how many people die of starvation or violence or drug overdoses in the Warrens and Lowlands every day? Many, many more than those who died in that pampered facility."

"I don't disagree, but if we do nothing, they're just as much at risk from collateral damage. This isn't over. Whatever happened, it's not the beginning, and it's certainly not the end."

Ciaran spread his fingers in one of his *as you say* gestures. "Then yes, to answer your question. I am familiar with the Warrens. The areas closest to the surface, generally, where people haven't quite given up completely."

"Is anything new happening there? Mayan mentioned his people have been looking for Lord Fool."

"Lord Fool does spend quite a bit of time there. His Revelry is . . . well, transient. Unpredictable. He is an Arcana with only one rule: thou must abide anarchy."

"And have you heard anything?"

"No. No, I haven't. But I can try."

"Fair enough."

Layne came in at that point with an ornate silver tray, on which were two fancy plates of bone china with oranges on them. Or orange products? The tops had been cut off, and the insides were filled with a type of pudding or custard.

"Buttered oranges," Ciaran said with relish. "Such a shame they're out of vogue. You're a peach, dearest. Thank you."

Layne nodded and withdrew from the room. *That* interested me, because they didn't try to stay or speak. They behaved like an apprentice.

Absentmindedly, I took a bite of the custard. Then I groaned. "Oh, my gods. Oh, my gods." Spooning more into my mouth, I said, "Is there an entire stick of butter in here? We need to put this everywhere. Everywhere. We need to put this in soap dispensers and toothpaste tubes."

Delighted, Ciaran nibbled on his own.

With my spoon, I pushed the orange aside to admire the plate. It had arched patterns of blue and red around the edge. In the exact center, below the orange, was a tiny red ship with a white star in the middle.

My spoon clattered to the plate. I stood up. I looked around me with new eyes, and didn't even realize I was chewing on a nail until apple bitter swarmed my taste buds.

"Holy shit," I whispered. "Ciaran, is this the *Titanic?*"

He shrugged.

"Ciaran," I repeated, louder, because a shrug just didn't cut it. "Am I standing in the *Titanic?*"

"A part of it. Just a little part. These are the first-class baths. And I may also have a first-class smoking room. Down there." He waved a lazy hand behind him.

"Oh, my gods, Ciaran, this is . . . Do you know how furious the human world would be if they knew you'd . . . you'd . . ."

He blew a raspberry.

I went over to a wall of photos. I don't think they were part of the original design: they were reproductions—or actual?—photographs from the voyage. Mostly the launch, where the photographers were able to escape the doomed vessel before it sailed from England.

I looked at the black and white faces, shaking my head. "I'm in the *Titanic*. You have a piece of the *Titanic* in a big cement bunker. How did I not know this? How—"

I slammed a hand next to one of the photos and leaned close. Pressed my nose to the glass. There was Ciaran, waving from a railing.

"You were on the Titanic," I whispered.

"I don't like talking about it. I was ill and recovering at the time. But yes. I saved who I could. It was . . . Well. In its own way, that night was a war, and one never forgets one's wars."

It was too much. I hadn't come here with the intention of spilling secrets, but this was too much. It was amazing, and extraordinary, and spoke to the depths of the person eating a dainty bite of buttered orange. It loosened my tongue, and the words just tumbled out.

"Godsdamnit, Ciaran, I know who you are."

He beamed. "Do tell. Use adjectives."

"Ciaran, I'm serious. Do . . . do you not trust me? Do you think I wouldn't keep your secret? I would. I value you so much."

The coyness washed out of his face. Slowly, he placed his spoon alongside the plate.

"My secret," he finally said.

"I figured it out ages ago. I'm half-convinced you deliberately left me clues."

"Clues," he said. "Because I am?"

"You're the Magician, Ciaran," I said on an exhale. "I don't know who that man is who sits on the Hex Throne seat, but he's not in charge. He's not the real Magician. You are."

Ciaran stood up, went to the other side of the room, and stared at one of the round wall murals. Portholes. I now saw that they were painted like portholes.

"Does he know?" Ciaran asked after a very long minute.

I knew who he meant. There were certain people in Atlantis who you spoke of in pronouns, and it was simply understood. "I don't think so," I said. "I never told Lord Tower. I've never even had a discussion with him about it. But why—"

"Clues," Ciaran repeated. "What clues did I leave?"

"When we were fighting Rurik, you had a strong reaction to the idea that Ashton could breach the defenses around the Magician's Westlands compound. You got mad about that a couple times, actually. And in the Sunken Mall that time, you were really interested in the elementals' version of the Hex Throne. And then back when I was fighting Lord Hanged Man, you didn't just pull favors from the man I call Lord Magician. You overruled him, Ciaran. You pulled his leash. Who is he?"

He did not answer. Instead, he asked, "Why would you think I deliberately left clues for you?"

"I don't know. Maybe the same reason I took up my father's mantle."

"And you did that because?"

"Because I have people. So many people to protect. And I think, now, you do too. We owe you so much." My voice thickened with memory. "You saved Brand. That time in the Westlands, when he was fighting on the patio and I couldn't get to him, and you broke through the wall . . . You saved him. I would have lost him without you. Do you think I could ever repay that?"

He turned to face me, and his Aspect rose.

We were in a room, but not. There was the wall of a ghost ship behind him, and also a river current—a river of shining mercury, of magic in its purest form. The ripples of light I always saw in his eyes were now everywhere—sunlight playing across this imbued torrent of energy.

For a moment—for just the sliver of a second—I thought I understood that which we were not allowed to know on this side of the grave.

His Aspect faded into shining eyes.

"Lord Magician," I whispered. "Brother. Ciaran. I see you."

"I see you too, Lord Sun. Guard my secret, and respect my taciturnity. I do not wish to speak of this further right now."

"I understand. I'll gather Layne and leave. I will guard your secret, and I will guard your secret, and I will guard your secret." The force of my words flowed around us.

Ciaran sat down in a chair. His gaze fixed in the middle distance, and he said nothing else.

I picked up my buttered orange and hoofed it out of there, calling Layne's name.

Diana waited for me at the gates by the staff parking lot. As the minivan rumbled away behind us, Layne and I walked up to her.

"I didn't realize you would be off-site," she said evenly, with a quick glance at Layne.

"Things don't always fall apart the moment I leave," I said. "That's why you're here."

"That is not why I am here, right now, at this instant," she said. "I am here to address that which fell apart once you left. Are you familiar with the shed that was inside the elasmotherium's pen?"

"Did you just use the past tense?"

"Your youngest ward appears to have been teaching the elasmotherium to play fetch with a Frisbee, and the Frisbee landed on the roof of the shed. The elasmotherium made considerable effort to retrieve the Frisbee. There is no more shed."

My heart stopped, started, stopped, started.

Layne said, "Do you mean Corbie? Corbie was inside the pen?"

"Alone, yes. Apparently, he learned how to gain access by moving a specific sequence of wardstones."

"Where is he," I said.

"Still by the pen."

* * *

Corbitant Dawncreek hadn't had the easiest life.

He had no memory of his mother. His father died when he was just a baby. He'd lived in near-poverty, and nearly watched his sibling consumed by the Hanged Man's court. Two of his homes had been destroyed. *Two* of them. One of the fires had damaged his vocal cords to the point where he spoke in a constant hoarse voice.

For all that, he was a happy child. He was loved. He spent the weekends in ecstasy, when Max, Quinn, and Anna returned from school. He was morose when they left on Mondays, but we took turns keeping him occupied.

I'd known he was a curious child. Corinne and I, as a secret project, once magically tracked his movements on an average weekday morning. It amounted to this:

Jumping out of bed at dawn. Hopping around his room. Running down to the kitchen in his pajamas to see what was being made for breakfast. Then he would run from window to window on the first floor, excited to see if anything had changed. Then he did the same on the second and third floor, which presented challenges, because many of those rooms were occupied. Apparently, he'd been racing in and out of my bedroom without waking me up; but I've heard Brand bellow more than once.

Then Corbie would put on giant Wellington boots he'd found in the basement and go see if there were tadpoles in the garden pond; or if the new groundskeeper would let him throw hard corn at the chickens; or if the waves in the ocean looked particularly bouncy.

I knew he visited Flynn constantly. He'd even been the one to name the dinosaur after an old neighbor's much-loved cat.

I did not know he'd ever, ever been past the wards without a chaperone.

It's possible I would laugh about this someday, but not now. There was nothing humorous about this now, not when it involved a six-year-old boy, not when it involved a several ton creature with a horn that could crush concrete.

* * *

The boy in question was standing by the warded pen with two guards and Quinn. His face was fixed into his crafty I'm-just-a-little-kid-and-don't-understand-any-of-this expression of carefully scrubbed innocence. Behind him, on the other side of the wardstones, stood the Siberian unicorn. It had a florescent orange Frisbee in its giant mouth.

I stood and stared at Corbie until his eyes widened and he realized the little kid act wasn't working. Then I crooked a finger at Quinn and stepped away from everyone. Layne ran over to Corbie and started hissing words of angry worry.

"And you are here because?" I said to Quinn.

"I sort of saw it? It doesn't always happen this way."

"What doesn't happen this way?"

Quinn hesitated. "I don't think it's my story to share. It seems rude to talk about people before they become the people they become. If it helps, Flynn won't hurt Corbie. Flynn is . . ." Quinn chewed on his lip for a moment. He settled on, "Flynn is smart."

"Flynn is a wholly inappropriate pet for a child. Even if Flynn wouldn't deliberately hurt Corbie, that doesn't mean he couldn't crush or hurt the boy by accident. Did you know this might happen, Quinn?"

Quinn's worry faded into surprise, and not a good type of surprise. "I thought you understood me," he said in a hurt voice.

"I thought we understood each other," I countered. "Why did you not give me a heads-up?"

"Because you won't do what I tell you, and sometimes that makes the worst things happen. The *worst* things."

This didn't seem like the type of thing we were going to resolve on the spot, and I didn't want to get angrier than I was. I turned from Quinn and went over to Corbie.

Squatting down, I asked, "What did you do wrong? Can you tell me that?"

Corbie nodded quickly. "I threw bad."

I held out my arms. Corbie rushed into them like he was getting a hug, but I picked him up instead and walked us over to the enclosure. Flynn made a high-pitched sound and dropped the Frisbee in the grass. He sounded, nearly exactly, like a dehydrated porpoise.

"He would never mean to hurt you," I said, "but he's very big, and you are very small, Corbitant. What if you'd been standing next to the tool shed when it collapsed?" I turned to our left, so we could see the pile of splintered wood that had once held animal feed. "Plus, Flynn is old. He could have broken a leg. He could have been hurt."

Corbie sniffed.

"And now I need to find the person who told you how to get inside the pen, and I need to fire them."

"No one showed me!" he said in a raspy rush.

"But you saw someone else do it, right? Someone let you watch. That is irresponsible. I cannot afford to have anyone on this estate who would be so unintentionally careless."

More sniffles. Corbie rubbed his eyes with the sides of his hands. He buried himself against my neck and cried for a little while. Then he said, "Can I go lie down please? Please Rune?"

"I'll take him," Queenie said. I looked over my shoulder to see that she and Brand had joined the group.

There was also a third person with them, a strange man, though he'd remained standing at a discreet distance. I passed Corbie over to Queenie with a murmured *thank you*, and tucked my T-shirt back under my belt so that I looked presentable.

At a close distance, the strange man cleared his throat. I cut my eyes at Brand, who whispered, "Vadik Amberson. The late Lord Amberson's youngest son."

Shit. Vadik's aunt Elicia had died at the rejuvenation center. I'd extended an invitation to them for my coronation gala.

He was older than Addam, appearing as a man in his late thirties, perhaps early forties. He was almost handsome—a strong nose, lips, jaw—

except there was just too much *face* around his face. A large forehead, cheeks that seemed to swallow his cheekbones.

"Vadik Amberson," I said.

"Lord Sun." He bowed from the neck.

"Welcome to Sun Estate. Have we offered you refreshments?"

"Oh, yes. Your girl was most kind and efficient. She's a credit to your new staff."

"That's Queenie. She's been with us forever." I shook my head, and refocused. "Please accept my condolences for the loss of your aunt. It was tragic."

The politeness flickered in his eyes—a tightening that may have been honest grief. "Thank you. That's why I stopped by. I wanted to thank you for the floral arrangement you sent, as well as the invitation to your coronation. It was most generous of you to remember my family."

"The Ambersons were a loyal and valued part of my father's court. It was my pleasure to reestablish contact."

"I was hoping we may speak more of that," he said. "Over the last few years we've . . . recovered our status, you might say. My father's death was a heavy blow, but recent investments have placed us in a much less precarious position. We remain unaffiliated."

The invitation laid there, and I did not pick it up. From the corner of my eye, I saw Diana watching me closely, and she nodded at my lack of an immediate response. Her advice was in the front of my head—along with a gut reaction I couldn't entirely decipher, except that I hadn't liked when he called Queenie *your girl.*

"I'm afraid I have some estate matters to handle at the moment, but we'll make time in the near future. Will you be attending the . . ." Fuck if I was going to say coronation. "The party?"

"It will be our honor. My dear aunt would want it that way, I'm sure." He reached out and touched a sigil on his neck—a silver teardrop. "This was hers, actually. A family sigil. It's like she's with me. She would be pleased to see your estate looking so alive again. When she was younger, she spent—"

Layne cried out. They were bending down next to Quinn, who was on his knees. Quinn's eyes showed wide, shocked whites, and blood began to pour from his nose.

I had barely taken a step toward him when he yelled, "Assassin! Now! Inside! Blades and bombs—healing sigil! Healing sigils now-now-now go-go-go! Go! Run!"

"Layne, get Addam from the beach, he's got healing sigils!" Brand shouted and took off at a sprint.

I paused only long enough to watch Layne pull a box cutter from their pocket, expose the razor blade, and cut an abscess that was hidden beneath their yellow sleeve. Magic flared—Layne's unique form of necromancy activated by exposure to air, helping them cultivate and kill bacterial infections to fuel their abilities. When they began to run, it was supernaturally fast.

A whispered cantrip gave strength to my legs, and I took off. Brand was already half a soccer's pitch away. I let him go, and focused on my own pace, swiping fingers across a sigil to release a Shield. The sabre was already melting into hilt form, urged by my unconscious command.

I poured more speed into the sprint. I didn't bother with the front entrance: I vaulted over the patio balustrade, through the open doors, into the ballroom. All of my senses—magical and mortal—were on alert for signs of disturbance or struggle.

I passed a group of Germanic dweorg smoothing raw material into wall cracks, yelled at them to shelter in place. Turned a corner into the main hall, just as Brand ran out of the kitchen on the other side. "Clear," he shouted.

We heard voices from the back of the house, and raced toward the solarium. Both of us reared back when we saw a person in dirty jeans and a tank top—a woman, young—standing in the archway, her back to us.

"Feet," Brand hissed just as I saw she wore no shoes, and they were flaking with olive-colored mud.

It happened so quickly. The woman shouted, "Too many glows!"

She ran into the room just as Brand reached her, and his hand missed snatching her sleeve by an inch. I ran in the room and saw Anna, Corinne, and Queenie. Corinne had Corbie in her arms.

The girl was running at them with a knife.

Anna dove in the way, and the knife went into her side.

The woman staggered back from Anna, who went pale and began to fall. Corinne was already shoving Corbie at Queenie and grabbing Anna, turning her body to protect the girl from more injury.

The woman spun on me and I saw she had something in her other hand—a round sphere that glistened like liquid.

She threw it at me as I raised my Shield. The sphere sheared off at an angle and burst, so that only my shoulder was splattered by the liquid inside it. I didn't even stop moving—I spun into a kick that took the girl in the solar plexus, just as the hilt of a thrown knife slammed into her temple. She collapsed with an airless grunt.

I didn't worry about the shining liquid until it seared my T-shirt into burning threads, and began to dissolve my skin.

The pain was unreal. I lost track of what was happening. Shouts, orders, the sound of chairs being flung out of the way. I saw Addam arrive and go for Anna, his hands already simmering with Healing spells.

Brand, panicked, was saying, "Hold on, he's coming for you next, oh, fuck Rune, oh, fuck." I tried to look at my shoulder, but my body screamed in protest. It felt like the flesh was being fried from the bone. It *was* doing that, I could *smell it.*

Corinne was there. She grabbed me, kicked the back of my knees, made me crumble to the ground. When Brand tried to stop her, she screamed, "It's rainfire! It sinks with gravity—turn him around, turn him around, before it burrows to his heart!"

I was manhandled so that the point of my melting shoulder was facing the swept tiled floor. Orange droplets began to fall and burn through the stone.

My eyes closed.

They opened and Diana was there, her hands wreathed in their own healing energies.

My eyes closed, and opened, and Layne was there. Addam, Diana, Layne crowded around me. My shoulder felt like someone was grinding a torch into it. I said Anna's name, but my eyes shuttered right afterward.

And then they opened. I blinked, and stayed awake.

I felt the intense tingling of either Healing or shock.

I was on the table that Addam had bought me. He was on one side, Brand on the other. Addam was massaging my wrist; Brand had his hand on my head. I let my head fall to the left, and saw the woman—who did not look like an assassin—restrained in a chair.

Her arms were covered in infected scratches, and they wavered in my sight, because there was magic in the drugs. The Agonies. I'd seen marks like that before, down in the Green Docks. The woman looked like an addict of the Agonies.

"Her feet," I whispered. Then alarm brought back my memory. *"Anna!"*

"The stab missed all her vitals, she's fine. She's fine, Rune," Brand said. "Take it easy."

The woman was moaning. Sobbing. Every word was weaker than the one before it. She cried, "They said they would glow the most, but there were so many glows, there were so many glows."

I tried to tell them to heal her, because I could see that she was in danger. It wasn't just the drugs that pulsed with magic. She was under a spell, and her failure had triggered the shortest of fuses. Every admission pulled her further down the River.

I tried to tell them. I really did. But she died before I pushed a word through my numb lips.

THE GALA

"One week," I said, arms folded firmly across my chest. I stood at a window in the library, where Diana had moved a desk and computer for her own needs. "One week and nothing."

"Not quite nothing," Diana said. "Every attack on another court yields more info. It's a matter of time."

"*One week*," I stressed, "since my thirteen-year-old cousin was stabbed, and now we're all expected to present ourselves in public today."

What had happened at Sun Estate had repeated itself at two other courts: Lady Moon's and Lord Hierophant's. An insane homeless youth or addict managed to breach defenses in those cases and die in a suicide bombing. All incursions were thwarted.

While Brand organized transportation to the gala in the front drive, Diana, Corinne, and I vented frustration. I circled away from the window, a little puzzled at the number of limousines outside, and sat down on the edge of my new seneschal's ad hoc workspace. "We don't even have names to identify the bombers."

"No, but they all corroborate *something* happening in the Warrens," Diana pointed out. "All of the attackers seem to come from there."

"None of these is the most important question as far as I'm concerned," Corinne said. When we looked at her, she said, "Why was Rune first?"

That caused some tingles in the back of my brain; only I wasn't sure if it was a shiver or an insight. I said, "We should cancel the gala."

"We must not, we will not, and we shall be safe," Diana assured me. "And if we're not? While under the protection of the entire Arcanum? Then the entire city is unsafe."

I looked at the time on my phone and saw we were running late. "Let's go before Brand sends out a search party."

The three of us headed for the first floor.

I was in tight pants. Again. Formal court affairs had a particular style for men, and that style more or less started with the crotch and dressed from there. But, since I was Arcana, I was allowed what I called my modesty cape, which I could swish around in front of my lap. It was the cape that Ciaran had given me on the day I claimed my throne, threaded in garnet and burnt umber, my colors.

I saw more guards than usual as we walked through the house. We'd been loaned Arcanum forces from Lady Death and Lord Tower. They had their own private forces and could afford to spare their Arcanum allotment. Even with that, though, Brand had insisted on putting his own security protocols in place for our travel to the gala, which is why I suspected there were more limos than we needed outside.

The main hall contained a swarm of lovely, beautifully dressed people. Every male above their age of majority—which meant Addam and Brand—wore pants as tight as mine, but they didn't have modesty capes.

"That's not what it's fucking called," Brand said when I told him. "You know that, right?"

It's possible he was a little surly because everyone was whispering good-natured jokes about the fit of his pants. Addam had even given him a golf clap, which just about had knives being drawn.

Corbie tugged on Brand's sleeve and shook a mason jar. The word SWER was sketched on the side in permanent marker. It didn't contain just spare change, either. There were M&Ms, buttons, and a Barbie dress.

"Bill me," Brand said, maybe a little too gruffly. That led to him comforting the boy, who started to sniffle, and who already had dried tear tracks on his face. He would not be coming to the gala with us. Queenie—who had flat-out refused to attend as well—and Corbie would be relocated to the Pac Bell at Lord Tower's invitation.

Corinne came up behind them and said, "Just think, Corbie, you'll get to swim in an indoor heated pool on top of a skyscraper. That sounds so fun!"

He shrugged as if it didn't matter, but he also spared a quick look around the room to see if Queenie was ready yet.

"Huh," Brand said, sizing up Corinne's gown. And since Corinne had read the same manual on emotionally stunted Companion expressions of praise, she grunted *huh* back. The two had developed an unspoken détente ever since Corinne's actions during the attack had almost certainly saved my life.

"Okay," I said, clapping my hands. "What's with all these limos?"

"Diversion tactics," Brand said. "Each will travel to Lady Death's compound using different routes, and only one will be filled."

"Then let's get this show on the road," I said.

In the eighteenth century, Atlantis found itself heavily and secretly investing in the economies of the human world. We'd always had our interests in mortal territories—especially the oldest of them, such as Africa and the Amazon, where the magic was as ancient and as powerful, in its way, as our own.

In the early twentieth century, to make our families more palatable to modern convention, we adopted saint monikers to be shared among the direct descendants of Arcana. The name generally echoed some element of our historic duties, as pertinent or not as they may be in the twenty-first century.

Lady Death's family name was Saint Joseph, and her court, the Bone Hollows, had been built on a peninsula in the northeastern corner of Nantucket. The area contained a massive null zone; rumor had it that Lady Death's mother had nearly bankrupt the court to purchase it.

As we toured the nightshade gardens around us, I kept an uneasy eye on a massive stone building with no windows on the edge of the property: the Manse. Inside it was the null zone, and no magic would work there, not even the meanest cantrip.

And we were spending the night there.

* * *

The gardens had a VIP area, and I was the only VIP. Lady Death had insisted on a space where I could remain during the event—excepting the actual coronation—to choose who I wanted to see, and when I wanted to see them. I think she also knew I'd need breathing space, which was kind of her to arrange.

It would be an all-night affair. The minors would head home with Lady Diana and Corinne afterward; only Addam, Brand, and I would spend the night. Diana and Corinne, along with Arcanum guards, would pick up Queenie and Corbie on their way home and stand guard until we returned.

The horde of attendees was limited to the highest circle of each court, with a few side invitations for families such as the Ambersons. There was no black market for tickets—due to the recent bombing unrest, the guest list was carefully cultivated and definitively enforced.

As always, the blend of scions both impressed and bothered me. So much vapidity had seeped into our culture; so much squandered magic and vain spell-casting. But this crowd wasn't filled with your average scion. The sheer gathering of sigils and mass sigils filled the air with a galvanic hum.

"Is that the building we're staying in tonight?" Addam murmured, sliding up behind me.

I looked at the windowless building. "The Manse. Lady Death refused to give me details."

"She wants to surprise us, perhaps."

"Her exact words were: I want you to experience this suffocating tradition with all the joy I do." I looked over my shoulder at him. "Maybe we can find a broom closet inside and make out."

"Be careful, Hero," he murmured, crowding into my side. "Promises are tricky things in New Atlantis, if I decide to hold you to them." I smelled the heat creeping down his face, heating the cologne he'd sprayed on his neck. I inhaled sandalwood and leaned into it.

Brand came up behind us. "Should I drink? I want something in my hand. I hate not being a bodyguard."

Brand was under strict orders to be a Very Good Guest and leave security to Lady Death. That meant he had no idea what to do or where to stand or what to say.

"Order something," I said. We had a private bar on the elevated garden rise. "Order for me, too."

"What's good?" Brand said to the bartender, raising his voice.

"The caterer seems proud of this. He calls it Graveyard Mist." The young man pointed to a flute of . . . bubbles? "It's gin foam and Mongolian cemetery dirt."

"Fucking scions," Brand said. "Addam, you deal with this."

Addam gave Brand a little bow and smile and went about finding us beer. Nearby, I spotted Lady Death, who was climbing the flagstone path to our high green hill. She wore a strikingly simple red dress that looked marvelous against her dark skin.

Beside her was a young woman who appeared as a human in her late twenties, but centuries crouched behind her dark eyes. They might have been sisters except for that.

"Rune Sun," Lady Death said. "May I present my mother, the Dowager Lady Death."

The woman tapped her silver cane on the ground in place of a bow. It was tipped with a tiny skull, as silver-plated as the cane; only I'm pretty sure you'd find bone if you scraped deep enough.

"My lady," I said, and bowed from the waist, a generous but respectful response. "This is my Companion, Lord Brandon Saint John. And this is my—"

Holy shit. I fumbled. Boyfriend? Lover? *Shit!*

"I am his Addam," Addam said smoothly, bringing three bottles of beer to us. He knew Brand well enough that the caps were still firmly in place. "May I get you a drink?"

"The Mongolian grave dirt sounds awesome," I said with a straight face.

"I will find my own company," the Dowager Lady Death muttered, and tapped off to another section of the garden.

Lady Death grimaced. "My deepest apologies, little brother. She is not . . . social. I will have words with her."

"No, please," I said. "Please. This . . . what you've done here . . . it's amazing. I owe you so much. Please."

She hesitated, but nodded. "Most kind. And it appears the visits are beginning." She hid a finger point behind a cupped hand. At the bottom of the slope, several Arcana began to make their way up the path. Lady Priestess was in the lead, and Lady Justice was not far behind.

I snuck a look at Addam's face and saw an expression that didn't fill me with confidence. I think I was about to find out how Lady Justice felt about my co-opting her children and sister.

Brand twisted off a cap and handed me a beer.

"You're with me," I said to him. I hesitated. "Both of you. I want all three of us to greet guests. Will that be a problem, Addam?"

"It will not," he said, genuinely pleased.

"Should I get Anna or Max?" Brand asked.

"No. Not today. Let them be young a while longer. I told Max that he could have a glass of wine every ninety minutes."

"Did you say how big the glass could be?" Brand asked.

"Well, shit," I said.

Addam laughed. "Quinn will be responsible for them both."

"Which Quinn?" Brand asked. "The one in the cute bow tie? Or the one who steals boats? Because you never know which one will take charge."

We didn't have time to continue, because the Papess Throne was upon us.

Lady Priestess was surrounded by three of her children, including Bethan. Bethan's powered chair chewed up the incline with a motorized hum. Her mother was wearing a dress made of cobwebs. To keep the magicked material pliable, Lady Priestess's skin was heavily powdered and smelled like orchids.

We exchanged some pleasantries, and I kissed Bethan's hand, which made her blush. She said, "Mama Nataki has kept me up to date on your investigation. I was horrified to hear about the attack on your court. Is there news yet?"

"None. Mayan is coordinating our efforts, and I'm anxious to stay abreast myself."

"Mayan will figure it out," Lady Priestess said on an exhale, looking around her. She adjusted her cat-eye glasses on her nose. "And when he does, I'll become involved." There was nothing wispy about that last statement.

The Saint Brigid family moved on, and the Saint Nicholas matriarch approached.

"Is it sad that I wish the Tower was here right now?" I whispered.

"Any fucking port in a storm," Brand agreed.

"Perhaps allow me to . . . manage the conversation," Addam said carefully.

Lady Justice had dressed in white—white cloth, white feathers, and a thin white-gold coronet. The only distinction was her dark sunglasses. I'd half-expected her to be accompanied by her heir, Addam's older brother Christian, but Addam had mentioned that competing demands would keep him away.

"I will speak with Lord Sun," Lady Justice said bluntly, reaching us.

There was an odd moment when everyone else, including Lady Death, realized they'd been dismissed. Lady Death gave her sister Arcana a breezy glance, accepted Brand's proffered arm, and retreated to a distance.

"Would you like to look at the fountain?" I asked. "The nightshades around it are nice."

"I'm fond of nightshades. I use them in many of our court poisons."

Right.

We walked to the fountain, which was tiled in a rich red that gave the water a ruby shine. I didn't know many of the plant names except for the poisonous one used for the spring equinox celebration. Atlanteans didn't waste time on Easter lilies or Christmas holly: our equinox and solstice flora were all deadly.

Lady Justice stared at the moving water for a minute. I waited until she was ready.

"Diana," she finally said. "I didn't see that one coming."

"It's my understanding that she's always been a caretaker for your children. Is it so surprising that she'd follow them?"

"But . . . seneschal? To a—" She had the grace to pause. "To a newly founded court. People will talk."

"People always talk. But we're Arcana. We can change the narrative."

"Do not placate me," she murmured, "especially with such pithy statements. I am angry, Lord Sun. I am angry."

"I exerted no pressure. I made no offer, beyond friendship. They all came to me of their own free will."

"But we are Arcana," she fed back to me. "We make the narrative."

"I love Addam."

"You are so young," she said, and shook her head. "You pillage my court, and so now I must decide on consequences. They will not leave with my blessing, nor with any sigils beyond that which they've earned. Nor will they continue to suck on the teats of my treasury. My sister and son will make their decision in full awareness of the punishment. If—"

My Aspect rose, and flames licked upwards from my eyes. "Your son," I repeated.

She looked confused for a moment, then grimaced. "Sons."

"Let me explain to you, in exacting detail, why you deserve this moment," I said. "Let me explain why you deserve the loss of your greatest treasure. Quinn drove *all* of this into existence. I wouldn't even presume to guess when he decided to come to me. Perhaps he'd always planned it, because of what he Sees. All of those possibilities, all of those paths, and *this* is the one he chose. And Addam and Diana followed because Quinn is the heart of their life. I am barely beginning to understand the wonder of that boy—and you didn't even *mention* him just now."

"Little broth—"

My anger had no brakes. "I took Diana? I took Addam? Are you that clueless?"

Her anger was there too, but chagrin also twisted her lips. "You don't know what it was like in Old Atlantis. Our standards—the way we lived—how we lived after we *lost* it. Quinn was sickly. I come from a time when sickly children die, and emotional investment only makes the loss that much greater. And these gifts—his prophecy—I have always distrusted prophecy."

"And I don't? Do you know anything about me? I hated prophets until I met Quinn. But I never put my hatred above my intellect, and my gut, and my practicality. I saw that kid for what he was almost immediately. How did you miss it? How?"

"Dominika," Diana said sharply. She'd spotted us from the bottom tier of the gardens and marched up the steps; I'd watched her progress from the corner of my eye.

"We require a moment," Lady Justice said.

"There is a line of guests waiting to speak with Lord Sun. This is his coronation. *Manners,* sister."

Lady Justice whipped around to stare at her sister. She raked her eyes across Diana and finally pointed a finger at Diana's insanely small purse. It was barely enough to hold an ice pick, let alone an actual weapon. "That," she said. "You can take whatever you want from the armory, so long as it fits in that bag. The servants will help you pack."

"I've already packed, and mother left me quite enough sigils of my own," Lady Diana said with a dismissive flick of her fingers. "You'd do well to remember that courts rise and fall, and charity flows both ways along long stretches of the River. Come. There's a bar over here."

"I will not—"

"Tequila it is. Come Doma," Diana said. She strode off to the bar without waiting to see if her sister followed, which was just as well because Lady Justice did. She did spare me a single look of brutal exasperation, though.

I remembered I had a beer bottle in my hand, and took a long, long sip from it. And I blinked to make sure my eyes weren't still burning.

There was much mingling to be done, and every Arcana, if not present in person, sent functionaries to greet me. They all brought wrapped presents ceremoniously piled on a table next to a podium. From our position at the top of the tiered lawns, I would be able to speak to the entire assembly when the time came for me to symbolically accept my father's mantle. I'd scratched out a passably good speech last night, which was safe in my pocket, albeit damp from the number of times I made sure it was still there.

In our cordoned area, there was a space reserved for dancing to innocuous orchestra music. The grass was as green as actual emeralds and as springy as a mattress. How people were able to navigate dance steps in heels, I couldn't imagine—although Layne was in stilettos and spun like a dervish.

Just when I'd built up my courage to ask Addam to dance, a woman stepped in front of me. She placed her hand on my arm and gently tugged me into a dance. I was too surprised for discomfort, and answered her green-lipstick smile with one of my own.

She appeared to be in her seventies, with sharp, arresting features that were compelling if not conventional. She'd dressed in a jade-colored gown, and a modest collection of sigils sparked on her earlobes, neck, fingers, and forehead. The circlet, in particular, was quite beautiful—copper filigree that seemed deceptively fragile but vibrated with the intensity of a mass sigil.

I didn't know her name, but she was familiar, wasn't she? And everyone around us seemed to be having a good time. So I let myself relax into the sweep of the slow dance steps.

The woman raised her hand to my shoulder. Her sleeve rode down, showing blue veins and flaking psoriasis. She followed my gaze and lowered her arm so that her gown fell into place.

When I lifted our clasped hands to let her turn under them, I caught the faces of my family. Addam was smiling at me, and Brand gave me a brief, happy nod. Beside them, Max was drinking a heavy red wine, and Quinn—

The expression on Quinn's face was a slap of cold water. For a second, everything felt wrong. It was like smelling an unwashed face under heavy perfume, something hard to identify but undeniably off.

The woman put her hand on my cheek to force my eyes to hers, and I returned her smile. It was a rather nice way to spend a few minutes. Her nails dug deep, half-crescents of fire along my jawline.

"Our people have spit in the face of evolution," she whispered. "Atlanteans have crawled back into the mud and lost their legs. But you . . . You've got some spine to you, haven't you?"

She let go of me. I bowed deeply and smiled at her, and felt copper in my mouth. Had I bitten my tongue? I gave her an embarrassed look and excused myself, which she accepted with a regal nod.

Over at the bar, I grabbed a napkin and dabbed at my tongue. It came away a watery pink. Sighing, I put another clean napkin in my pants pocket, which wasn't as easy as it sounded because the pocket was barely three microns wide.

"I feel like I need a nap," Brand said, coming to my side. He wiggled a finger in his ear. "Maybe I need a coffee myself."

Over his shoulder, I saw that Quinn was making his way to me. He looked upset, which made me tense, but before he could reach me, Vadik Amberson slid between us.

Brand's back fused into a single line. There was only so far he was willing to push the no bodyguard experience.

"Vadik," I said. "I'm glad you could come."

"Again, the invitation was most generous of you," he replied, bowing. Not only were his court pants as tight as mine, but the crotch area was a different shade of yellow. "I'm sorry our conversation was cut short the other day. Such a disturbance at your estate! The papers have been oddly quiet about it, though."

That annoyed me, so I said, simply, "Yes. They have been."

"Perhaps we can continue catching each other up on the welfare of our houses? If you'd indulge me, there's a quiet area by the ice sculpture, and it's deliciously cool as a fringe benefit."

I glanced at Brand, who lowered his chin a fraction. He'd stay with me.

"Please," I said, and gestured.

Vadik gave Brand an unfriendly look when he followed, quickly smothered under a closed-lip smile. We moved past the rows of dark green flowers and vines, where a vast circle of ice, like an oversized coin, had been carved with my Arcanum seal. The ice of the stylized flame had been cleverly mixed with amber dye to give it a glistening, lifelike appearance.

"Pretty," Vadik said, with barely a glance. "And cool. These hot summers will be the end of me. It must be a challenge at the estate, updating old pipes and machinery and what-not."

"We're up to the task," I said. I drummed up a little more manners from my irritation. "Vadik, I am glad to hear the Ambersons are doing well. Lord Amberson maintained faith with my father until the end, and I won't forget that. Nor will I forget the hardships you suffered when that end came. I'm sorry your father isn't with us today."

"This would have delighted him. And my mother, if she had lived, too. We must toast this new cycle tonight."

"Then we will."

"And perhaps we can discuss other ways our houses may benefit each other."

They say the eyes are the windows of the soul. I agree. It's just that, to ascertain the soul, you have to stare right into someone's eyes, which has always struck me as a bit creepy, intimate, and unpleasant. I'd rather just get the cliff notes from Brand later.

In this case, though, Brand had already shared his opinion with me by assuming his bodyguard pose: he did not like Vadik Amberson. And I think I agreed. Vadik's gilded manners were just as impressive as a thin layer of gold plating.

"I think we should—" I started to say, but Vadik clapped his hands and made a delighted sound.

"I love this music. Argentinian. Very popular in the 1900s. We must dance."

He took my hand and tried to twirl me back to the dance floor, and my whole body locked up. I did not like to be touched by strangers. It triggered my worst impulses. And for some reason, those triggers were stunningly close to the surface today—I have no idea why I had such a panicked reaction to being grabbed by the hand for a dance.

And then Brand was there.

He took Vadik's wrist, pressed on a nerve that would have made the scion's hand go numb, and forced him a good three feet away from me. For a second, I thought Vadik was going to go for a sigil, but Brand said, "I'm going to save your life right now. You may not be familiar with Companions. We can't survive a sustained fight against a spell-caster. We rely on speed and terminal success. If I think you're going to release a spell, I will not hesitate. I will end the threat to Lord Sun. Do you understand?"

Vadik nodded, his cheeks mottled.

"Never, ever, ever lay hands on him again without his say," Brand whispered.

Vadik turned and walked away, his stiff gait the only sign of our quick confrontation.

Brand turned a glance in my direction to make sure I wasn't pissed at him. I wasn't. He was the best thing in the Universe. Everyone should have a Brand.

His anger melted into a crooked smile. "We're okay?" he said.

I nodded. "Can you get me another beer? I need a moment." I saw Quinn bouncing on his heels a polite distance away, staring rivets at me. "Quinn will keep me company," I added.

Brand left for my drink, and Quinn rushed over.

"Are you okay?" he demanded. "What should we do?"

"Nothing. I'm fine. He's just the son of someone loyal to my father, it's—"

"Not *him*," Quinn said. "The woman. What are you going to do about her? Have you called Lord Tower?"

"Have I . . . *What?*"

"Are you mad because I'm not supposed to know? I'll apologize later. Max found the sketch, so we took a picture and were doing reverse recognition searches to see if we could help you."

"Quinn, what the hell are you talking about?"

He pulled out his phone and thumbed up an image from his photo file. It was the pencil drawing Mayan had given us on Subject Jade.

"What are you going to do about her?" he asked again.

"We're going to find her. What do you think we're going to do?"

"But . . . she's *here*. You danced with her."

"What?" This conversation made no sense. "Of course I didn't. Do you mean that lady? She looked nothing like that."

"She looked *exactly* like this. She's even wearing *jade,* which seems a little like she's mocking us if you ask me." He shook the phone at me.

"Quinn, the woman I danced with isn't a bad person. She was very nice."

He watched me for a few beats, then shook his head slowly. "Rune, can you not see that this is her?"

"Quinn, I promise, it's not. It's really not."

"I think... I think I need to be very quiet now," he said. "I think something is happening I shouldn't mess with."

Max was pretending he wasn't eavesdropping, which may have been believable if he'd ever really had an interest in ice sculptures. I snapped him over.

"How much wine have you given Quinn?" I asked.

"None!"

"Well, get him some. Keep an eye on each other. My head is splitting, and I think I need to give a speech soon."

I hurried away, reaching for the used napkin in my pocket, because I'd bit my tongue again.

The next hour was a scattered dash of congratulations, all leading toward the podium. Other than the Arcana I'd already greeted, I met with Lord Hierophant (who always took the opportunity to remind me to keep my mouth shut about anything I'd spotted at his house in the Westlands); Lords Chariot and Judgment; and Lady World, who greeted me as a friend. We'd bonded over the Hanged Man raid.

Others sent envoys, including the Magician, Strength, Temperance, the Devil, and the Moon. There was a wealth of politics in these gestures. Did the Magician know I knew he was a puppet ruler? Strength and Temperance had both lost children because of me, and I always worried if their acceptance was covering a long game. Lady Moon had once been an ally of my father, along with Lord Star, my late mother's old court. Lord Star was now buried alive beneath the earth and widely known as the Anchorite, and Lady Moon had turned her back on my court when my father died. I wasn't even sure I could trust an overture from her. As for Lord Devil? I'd be perfectly happy if circumstances never drew me into his orbit.

"It's time," Lord Tower murmured in my ear. "You must speak to the crowd and name your throne."

I blinked and saw him at my side. Addam and Brand stood behind him, along with Diana Saint Nicholas.

"Okay," I said. "Okay, I've got this."

Lord Tower glanced over his shoulder. Addam and Brand stirred and backed away. When we had the assumption of privacy, he turned back to me, and urged us in the direction of a small stage that held a podium. I'd asked Lady Death not to plan a series of speeches. I would have a few remarks, and then encourage people to snack and drink. That was enough attention for me.

"I did not expect this to happen so soon," Lord Tower said as we walked. "I thought we would have years to prepare you for the throne."

"Sorry about that."

"You shouldn't apologize. It's occurred to me that if you waited until I thought you were ready, then that very fact would mean you *wouldn't* be ready. I believe, now, things happened as they must. I will reserve the right to be worried, though."

"I'm okay with that. You know you got me here, right? That none of this would exist without you? Not my court, not this moment. Not my family. Not Brand. Not me. You saved us."

Lord Tower looked into my eyes; only it wasn't like with Vadik. This was a connection I welcomed.

Lord Tower said, "I am so very, very proud of you."

I swallowed. My eyes burned. Not the fiery type of burning. I discreetly wiped them with the napkin in my hand.

"Now go," he said. "Go and tell the world the Sun Throne has returned."

The garden quieted.

I allowed myself a few seconds to gather it all in—spotting Arcana and envoys and family. My gaze lingered there last. Layne's face glowed as they smiled at me. They stood with Ciaran, and Layne had their hands on Anna's shoulders. Max and Quinn were trying to hide their newly filled wine glasses from Addam. Diana and Corinne stood side by side. And Brand and Addam had eyes only for me.

Reaching into my pocket, I felt for my speech.

No speech. No paper.

For a second I thought maybe I'd used it to blot my tongue, only that wasn't as important as the fact that it *wasn't fucking there.*

I saw Brand sigh and shake his head. He pulled what appeared to be a copy of my speech out of his pocket.

Only, for some reason . . . I decided I didn't need it after all. It was like the world had taken a deep breath around me. The panic washed away. This was never something I worried about. I'd spent too much of my life where I only had words to back up my limited collection of sigils.

Besides, I controlled my narrative.

"The human world suffers through a pandemic," I said into the microphone. "We suffered along with it until Atlantean magic and ingenuity carried the day. But we still spent a long season inside our homes, sheltered from a microscopic enemy. The last thing I want to do, now, is to make you stand in place a moment longer than you need to. Please. Drink, and eat, and dance, and reconnect with each other. Pandemic aside, our city has experienced a generation of prosperity, and my court stands ready to experience it with you. My father's throne is filled again. I have claimed his mantle. New Atlantis once again has a Sun Court."

"The Sun Court!" Lord Tower cried, lifting his glass.

A tidal roar, a wave of raised glasses shining under the low evening sun, reflecting the orange and purple horizon.

"The Sun Court!" Lady Death shouted, and arms went up again.

But our powers happened in three, so the head of the Arcanum, Lord Judgment, resplendent in his deep red and black court colors, slammed his staff of office against the ground and shouted, *"Rune Sun, Arcana of the Sun Throne!"*

The shouts from my family alone deafened me.

Presents came next. I knew it would be a showy affair, I just didn't expect it to be so insanely lucrative.

The first box I opened contained a sigil from Lord Judgment.

Lord Judgment had bought me a *sigil.* A fucking *sigil.*

Twenty years with six of my own, before adding Lady Lovers' emerald ring and Quinn's platinum disc to my collection. Twenty years of limited options for spellwork, and now this. A gold sun pendant on a dwarven steel chain.

I stared at it for a long time before putting it around my neck. The crowd roared. Lord Judgment clapped me on the back, spoke the words to assign ownership of the sigil to me, and just like that, I had an eighth sigil.

Mikhail Saint Guinefort, son of Lord Devil, presented me with a bar of iridium meant to be melted down for a weapon. Lord Star, the Anchorite, somehow managed to deliver a bone toothpick, which just about made me piss my pants. No one spoke about what the Anchorite did to be imprisoned.

Precious metals. Gemstones as big as goose eggs. Literally as big as goose eggs. I had a flash of memory: being on the roof of the Lovers mansion, watching a fugitive Lady Lovers vanish through a portal, thinking about what sort of treasure she was going to collect. *Visions of gemstones the size of goose eggs danced in my head.* Now I actually owned some.

Some of the gifts were practical. Some were pain-in-the-ass sleights. Some contained hidden political meaning, layers upon layers of meaning that made my head hurt. There were plenty of gifts for Brand, too, which had him bouncing on his toes to get a better look.

Lady Death had told me that only a personal list of friends would spend the night in the Manse, and their individual gifts would be presented later. I could barely imagine how they'd compare to this fortune.

"One drop in every drink," Corinne said, stuffing the vial of cloudy liquid into Brand's hand. She wanted him to use it during our overnight stay, since she wouldn't be there. "It'll curdle if there's poison."

"Have I ever let him be poisoned before?" Brand demanded. Then he gave the vial a reluctant look. "Where'd you get it?"

She rolled her eyes and stepped back to put hands on Anna's and Layne's shoulders. "We'll leave you to it. I'd like to collect Corbie and Queenie before it gets too dark."

Max came over and gave me a huge hug. He opened his mouth to say something and hiccupped instead.

"Next time I'll remember to say how big the glass can be," I told him. I pulled him into another hug and pounded on his back. "Look after everyone tonight?"

"I will," he promised. "You were really, really awesome today."

"That's what the T-shirt will say," I agreed. I put an arm around his shoulder and turned him to look for Quinn. He and Addam were talking, so I herded my potentially drunk adopted little brother over there.

Addam was saying, "Are you sure you're well?"

"Yes," Quinn said, but he didn't look very happy about things.

Addam's lips twisted ruefully. "Are you mad I'm sending you home? Am I a bad brother?"

Quinn took the question seriously. He stared at his brother for a very long moment. His eyes went glassy. He finally said, "You're the best brother anyone has ever had."

Of course that made Addam's eyes go glassy too. He pulled Quinn into a hug and kissed him noisily on the head. "The second-best brother anyone ever had," he corrected.

Corinne started to gather everyone who was leaving, as Lady Death gathered the all-night guests on the white-sand courtyard in front of the Manse. I passed Max off to Brand and went over to Quinn once he and Addam were done being soft.

"Are you really okay?" I murmured.

Quinn rubbed his sleeve across his face. "I am now. I mean, once I knew I had to be, I was. I just wanted to enjoy everything."

"You're not still worried about that woman, are you?"

The fifteen-year-old sighed. *Sixteen.* He'd had a birthday recently. I couldn't believe I'd known him long enough to see him grow up, even a little. "I can't talk about that anymore, I don't think. It's too late. But you'll all look out for each other, right? You'll look out for Addam?"

"If you don't know the answer to that, we'll have to replace your crystal ball. Quinn, are you sure you and the others will be okay leaving? Do I need to worry about something?"

"You need to worry about what's here. My path is . . . clear. My path is clear. I'm more worried about you."

I turned and pointed. "Addam. Brand. Ciaran. Lady Death. Lord Tower. Quinn, if I still need help with all them here, then we're all screwed. But I'll be careful. I promise you."

He nodded, turned, and then kept turning until he was swinging back to face me. "And I suppose it's okay to share your cheese, though it's a situation you will want to *closely* manage."

Then he was off.

Brand came to my side and whispered, "Everything fine?"

"Eyes ahead," I murmured.

Brand's face shuttered. A half second later, he made himself smile, and clapped my shoulder. It wasn't a bad acting job, all things considered—since I'd just given him one of our codes for staying alert. Quinn's behavior had me on edge.

That's as much as I'd tell him until I knew we had our privacy.

We stood on the soft sand that formed a courtyard in front of the Manse's elaborate, nine-foot-tall, closed doors. The sky had darkened with true night, and a full moon brightened behind thin clouds, creating lacelike patterns.

Lady Death said, to the small crowd of people, "As you know, the Manse is only used on special occasions, and has a rather stifling list of rules—"

"*Daughter*," the Dowager Lady Death hissed. Because, fun, she was invited too.

Lady Death smiled tightly. "Magic, naturally, is forbidden within. As are lights. In the old days, we called a building such as this the Midnight Manse. In denying our sight, we repair our other senses, and form bonds among each other through the shared experience of our blindness."

At my side, Brand patted down one of his pockets. I could already see the arithmetic in his head, adding up how many devices he packed that could serve as flashlights.

"One other tradition is to take a long look at one you hold dear before entering the darkness. You can hold their image in your mind's eye to light your way."

That sounded potentially awkward. As Brand and Addam turned to face me, I stepped aside and looked at *all* of them. From a well-behaved Ciaran; to the Tower; to the man I intended to choose as a consort one day; and the man who'd always been the best part of my soul.

That was one hell of an image to hold in my mind's eye.

The immense double doors opened on soundless hinges, showing nothing but darkness ahead.

THE MANSE

I took one last glance around me as the party began to move into the darkness. Lord Tower was near the front of the crowd. He'd mentioned Mayan was going to stay at the Pac Bell and run our security detail for the night. It was Mayan's gift to me—he'd be looking after my friends and family while I was locked in the Manse.

Past that, there was a small handful of Lady Death's people, along with Lady Priestess, who stood behind Bethan Saint Brigid's wheelchair. Lady Priestess had asked to join us, and Bethan seemed delighted to be included as well.

My gaze wandered to Lady Death's friends. Her seneschal, Fiore, had been introduced as nonbinary. They had a white braid that reached their waist, and wore a black jumpsuit with a transparent, gauzy skirt. They looked comfortable—all of Lady Death's people did, eschewing scratchy formal wear for looser leggings and shirts. They didn't have the polish of the average scion, and weren't draped in sigils or expensive jewelry. They reminded me of my own inner circle, actually.

"These are your peeps," I whispered to her. "Aren't they? These are the kids who you smoked cigarettes with behind the gym!"

She rolled her eyes at me but didn't deny it.

The only person who stood out was the kind, elderly woman in green. She stood by herself and waited for her turn to move forward. It amused me to think that Quinn pegged her as a potential threat. I couldn't think of anyone less threatening. Wasn't she a member of Lady Death's court?

The crowd hushed as the first line of people vanished inside. It was so quiet that I was able to hear the nearby ocean for the first time. Its susurrus accompanied my final steps inside the yawning blackness.

Then the doors closed behind us, and we were in complete, relentless darkness. I couldn't even see my hand in front of my face.

Lady Death spoke.

"Thank you for honoring our most ancient of traditions, and refraining from using any light source while you remain in the Manse. There are only a few illuminated spaces, including the baths and the chapel. Your overnight luggage has been deposited in your rooms. I'll give you instructions to reach them next. Please feel free to do as you wish for now, and we'll meet for a midnight feast at the bell. Fiore, dear, would you please accompany Lady Anuarite to her suite?"

"I am capable of finding my way, daughter. I built this manor."

Lady Death audibly sighed. I heard a shuffle of movement and the receding clip of a cane on hard tile.

"Rune," Lady Death said. "I have two suites set aside for you, Lord Addam, Lord Ciaran, and Lord Brandon. There are two bedrooms in each suite. I will ask each of you in turn to approach my voice, and I'll show you how to navigate. Feel free to rest or make use of the baths. My seneschal, Fiore, will gather you when it's time for dinner. Follow my voice, little brother."

I made my way to Lady Death and felt the comforting bulk of Brand at my back. From the sound, Addam was just behind him, and then maybe Ciaran.

"I'm taking your hand now," Lady Death said, and I felt cool fingers and slick nail polish against my hand. "There are a series of cords throughout the building. Follow the felt cord to reach your cul-de-sac of rooms. If you wish to use the baths, follow the metal link chain from those rooms. If at any point you feel a knot in the cord, be careful—there is likely a step up or step down ahead. You understand?"

"I do. Thank you, Lady Death."

"It's time you start calling me Zurah."

"Zurah," I repeated.

I felt her guide my hand to a nest of cords. She played my fingers along each one so that I could tell the difference between felt and the other tactile sensations—silk, velvety tassels, wool, samite, smooth beads.

"Please," she said. "Rest. Enjoy the baths. Find sight in sightlessness. Go in peace, Rune."

I took a quick breath, isolated the felt thread, and began walking forward.

"I thought Lady Death was supposed to be a master tactician," Brand complained the second time I bumped into invisible furniture. "And yet, there you are, first in line."

"I can't see a fucking thing," I announced.

"Are we ready to cheat yet?" Ciaran asked from the rear of the group. "I want to see if my cell phone works."

"No cheating!" I called out. "We're going to honor their traditions. It can't be that difficult." I was running my hand along the wall for extra support and felt the bump of a mirror or painting. I managed my way around it without another bang.

"I have a flashlight," I heard Brand mumble to Ciaran.

"No flashlight," I said. "And if you need something to distract you, start thinking about the fact that you're going to be sharing a suite with Ciaran."

"He snores," Brand said in outrage.

"What did you say?" Ciaran asked in surprise.

"You. Snore."

"You cannot possibly know that," he said.

"Can't I? How about one of the dozen times you've swanned off into dreamwalking and left us holding your snoring body?"

"Well then, I suppose you're lucky there are two bedrooms in our suite," he said airily.

"Negative," Brand said. "We're going to share one suite. It's a body-guard thing. And since you're one of the people I protect, don't bother complaining about it."

"Aren't you off duty?" Ciaran asked, at the same time I raised my voice and said, "Knot! There's a knot in the felt. Look out for a stairway or something . . ."

"Absolutely fucking not," Brand said. He muscled around me and took the lead. A moment later: "It's a step up. Two steps. Come on."

We navigated our way down another hallway until Brand said, "The cord ends. It's tied to a few other cords—I think I can feel the metal chain. We should go to the baths in an hour." As he said this, he fumbled for my hand and tapped the back of it. We were on the same page: stay together, find a space where we could privately talk. A bath would have shower-heads, and running water was a handy noise buffer.

Brand continued to narrate his quick exploration of the dead end. He found two doors, picked one, and we entered the dark suite.

We bumped our way to the middle of the room. It appeared that all furniture was gathered around the edges, and Brand found the doors to the two bedrooms and a shared bathroom.

"Well, that's the tour," I said. "I'm taking a nap. Shotgun on Addam! He's the pillow I brought with me."

"I support this shotgun privilege," Addam said from the darkness on the other side of the room.

"If anyone finds any earplugs, let me know," Brand said.

"It's as if you're not worried I'll walk into *your* dreams," Ciaran told him.

Brand huffed and went into one of the bedrooms. Ciaran followed and shut the door behind them. I told Addam to wait, counted to twenty, and sure enough, the fuckers lit up their phones and flashlights. I could see the glow under the door.

"I'm following the rules," I said.

"Most admirable," Addam said. He took me by each hand and backed me into one of the rooms. It turned out to be the bathroom and not our bedroom, which we figured out just before he tossed me across the bathtub and not a bed. We retraced our steps and found the second bedroom.

Inside, he nudged me onto a soft, massive mattress. Clothing rustled. Addam sighed theatrically and said, "These pants were so tight that the rivets left marks on my legs. Feel." He took my hand, brought it to his thigh, and let me trace the indentations along the outside of his leg.

We lost a few minutes as I found each and every one of them. I thought it would be romantic if I kissed them, but that was just too forward and suave, even in my imagination. I settled on pulling him onto the mattress next to me and reaching for his face. I found a cheek, let my fingers trail down to trace his smile.

"Why," Addam whispered, kissing the side of my hand, "have you been so nervous around me?"

My brain filled with static for a second. Did he? He did. I opened my mouth to protest his timing, and realized we'd both been treating the subject like sniper fire. I was on shaky moral ground.

"Rune," Addam said patiently. "We are not so delicate that we will fall apart if you are angry with me."

"I'm not angry with you," I said, and then the dam broke, because him thinking I was mad was the last thing I wanted. "Addam, no, that's not it. It's just . . . it felt . . . I worry that, in your mind, you're . . . settling. That you think you have to settle. That I've already given you everything I have to give. Because I haven't. I've just *started*. I want to give you the world. I want to share the world with you. Brand and I . . . it's different. It's different. What I have with you *is* love, and it *is* unique, and I don't share anything like it with anyone else."

"This," he said after a pause, "is about what I said at the Enclave. Isn't it?"

I didn't say anything.

"This is about when I told you that I knew I was not the love of your life," he added. Now his fingers were on my face, feeling my muscles in the darkness, trying to find the shape of my mood. "May I admit something, Rune?"

"Will it make me feel bad?"

"No. I wish to tell you that in the months between that moment—the moment in the Enclave, and this, much has happened. We were separated by a pandemic. We came together at Sun Estate. We have made a *home* at Sun Estate—we have made a family. A real court family, filled with many mothers and fathers and siblings and children. I would have never expected you to adapt so well. Nor Brand. You were very committed to your Half House. So it is simply not possible for me to know how much you have to give. You keep surprising me."

"But it's not a competition, right?" I said, still anxious.

"It is not. And I did not mean to imply that I was settling. The word makes no sense to me, not in this context. Does one settle for a happy life? Because I have a happy life."

"Good," I breathed. There were other things to say—discussions to have, about Addam's place in my court. But not now. Not just yet. Quinn's vague warning still lingered. "Um. Do you want to talk about this some more? Or can I go back to counting rivet marks?"

He laughed.

I woke from a nap and gave a huge, spine-cracking, indolent stretch. I was barely halfway through it before Addam sighed and ran his hands over my belly.

"How long were we asleep?" I asked.

"Three Brand knocks," he said.

"We should go to the baths. It would be nice for all of us to relax and—" I reached out to squeeze his hand hard, "*talk* in the baths."

Addam remained absolutely silent for a moment. Then he squeezed my hand back. He understood.

"I like you, Saint Nicholas," I murmured, and tried to kiss his neck. I got the shoulder instead.

I swung out of bed, felt around for my overnight bag, and got undressed. There had been a guest bathrobe folded on top of the luggage, along with a soft towel. I took advantage of both.

In the main room, Brand and Ciaran were arguing over how Ciaran had got a deviated septum. Brand appeared to be willing to bet money on the 1980s. We lined up and went outside to find the metal chain.

Brand took the lead without challenge. Which meant, of course, that he took pleasure in calling out every possible obstacle before one of us could trip over them, as opposed to my own warnings, which had amounted to a swear as I collided with something.

The baths weren't far. By the time we'd made our way down a single corridor, I could already smell the bleach. The air was warm and damp, too.

"The baths," a voice announced ahead of us. "Please lower your eyes."

I did, and the attendant opened the door to the chamber. The coal glow from within burned like sunlight. I blinked watery eyes against the reddish light and made my way into the room.

Braziers filled with hot embers gave the baths a medieval glow. The red light felt hot and heavy, spreading like melting wax on our skin. The space was as large as the Sun Estate solarium, and featured hot and cold pools, showers, steam rooms, and saunas. We were the only guests to be taking advantage of them.

Brand and I chose the baths because it seemed like the best place for unexpected privacy. But it hadn't occurred to me I'd need to get naked in front of everyone. Maybe Ciaran would feel weird about it too? I looked over and watched him shuck his robe. Underneath, he had on a one-piece bathing suit from the 1920s. It went down to his calves.

"What?" he said, seeing my stare. "I have an extra if you'd like. Are you wearing Spider-Man underwear?"

"Let's clean off first in the showers," I said stiffly, tightening my bathrobe's sash.

"That's rather forward," Ciaran said. "Will there be suds? I vote for suds. Why are you wearing your bathrobe into the shower?"

Brand barked him forward into the separate room. Inside a sandstone-colored shower room, Brand went faucet by faucet to turn them on. He wore only a towel around his waist, though I saw a sliver of a knife hilt poking from the small of his scarred back.

He put himself in a dry corner when he was done, so that he had a good view of the archway. I wordlessly gestured to everyone to join. By that point, it was clear something was up, and even Ciaran mutely complied.

"Quickly," I whispered under the sound of pressurized water. "Quinn thinks that . . . Well, he didn't exactly *say* shit might hit the fan, but it seemed implied. We need to stay alert."

"Is this related to the attacks on courts?" Ciaran asked. "The matter at the rejuvenation center?"

"I think so. I don't know. He seemed focused on one of Lady Death's guests, but he's off base there."

"Which guest bothered Quinn?" Addam asked.

"The woman in green. I danced with her?"

"Why did that bother him?" Brand asked in confusion, to which I shrugged.

"What about Corinne and Aunt Diana?" Addam asked. "Has Quinn warned them?"

"I've been texting Max and Mayan to keep them extra alert," Brand said.

"It's strange you only texted when you needed to move around the bedroom and keep from smacking your elbow on things," Ciaran murmured into a hot jet of water.

"I trust Mayan to stay on top of home security," Brand said, ignoring him.

"What do you suggest we do?" Addam asked. He removed his bathrobe and started to take a comfortably naked shower. "Sigils are useless. Will your sabre work in a null zone?"

"No. At least it never has before."

"It's actually not a bad set up," Brand said. "Every spell-caster will be at a disadvantage, but Rune and I have our training. We'd be safer if Rune wasn't so distracted by a penis, though."

I snapped my gaze upwards.

"Not just any penis," Addam murmured.

"Listen," I said. "I'm going to find a way to the Tower, because we need him on alert too."

"What about Lady Death?" Ciaran asked.

"I'll talk with her," I said after a moment's reflection. "I'll talk with her and . . . I don't know, follow my gut. I think she's a safe ally."

"I concur," Ciaran agreed. "But stay out of earshot of her mother. That one has house fires in her eyes."

In the room outside, I heard the door squeal open. The attendant announced, "Lady Death."

I glanced at our small group, tightened my bathrobe's sash, and went back through the archway. Lady Death stood by the brazier with a cup of water, which she poured over the coals to release a roar of steam. She wore a simple white shift and red crocs.

"They told me you were up and about," she said. "What do you think so far?"

"I like the idea that I can go to a dinner party and not comb my hair," I said.

That provoked a smile. "You appear to have remained somewhat dry. Were you planning on bathing, or could I tempt you for a private cocktail?"

It would give us a chance to talk, which I needed. So I went back into the showers—and now Brand was naked too, godsdamnit. I told them I was going to spend some time with Lady Death and I'd find my way back to our rooms afterward.

"I'll be fine," I told Brand's mulish expression. "It's a chance to explore the Manse layout."

"Half an hour, then I come looking for you," he said.

"Half an hour, plus an extra fifteen minutes when you remember I can't see the time anywhere," I agreed.

Back in the hallway's darkness, ember spots danced in my vision, but Lady Death took my hand and led me. She didn't bother with the cords at all. Her suite was on the second floor, and the stairway we climbed had wide and long steps, easily traversed.

"Have you felt a heightening in your other senses?" she asked as we made our way down the hallway above the baths.

"Yes," I said. "I feel each and every bruise."

Her throaty laugh filled the hallway. "In my mother's era, we spent several nights a week inside the Manse. I've relaxed that obligation to only special occasions. I enjoy reading before bed too much. Here we are."

I heard a door open, and we entered her suite. The darkness was just as pitiless as the hallway, but the vibration of our voices changed. Maybe my senses *were* getting better. I could tell, without feeling, that we were in a much smaller space.

"Is this the antechamber?" I asked.

"No. It's the smallest bedroom in the building. I chose it instead of the master suite—it messes with people's expectations. If you move directly away from the sound of my voice, you'll find a small table and sitting area. Please, relax. I'll pour us a gin and tonic if you're amenable."

"So amenable," I said. "And what's the secret?"

"What secret?"

"About this room?"

That disembodied, throaty laugh again. She did not reply. I followed the sound of her progress: glasses sliding across a surface; the click of ice cubes; the lazy gurgle of liquid being poured, and the snake-hiss of carbonation. The scent of limes flowered.

"Why do you say that?" she finally asked.

"Because I live with Quinn. I'm used to evasive statements that hide what he's really saying. You didn't choose this room because of what people thought."

"Come here," she finally said, while depositing my drink at the table. "Over here." She took my hand and led me to a corner of the room.

"This is the northwestern edge of the Manse," she said. "And it sits, as it is, a handful of feet over the null zone."

She whispered a few words, and a ball of frost-blue light appeared above us. I squinted my eyes against the flare, and the room hung in my brain like a snapshot: Lady Death in her white shift, a space barely larger than my own bedroom at Half House, and a collection of mismatched furniture. Everything had been picked for comfort and tactility, not décor.

"You're so damn clever," I said. "How did you ever figure it out?"

"Throwing a tantrum and hiding from my mother when I was six. The stone is still pitted from the Frost spell I cast."

I was able to blink my vision back and saw the divots in the stone she'd mentioned. With a twist of her wrist, she dissolved the light cantrip, sending us back into darkness.

"Smart," I said. "And reassuring. Null zones freak me out."

"Because of Rurik," she said.

A messy, full-throated roar of memories rose and were quickly pushed aside. "Someday I'll have to find out what you all knew of me before I got a seat at the table," I said. "But yes. Sort of. Rurik could manipulate—and *move*—null threads. He literally could make them scissor back and forth across sigils and destroy them. Scariest trick in the world."

"I can imagine. Would you like to sit?"

And so we sat at the table and toasted the evening.

"Did you throw a lot of tantrums when you were young?" I asked.

"You met my mother, didn't you? Such a friendly sort. Rainbows practically fly from her arsehole."

That startled a laugh out of me. She laughed along with me. "But, yes, there were a lot of tantrums. Anuarite is very much a traditional Atlantean—home-country Atlantean, not New Atlantis Atlantean. So stiff and inflexible that she's easily broken. When she was hurt in the War, I had to step up and take the throne."

"You took the throne because you were the most powerful spell-caster of your generation," I said. "Not because she was breakable."

I heard a sound of demur. She changed the subject by asking about my own mother.

"I don't remember her at all," I said. "Brand doesn't either. She died when I was an infant, and my father rarely spoke of her. All I know is that it was a political arrangement. My mother came from Lord Star's court, which at the time was part of an alliance with the Sun Throne."

"The Celestials," Lady Death said. "I remember. It's hard to think Lord Star was once an ally of anyone."

"Do you know he gave me a bone toothpick for a gift?"

"How did he even know it was your coronation?" she wondered.

"That's a problem for another day." The spots of glacier-light, afterimages of her cantrip, finally faded from my eyes. It drew my attention back to the wall. "Does the . . . does *our power* work inside the null zone?"

"No. And this room is soundproofed—you may speak freely. I've meant to ask if you've received any training yet on the Majeure."

"Just the dangers of it. Lord Tower told me. I know enough to understand you gave up some of your life to help me save Anna, Corinne, and Corbie. When you summoned the ghost steeds."

"It was important to you."

"How much time did you lose? Are you able to even quantify it?"

"Ach, we each have our way, or so we believe. Perhaps six months and a new gray hair? It's not usually such an extravagant cost, using the Majeure—but my ghost steeds are a powerful, powerful magic."

"Thank you. For being honest. Lord Tower would have never confessed anything like that to me. It's so important for him to be perfect. It's why I have a tough time admitting insecurity around him—because I assume he doesn't want to see that in me, either."

"Then perhaps we should agree with each other, here and now, to be candid with each other. I like having you in my life."

"I like having you in my life too."

It wasn't exactly a vow—and I felt no magic—but the words nevertheless seemed to cement something between us.

I heard a rustle as she relaxed in her chair, then the scrape of her glass. "You talk about insecurities. No one can give you rules for being an Arcana, Rune. If anyone tries, it's an illusion. It's too intensely personal an experience to accurately share. Nothing in your life prepares you—not experience, not history books, not observation. How can anyone understand what it's like to command power like this until one has worn the weight of it? Our lives are outside all semblance of precedent. We are as unique as our Aspects. But for all that . . . For all that, there are some common mistakes. If I can help you step over the occasional land mine, I will. If you're open to feedback."

"Wide freaking open." Then I hesitated. I stalled by taking a sip of my drink. The sour citrus made gooseflesh rise on my arms. "In fact, I need your help now."

"What's wrong, Rune?"

"Quinn was very nervous today. He was nervous leaving me, Addam, and Brand. It's making me cautious."

"I see," she said carefully. "His abilities?"

"Yes."

"And his concern. Now? Here?"

"Possibly," I said.

She got up, went to the wall, and cast another light cantrip. She stayed there to keep the spell alive. "I need to see your face," she said. "Tell me what has happened."

"Nothing yet. But I'm feeling . . . alert. He mentioned one of your guests."

"One of *my* guests?"

"The woman in jade. With the pale green lipstick?"

Lady Death's face drew into a frown. "I . . . think I know who you mean. She's with your party, though, isn't she?"

"No."

"Ah, well, I don't sense any harm from her. Do you?"

I started to reply and realized I didn't know what to say. It was that really irritating not-knowing-what-to-say sensation, like when you had the answer waiting on the tip of your tongue a half second before the question was ever asked—but the mere fact of being asked made the answer skitter away.

"No, of course not," I said, and the feeling subsided. "I can't even remember the details of what Quinn said. The thing is that occasionally what he Sees is . . . maybe not *wrong,* but *not-what-happened-in-this-timeline.*"

"There is no harm in paying attention to his warning. We will keep our wits about us."

She took a healthy sip of gin and tonic as she said this, which was just the sort of way I liked keeping my wits about me, too.

"On the plus side," she added, "if anything happens, perhaps you'll do me the favor of breaking things. Anything. Feel free to literally tear a wall off this place."

"Easiest promise I've ever made," I said.

I told Lady Death—*Zurah,* I reminded myself—I could find my way back. She reminded me the metal chain would lead to the baths, and the felt cord to my block of bedrooms. She warned me not to confuse the felt with samite—which I remembered as a scratchy silk. Apparently, the friction of decades had given it a misleadingly smooth appearance.

Naturally I grabbed the samite cord by accident once I reached the baths. Since I knew my rooms were close, one would think I wouldn't get too lost, but a minute later I was in a stone corridor far colder than any corridor I'd walked through. It smelled of must and wet rock.

I felt around for any hints of my location, discovering in the process that even the paintings of the Manse were tactile. The raised surface of the image was almost a type of Braille. I felt a tree, and maybe a cloud or whale? But no doors to knock on.

Unease prickled the back of my neck.

Was I being watched?

Usually my gut instincts were tied to a visible cause. This was a wholly new experience, and I didn't like it. I *truly* felt like I was blind, and I couldn't understand why. I was missing something large. Something significant. Like I was meant to jump into a fight, but there was no actual threat in front of me.

Footsteps sounded. A voice sighed, "It's me."

"Brand," I said. "Do you feel on edge?"

"Yes, because you went and got lost."

"How did you find me?"

"Our Companion bond still works. I followed the vague feeling of helplessness. Come on. Grab my belt loop."

He got me back to my room, where I was told we had an hour to kill before Brand and I were expected in the Chapel for gift-giving. It was to be a private affair, which piqued my interest.

Addam, feeling challenged, also made it a point to pique my interest, which meant I spent a nice hour with him behind closed doors.

At the appointed time, Brand and I followed the instructions given by a staff member. We took the metal chain to the baths, and corded copper wire to the chapel. I remembered Zurah telling us that the chapel was one of the two places with lights—but not until it was too late to go back and comb my hair.

The first thing Brand said when we stood within the soft and unsteady torchlight of the chapel was, "Jesus Christ, you were only with Addam an hour. You look like the after picture of a prom date. Tuck in your goddamn shirt at least."

I tucked in my shirt, which was hard because I'd picked comfy pants without a belt, but my buttons were off, so I untucked and fixed them. Halfway through the process I realized I was showing the Dowager Lady Death my pale gut.

She sat in a pew near the front, her dark eyes narrowed in dislike.

"My lady," I said, and quickly finished buttoning. "Apologies. I didn't realize you were here."

"My daughter delights in loopholes. This is not how the chapel is meant to be used. Its light is a gift, meant to be part of an act of devotion."

I looked around me. The chapel was small, stuffy with smoke, and fitted only with those hard pews. A spider web floated down and momentarily caught fire on a torch.

"My lady, would you mind if I asked you a question?" I said.

She folded her young, smooth hands along the head of her cane.

"Have you seen the video from the rejuvenation center?" I asked.

The woman stiffened. "Excuse me?"

"I heard roundaboutly that Lady Death was going to show it to you. The woman in the video speaks with an old Atlantean accent. I don't know enough about the accent myself, but wondered if it betrays any sort of regional influence."

"I watched that video. I know nothing. I am unclear why I must discuss it again. How exactly am I to be involved?"

"Ah," I said, unsurely. "You don't need to be, of course."

"And here, of all places? *Profane,*" the woman hissed.

"Mother," Lady Death admonished from the doorway.

"This topic is unseemly. I will leave you to your. . .*gifts,*" she said, and tapped her way out of the room. She did stop at the door, though, and turned her body to face me. "You best hope this woman is not as old as her accent suggests. Blood ran thicker back then. We bowed to actual power, not simply the inheritance of such."

When she was gone, Lady Death rubbed a pulse on her forehead. "Letting it go," she whispered. "Anyway. Lord Tower will be along in a moment. His gifts to you are private, but do know that one of them is in part from me, and you earned it. I'll send one of the staff to bring you to dinner in an hour. There is a charcuterie board by the altar—please help yourself. And if you see a long skinny rat, don't panic. He's a ferret and his name is Remus. He hunts down rodents in this part of the Manse. He's quite well-behaved unless he likes you."

She patted the frame of the door in goodbye. Lord Tower must have been waiting in the hallway to politely pass. I heard them murmuring greetings.

I went over to the food, because it was food. There were several different types of crackers, meats, cheeses, and fruit. I saved all of the fruit for Brand, and loaded a cracker with salami and cheese. It was probably a good thing I'd been warned about Remus, because he apparently liked food too, and was sitting on his hind legs by the tray.

"*Very* nice manners," I said. "I can't even tell if you've stolen anything yet."

Remus stared at the cheese on my cracker. He looked at me, at the cheese, at me, at the cheese, at me, at the cheese—and then paused to see if I was smart enough to pick up on his hint. When I didn't move, he looked at me, at the cheese, at me, at the cheese—

I gave him a cube, and laid some meat in front of him.

Brand came over and grabbed a grape, which he was in the process of chewing when the Tower entered. Lord Tower had changed into one of his silk pajamas and was barefoot. That half-chewed grape saved us all a one-liner, I'm sure of it.

"Gifts between close allies," Lord Tower said, "has always been a private affair. When done right, they are assets to be concealed—aces up your sleeve."

"If this ends with a pony I will be all sorts of happy," I told him.

"You could buy a thousand acres filled with horses, with these gifts," he said. He went to the altar, reached behind the podium, then came to us with three boxes. All of them were bright silver and tied with black ribbon. One was flat and square; another was the size of a large pen; and a third was a jewelry box.

Brand got the last two, and I got the first. I might have expected some snark, but Brand just looked puzzled that he'd got a gift at all, let alone two.

"Please," Lord Tower said. "I wish we had more time to enjoy the process, but we'll need to move to the dining room on the hour."

"Who should go first?" I asked Brand while ripping the silver wrapping paper from my gift, which got me the sour look I was fishing for.

"That is a gift from Lady Death and myself," Lord Tower told me. "We each donated a portion of our claim on Lord Hanged Man's estate in order to secure that. We'll discuss it in a moment."

Under the paper was a beautiful box inlaid with coral and volcanic glass. I opened the lid. Inside, laying on white silk, sat the Hanged Man's noose.

The box hit the table. I got up and went to the other side of the room.

Remus chittered and jumped off the table, scurrying after me. I may have put a cracker and extra slice of prosciutto in my pocket earlier.

Brand gave Lord Tower a plaintive look.

"Hear me out. You have a choice," Lord Tower said to me. "No sigil is greater than another. No mass sigil is greater than another. Yet the base functionality of the object the sigil is shaped into, along with its history or notoriety, does have a considerable impact. That is the noose of the Gallows. It is timeless. If you were to sell that gift, it would quintuple the investment. And since you can easily claim this mass sigil through conquest, it is entirely your decision to make."

Sigil-making was a lost art and our supplies were finite. Sigils remained relatively plentiful, if anything with a six-digit price tag could be called plentiful; but mass sigils were items of singular rarity. You'd need to add another digit to the price tag to get close to its worth.

Inside that silver box was more money than I'd made from my share of the raid. It was a staggering gift. And . . .

"Oh," I said. "I could exchange it for more mass sigils. Or a combination of mass sigils and sigils. Jesus wept, Lord Tower—I could double my personal arsenal."

"As you say," he agreed.

I wanted nothing to do with that noose. It wasn't even a decision. The idea that I'd use it to protect people I love was anathema. Toxic.

"I could set up a private showing of sigils and mass sigils with the Arcanum's preferred vendor," Lord Tower suggested.

"Please. Yes." I gave him a wary look. "Just out of curiosity, would you have decided to sell it?"

Lord Tower crossed the room to stand in front of me. He made sure our eyes met before he said, "You can stop asking me that question, Rune. Trust your own decisions as I do."

"This is . . ." I swallowed and looked back at the silver box. "This is significant. This is far, far more than a new court should expect for a gift. I can barely wrap my brain around what this will mean. Anton, thank you."

Brand made a sound. I glanced at him. He had a look on his face as if to say, *When did this Anton business start?* I shrugged to say, *It's a thing now.* So he gave me an exasperated expression because I'd always told him I'd drop the Tower's name the first time I needed a really big favor.

"I sort of played that card," I sighed.

"On what?" he whispered.

"He . . . allowed Julia to remain . . . employed. After hearing that video that alluded to the Majeure."

Brand's eyes widened. He really, really wanted to talk about my choice of favors, but decided it wouldn't be a good look on him. He settled for a single, fixed eye roll at the ceiling.

"Few things amuse me more than attempting to understand your shorthand conversations," Lord Tower said. "But for what it's worth: Julia has been promoted to field lead for all of Germany. She sends her thanks to you."

"She didn't even mention my name, did she?" Brand asked.

Lord Tower smiled. "Now. Brandon. Your presents. The larger box is a gift from Mayan."

"Mayan bought me a gift?" Brand said.

"He did. It's an invention of his own design. He has one himself."

"Oh, weapon," Brand breathed. He shredded the ribbon and wrapping paper to get to it. Inside the box was a metal tube that resembled a police baton.

"There's a—" Lord Tower started to explain when Brand found the button that made metal wings pop out. The Tower smiled. "Mayan calls it a dart-bow, a dart gun-crossbow derivative. It contains hollow needles that pierce and dissolve under the skin. There's a clockwork device on the tube that rotates cartridges of various toxins with different levels of lethality. It's exempt from the city's firearm ban, too. Mayan has put instructions in the box."

"It's amazing," Brand whispered, running a calloused fingertip along the slick metal surface.

"The smaller box is from me," Lord Tower said.

Brand put the dart-bow down reluctantly and opened the jewelry-sized box. Inside, nestled on a bed of white silk, was a belt buckle.

"Volcanic glass," Brand murmured. He hid his confusion as well as I did though. There was nothing particularly intricate about the design.

"If you snap the buckle," Lord Tower explained, "you'll find a sigil shaped as a white-gold coin inside. I've stored Fire within it. You can't use sigils, of course. And if you want, you can break the buckle now and give it to Rune, but the idea is—"

"The volcanic glass masks the sigil's signature," Brand said, his voice rising. "If we're captured—if our weapons and sigils are taken away from us—they might leave this behind. This could save him. This could save Rune, if I can get it to him."

"Indeed. Though I prefer to think that it would save the both of you."

Brand gave the buckle a stunned look. "You bought me a sigil."

"Just because humans can't use sigil magic doesn't mean they can't own one." Lord Tower walked over to Brand, picked up the buckle, and laid it in Brand's hand. He covered it with his own fingers. "Brandon Saint John, I give you this sigil. Its will is now your will."

Brand gasped and nearly dropped the sigil. With his free hand, he touched the raised hairs and skin along his arm. "I felt that," he whispered. He laughed. "You bought me a sigil?"

"I did. Once the glass breaks, you'll need me to replace it, or another practitioner of gemstone art."

"Meaning you," I said, since the ability to melt and paint with gemstones was a very rare skill.

"At some point, Brand, Rune can tell you the words to share the sigil with him, so he can use it if you find yourself in need. But . . . Well. That is the gift."

Brand put the buckle down gently on the silk, covered the box, and hugged Lord Tower.

The statement repeated in my brain three times with a different emphasis each time—on the *he, hugged,* and *Lord Tower.* A million jokes, and all I could do was watch my vision skid left and right as tears filled my eyes.

"This will help me save him someday," Brand whispered. His arms were tight around the Tower, and the Tower returned the embrace. They stood like that for a few seconds until Brand sniffed and pulled back. He said, "Fucking hell, I can't believe your pajamas let me do that. They've got to have six different ways of setting me on fire for breathing in your direction."

"Not untrue," Lord Tower agreed. "Although we *are* in a null zone."

Brand's face exploded into insight. He snapped his fingers and said, "His hairclip. Mayan always wears that obsidian hairclip. I've wondered why for *years.* He's not that sentimental. Shit, I was betting it had a lock-pick inside it."

Lord Tower laughed, which was almost as rare as Brand laughing. And then Brand started laughing.

Since it was a moment for the ages and meant to be shared, I made a salami and cheese cracker for Remus.

Dinner was an experience.

None of the foods were hot—including the tea and coffee. Everything was tepid to avoid the burns that accompanied easy spills in the darkness. And the foods were a surprising blend of spices, sours, and sweets—each bite hit my palate like a SWAT team.

"Try the mushrooms at nine o'clock," Lady Death murmured to me. She was at my right hand, and Brand was on my left. "You may recognize the source."

"If these are those mushrooms that grow out the heads of worms, I am done," Brand announced.

"Insolence," someone hissed, to which Lady Death sighed, "Mother."

"Did you really take over the Hanged Man's mushroom farm?" Lady Priestess asked with genuine interest. "That's so . . . practical of you."

"I did," Zurah confessed.

"But she evicted the elderly dinosaur first," I said.

"You're welcome to return it."

I banged the end of my knife on the table. "Zurah Saint Joseph, you visited Sun Estate and convinced Corbie to *name it*. He calls it Flynn."

Her throaty laugh filled the room.

"This one was probably a battlefield general in her last life," one of her friends giggled. "You don't even realize she's outsmarted you until your nose is squashed against a corner."

"Shush now," Lady Death murmured. "I look out for my friends."

Her friends all agreed, made a lot of noise, and hoisted glasses for a toast.

"Mushrooms," a voice to my far right said. "The city slides into obsolescence, and you show pride in *farming*. Your efforts do not match your bloodline. You are the Bone Hollows. Your kind once created sigils. *Sigils.* And mass sigils! One of your ancestors even wielded a planetary sigil, once upon a time. And now . . . mushrooms."

No one responded.

My skin crawled even as my brain accepted this as a normal turn of conversation. I felt, a little, like I was going insane, only I didn't know why.

"You," the older woman's voice snapped. "Dagger Throne. You lead this city."

"The city leads itself, as it always has," Lord Tower said in a friendly voice. "I simply help it . . . paint between the lines."

"You speak like a politician, not an Arcana. Very well then, Councilor Tower. Address the assembly. Tell us where the paint is in danger of spilling outside the lines. Have you deduced yet who killed all those poor people at the rejuvenation center?"

"Not as such," Lord Tower said. "We are exploring several lines of inquiry."

The woman didn't speak for a long moment. Then, in a much colder voice, she said, "You evade me. Let's try that again, shall we? Whom do you suspect?"

Lord Tower cleared his throat, an uncomfortable, drawn-out sound. "We are not sure. We suspect Lady Jade—"

"*Lady* Jade now, is it?" she laughed.

"Subject Jade. Lady Jade. Temporary monikers."

I listened to Lord Tower share privileged information in a casual setting, and it was wrong, but I didn't exist. I had no better way to describe the way I suddenly felt. *I did not exist.* I was a stage prop until it was my turn to utter a line of dialogue. This was not my story; none of this spun around me. It was as if I did not even exist.

"We suspect Lady Jade is very, very old," Lord Tower said in a voice showing signs of stress. "Centuries. She possesses abilities that are . . . uncommon, in modern society."

"Does she," the woman murmured. "But you must admit, even if only to yourself, that there's another explanation. You're smart enough to have figured that out." Her fork clicked against her plate, and I heard the scrape of a wineglass. "Lady Jade," she repeated. "I should have picked the Cerulean suite. I'd look much better mocking you in blue."

"You," Lord Tower whispered, and his voice strained. "You have played your game too far."

"What?" Lady Priestess cried, her voice stuttering. "My head is pounding . . . what is this? What is happening?"

"Very well. See your world through clear eyes," the woman said. She whispered a few words, and light cantrips sprang from her hand and circled the table. Five, six—seven of them. Seven light cantrips, juggled simultaneously, in a null zone.

Then she snapped her fingers and broke apart the spell keeping us all in thrall.

Rationality returned as the mind-fogging spell broke apart. I suddenly knew who she was. I understood every bloody word Quinn had told me. But I could not move. My muscles refused to obey. It didn't feel like paralysis—it felt like my arms and legs were simply ignoring the neurons firing at them.

I panned my eyes left and right. The lights now showed a rather average dining room, devoid of the types of furniture that might be inconvenient in the dark. The white walls were splattered with blood.

Lady Jade looked at the bloodstains and shrugged a single shoulder. "I'm afraid I had to discipline some of the servants earlier. Don't worry, I put what's left in the freezer."

Lady Death made a sound, her face drawn into a pained rictus.

"You're got some life in you, haven't you?" Lady Jade laughed. She folded her age-spotted hands atop each other and leaned back in the chair.

Her attention turned back to the Tower.

"By all means," Lady Jade said. "Run off and gather with the other pawns. Discuss matters. Perhaps you'll even be smart enough to spin events into your favor—by seeking mine, eventually, of course. But for now, above all else, leave me alone. Are we understood? Come at me at your own peril." She tapped a finger in my direction. "That includes you. For the life of me I still don't know why you're such a threat. But you are. I'm not without my own access to the Sight." She tutted. "Don't let your importance in events go to your head, though. I haven't decided what you are yet: cog or catalyst. But if you fuck with me, I will fashion a hell from your nightmares and lock you in it. It will be violation unending. *Heed me.*"

"Cantrips," Lord Tower gasped, pulling the attention back to himself. "Null zone."

"Don't flaunt your ignorance," Lady Jade said. "It's unseemly. You don't even understand what these are. Null zones? They are anything *but.* What you call the absence of magic is actually the saturation of it. Your failure to draw on it as a resource is an *allergy.* It shows how much ability our people have lost. The raw force of these zones constipates you."

Lord Tower stopped struggling. He stared at her levelly.

Whatever calculations occurred in that moment were quickly decided.

And the Tower stood. It was not graceful. It happened in jerks and starts. But he began to stand.

Lady Jade slammed her hands on the table, overturning a glass of red wine. Power spiraled out of her—I've never felt anything like it. It was like an Aspect rising, or the Arcana Majeure. And yet, for all that, she wasn't using the Majeure, and it was not an Aspect. This was her baseline.

I was scared shitless.

Lord Tower struggled against her magic as she pushed back. The air between them distorted and wavered—heat off an engine block, the view through old, warped glass. Sweat beaded on the Tower's forehead. In the rotating light of the cantrips, his face did not look real or substantial; it was an absentminded pen sketch, more scratch marks than true lines.

Lady Jade let out a frustrated sound and strained harder—

And then there was a single, fleshy bone snap. She screamed and put a hand to her collarbone.

"This frail body," she hissed. "Godscock! Don't expect that to work a second time."

Lord Tower still couldn't move his arms or use his magic. He didn't need to. He just wanted to bait her rage and shatter her concentration, because it took concentration to sustain magic.

On my left side, Brand took advantage of the break in Lady Jade's willpower to pull out his new dart-bow. He snapped the wings of the device open and fired a dart into the V of pale flesh above her cleavage.

Whatever poison was in the dart was fast acting. Lady Jade yelled in pain, swept out her arm, and I went flying backwards into the wall. Everyone did—pinned by momentum for a single heartbeat before sliding to the ground.

"I don't yet know your value to my court, which is the only reason you'll survive this moment," she said, panting in pain. "But by all means, let's test your resourcefulness. If you're among the best the city has to offer, you'll see sunrise."

She touched a diamond bracelet on her wrist. A funnel of swirling air appeared above her. She gestured, and the point of the funnel cloud anchored to the wall and turned into a portal. She walked through it, the portal closed, and we could all move freely again.

The cantrips died. I heard someone spring to their feet.

"Oh, sweet River," Lady Death gasped. "Fiore, check the kitchen, find any injured! We—"

Below us, the floor moved—the massive roar of an explosion followed by its earthquake sonics.

"The vault," Lady Death said.

"She's after your sigils," I stammered.

"It's not that type of vault," Lady Death said. "Dagger Throne, Sun Throne, with me. Ciaran, too, if you please. The rest of you find any wounded and gather in the baths. Do you understand?"

"Why would we—" the Dowager Lady Death began to say.

"Because *I said so*," Lady Death snapped. "We need light. I can't make my cantrips work—I don't understand how she did."

"Lights!" the Dowager Lady Death cried. "I will be forsaken! I swore I would never betray our rituals when I built the Manse."

"You are not forsaken, mama, because the decisions of the court are no longer yours. Brandon—light!"

I felt a quick flash of pride that she knew my Companion that well, and then Brand had his small, powerful LED light in his hand. All of the other cheaters followed suit: cell phones, keychain lights, a Zippo. Lady Priestess actually pulled a huge, metal, 1970s-era flashlight from an oversized purse and bounced the beam around until it settled on her daughter. Bethan had fallen from her powered chair when Lady Jade slammed us into the wall, and was muscling her way back into it. Addam quickly stepped over to help her. He looked as shaken as I felt.

Fiore came back into the room with two members of the kitchen staff. Their aprons were stained with blood, and they had the wide eyes of shock victims.

Lady Death took in the small number and whispered, "The others?"

Fiore shook their head, jarring loose a tear.

"Right," Lady Death said, and swept her grief aside. If she was like me, it would be sitting in a mental box labeled *To Haunt You at the Worst*

Moment Possible. "Right. As I said—all of you move as a single group to the baths. Nataki, would you and Bethan lead the group?"

"They are under my protection," Lady Priestess said.

"Have them contact my guards. Have the guards assemble outside and wait for my signal."

"Trust the details to me," Lady Priestess said. "Go—find what happened below us. The bitch has laid a trap. Find what it is before its jaws close."

"With me," Lady Death announced, and swept from the room. Lord Tower was at her side; Addam and I were a step behind. Ciaran and Brand followed, but I noticed that Bethan Saint Brigid grabbed Brand by the elbow first to whisper something urgent to him.

We strode down hallways now laid bare by the disorienting beams of light. The system of fabric cords prominently adorned the walls, and the décor had blindness in mind. No painting frames had sharp edges; vases were cleverly attached to the surfaces of tables; and the flowers were chosen for their scent, not beauty.

"Can your guards breach the Manse?" Brand asked from the rear. "Shouldn't we gather at the front doors?"

"The building may look ancient, but the doors and walls have metal cores. Make no mistake, this is a bunker," she replied. "We'll have to tackle our present circumstances one fuck-up at a time."

"Who *is* she?" Addam said. His voice sounded hoarse and dry.

"A very good question," Lady Death said. She looked at Lord Tower. "That level of psionics and compulsion? Time magic was at play. Agreed?"

"Agreed," he said, almost too soft to hear.

"You know what this means. If there was one fugitive, why not two?"

I had no idea what she was referring to. I had even less context for the Tower's reply. He said, "Powerful enough to survive the stream? To *emerge* from it?"

"Down there," Lady Death said, pointing to the stairwell ahead. She spared the Tower a troubled expression at what he'd just said, but refrained from replying.

Emerging from a stream? Fugitives? I'd been upset weeks ago that I hadn't had a seat at the table, but I'd never suspected I was sitting in another room entirely. That paradigm would change, and soon.

The staircase scissored back on itself three times, taking us far lower than a single floor. At the bottom was a metal and wood door with a modern keypad next to it. Lady Death hit six numbers, and the door slid into a wall recess. Brand gave me a glance at this, which I didn't even slightly understand, meaning he was already three conclusions ahead of me. What had Bethan told him? I knew that look on his face—he'd got the scent of something.

The room on the other side was thoroughly of this century: thick metal walls and white linoleum under fluorescent lights.

On a wall to our right was an open vault door ringed in twisted metal. A woman stood in front of it. She was making soft, pitiful noises as her body spasmed. I heard the snap of bones, saw the bulging of joints where no joints should be. Her face was pale; a long scrape down one cheek showed bloodless, raw flesh.

She saw Lady Death and mouthed a word. Lady Death started to her, saying the name *Jabuela,* but Brand grabbed Zurah's sleeve and yanked her behind him.

He shouted, "Back back back back!" I turned and shoved at people, getting them on the other side of the door we'd just come through.

The woman Jabuela screamed, a sound that started as an ice pick–piercing shriek and kept climbing higher. A shockwave of magic rammed into our crowd. The worst headache of my life split my vision in half. I went down at the same time as Addam, who grabbed me against him and took the brunt of the landing.

"What," I whispered, disoriented.

Memories forced their way into my head. There was no context, no precedent, to explain what it felt like. One second, there was me. And the next, shards of someone else's soul became my fact. I was a heavy smoker, only I wasn't. I liked Bloody Marys and sunrises. My childhood dog was named Asher. I died while remembering the feel of his fur under my hands as the healer put Asher to sleep; I died while remembering Asher as a puppy jumping in my lap and licking my face; I died while falling asleep in a bed with blue sheets and a brown afghan, the whinnying breath of my sleeping dog beside me.

"Did we have a dog?" I asked Brand. I was crying. I tasted the tears on my lips. "When did Asher die?"

"I had an affair with my sister's boyfriend," Brand said. "How could I forget that? I still see her screaming at me, she's so mad, she's so fucking *mad.*"

"Kakodaimōn," Lady Death grunted, rubbing her knuckles along her forehead, face a mask of pain. "Oh gods, Jabuela released a kakodaimōn."

"She's gone, she's run!" Addam shouted, lifting me to my feet.

There was an open door on the other side of the room and no sight of Jabuela.

"What was that?" Brand said.

"Kakodaimōn," Lord Tower said. His cheeks were the color of chalk, which right then and there became the scariest part of the moment. I'd never seen him so unsettled. "Ancient Grecian spirit. The headache will fade, but—" He didn't finish the sentence.

I didn't need him to. If a kakodaimōn had infested Jabuela, it had shattered her mind and sent a lifetime of memories flying out like shrapnel. We all caught a piece of them. They were our memories now. They were *us* now, though the intensity, thank gods, would wear off.

Brand staggered over to the vault. He scrubbed a fingernail along the bent metal, looking at the marks of the explosion. Lady Death went to the mouth of the vault, reaching out to squeeze Brand's shoulder as she did. Past her, I saw a small space filled with shelving units. There was a modest collection of bottles, casks, locked boxes. On the ground was broken blue glass and a clump of umber-colored wax, now cracked down the middle.

"What is all this?" I asked quietly, going to her side.

"Containment," she said. "You'll have your own vault in time, of things you've defeated that cannot be killed, or allowed to walk free."

"What will this . . . this cacko-demon do?" Brand asked.

"It possesses animal intelligence," Ciaran said. He ran a shaking hand along his mouth. "And I appear to have a very strong diet soda habit now." He bit his lip and shook off the thoughts. "Animal intelligence. Its entire purpose is to infect, consume, and move to the next meal. It'll leap body to body."

"What happened to her?" Brand asked. "The bone cracking?"

"The kakodaimōn transforms the host," Lady Death said. "Stronger, quicker. Able to scale walls and crawl along the ceiling. It doesn't feel pain, once the host's memories are dispersed. Jabuela is . . . she's gone. She's just gone. What's left is cowardly—it will retreat against overwhelming force. Its primary directive is to extend its existence through transference."

"Good," Brand said. "We need a plan, and we need it now."

Zurah went over to a panel by the vault door. It was scorched, but functioning. The blackened bits smeared her hand as she punched a button.

Overhead, from speakers built into a ceiling panel, I heard an electric crinkling.

"This is Zurah," she said, her voice an echo delayed by a half second. "A contagion is loose in the building. Lock yourself in a room and barricade the door until you hear my all clear. Fiore, contact the guards and warn them they must not breach the building under *any* circumstances."

Brand hissed the word *vents* to me. Lady Death heard that and shouted, "And vents! Block all vents. The contagion is a parasite that requires living hosts—block any exit a person can enter through. Secure yourselves, and wait for help."

She let go of the button, wiping her fingers on her pants. She gave Brand a grateful look. "Never whisper good advice to me again, little brother. I would have never forgiven myself if I had missed that."

"The plan," Lord Tower prompted. "Do we head to the front door or the baths?"

"The baths," Lady Death said without hesitation. "I have an idea. We need to move quickly. Follow me."

As we rushed toward the baths, Brand barked orders to make sure everyone had a direction to watch. I snagged Lord Tower's arm and pulled him to the rear of the crowd.

"There's no one else I can ask this," I whispered urgently. "Please. Please, Lord Tower, if I get infected, before my memories are shared—"

"Only if you kill me too, if I get infected," he said grimly.

We stared at each other, and we'd never been more on the same page.

"Agreed," I said.

Somewhere ahead of us, the kakodaimōn shrieked. I pushed through the crowd, taking the lead with Brand. Lady Death was about to complain, but demurred; she knew Brand and I were trained for field action.

"We need to pare down the group," Brand whispered to me. "Lock civilians in a room, keep everyone we trust together."

"Okay," I said, and I *really* wanted to know what Bethan Saint Brigid had told him, and who Brand no longer trusted.

"Everyone watch your direction," he called out. "Shout if you see anything. Give Rune and I a ten-foot lead."

We shifted into action mode. Brand gave me one of his knives since he had his new dart-bow. Then we rushed down corridors, following Zurah's backseat driving.

It didn't take long until we spilled into the damp, red heat of the baths. The larger group from dinner was already there, and none of them had seen the kakodaimōn. Brand infiltrated the crowd and started asking quiet questions—he seemed very intent on talking with Zurah's seneschal, Fiore, in particular. I also noticed Bethan watched his progress with worried eyes.

"Daughter," the Dowager Lady Death hissed. "What happened to my Qing vases?"

"I swapped them out for resin reproductions that won't turn into expensive shards," Lady Death said distractedly.

"The state of our Manse is—"

"Excuse me, ma'am," I said, and stepped between them. Rude but effective. "Zurah, we need to talk. Can we secure the bystanders?"

"Fiore." Lady Death raised her voice. "Take all the members of my court and secure them in a nearby room. Check the vents. Shelter in place until I come for you. Our guests from the other courts remain with me."

"As will I," the Dowager said firmly.

"Make it so," Lady Death told Fiore, and trusted them to carry out the orders. Her attention narrowed on me. "What do you know?"

"Brand's investigating already."

So we waited impatiently while Fiore escorted people to nearby rooms and saw them lock themselves in. Addam and Brand helped, watching the hallways for signs of ambush.

As soon as we were down to Arcana and their inner circle, Brand closed the door, stationed people at the three vents he'd already located, and pulled Zurah aside. I was sick of being clueless, and forced myself into the discussion.

"You've been betrayed," Brand whispered. "Are you sure you want all these people here when we discuss it?"

"By without or within?" she asked. "The betrayal?"

"Within."

"I am responsible for the actions of my court," she said. "If I have wronged guests, I will be transparent about it."

Brand gave her a single nod, backed up, and addressed the room. "We need to secure the person who set the kakodaimōn free, and then we need to connect with the guards outside. None of you can help in a null zone— you need trained troops with weapons."

"Secure *the person?*" the Dowager Lady Death said. "The woman, Lady Jade—she already fled!"

"Whoever Lady Jade is, she's not omnipotent," Brand said. "She just wants you to think that. The idea she could let the kakodaimōn free without help is just smoke and mirrors."

"How could you possibly know that?" Addam asked, though not critically.

"Because that's the way it happened," he said.

"If this Lady Jade did have help, how could we possibly figure out who right now?" the Dowager said in exasperation. "Most of our staff is out there, not in here! You can't already know—"

"It was you, you, or you," Brand said immediately, and pointed to Zurah, Fiore, and the Dowager Lady Death herself. "You all have the code to the vault room."

"So do a dozen others," Zurah said in confusion. "So did Jabuela."

"But Jabuela didn't have the code to the vault itself, did she?"

Lady Death blinked, still confused. "The vault was blown open."

"No, it wasn't," Brand said. "Did you see the explosion marks? There were at least two structural steel bolts that didn't break. That door didn't swing open on its own. Smoke and mirrors. I've been asking questions, and only you three have the vault code."

"Brandon," Lord Tower finally said. "You need more."

Brand turned to face the Dowager. "That sigil," he said, and pointed.

The Dowager Lady Death looked down and seemed to notice for the first time that a sapphire and porcelain pendant had been jarred from under her blouse. She grabbed it and put it beneath her collar.

Lady Death went over to her mother, ignored the woman's attempt to swat away her hands, and pulled the pendant back into the torchlight. Since the Dowager wore more than one necklace, several ended up dangling there. "Mama?" she whispered. "Where did you get this?"

"From the armory. I found it in the back. It hasn't been used in decades. Am I not allowed use of our armory?"

Lady Death ran a thumb across the sapphires. "I have no connection to this. It is not a family sigil."

"Bethan?" Lady Priestess said sharply. Her attention was on her daughter, who was pale and wringing her hands. "Do you know something?"

"Yes, mother. That sigil . . . it bears a very strong resemblance to one from the audit."

Lady Priestess wheeled on the Dowager, and her normally scattered expression reddened with rage.

"The audit of sigils taken from the rejuvenation center," Bethan whispered to the rest of us.

Brand said, "And now that we know that, it's a later problem. Getting to the guards outside is a *now* problem."

"Barricade yourselves in this room," Lady Death told us. "I need to reach my bedroom. I have an idea, but I need help. Lord Tower, can you seal the building if I create a temporary breach?"

"Once outside, I can," Ciaran offered, touching his bone necklace.

"Good. Then I know a way out. We'll reach our guards, organize, and return with fucking flamethrowers. Mother, you will stay by my side."

"Daughter, you cannot believe—"

"ATTEND ME!" Zurah roared.

The Dowager dropped to one knee, awkward with a cane. She kept her head bowed and didn't say anything, acknowledging the head of her court.

"I could stay behind and patrol the corridors," I said, and then caught Brand's narrowed eye. "You don't mind, right?"

"How do you even fucking recognize me in the morning?" he said, just loud enough for me to hear.

"We can stay together?" I whispered back.

That was when a woman screamed—the stuttering, rising scale of shock and surprise.

"Lady Death, Ciaran, Rune, Tower, Addam, *now,*" Brand said. "The rest of you barricade the baths, wait for our return, let's go!"

He and I rushed the hall. I noticed that Lady Priestess whispered a few worried words to Bethan, and followed us without invitation. She positioned herself directly behind the Dowager, who Zurah dragged by the wrist.

As soon as we were in the hall, I spotted the kakodaimōn. Jabuela was barely recognizable—her skin was alabaster, her arms and legs had extra joints, and nothing more intelligent than sibilant hisses came from her mouth.

"I'll distract it," I hissed before Brand could stop me. I sprinted at the kakodaimōn, holding my Companion's knife in the type of grip he'd trained me to: all fingers wrapped around the handle in a fist. The creature stopped trying to break down the door and wheeled on me. Half a yard before I reached it, I slid into a home run position, using the knife and my raised arm to keep the creature from falling on me.

For a few seconds, I was everything it wanted. Its fingers and mouth dripped with a gelatinous fluid that would transfer its essence into me. It tried to grab my mouth in a two-handed grip to force its fingers past my teeth.

Using my distraction as cover, Brand vaulted over the kakodaimōn, kicking off a wall to power the jump. He landed, wheeled, put the creature's throat in the crook of his arm. Before the demon was even aware of it, Brand had severed the jugular. There was no spray, just a thick plopping of congealed blood.

The creature shook loose with inhuman strength and fled.

"Upstairs," Lady Death said. "Quickly!"

It took almost no time at all to run up the stairs and reach her corner room. Inside, she told Brand to shine his light on the corner.

"Do you need help?" the Tower asked.

"I only need everyone to stand back."

"Daugh—"

Lady Death went over to her mother and shoved her into the wall. The woman's short scream ended in a gasp as Lady Death's forearm creased her windpipe. They exchanged a look for a few long seconds. When Lady Death released her, her mother stayed quiet.

Zurah Saint Joseph was more than just an Arcana and sigil user. She'd devoted her entire life to the discipline of Frost magic. Without sigils, she could still manifest magic. And when aided with sigils, her innate Frost abilities were a fearsome weapon.

She pressed her hands along the stretch of wall outside the building's null zone. The ground began to rumble, softly—growing louder and louder until the rock began to groan to its breaking point. Ice began to scale the stone, cracking and showering the ground in flakes.

There was a thunderous noise—a deep, vibrating *CRACK*.

The wall blew outward. Starlight and cool air rushed in.

Outside, we immediately organized the guards who ran to the site of the explosion. They sent a unit to the armory for weapons, while Ciaran released a powerful Shield spell capable of sealing an entire building. How the fuck I ever doubted he was the Magician, I didn't know. Even Lord Tower nodded in approval at the slick work.

"Levant," Zurah said to a tall black man in royal blue and black, her house colors. "Take this woman to a cell."

Levant didn't understand what she meant, because Lady Death had put a hand in the small of her mother's back and shoved her. "Take . . . the Dowager Lady Death?" he said.

"Strip her naked. Remove all sigils, all jewelry. Lock her in a cell, and guard her. Give her no food, no water, no comfort until I say otherwise."

"Zurah," the Dowager said in a soft, intent hiss. "We must *talk*. You are putting yourself on the wrong side of things."

"I don't think she is," Lady Priestess said.

"Nataki," the Dowager said desperately. "You know me. You know that I would never—"

"I know *nothing* about what you are or what you've become. *Graverobber*," she spat. "Draped in the loot of corpses. Profiting from the death of people *under my protection*!"

Lady Dowager rose to her feet with the help of her cane, and dark crimson lines branched across her face. She spat the word, *"Ignorance,"* as her Aspect rose. The words were magic, whipping across Lady Priestess's face like a cat-o'-nine-tails, raising scratches on her flesh.

Lady Priestess's Aspect answered the challenge.

Her face began to glow with multicolored light, turning her into a living statue of stained glass which shone from behind with the force of afternoon sun. The stained-glass light fell across the Dowager Lady Death, who screamed and dropped to her knees. Lady Priestess's Aspect was a thing of legend—a rare hereditary Aspect that they called the Glory. The light was not light, and it judged.

As the Dowager broke into tears, my phone began to buzz.

Addam jumped, as his own phone vibrated.

And Brand's. And Ciaran's. Finally Lord Tower's phone went off as well.

Confusion reigned. Brand was talking with our house guards, I think; Addam with Corinne; Ciaran with Layne; the Tower with Mayan. I looked at my own phone and saw Diana's name.

I didn't even have time to say hello before she told me that Max and Quinn were missing.

THE ARCANUM

I woke and, after a few minutes of aimless blinking, swept a hand over Addam's side of the bed. The sheets were cold. I buried my face in his pillow for half a minute, inhaling sandalwood and amber.

I'd hoped he would have slept in. Yesterday had been awful.

Feeling decades older, I got up and dressed without wasting time on a shower. I had a Band-Aid on my finger—Corbie had bled me last night, to make the large Sun Emblem in his bedroom light up—which I pulled off and threw away. A quick glance in the mirror convinced me to finger-comb my hair, too. There'd be time enough later to clean up properly—I was due for my first meeting in the Arcanum's war room at lunchtime.

I already knew where Addam would be. He'd taken over an old classroom on the fourth floor as his own personal war room.

The first thing I did when I opened my bedroom door was to whistle for Asher. Halfway through the whistle I realized I was calling for someone else's dead dog, and a shiver went up my back. I decided not to think about that. It would take a while for the brunt of these effects to fade, and the memories to detangle.

I made my way through the mansion and fought, with bare success, to keep other dark thoughts at bay. When I entered the old classroom, the first thing I saw was Addam sitting straight in a chair with closed eyes. I froze on the threshold until I heard his soft sleep-breathing.

Oh, Addam.

Around him, on a folding banquet table, were maps, first-hand accounts, handwritten journal notes . . . Anything he could find on the internet about the Warrens and Lowlands. We suspected Quinn and Max were being held there, so finding intelligence on the terrain in anticipation of a rescue attempt was the best way he knew to contribute.

I walked over to the table and quietly picked up two letters set to the corner. One was in Quinn's handwriting. The other was a three-line message on heavy rag paper that smelled like lilacs.

The message said this:

The boy is an advantage I cannot allow you at the moment. I will treat them both as prisoners of war under the oldest of Court rules. So long as they comply, their safety is assured.

My fingers shook with anger as I shuffled the message behind Quinn's letter. Quinn had written:

Addam,

I need you to trust me now more than ever. Nothing is more important. Please, please, please understand that I'm doing what's best.

I know she's coming for me. I'm going to go willingly. It's the only way you all have a chance of surviving—it will give Rune the best path to saving our family.

She will treat me well, because she comes from a time when there were rules around taking noble prisoners.

Pay attention to the pill guy so you don't waste time. Or both of them? It's all foggy now. I don't know anything else, but that was important. You need to be able to move fast and not waste time, so make sure Rune and Brand know this too.

I really, really love you.

Q

"You've had word," Addam slurred, anxiety sharpening his accent.

"No," I said.

His face fell. I put down the papers and went behind where he sat, to rub his shoulders. "You're exhausted. Why not get some rest? You need to be in fighting shape when we move."

"When?"

"I don't know. I'm assuming the Tower has a plan, since he called a meeting of the Arcanum."

"He should have come here yesterday," Addam said, and not for the first time.

"You know how he feels about Quinn. He's working on this, Addam. Trust me—by the time I come back, I'll know more. I'll have a plan."

"You are so calm," Addam whispered. The shoulders under my hands went tense.

"That's just what I want people to see," I said, and meant it with all my heart. "Because I'm planning on killing a whole lot of people over this."

He turned in the chair and looked up at me. His eyes were rimmed in red. Closing them, he buried his face against my chest.

"He's lying," Addam whispered. "The letter . . . I know how he *evades*. He says he will do what's best, but he doesn't say he's doing what *I* would do. He says it's the way that *you* have a chance of surviving. That it will help you save the family—but he says nothing about him or Max." Addam bunched my T-shirt in one of his fists, kneading the cloth. "He is protecting me. I've lived for years with this . . . this *fucking* fear. That he's waiting for the best possible moment to throw himself on the pyre. That . . . that eventually all the different options would be too much, and he'd give his life to buy the best one."

I pressed my lips against his head and said, fiercely, "We will find our kids."

I met Brand by the carport on the side of the building. He was finishing up a maintenance check on his motorcycle, which surprised me. We'd been driving around in armored SUVs since the attack on the estate, courtesy of Lord Tower. I had wondered if he'd switch up our mode of transportation eventually.

"I wish we knew where we were going," he grumbled, seeing me. He was decked out in full black tactical gear. I noticed he'd retrofitted one of the many holster loops to hold the dart-bow, and the array of knives along his chest were tipped with coral, obsidian, and vulcanized coal dust. He could slide into any type of field action without a moment's pause.

"Did Mayan text you?" I asked.

"Yeah, but only to tell us what time to text him back."

I frowned. "But where are we meeting the Tower's car?" I was under the impression we'd be meeting at a second location, and from there we'd be transported to the Arcanum's secret bunker—something I'd barely known existed, let alone located.

"He's fucking showing off. He just said to go to a random place we normally wouldn't go, and then text."

"Are you sure it's safe to take the motorcycle out?"

"No, Rune, it's fucking dangerous. I'm just trying to lose you too, and make all three missing people a hat trick."

"Brand," I said.

He wiped at a grease stain stubbornly.

"You didn't lose them," I said. "None of this is your fault."

"Really? Because I'm in charge of security. It sure the fuck seems like my fault."

I went to his side and sank to a crouch so that we were at eye level. "That woman mind-fucked *the Tower*. We have to assume she has people at her side who are just as deadly. What do you think your people could have done? Or Mayan's people? Any guards who got in the way would have been slaughtered. And if you honestly think Quinn didn't know that, you don't know Quinn. Lady Jade may have sent someone to take him, but he offered himself up first."

"And Max? Quinn didn't mention Max in the letter. He didn't know Max was coming with him."

"If Max caught Quinn sneaking out, he wouldn't have left Quinn's side."

"So we just hope that they're safe?" Brand demanded. "That they'll be treated well?"

"Yes. That's how we keep moving forward."

"Until we have a target," Brand added.

"Until we have a target," I agreed.

Brand snagged a helmet hanging from one of the handlebars and stuffed it into my gut. Thirty seconds later we were on the bike and heading around the side of the estate, loud enough that curtains in the mansion twitched as we shot by.

I expected him to head for either the main driveway or maybe the old visitor's lot, but instead he shot down a newly paved walkway through the orchard. A wall of brambles blocked the path in front of us, which seemed very problematic until Brand pressed a button on his console. The brambles shuddered and rose, revealing the electric gate they were attached to. On the other side was a tunnel of foliage and branches I barely had time to be impressed with until we shot out on an access road that led to the city streets.

"You built a secret tunnel!" I shouted in his ear while pounding his shoulder. "That's a Tower trick!"

The whipping wind stole my compliment, but he felt my approval, and gave the motor a quick rev.

The random part of the city that Brand picked was a street packed with elegant, multi-story buildings that housed department stores. We'd never been fans. To us, department stores were more or less a big bin of negative emotions: things we couldn't afford, people we didn't want to see, hundreds and hundreds of ambush points.

Brand parked his motorcycle down an alley, locked it, and texted Mayan as we walked back to the street. Half a second later—nearly quicker than thumb typing—a blue taxi pulled over and glided to a stop by the store. A woman got out wearing the runway-shopping ensemble of the very wealthy, passing me with a wink.

Brand and I got into the car with no small amount of suspicion. The smoked-glass partition was up between us and the driver, and the car began moving without a single instruction. I wasn't even sure there *was* a driver.

"Okay, they followed us," Brand said. "That's the only thing that makes sense. There's no way they'd just happen to be in this area."

"The last time you let a car follow you, I was pushing it from above with baby fingers," I said.

"Then how the hell did it know we were going to be here?" Brand asked.

Tactically, Brand was better than me. But when it came to the Tower? I always figured it out first. Laughing softly, I looked through the darkened glass at the streets around us. "Have you ever been in one of these blue cabs?" I asked.

"Why would I spend money on a cab?" Brand asked. "That's fucking stupid."

"But you've seen them?" I said.

"Of course I have."

"Because they're everywhere. Half of the time they have an out-of-service light on. This must be one of his tricks. Remember the bless-fire ring?"

For years and years, I lived at and visited the Pac Bell and never knew that there was always a small squad of fake pedestrians surrounding his building at every given moment, prepared to raise mass defenses against an attack. When we'd been on the run from spectres, Lord Tower had revealed the defense to save us.

"He owns the cars," Brand murmured. "He keeps them on the streets at strategic points."

"Dozens and *dozens* of cars," I marveled. "All within seconds of him should he ever need a quick getaway. Complete with fake passengers! That man."

"God," Brand said after a long, heartfelt pause. "We need to be that fucking rich."

The taxi turned onto a major artery and drove halfway across the city. After about twenty minutes we entered a neighborhood of midrange office buildings, and drove into an underground parking structure. On the lowest level, a gate soundlessly rose as we approached.

The taxi turned and drove straight toward what, from my awkward angle in the backseat, appeared to be a cement wall.

My flinchlessness was rewarded: we drove through it, and into one of the New Atlantis subway tunnels. By this point Brand had brazenly rolled down the window so that he could stick his head out to see what was ahead.

"We're driving onto the back of a subway car," he announced. "This is some serious spy shit right here."

"I wonder what kind of food they'll have?" I said.

He leaned back in the car long enough to stare at me.

"What?" I said. "It's the Arcanum's secret war room. They've got to have a personal chef and barista, right?"

He leaned back out the window.

The subway ride was short. We barely had time to find the light switch in the backseat before we were reversing down the ramp of the converted carriage car.

The new space was a dead-end access tunnel converted to a rudimentary parking lot. There was one other blue taxi there, along with dark town cars and a rather well-behaved pegasus.

Mayan stood in front of an open, rusted metal door. He waited until we'd stopped in front of him before he visibly swallowed and said, "It's my fault. It was my watch. I had one job—*one*. To keep your family safe while you were off-site."

"Oh, not you too," I said.

"It's both our fault," Brand told Mayan grudgingly.

"*No*," I disagreed. "Not that either."

Lord Tower slipped through the door and gave both Companions an exasperated look. One hand was wrapped in fresh gauze, and the fingers under the shape of the gauze were once again finger-length. "Enough. No one could have stopped a clairvoyant of Quinn's caliber. You diminish him by suggesting otherwise."

"Hear, hear," I said. "Now, let's grab a snack before the meeting."

The Tower flicked a gaze down to my empty arms. "The new guy usually brings donuts," he said, and turned and led us all through the corroded door.

On the other side was a waiting room, unassumingly dank and bare. Whoever had designed the secret bunker had leaned hard into the illusion, making me a little eager to see what the heart of the complex looked like.

"This is where you part ways," Lord Tower said. "Mayan will take Brand to a Companion area. The war room is this way."

I stopped sightseeing. I could feel the warmth drain out of my gaze. Maybe I was on a shorter fuse than I thought, because the most I could say was, "Excuse me?"

"Rune," Brand murmured, a little embarrassed. "It's okay."

"It," I said, "is not."

Lord Tower turned to fully face me. "Only Arcanum are seated in the war room. It allows us to be candid."

"I'm feeling pretty candid right now," I promised him. "That makes no bloody sense. Mayan and Brand are half our *brains*. They're our strategy and defense. Why the hell wouldn't I want Brand's counsel at my side?"

"It is not meant to be a slight," Lord Tower promised.

"Rune," Mayan said, and showed me the palm of his hand in a calm gesture. "I've got a lot of things to tell Brand. I need him. While you guys are still arguing about who speaks first, we'll be moving onto our third or fourth plan."

Lord Tower rolled his eyes at that, which was a wholly unguarded expression, and perhaps the only thing that convinced me to back away from the ledge I was about to leap off.

"Fine," I muttered.

"Oh, this is going to be fun," Lady Death said from the mouth of a nearby hallway. Despite the energy she tried to put in the words, her face was drawn and tired. "Allow me to show our little brother his office. We'll be along shortly. Yes, Anton?"

"Very well," Lord Tower said.

I didn't move until Brand gave me a nod. Once he did, I walked over to Zurah without another look at the group. Quickly, the weary expression on Zurah's face become my focus.

"Are you okay?" I asked softly as she led me down another plain, cement hallway. Bare light bulbs overhead lit our way.

"Are you?" she asked.

"Not even a little. I'm sorry about . . . everything. Your mother. Your friend."

She put a hand on my arm and said, "Having a piece of Jabuela's thoughts in my head has been . . . difficult. Come. Let me show you your room. We meet in twenty minutes."

"I have an office?"

She pointed a little way down the hallway. Metal doors—just as old and rusted as the one from the underground parking lot—lined each side. We went to the door she indicated. I tried to open it, but it was locked. Lady Death nudged me aside and put her shoulder to it. The door scraped open like nails on a chalkboard.

The room inside was not a lavish secret bunker. It was a dirty old office space with mismatched furniture, cartons of old paperwork, and about six or seven recycling bins full of empty soda cans.

"My office was a storage room?" I said. I pointed to the blue bins. "And storing these in an empty room kind of defeats the concept."

"Your seat has gone unfilled for a long time, little brother," Lady Death said.

"This was my dad's?" I said.

"It was."

I looked at the crowded space with renewed interest. Then I remembered there were still more important topics. "The kakodaimōn. I meant to ask. It's contained again?"

"It is."

"And Jabuela? Your friend?"

"She was the head of my security team. And yes, my friend. At least

I thought she was. She's gone. She was gone the moment the creature entered her mind." Lady Death made a frustrated noise and rubbed her forehead. "I'm tired and making little sense."

"I know the feeling. I'm . . . Well, I'm either undercaffeinated or over-caffeinated. I forget which. But my thoughts are scattered. I'm sorry about Jabuela."

"She . . . was involved in these events. Another thing my mother will answer for. The Dowager has been uncooperative, but we've been able to learn more by searching Jabuela's quarters. I'll share details as soon as we gather. Fifteen minutes? Someone will stop by and collect you."

I spent a few minutes just squinting at the disorder after she left. The room wasn't completely what it seemed. Despite the mess, strong domestic wards hummed in the background, handling the worst of the mildew, mold, and allergens. I didn't see any vermin scat on the ground, either.

A mug on the nearly buried desk caught my eye. Picking it up, I saw that it was filled with a fine layer of dust and old tea stains. Had my father left this here once? Thinking he'd return?

"Rune Sun."

Lady Justice stood in the doorway. She didn't quite enter, just hovered on the threshold.

"I'd offer you a seat, but they're covered in old Tab cans."

She gave me a wry smile. "As you might have guessed, the Bunker is not staffed. That's what we call it, by the way."

"Did you want to talk to me?" I asked her bluntly.

She entered the room. All her nerves moved to her hands, which fidgeted along the surfaces of boxes and bins. "I wanted to apologize. My behavior at your coronation was . . . petty."

"None of that matters now. None of it."

"Agreed," she said. "We must find my son."

I think it was the first time she'd ever spoken of Quinn without prompting.

"Did you bring the letters?" she asked. "I saw the scanned copies, but . . ."

I pulled a plastic bag from my pocket. Inside were the two letters—one presumably from Lady Jade, the other Quinn. She shuffled Lady Jade's letter to the back without reading it, and took her time on Quinn's note. From the minutes that passed, she may have read it two or three times.

"He only has heart for Addam," Lady Justice whispered. "Not a mention of me. I am not being arrogant. It's a simple statement. He finds himself in danger, and he calls for Addam. He calls for you. I have failed my sons badly, haven't I?"

"Yes," I said, still stubbornly blunt. But that was my emotion talking, and it wasn't fair to Quinn. "But your youngest son has an endless amount of patience for the shortsightedness of others."

"We shall see. I cannot . . ." She broke off again. Took a short breath. "I cannot retract what I said. If my children, if my sister, move to your court, there must be a separation in finances."

"Addam runs his own business. He doesn't need your money."

She flicked me a look at that but said nothing for a moment. "But perhaps . . . the separation . . . needs not be so absolute. I can't lose all of them."

I didn't take the apology for more than it was worth. It was too shiny and new. But it was progress of a sort, at least.

"We should join the group," she offered, and held an arm out. She wore a sharp white suit today, with a raised design in the vague outline of feathers.

I took her arm and let her lead me to the war room.

The origin of the Arcanum is lost to the millennia. As far as our people are concerned, it has always been. Arcana have shadowed all of earth's history—the puppet masters and catalysts, influencing global events in order to serve our deeply rooted survival instinct.

When Atlantis revealed itself last century, it wasn't just humanity that was irrevocably altered. Our way of life changed as well. Influencing events had been easier from the fringes; we were unprepared for how blistering the spotlight of the world could be.

There were twenty-two seats in the Arcanum, once upon a time. The Emperor was dead. The Lovers had been dismantled. The Hanged Man was dead. The Empress had vanished into the Americas.

In a way, paring down the seating arrangements had simply consolidated our power bases. We were at a pivotal moment as a people—I'd always believed that. The world demanded we adapt. But there were so many unknown variables in how that might play out.

Present were the Lords and Ladies Strength, Hermit, Justice, Chariot, Magician, World, Hierophant, Priestess, Judgment, Tower, Death, and Sun.

Absent were Temperance, Wheel, Devil, Moon, Fool, and Star, who was imprisoned underground for his dark crimes.

For all that, my first thought was more prosaic.

"Is that from your living room?" I said to Lord Tower, looking at the chair that Lady Justice showed me. "Isn't that from your wicker phase in the two-thousands?"

A mismatched collection of chairs ringed a dark glass table. The room was just as cement and barren as everything else I'd seen. The floor was cleaner; I saw a broom propped in the corner of the wide space. The ceiling overhead, with its wire cages around bare light bulbs, was so low that Mayan or Addam, two of the taller men I knew, might have hit their head on it.

"It surprises you that we don't allow interior designers into the most heavily warded room in the world?" the Tower said.

"Yes? Maybe? There's no shrimp, is there?"

He handed me a bottle of warm water and took a seat next to me. His wicker chair had a wide, fanned back. There weren't even candy dishes on the table. It was as if the Arcana had got together with odds and ends from their basements and built a members-only tree house.

"The room keeps us humble," the Hermit said.

Zurah blew a raspberry. "We're also very lazy."

"Though we keep meaning to settle on a color scheme and paint the walls," Lady Priestess added absently. She was flicking through documents on an electronic notepad.

"I would think you're used to roughing it, Rune," the Magician said, taking a seat in a burgundy leather office chair. He wore a segmented belt with domino-shaped links, and each link vibrated with the power of a mass sigil. It was a show of force, which meant I was now jealous in addition to being snitty about the comment.

How had I ever believed this man was authentic? As long as I'd lived, he'd been the face of the Hex Throne. Square-jawed, movie-star good looks. Stupidly powerful. Insanely rich, due to his monopoly on portal magic. He was—he'd always been—too good to be true.

I was dying to figure out how Ciaran had carried out this spectacular ruse.

"You stare," the Magician murmured while laying a slim portfolio of documents in front of him.

"I like the new haircut," I said evasively.

His gaze snapped up to me, genuinely puzzled and maybe a *little* suspicious. The Tower's eyes also narrowed, which made me wince internally, because I vowed to Ciaran I'd be discreet.

So I set aside my pettiness. It was time to put this table, and the people around it, into my service. I had no other priority.

"I'd like to make a request," I said.

Lord Judgment—the aging quarterback of the Arcana, dressed in dark clothes with a gold circlet on his forehead—leaned his massive staff of office against the table. "Go on. We only stand on ceremony in the Iconsgison," he said. "If matters are urgent enough to require a quorum in our war room, then we all must speak freely."

"Great," I said. "I'd like to include Companions in this discussion. Their strategic perspectives would be invaluable."

"Noted, but denied," he said. "If we require them to bear or give witness, we'll call them in. For now, the Arcanum is in session."

He grasped the staff of office and gave it a perfunctory tap against the ground. It was not a magical gesture, but it had the force of authority.

"You've all read the reports," Judgment said. "Let's not waste any time on the basics. I want to hear about new developments. Lady Death."

Zurah sat up in her chair and folded her hands in front of her. She stared at nothing in particular while she spoke. "For the sake of shared vocabulary, we have identified a body of conspirators loyal to this Lady Jade. My mother was turned to her side, and she then turned my head of security, Jabuela Ducaale. They helped get Lady Jade access to my estate, the Manse, and my secure vault."

"Two questions occur to me," the Tower said. "Why was their assistance needed, and what is the purpose of this conspiracy?"

"It's true, then, that Subject Jade overwhelmed even your mental defenses," the Magician said.

Lord Tower smiled at him. "As she did the mental defenses of Lord Sun, Lady Priestess, and Lady Death. As well, I'd surmise, as any of you who attended the coronation and possibly saw or interacted with her."

"It was a clever spell," I added. "Not Invisibility or Camouflage—she just rendered herself harmless to our perception."

"Clever people are somewhat overrated," Lord Strength said without looking at me.

"Tell me," the Tower said. "When did you first learn to use a null zone to power spells?"

That shut Strength up.

The Tower wasn't done. "Because I first learned how to do it from *her,* after she immobilized four sitting Arcana in her presence."

Well, that shut me up, too. Partly because it made so much sense. I remembered how the Tower pushed back against Lady Jade. I hadn't realized he'd simply heard her argument about the true nature of null zones, believed it, and adapted his lifelong outlook on reality accordingly.

"Are we ready to return to the questions at hand?" Lord Tower asked. Lord Strength, jaw set mulishly, nodded.

"She is not invulnerable," Lord Tower said. "Nor is she omnipotent. While Lady Jade displayed ability, she also relied on help to make certain that parts of her plan were more effective—such as accessing the vault. Lady Death, why was your court member susceptible to being turned?"

"Jabuela," Lady Death said. "She comes from a . . . disadvantaged childhood. It left its marks. I suspect her past was the lever used to convert her."

"She was paid?" Lord Hierophant asked.

"I don't think so," Lady Death said. "It wasn't financial gain. I spoke with the people closest to her, and she'd made occasional comments about citizen rights, and a rising movement belowground. And that echoes some . . . memories that I absorbed when the creature broke her mind."

"The Warrens again," I said. "The mud on Lady Jade's shoes."

"We found traces of the same mud in Jabuela's room. I looked for it specifically." Zurah double-tapped a panel of glass, and the tabletop flickered to life as a monitor.

I looked at the forensic report that popped up before each place setting. The location of the clay wasn't identified, just general confirmation that it's a strata of soil well below ground level.

"But . . ." I trailed, gathering my thoughts. "That can't be the same reason your mother was turned. No offense meant, but she doesn't seem that concerned with money or the plight of the average citizen."

"Yes and no," Zurah said. "Much of the Bone Hollows is deeded to the sitting Arcana. When she stepped down, she gave up everything. That was why it's so easy to believe her loyalties could be swayed by gifting her an unattached sigil. She has access to dozens of *family* sigils, but none linked only to her. And on a larger level, regarding commoner rights, my mother may not care about those *led,* but she has very strong opinions on those *who lead.*"

"Vivid opinions," Lady Priestess said. "We all knew her. She's an isolationist, on top of everything, like Lord Devil and Lady Moon—who, I note, are conveniently absent. And the Dowager doesn't just believe we should cut ourselves off from the human world—she believes it's our right to subjugate it. She'd show her belly to a true Power, especially one that thought like her."

"Or someone who simply *said* they thought like her," I cautioned. "Lady Jade is playing more than one chess game. I'd bet the Tower's bank account on it."

"Much appreciated," the Tower said wryly.

"When Mayan's team combed through the rejuvenation center," I asked, "did they use Psychometry spells?"

Psychometry was a very handy investigative magic, and I'd used it often in the field. Strong emotion leaves imprints. Psychometry can let an Atlantean tap into those echoes—either with visual, auditory, or emotional feedback.

"Excellent question," the Tower said. "A senior security officer used Psychometry. The feedback crippled him—he remains in critical care due to the backlash and can't recall a thing he saw."

"The Psychometric feedback on Rurik brought me to my knees," I remembered. I looked at the others and said, unnecessarily, "The lich."

"Powerful people leave powerful footsteps," Lady World said, shifting in her chair for the first time. "One of us could try. Or we could adapt the magic to muffle the feedback?"

Lord Tower tipped his head at her. "I have specialists working on it. I'm close to a potential solution."

"That may help isolate her bolt hole in the Warrens or Lowlands," I said. "Because she has a bolt hole. She has a compound. I'm sure of it—we know she has followers and soldiers, and they need to gather somewhere. But we haven't talked about the biggest potential link. Where," I said, "is the Fool?"

"He has one compound in the Warrens, and another aboveground in a wooded swamp," Lord Tower said. He tapped a few commands into a tabletop keyboard, and a map of New Atlantis filled the middle of the table. A red circle appeared around an oblong temple near a northern swamp. "Both compounds are deserted. I've tasked our satellites to watch for movement at the aboveground facility, and have spotted only the odd individuals, but no gatherings. The Warrens is another matter, of course. It's harder to send large teams there."

I bit my tongue before I could blurt, "We have satellites?"

"And Lord Fool is connected how?" the Magician asked.

"By his followers," I answered. "Has Mayan confirmed it yet?" I glanced at Lord Tower, and damn if I hadn't guessed right.

"Yes. The assault on courts were carried out by current or estranged members of the Revelry. We just made the last connection this morning."

"They looked like members of the Revelry," I said. "Indigent, mavericks, anarchists—the lost children of Atlantis have always been drawn to Lord Fool, and he's always taken good care of them. It's a bigger population than most people suspect. But I've never known them to be organized or violent, though."

"We've never known null zones to power spells, either," the Hermit said. "The world has been changing around us for a long while now."

"Which leads to the elephant in the room," Lord Strength said. "Who the hell is this Jade bitch?"

Apple bitter flooded my mouth. I discreetly spit a piece of my nail into my hand and lowered it to my side.

"One question," the Hermit said. "Has the Empress returned?"

"No," Lord Tower said. "Or at least, this isn't her. Not just in personality, but the power signature is different."

"I've also seen the Empress rejuvenate to a much younger age," Lady Priestess said. "The lack of rejuvenation is important. Lady Jade's rage was not false."

"I agree," I said. "So let's talk about the second elephant in the room."

Lord Tower turned his head, slowly, to blink at me.

"What fugitives live in the timestream?" I asked. "That's what you meant by stream, I assume."

By the reaction around the room—mainly different levels of knowing and discomfort—I knew we weren't all playing from the same handbook. And I'd had just about enough of that.

"Maybe it's time we get candid," I suggested.

Lady Death sighed. "Rune, it's not as if we have orientation materials for new Arcana. There's not a training module titled *Shit We Keep Secret*. There are a lot of things you'll learn—terrible, but generally highly *unlikely*—things. I promise, we have every intention of discussing this now."

"When I made claim against the Hanged Man," I said, "the turning point—the moment when many of you dropped everything to support me—came when you found out he was using Time magic. At one point, I was told it could open a door not easily closed. Does all that have to do with the Hourglass Throne? Do you suspect it was never truly dismantled—or that a new Arcana is rising to take control over it?"

Lord Tower tapped a button, erasing the table screen. He leaned back in his chair and exchanged a quick look with Lord Judgment, who inclined his chin.

"Not exactly," Lord Tower finally admitted. "The Hourglass Throne was thoroughly destroyed in a raid over a thousand years ago, for crimes against Atlantis. It no longer exists . . . but its final ruler may. Records from that time indicate that Lord Time attempted to escape into what we call the timestream during the fall of his court."

"*Lord* Time," I said, and a long, drawn-out *aha* stretched across my brain. "That's why you were so hyperfocused on gender during the attack on the rejuvenation center."

"There are no records that indicate a woman of Arcana-level power existed in their court at the time the Hourglass Throne fell," Lord Judgment said. "Lord Time's sons were his heirs, and they died during the raid. He was married to several women, but none allegedly possessed the Majeure."

"And the Arcana Majeure is an essential fact here," Lady Death said.

"No Atlantean could withstand the forces of the timestream without it. To use it as a refuge? And emerge at another point in time? It is a fantastical possibility."

"And yet, we have Lady Jade," I said. "Fantastically powerful. You say that the compulsion at the Manse was underlaid with Time magic—and I'll need to take your word on that. So we're left with the possibility that there . . . What? Was another heir who escaped with Lord Time? Does that mean Lord Time is still out there too? Or maybe Lord Time transitioned genders—I know it happens much more in modern times, but it wasn't unusual even back then."

"That would be a mercy," Lady Priestess said. "One of them is going to be difficult enough to corral, I'd rather there not be two. Let's be honest amongst ourselves, if not outside this room—we are not like the Atlantis of old."

"We should not inflate our adversary," Lord Tower said, though politely. "The amount of time spent in the timestream is *objective*. Let's assume Lady Jade went in a young woman. Even considering the pace of our aging, it's unlikely she spent more than a hundred years in it, since I can't imagine she had access to rejuvenation technology. And if she was able to somehow survive her journey in the timestream, she would theoretically be able to appear at any point."

"It's just as possible, then, that she was an old woman who spent ten minutes in it," Lord Magician argued back.

"It is," Lord Tower said. "Except for the fact that she used modern slang, in addition to Old Atlantean. She appeared to be relatively well informed on current events. She has followers, and she appears to be developing an inner circle." His face momentarily contorted into a disgusted look, a rare sign of frustration from him. "All our suppositions conflict themselves. There is much we do not know."

"We know enough to guess the Hourglass Throne may exist after all," Lord Strength said. He gave me a thin smile and his full attention. "Our little bulldog now has a brand new Arcana court to destroy."

BANG.

Everyone jumped before staring at Lord Tower's hand, which had slammed down against the table.

He said, in a soft voice, "A failed insult, and an unnecessary reminder of your traitor son."

My phone buzzed in my pocket, giving me a perfect excuse to duck my sight from the moment. Brand had texted me a quick, *Talking about time yet? figured something out.*

I thumbed back a quick *Yes,* and then, *Ducking interrupt us pls.*

There was another *bang,* and I looked up to see Lord Judgment standing with his staff of office gripped in one hand. "Ill-advised comments on both sides," he said. "We will be better than this."

"And yet . . ." the Hermit said. "Perhaps there is some wisdom in our barks and bites. We have instantly invoked words like *adversary* and *attack.* Are we so sure this isn't an opportunity? The death of a court injures us all. The Hanged Man—and please understand, I condone his actions in no manner or fashion—ruled his court for hundreds of years. When he died—suddenly and without the structure of a well-developed raid—we lost unfathomable institutional knowledge. We are less because of that. What opportunities might an Atlantean of old represent?"

"Lord Hermit," I said. I had a middling friendship with him. At the very least, he told me on at least one occasion that he views himself as being in my debt. "I've spoken with Lady Jade twice now. If we use words like *adversary,* it's because she has openly made moves against this ruling body. She does not want to co-exist. She wants to lead. I truly believe that."

"My mind is not settled," he said, with a tip of his head. "I merely provide conjecture. It is the nature of a hermit."

"It's a fair point, and diplomatic envoys will remain in our bag of tricks," Lord Judgment said. "But first we must confirm whether this woman is, in fact, a scion of the Hourglass Throne. We must learn her location. We must learn what actions she's taken to mobilize a base since she's returned, if that also, in fact, is true."

"Can I ask a question?" I said.

He flicked a finger in my direction.

"What were their crimes against Atlantis? No surviving texts from that period are clear. If I had to guess, they nearly created a paradox."

"They nearly did," Lord Tower said. "From what I've learned over the years, the Time Court fell during a plague that severely depopulated the Atlantean homeland just over a thousand years ago. Three of Lord Time's adult children initially died."

"Initially?" I said.

"He used Time magic to extract them from an earlier timeline and move them to a point after the epidemic subsided."

"He cheated death," Lady Death said. "He stole from the River. He unleashed doppelgängers into our true timeline. I can barely imagine what the consequences may have been. Destabilizing the timestream is potentially a world-ending event. And these were simply the crimes that were recorded. Gods know what else they may have done in service of their own interests."

"Our Companions may have some new thoughts about this," I said, hearing footsteps echo from a nearby hall. "They just texted me. Could we hear them out?"

Lord Judgment waved a hand and sat back down.

Brand and Mayan strode into the chamber, Mayan a half step ahead. "With your permission?" he asked Lord Tower, who nodded. Mayan flicked a hand off his notepad, and the tabletop screen pinged. The frozen frame of a video appeared before us.

The pharmacist, I said to myself. It was the beaten pharmacist from the rejuvenation center, who'd made one of the videos of Lady Jade.

And then I thought—via the thunderbolt insight that so often accompanied one of Quinn's insanely vague prophetic hints: *A pill guy.*

Mayan picked up a white pen from a tray attached to the side of the table and handed it to Brand. Brand gave Mayan his *what the fuck am I supposed to do with that* look, so Mayan took the pen back, went over to the frozen image, and circled the man's hand. A bright red circle attached itself around the image, and moved with the motion of the hand as soon as Mayan hit play. I watched professional interest and jealousy peek through Brand's scowl, which was nice, because he was hard to shop for on holidays.

Mayan gave Brand a blank look until Brand, somewhat uncomfortably, went to my side and spoke. But just before he did, he snuck a dental pick into my hand, presumably because the apple bitter–flavored nail caught between my teeth was irritating our bond.

"Mayan told me about the Hourglass Throne," Brand said. "We began following up on possible ways to confirm its presence, when it occurred to me that we already had a witness. Someone already confirmed that the Hourglass Throne was involved in the rejuvenation attack."

"The pharmacist did?" I asked. "Before he died?"

"He told us," Brand said. "Remember?"

"He . . ." I trailed off and tried to remember the video. He'd only been conscious for moments, hadn't he? He'd pointed the finger at a guest of the center.

"He said it was a guest," Lord Tower told the room, echoing my thought.

"Not exactly," Brand corrected. "He said it was *our guest*. String that together and make sure you break *our* into two syllables."

"Hourglass," I whispered. "He was saying Hourglass."

"And watch his hand. He was giving us a sign all along. But his hand moved so slowly I thought he was just twitching."

The image with the anchored red circle moved. The camera spun out of the man's reach when he pushed it under a desk. The last few frames focused on his fingers, which did look like they spasmed. Mayan tapped a button on his notepad, and the image jumped into double speed. The twitching began to make a pattern.

Mayan drew an X on the tabletop with the white pen and capped both the top and bottom with a straight line. It now looked like a very angular hourglass.

"This is suggestive, but not conclusive," Lord Judgment said, but with definite interest.

I caught Lord Tower's eye and mouthed the word *Quinn*. Clearing my throat, I said, "I have access to clairvoyant resources. We were told to pay attention to a man with pills."

"Suggestive and convenient," Strength said. "I would like more facts before we tear the Warrens apart in a hunt."

"I'd like to examine the Fool's compound," I said. "I'll take Brand and Addam. If we can find where the Revelry's followers have gone, we'll find Lady Jade."

"Done," Lord Judgment said. "Coordinate with Lord Tower. In the meantime, we'll explore other avenues, and I'm asking all courts to move to wartime footing. Be prepared for anything, and at any moment. Am I clear?"

"What about those absent?" Lady Priestess said. "Where are the Devil and Moon?"

"They opted to remain outside the closed border," the Hierophant said. "I spoke with Lady Moon. She and Lord Devil were vacationing elsewhere when the pandemic struck."

"Is there a reason to suspect they may be involved?" I said. "Lady Priestess, you mentioned they were isolationists."

"They are, but that's a tenuous connection. I have no real evidence to doubt them, just a few curious coincidences. I'll look down that particular rabbit hole."

Lord Tower turned to me and said, "If you can spare an hour, I'd like to show you something first?"

The Tower led us through a short maze of corridors. Brand and I hung back, because I had something to say to him.

"Is that a juice box?" I hissed.

Brand looked down at his hand. "Yeah. They've got this posh Companion room with granola, drinks, and a low-fat chocolate yogurt fountain with fruit."

"Do you know how many doggy bags I've brought you from restaurants, you fucking ingrate?"

"You know," he said with real exasperation, "this is why you should haul your ass out of bed earlier and eat a real breakfast."

I didn't have time to respond, because Mayan had muscled a metal door open. On the other side was a large room filled with banquet tables. From the scuff marks on the ground, it looked like they'd just been set up.

And then I didn't notice anything else, because I'd closed my eyes and was bathing in the relentless, tidal wash of magic.

"Unbelievable," I whispered. "It's like an ocean."

I heard Mayan explain to Brand. "Those are all sigils. Mr. Dean is a preferred vendor of the Arcanum."

Opening my eyes, I cut a glance to Lord Tower.

He said, "Mr. Dean is already aware you'll put forward Lord Hanged Man's noose as collateral for the trade. He will make you a fair offer."

Mr. Dean was a short man with a weathered face and nicotine stains on his fingers. His eyes had the dull yellow sheen of a longtime smoker. In a raspy voice, he said, "Welcome, Lord Sun. I brought a large collection of items for your review, including both standard and mass sigils. I imagine that the price of the noose would easily allow you to purchase two mass sigils, if you desired."

"Easily," I said. "One may have already calculated that the noose is worth up to five."

The man's smile grew a bit fixed. "I am always open to negotiation, of course."

The Tower and Mayan stepped to the side to have a discussion, while Brand joined me at the tables. Claret-colored silk scarves had been laid out to cushion the artifacts. A dizzying display of sigils were in front of me. The pulse of their very existence was strong enough—but the force of the mass sigils laid out on the next table was nearly thunderous.

The possibilities weren't endless, but they were absolutely staggering.

I could walk away from this room with a few new mass sigils along with several new sigils. Hell, I could buy sigils that *matched.*

In video game terms, I was about to level the fuck up.

The first item I knew I had to own was a brooch. It was shaped like a silver dove in front of a rising sun, and yellow topaz glinted as its eyes. It reminded me of Anna's growing Aspect—whenever it rose, I heard the sound of wings. She needed a sigil of her own; it was time I began training her and Max in earnest. Corbitant was too young, and Layne had made clear that they only wanted to train their innate necromancy.

"That'll so get yanked off you in a fight," Brand said, seeing my fingertips graze the surface of the silver bird.

"It's for Anna. It would be good for training."

A quick stutter of conflicted emotions hummed along our bond—approval because Brand loved the kids, disapproval because that would be one less sigil I might have depended on in a fight.

"That's nice," he finally sighed. "Now be greedy."

"Gladly. I was thinking I would—" My breath caught, landing on a gold belt buckle in the shape of two interlocked infinity symbols. "Oh, Brand. Brand, that's the symbol for Companions."

"It is?"

"An old symbol. And I think . . ." I picked up the sigil and felt along the curves of the infinity design. It was not one piece of art—it was two interlocking sigils. "Two of them. This stores two spells."

"A rare find," Mr. Dean said, clearing phlegm from his throat as he gave up the pretense of not eavesdropping. "I see you like it. It's quite expensive, but surely within your budget."

"Okay," Brand said. "You're getting that look on your face that shopkeepers get when a dumb shopper indicates they love something that doesn't have a price tag on it."

"I promise you, my lord, my prices are quite fair, but this really is an *exclusive* design that—"

"Oh, Lord Tower!" Brand said, raising his voice, while I tried not to slap a hand over my eyes. I did that a lot around Brand.

The Tower turned his head and gave Brand a mild but well-defined look of long suffering.

"Do we need him to come over?" Brand asked Mr. Dean.

Mr. Dean swallowed and shook his head.

"Excellent," Brand said. He raised his voice again and told the Tower, "I like your shirt. As you were."

I browsed the sigils some more and then moved to the mass sigils. I'd already made a few decisions in my brain, even before coming here. As tempting as it would be to walk around with a mass sigil, I had so few that they were more important for estate defense. If I could bury enough and link them, I'd have a defense spell as powerful as the one that used to protect Half House. So I ignored the more fanciful mass sigil designs, and simply focused on solid and functional discs.

At some point, Mayan and Brand moved off to talk about my upcoming investigation, and the Tower waited by my side.

"Last year, in the Westlands," I said absent-mindedly. "At the Moral Certainties compound. That was one of the first times I filled a mass sigil for personal use. It wasn't as easy as I expected. It was like filling an ocean with a bucket."

"There's a trick," the Tower said. "At least, there's a certain trick that I use. I imagine that my magic is loud and heavy, and the mass sigil is a cavern. When my magic hits the walls of the cavern, it ripples and echoes. It amplifies the pace at which I store the spell."

I blinked, realized it was gorgeous advice, and smiled at him.

"I see you pulled aside that brooch," he said. "An unusual choice for you."

"It's not for me. It's for Anna. I need to start training her. Whether she really ends up being my heir or not? That's up to her. But she's too strong not to start sigil training as soon as possible."

The Tower picked up the brooch and smiled down at it. "It reminds me of a sigil I gave my Amelia. My youngest child, but always the smart one. A fearless, loving girl—until she got old enough and her mother forced her into the public eye." The Tower's eyes shuttered. "Amelia didn't react well to that. She wants nothing to do with politics and publicity. And it ruined Dalton, too, but in a different way. He took to public life just a little too much. It's why he spends so much time in the human world. The level of adoration is disproportionate."

"I like Amelia," I said, because I felt I had to remark, and I wasn't about to say anything about Dalton Saint Joshua.

Lord Tower angled a quick look at me. "Let's settle up. I don't want to keep you too long. I'll advise on the final negotiations."

With the Tower's help, I settled on the brooch and Companion symbols, and three mass sigils. The shopkeeper grumbled, but he was pocketing at least a million-dollar profit once he auctioned the noose as a collector's piece.

Ten.

Just like that, I left the place with ten sigils to call my own.

THE REVELRY

The monster on my chest twitched its whiskers, which was unthreatening enough to keep me from yelling.

"Holy shit," I said sleepily. "I know you."

Remus squeaked, tumbled off my chest, and slithered off the side of my bed. I rolled to the edge in time to see him disappear into my overnight bag, which was still lying on my bedroom floor from where I'd dropped it after the night in the Manse.

"You're a stowaway," I accused my handbag. "Have you been hiding there all along? You know, Brand told me if I adopted one more kid, he was going to lock me in a room with everyone under the age of twenty and a twelve-pack of soda."

The bag shimmied a bit, but Remus didn't reappear.

"You probably don't know this," I told him while groaning my way out of bed, "but I think there's this really weird prophecy about you. You may want to stay away from Max."

I'd barely caught four hours of sleep and it was dawn, combining into two of my least favorite things. (Except for the nagging memories of Jabuela, who loved sunrise, but it fucked with my head to think of that.) Most of the afternoon yesterday had been spent in my sanctum, meditating over an array of spells to store in my suddenly sufficient personal sigil armory. It felt bizarre to have that many on me at once. The average scion was rarely without a dozen of their own, which meant, for the first time since I was fifteen, I was nearly on the same playing field.

When I'd tried to explain that to Brand, he'd snorted and glared, saying, "You can do more with one sigil than most do with five. Jesus Christ, Rune, these are not the days to act fucking humble."

I took the advice to heart, and spent the extra hours storing some of my most powerful spells. If it took a little longer than usual because I kept stroking my new sigils lovingly, no one needed to know.

Fifteen minutes later I was geared up in my best field outfit, including my black leather jacket and boots, all fitted with basic wards to give me a slight edge in combat. I spent a final minute smiling at my double-Companion symbol belt buckle sigil, and headed downstairs to meet up with Brand and Addam.

Anna waited for me in open ambush, splayed across the bottom step of the second-floor stairway with an open iPad.

She gave me the teenage look of long-suffering. "I want to talk to you," she said.

"Can we talk later? Addam and Brand are waiting."

She gave me her blank look, which meant she knew I was heading into the field, and maybe that was why she was camped out on the bottom step of a stairway landing.

"Here," I sighed, and walked into an empty room. It'd been a guest room, once upon a time. The estate contractors had removed the rotted and mildewed furniture, leaving behind stained wooden floors and scabrous patches of wallpaper.

"I need to help," she said once I closed the door.

"Okay," I said slowly. "Why don't you pick up where Addam left off? You know he's been researching the Warrens and Lowlands."

"You're heading *into* the Warrens today, aren't you?"

"I don't think we are. We're going to try to find Lord Fool at the Revelry."

"Which may lead to the Warrens or the Lowlands, right?"

"Anna, you're not ready for the field. This isn't a discussion I'm prepared to have with you."

"But I can be useful!" she hissed, lowering her voice. "I can help you! I can use the—"

She bit off just before mentioning the Arcana Majeure, which we'd agreed was a topic that would not even be *breathed* between us until she was a little older.

I bent my knees so that we were at eye level. I felt the warm presence of my Aspect turn my eyes orange. "Go on. Finish the sentence. I double-dog dare you."

She shook her head but maintained a stubborn look.

"Do we need to have this talk again?" I said.

The thing was, my cousin had potential. Massive, massive potential. I'd only learned what the Majeure was myself over the last year, and I'd only manifested my use of it in the last few years. According to Lord Tower, for Anna, at her age, to be showing the ability was exceptionally rare. She was destined to lead a court—mine if not another. At the very least, her use of the sigil-less Majeure magic marked her as a budding principality.

"I haven't told anyone," she swore. "But that doesn't mean it's not *there*. I can help! They . . ." She trailed off and wiped stubbornly at one eye. "They left me. I thought they were my friends. But they *left me*."

"We don't know how it happened. I don't think Quinn meant for Max to go with him. It's not a field trip, Anna—they put themselves in unspeakable danger. Do you—"

"Your eyes are on fire," she whispered as I saw my flames reflected in her eyes.

I closed them and banked my Aspect. This was exactly why I hadn't given her the sigil yet. She was as headstrong as I was. "Please do not do anything stupid, Anna. I couldn't bear it."

"I'll do the research," she said.

"Thank you. I really need to go now. Okay?"

She nodded but didn't meet my eyes. I thought about forcing her into a vow for a wild second, but you just didn't do that with children. They screwed up too easy, and the consequences of breaking a vow could fracture their abilities.

I continued down the stairs to the main hall. Layne waited there, the second point of ambush.

"No, you can't come with me," I told them.

Layne wore jeans and a purple blouse, and their face was flushed with fever. In anyone else that would be worrisome, but Layne fed off infection to power their immolation magic, a rare form of necromancy.

Then I realized maybe it *was* worrisome. Layne wouldn't be actively feverish unless they were storing up power for expected use.

"Do you have time to talk?" they asked me, shifting weight nervously from foot to foot. "It's important."

"I'll make time tonight," I promised them. "Tonight. Addam, Brand, and I are going out now to learn where Max and Quinn are. I really need to go, Layne. Please?"

They gave me a disappointed look and shrugged.

"Tonight," I said. "I promise. Can you keep an eye on Anna?"

The disappointed look seamlessly phased into an eye roll, and they gave me a much less casual shrug.

"Thank you. I need to go. Do me a favor and tell Corinne and Diana that they're in charge. I'll see you tonight."

When Layne didn't move, I slunk gracelessly around them, feeling awful, but I could sense the impatience thrumming along my bond with Brand.

I found them outside, parked in the circular drive. Addam had driven one of his sports cars from the staff parking lot. Brand waited for me at the bumper.

I watched his eyes flick across my new sigils in approval. "Loaded for bear?" he asked.

"I'll hold my own."

He squinted at the gold sun pendant in particular, then pointed at the chain. "Is that really dwarven steel? Nothing breaks that shit. You could choke out someone with it."

"Brand, do I need to tell you never to choke someone out with my magical artifact?"

He rolled his eyes. I opened the back door for him. We both got in, leaving Addam to drive alone in the front, which made him turn in the seat and give us a plaintive look.

"I need to watch the rear for attack," Brand explained.

"And Rune?"

"Who the fuck knows. If he's smart, he's remembered you're rich and is checking the cushions for lost money clips."

"Look," I said. "I get it. We're all ready to hit something. Let's put the adrenaline to better use. The Revelry awaits."

Gereja Ayam came from the hills of Magelang in Central Java.

It was a newer translocation from this century. The building had been created by a man who claimed to have communed with the Christian God.

In its original design, it was a temple shaped like a dove facing a nearby volcano. In reality, it looked like a basic stone sketch of a hen. Locals had called it the chicken church, and it had been abandoned before completion.

Lord Fool had translocated the temple onto his private acreage. It was located in a swamp just south of Lady Death's peninsula, a tract of land formerly known as Squam Swamp. It was both beautiful and dismal: large hardwoods, seasonal ponds, and profuse fern and shrub growth in the underbrush.

The air was brackish, heavy with the smell of mud and vegetation. There were no sounds except what you'd expect to hear in a swamp.

"Lady Death wants us to wait," I said, showing Brand the text message. My phone had buzzed just after Addam parked the car in a dirt lot.

"Why?" Brand said. "What did you do?"

"Why do you always say that?" I asked. "When exactly are these vast swathes of time I apparently have to screw up when you're not hovering at my shoulder?"

Addam had pulled out a small but powerful LED flashlight. Shadows and light played tag with each other along the dripping canopy. "I can't even see the residences from here. Are you sure they have separate dormitories?"

"I'm not," I said. "I only know that they don't sleep in Gereja Ayam. It's hard to know for sure: Lord Fool doesn't let many outsiders on his land, and he's got some of the best Shield and Deflection magics on the island. Mainly because he wants to be left the hell alone."

I whispered the words to a light and lens cantrip, then sent a powerful searchlight beam into the foliage around us. There were at least two well-trodden paths. One led in the direction of the giant bird head of the translocated temple, just visible through the dense canopy. I danced the searchlight along the second path and found only old footprints and overgrown weeds.

"The Arcanum had satellite images of the property," I said. "Lord Tower seems to think the Fool hasn't been here in a while."

"What about his people?" Addam asked.

I shook my head. "I don't know. He has a compound underground in the Warrens, but it's off-map. They could all be there."

"I haven't even asked you what the Arcanum's meeting was like," Addam said. He gave me a guilty look. "I have not been attentive."

"Your attention has been exactly where it should be," I told him. "There is nothing more important than finding Quinn and Max."

Addam blinked a few times and took a breath. "It must have been strange, being around the table with so many Arcana at once."

"You don't know the half of it," I admitted. "It was so uncomfortable! I didn't expect that."

"They were unwelcoming?" Addam asked.

Brand barked out a laugh. "I love how you sometimes don't take Rune literally. When he says uncomfortable, you realize he's talking about the lack of stuffing in the seat cushion under his ass, right?"

"Well, it was strange," I said. "The entire room looked like it came from a yard sale."

Addam's distracted look sharpened into a small smile, and he shook his head at me. He was probably about to say something nice and sweet, but at that point the forest's stillness broke under a sharp sonic whistle.

Zurah Saint Joseph descended from the sky like a bullet and landed with a ground-shaking crack. Our flashlights crisscrossed her as she straightened to full height. She wore deep red leathers, nearly black; hair drawn into a thick braid; and around her waist was a belt fitted with a dozen small silver wands, each half the size of a barbecue skewer. They shimmered with the ardency of sigils.

"You're coming?" I said in surprise.

"You didn't think I'd let you have all the fun, did you?"

"Oh, we are going to fuck shit *up*," Brand said.

"If needed," she agreed. "But I'm also friendly with Lord Fool. If he's here, he'll listen to me." She whispered a quick word and manifested a light cantrip above her head. With a sharp flick of her finger, she sent it zooming down the path leading away from the temple. "The RVs are that way. Let's start there."

"The what now?" I said.

The dormitories of the Revelry were, indeed, a trailer park. A huge circle of RVs and campers, their wheels long since sunk and dry-rotted in mud, surrounded a fire pit and coal barbecue stands. Holiday decorations from a long-past equinox were still strung along lampposts. The colors were vibrant in the marsh, like the slash of a child's paintbrush across dirty paper.

Rain had begun to fall in the post-dawn dimness, so light it didn't even make ripples in the potholes around us. There wasn't a soul in sight.

"What are we looking for?" Addam asked in the stillness.

"Bodies," Lady Death said.

I combined my lens and light cantrip again to swing a searchlight around me. No signs of violence. No overturned chairs, no bloodstains, no weapon gouges in the tables or lampposts. "What are you seeing that I'm not?" I asked her.

"People have died here," she said grimly. "It makes the back of my eyes itch. My bloodline is good at sensing the . . . echoes, I suppose, of a soul's passing."

I didn't question her. My bloodline was unusually good at sensing the presence of magic. Each court had its own little bag of genetic tricks.

"Can you tell where?" I asked.

"I don't smell rot," Brand added. "But the swamp fumes may be covering it up."

"It's here. There's been death here recently," Zurah said.

Brand turned in a slow circle, eyes high, taking in tree limbs large enough to support a person, checking to see if there were any vantage points from the nearby temple that would let anyone spy on us. "I'd rather clear the compound first before we start rooting around."

"Let's just check a couple of trailers first," I suggested. "Look for signs of *how* people left. Check for luggage, full closets, perishables, personal keepsakes. Zurah, have you been here before?"

"Once or twice," she said. "It was always crowded. Lord Fool is zealous about privacy, but don't confuse that with accessibility. His court has long been considered a last resort for the disenfranchised. He takes care of people who have little else. Many struggle with addiction, poverty, homelessness, mental health issues, unemployment. There's a lot of mobility in and out of these residences."

"They can't all be dead," I said. "We've identified some of his members already as being in service of Lady Jade. What the hell happened here? It's beginning to look more and more like a—"

"Raid," Lady Death finished. Her mouth set in a grim line. "It's looking as if there's been an unsanctioned raid on Lord Fool's holding."

"We raid to destroy," I said. "We raid for material gain. I can't remember a raid on record where the goal was its *people*."

"And yet," Zurah said, "it's a quick way to establish your own power base if you have no people of your own."

"Did you store the X-ray spell?" Brand asked me. "Can you use it on the RVs to flush out traps or ambush?"

"Good idea," I said, and brushed a thumb along the left side of my interjoined belt buckle.

X-ray was a spell with limited versatility. It did one thing very well, unlike an elemental magic such as Fire, which could fold into offensive and defensive capabilities at my command. With my new batch of sigils, though, I finally felt like I had the flexibility to take risks on the spells I stored.

The world jerked back and forth between darkness and lightning-blast white. As the magic balanced, a sharp migraine stirred sluggishly into motion behind my eyes. It wasn't like comic books—X-ray vision didn't let me see everyone in their underwear. You can peel away layers with the spell, but you still needed light to see things, and there just wasn't enough of that under, say, Addam's tight trousers.

"Flood the RVs with light cantrips," I said. "Shine them in windows. Follow my point—I only have a minute or two of this."

I heard Brand order people around through the hammer-hits of my migraine. They placed themselves at the RVs and began to shine cantrips or flashlights through open or undraped windows. I peeled back layers of steel and aluminum to see the trailers' grayish interiors, occasionally getting lost in grains of wood or Formica.

"Half-filled water glass on the table. Pillows and sheets on the ground. An open closet with just wire hangers in it. A shattered vase. A wall covered in Scotch-taped photographs." I pointed as I said everything. "Food on the table. Brok—" I stopped midsyllable. "There. What's there?"

One of the trailers was parked at an angle, an odd misalignment in the rough ring. Crates and trash bags had been piled at the base of it, keeping light from shining into the foundation. It looked sloppy and hurried.

Brand went over, extended a police baton, and used it to hook the trash bags and fling them away from the trailer. "Drag marks," he called out. "The RV was moved recently. Stains, too. Might be blood."

"It is," Lady Death said quietly.

"There's a hollow under the trailer," I said. I tried to peel away the mass of metal, but there just wasn't enough light to make out more than the edges of a pit and freshly turned soil. "Addam, can you move it?"

Addam strode out of my peripheral and joined Brand at the base of the trailer. He ran a thumb along one of the platinum discs threaded through his belt, and a blurry wash of power coated his hands. He began to step away from the RV while lifting his arms. The entire vehicle shuddered with metallic coughs and groans, then lifted a few inches from the hard-packed dirt and slid backward.

Light fell on the mass grave. Too many bodies to count in a single look, though not more than a half dozen.

"Weapon marks," Brand confirmed. "There's a thick layer of powder on the bodies. Lime powder or something alchemical. It hides the smell of decay."

"Infiltration," Lady Death guessed. "Lady Jade infiltrated my court. Turned one or two key people. I stopped it early enough, but Lord Fool didn't. That would explain the different signs we are getting. Some people packed and left; others left hurriedly or were harmed. His court was infiltrated and broken, and the greater part of it has been absorbed elsewhere."

"If it's her, she took pains to hide the bodies," Brand pointed out.

"To buy time?" Lady Death guessed. "This wouldn't go unanswered. The Arcanum must act. Raids are regulated for a reason—they permit power plays and a change of leadership while preventing a loss of total mass from New Atlantis as a whole. Unstructured raids dilute our resources and artifacts. Our society works because power remains in the hands of courts."

"Does it, though," I murmured, but loud enough to have Zurah shoot a chagrined look my way. She thought I was upset because she had obliquely referred to my father's court. I wasn't. I was just becoming more and more concerned about the way we *did things.*

Brand's phone began to buzz. He pulled it out, answered it, and then started rubbing the skin between his eyes. "Thank you for sharing," he finally said, and hung up.

"What?" I asked.

"Corbie found a green marble." He put a Bluetooth adaptor in his ear so he wouldn't need to use his hands again.

Zurah made a sharp sound of discovery. As my X-ray spell flickered and died—taking my headache with it—I watched her go over to a table on the other side of the clearing. A bedsheet had been laid across the top of it. She lifted the hem and reached low, and when she straightened back up, there was a small dog in her arms. It was muddy and brown and seemed to carry the genetic strain of a dozen different yappy-type dogs.

"This is the Fool's hound," she said, setting the dog on the ground and checking it quickly for injuries. "She's rarely outside his presence. This is not a good sign at all, Rune. Lord Fool would never abandon her. He simply wouldn't."

"Let's check out the temple," Brand said. He glanced at the mass grave, and then at Addam.

Addam nodded in agreement, lifted his arms, and moved the trailer back where it'd previously rested. Whether to preserve evidence or show dignity to the dead, I'm not sure. But I appreciated the thought.

The unfinished nature of Gereja Ayam made it seem like an older structure than it actually was. Lord Fool hadn't made much effort to complete construction. We skirted around crumbling balustrades and let ourselves through a side door. The windows—once glass inside a leaded floral design—were broken, allowing a cold swampish cross-breeze to whistle through the large interior.

The roof overhead reminded me of the hull of an overturned ship. Bright graffiti in neon colors covered large swatches of concrete. I spotted a collection of rooms at either end of the chicken church—ass and beak—and a large circular stairwell led to what once had been twelve rough basement chambers. Birds flew unseen around the rafters, disturbed by our presence.

The windowless walls may have provided dubious shelter, but they did help us in one way: the swamp's odor wasn't as overpowering, which gave us the warning we hadn't had outside.

"Bodies," Brand said.

"Recent deaths," Lady Death agreed.

I didn't need to agree. It was obvious. Fiction never completely gets it right—sometimes death isn't gore and blood spatter, sometimes it's just shit. It's the smell of everything that pours from our bowels at the moment of death, life's final ignobility.

Lady Death flipped a hidden top off one of her rings, revealing a metal flange. I wasn't sure what I was seeing until she rotated her arm like a gun, using the flange as a scope.

"Huh," I said.

"Helps me visualize my aim," Zurah said, noticing my attention. "You've never seen my ice arrows, have you?"

"Would a ring like that improve Rune's aim?" Brand asked while I loudly said, "My aim is fine."

Then Brand froze. "Birds stopped making sound," he whispered.

Lady Death ran a hand along one of her skewers. A whoosh of air ruffled her braid as it spiraled away from her. I felt the gust probe and whip past my face. She was sensing the presence of living beings—a spell I used often myself.

"We're surrounded," she breathed. "Six life signs."

"Take a point," Brand snapped. "Back-to-back."

We formed a rough circle, each taking a direction. As she moved, Zurah raised her voice to a shout. "I am Death of the Bone Hollows. By my will and word, Lord Fool's compound is now under the interim regency of the Arcanum. Step into the light and lay down your weapons or be treated as our enemy."

Attacking us would be an incredibly smart or stupid action. There was no middle ground. Unless it was Lady Jade herself, the chances of an attack succeeding were so slight that either they would be fools to fight us, or smart enough to know that sudden and decisive action was the only chance they had at winning a battle.

They attacked.

Five figures in unrelieved black, including gloves and balaclavas, stepped from behind hiding spots. They had compound bows in their hands.

Two of them dropped and died before they hit the ground, each with one of Brand's knives in their throats. The others pulled back on their strings just as Lady Death lifted an arm and expelled a huge burst of magic. A moving Mobius strip of subzero temperatures slithered around the circle we'd made, shattering the arrows that hit it.

Addam released an Earth spell, made a snatching gesture, and pulled a crumbling column down on the head of a third attacker. The assassin vanished in a plume of dust and blood spray.

I uncoiled my sabre from my wrist, hardened it into its sword hilt form, and fired at one of the two remaining attackers. The firebolts hit Lady Death's protective barrier and turned into hisses of steam.

"I've got them," Brand said, pulling out his dart-bow. "Zurah, can you lower—"

A chunk of ice the size of a cannonball hurtled from the ceiling, passed through the ice barrier, and hit the middle of our circle with concussive force. The next thing I knew, I was on my hands and knees, covered in scrapes, not to mention patches of frostbite from Lady Death's barrier, which luckily had begun dissipating the moment we were knocked off our feet.

"Rune, man on your left!" I heard Brand shout hoarsely.

Trained instinct had a stiletto boiling up from my sabre hilt. At the same time, I turned and stabbed upwards. The garnet blade slid into the soft space under the assassin's jaw. I saw flashes of red light from inside his mouth before he slid lifelessly to the ground next to me.

I wheeled away from where I'd been laying, to put distance between me and an aimed attack. As the world spun with my scramble, I saw Addam helping a dazed Lady Death to her feet. Brand was in hand-to-hand with the fourth and fifth assassins. And floating above us, now just a few feet from the ground and clad from head to toe in scaly green leathers, was someone new—the person who had launched a Frost attack against us.

Oh, please, please monologue, I thought. I ignored the burning, bleeding scrapes on my hands and pushed to my feet. From the side of my vision I watched Brand dispatch his attackers.

"I've got strong opinions on people who go around in masks," I said loudly. "Would you like to hear them?"

The floating figure pivoted with arms outstretched. A thread of pebbles wormed into existence between his palms, forming a boulder with astonishing speed. The figure thrust, and the rock whistled through the air and slammed into the ground a hand's length from where Addam and Lady Death had been sitting. Addam used Telekinesis to slide them both away at the last second, but Lady Death cracked her head against a pillar in the process and sagged in Addam's arms.

Brand had trained me to identify obvious weaknesses immediately. Sometimes those weaknesses were psychological. So when a person with a mask attacks you? Their weakness was the identity they clearly sought to conceal.

We'd practiced this moment in training, but never in real life.

I began running while shouting, "Brand, cover! Addam, slide me home!"

A sphere of stone crashed to the ground behind me. I dropped to a slide tackle, felt Addam's Telekinesis grab my stomach like an iron vice which tripled the momentum of my slide. More skin tore and blood ran down into one of my eyes. I ignored it, focused on the gold chain around my ankle, and let its spell pop loose. The world flickered in color negative.

When I was under the figure, I tensed my muscles and shoved upwards into a jump. I grabbed their ankle and sunk my Psychometry spell into them.

There was a reason that Psychometry magic was only meant to be used on inanimate objects. The echoes of powerful events were difficult enough to face through unfiltered magic; the idea of using a blend of clairvoyance and psionics on a living being was a staggering onslaught of images and sounds.

As I fought through powerful memories of love and location, of breakfast food and rough sex, of fealty and betrayal, I managed to cough out one single word:

"*Vadik.*"

"Vadik Amberson's involved!" Brand shouted, his hand against the Bluetooth adaptor in his ear. Two bodies were at his feet. "Send a team to the Amberson family house, Lord Tower!"

The scaled mask turned my way. Our gaze locked for a moment, and Vadik shot upwards to a broken skylight and vanished into the early morning gloom.

"Shit," Brand said. "I'm really going to call Mayan now."

I was already on my way to Addam and Zurah. Addam had activated a Healing, and was heating the bleeding wound on her head to a cauterized, thin line.

"Vadik Amberson?" she said to me.

"A House scion," I said, as Addam turned his healing magic on my head wound. "Once tied to Sun Estate. He was at the gala. I think he's a principality."

"I see." Zurah groaned, took my outstretched hand, and let herself be pulled to her feet. "And I feel like a fucking amateur."

"You'll get the next one," I said, and tried to keep the teasing smile off my face.

Since I have almost no skill at hiding my emotions, Zurah spotted it with narrowed eyes. "Is he always like this?" she said to Brand.

"Oh, I could write a fucking country song about it," he said.

"A moment, please. A principality?" Addam said. "How would you know that? And how is that possible? Is he rogue?"

"He must be," I said. It took me a second to realize why my brain was starting to make impatient noises in the back of my head, which was already starting to throb under the weight of active magic. "Shit, I'm burning through my Psychometry spell. Brand, can you guide me around?"

Brand came back over while tucking his phone in his pocket. "Mayan dispatched a team to the Amberson estate. Hands out, Rune. Watch what you're touching."

"Wait," Lady Death said. "The buffer. Don't forget the buffer spell. Lord Tower taught me it last night."

The last man to use Psychometry to track the movements of Lady Jade had wound up in the hospital. Lord Tower had mentioned in the Bunker that he was developing a spell to muffle the backlash. Zurah touched another one of her skewers. The release of magic made a *wuumph* noise, like the inhale of atmosphere before an explosion. She sent the magic streaming toward me, and almost immediately my headache vanished.

"Gods," I whispered. I backed away from them while moving in an unsteady circle. "Buffer doesn't begin to describe it. What is . . ."

Normal Psychometry was a tactile ability. Touch let you tap into the echoes of strong events, some auditory, some visual, mostly emotional. Voices and images would flicker past like a speeding carousel.

This was different.

Independent of touch, my Psychometry spell reached out with greedy and grasping efficiency, instinctively piecing together sounds and sight into layers of ghostly film. Entire scenes were projected around me in dull, old colors. It wasn't quite vision—it was the anticipation of vision based on intangible elements like echolocation and the overlapping memories of those who had stood here. The entire spell depended on those memories, actually: in any given moment, there were slices of the room that hadn't been included in the cone of vision that every person saw, leaving grayish-black spots scattered across my field of view.

"Narrate," Brand said, loudly enough to get my attention.

"Lots of things. So much. It reaches back so far. But these images are brightest—" I gestured to the rear of the temple. "Division. Argument. Speeches. A man tried to stop them."

"Who did?" Brand asked.

"I think he's Lord Fool's seneschal? He tried to stop people from leaving. They turned on him, in the end."

I walked through a ghostly mob of people dressed in torn jeans, mismatched clothing, and fabric that would be riotous with color under normal light. A man—too rugged to be pretty, too pretty to be handsome, but wearing the Fool's seal of office—was gesturing to the crowd that was slowly backing him to the wall.

As I focused, his words whined into a distorted, vibrating clarity.

"It is *not* the way forward!" the ghost-seneschal shouted. "You're retreating to a myth. The Lowlands compound is a trap!"

"Lowlands compound," I repeated. The dust in the air made my voice rasp.

The visions were beginning to flicker and fade. Psychometry was a fleeting magic. I'd have needed to meditate for a massive amount of time to power the sigil spell for more than a brief handful of minutes—and I hadn't had the time.

I picked up my pace to a jog, hearing the reassuring sound of Brand's footsteps before me. Moving in dizzy loops, I tried to isolate the thickest gathering of images, trying to sense any pattern that may provide valuable information.

"Zurah," I said. "Are the rooms beneath us still unfinished? Like they were when the temple was translocated?"

"Yes. They're used for storage, I believe."

"Movement. Paths," I said, seeing all the overlapping traffic, but all toward the hewn stone stairway. Why go down to unfinished rooms? "People—"

Psychometry died with a brief monochromatic flicker. The buffer spell that had been twined around it remained, but I didn't like the feeling— like cotton batting being wrapped around my head. I flicked a hand and dismissed the spell.

"People what, Rune?" Addam asked.

"Most of them went that way. There's got to be something down-stairs."

* * *

Brand traced the rim of the tunnel entrance with his flashlight.

"It angles down," he said. "Pretty sharply."

"Perhaps it connects the temple to Lord Fool's underground property," Addam said.

"At the very least, it's a sure bet it goes into the Warrens, if not the Lowlands," I added.

"We need support," Zurah said. It had taken a second healing spell to keep her on her feet, and her voice was not steady. "We need to check in with the Dagger Throne to see if they found Vadik. We need to see if any of those attackers are alive and able to be questioned. We need to tell Judgment that we suspect Lord Fool is the victim of foul play."

"You're right," I told Zurah, "but that doesn't change the fact that I'm going down that tunnel now."

"Little Brother," she began to say.

I held up my hands. "This is not me being headstrong or impulsive. The people who attacked us may have been guarding the tunnel, which means their absence may be reported. We have a very, very narrow window to take advantage of that."

"Rune, I have great respect for your abilities, but Lady Jade had us all pressed tight under her thumb. You remember that."

"I know, and trust me, I have no desire to go into battle against her unless I'm there to hold the Tower's jacket. But this is a chance to learn more about what's happening. You heard Mayan—sending teams into the Warrens is problematic. Large, armed parties attract the wrong sort of attention. But just me, Brand, and Addam? We could slide in, observe, learn."

"One hour, and then I'm coming after you," she said. "I'll stay and make the arrangements up here."

I shifted my gaze to Brand and Addam, mutely asking if we were all on the same page. I needn't have bothered. They'd dig a tunnel with their own bare hands if it brought us closer to Max and Quinn.

"Will you look after Lord Fool's dog?" Addam asked Lady Death, because he was Addam.

"Of course."

"We will contact you within the hour," Addam said.

"Then go," Zurah said. "Stay safe, and gods' speed."

THE WARRENS

The tunnel had been built with magic—that much was obvious. The three of us were able to walk abreast, with Addam's and my cantrips bouncing ahead to light the way. The walls were smooth and seamless, and lacked any sort of tool or engine marks.

It was also cold. Brand's swears hung in front of him as frosted mist. The latest swear was directed at me, because he didn't think I was being observant enough.

"I'm always more observant than you think I am," I complained.

"Since when?" Brand shot back. "Since you packed a ferret in your overnight bag?"

"I should never have told you that," I said. "And crap, I forgot to mention to Zurah that I stole one of her pets." Brand's mouth opened, so I pointed at it. "If you mention the goldfish, I will lose my shit."

"Goldfish?" Addam asked me.

"Brand doesn't think I know how to care for pets," I said. "And I was fucking five years old."

"You suffocated it. You literally drowned a fish," Brand said.

I stepped on something. With a flick of my finger, my light cantrip spun back to me and illuminated a sparkly red hair band. It was the sort of thing members of the Revelry wore.

"Lots of footsteps in the dust. Even on the edge," Brand said. "Large parties of people headed this way, and I don't see that many footprints leading back."

Our conversation subsided, and we continued to walk. Occasionally the sloping trail switchbacked, but only downwards, never up.

"That was a nice use of Telekinesis back in the trailer park," I told Addam. "I don't think I've ever seen you lift something that large."

"Large is easy," Addam said. "Precision is more difficult. But when you're holding a baby in the air with your mind, you learn."

"Quinn? You used to move Quinn around with your mind?" Brand asked. "Is this a fucked-up scion thing?"

I'd sent my light back down the tunnel, but I could hear the smile in Addam's voice. He said, "Quinn was a very fussy baby. He slept poorly. But he loved being rocked in the air. It always put him to sleep. That's when I started storing Telekinesis spells as a matter of routine."

"You are so fucking soft, Saint Nicholas," Brand said.

I kicked Brand in the shin—or at least aimed a general kick where his shin should have been. He must have felt the whiff of air, because I sensed his grumble along our bond.

"We'll find him," Brand finally said. "You know that, right? And it's not like Quinn is defenseless. He and Max are tougher than we give them credit for."

Addam went quiet for a few moments, too long to be thinking of a response.

But after a minute had passed, he spoke again. "Quinn has so little life experience. I . . . it was . . . It was always hard for me to see him socialize with others. I remember this one time I thought it would be fine for Quinn, who was six years old, to have play dates with other children. He'd made a little friend at the Russian compound where I was stationed at the time. Quinn was invited to his friend's birthday party, and he shopped for the gift himself—quite seriously, picked it out himself. I remember watching Quinn from the sidelines with the other parents. I was holding my breath, but I was so proud of him, standing there with his present tight in his arms as he went to offer it to his little friend. He was so *hopeful*. So *happy*. And then the boy opened the gift. Quinn had bought Mikhail a fire truck, because Mikhail secretly wanted to be a firefighter. Apparently, Mikhail had never told anyone this. His parents were rich and Atlantean, and would have laughed at the idea. I believe the boy realized Quinn had read his deepest desire, and instead of being surprised, Mikhail was scared and angry, and started calling Quinn awful names. My heart had never hurt so much in my entire life. Until Quinn's coma. Until today."

"Are," Brand said, and his voice sounded a little sniffly. "Are you *fucking kidding me?* Now? You tell a story like that *now?* Have . . . Jesus fucking Christ, have we taught you nothing about timing?"

"Rune does seem to mention that often," Addam mused.

And we kept walking.

"Are you tracking our distance?" I asked Brand at one point.

"Yes, but I'm almost out of fucking breadcrumbs."

"I'm serious. I think we're well over a mile down. If we go much deeper, we're in Lowlands territory."

"Yeah," he said, and I caught the thread of worry he'd been trying to hide. "I don't know if we're geared up enough for that. Even just for recon."

"Wait," Addam said quietly. He whispered a few words, and a glimmer of air appeared in front of his eyes. A quick and dirty lens cantrip. "I think . . ." he breathed. "Rune, cancel your light cantrip. I think there's light ahead."

I flicked a finger and my ball of light, some yards ahead, dissolved. Addam did the same. And he was right—ahead, we could now see the grayish-white shine of torchlight fighting its way around the twists and turns of a dark tunnel.

In this more forgiving darkness, we resumed forward without light cantrips. Brand was the first to notice that we were passing into an older complex of tunnels. "The walls ahead were hand dug. Getting narrower."

"And branching," I said. "Look—it's darker over there. That's a new tunnel branch. Shit."

"I think . . ." Addam said and walked to the edge of the tunnel. "I think there is writing here? These do not look like dig marks."

Brand chanced his flashlight, getting up close so the beam didn't bounce around too much. "Nice spot, Addam. These are underground symbols. That mark indicates a split in the tunnel. The fork on the left means food is served. The dome with a large dot inside it means that a gang has taken over. That's on the right."

"Could the Revelry be the gang? Or Lady Jade?" I wondered.

Brand tapped the left symbol. "Food could mean an underground market. Any place where people can buy things or eat is a place that Addam can bribe people for information. It's the safest approach."

"I agree, except for the part where you shake down Addam for cash."

"I found a twenty in his back seat," Brand said. "We're good for the first bribe."

"You lie," Addam said. "I know that is a joke. Quinn and Max regularly raid my sofas and change trays."

"Fine, I have a twenty, and I'll donate it to the cause." He pulled a small vial out of one of his pockets and placed his thumb at the top of it. "Both of you close your eyes. I'm going to spray this on your face, and then smear some dirt on you."

"What is it?" I asked.

". . . water," he said. When I didn't budge, he slapped a hand over my eyes and sprayed a fine mist on each cheek.

"That smells like WD-40," I complained. "Some got in my nostrils!"

I opened my eyes to see Brand scooping a handful of loose soil into his palm. He came up to my face again and said, "Close your eyes. Serious, Rune. You'll get to do the same to me."

I closed my eyes, heard him puff, and felt a fine sheen of dust billow into my face.

"Smear it," he said. "And presto—no sigil, no spell, just plain old human brain magic. You both let me do the talking. This is not the type of place for a guy who owns a razor carved from a meteorite, or a guy who catches fire when someone looks at him the wrong way."

The translocations that began in the 1900s—culminating in a frenzy of teleportation and city-building in the seventies and eighties—was never a practiced science.

The Atlantis homeland had few translocations of their own. We didn't need buildings steeped in traumatic residue to create a source of magic.

We lived on an island that had been steeped in magic for thousands of years. But the forced, desperate creation of New Atlantis required a quick source of power, which necessitated the Arcanum—using powerful secrets from the Hex Throne—coming together to provide the raw ability needed to create a city.

Many of those early translocations failed. Either our magical estimates were off; or the earth was unstable; or, metaphorically speaking, we simply bit off more than we could chew. Some structures ended up below the ground. Some sank. Hell, once I found an entire mall hidden in the bedrock of the ocean offshore.

The Warrens were the product of bad translocations, connected to the surface streets by tunnels, sewers, and deep basements. They were stacked on top of each other like iron filings clustered around a magnet. Deeper than that—much deeper—were natural cave systems and deliberately secret translocated compounds that were, collectively, called the Lowlands. There were no maps of the Lowlands, very few facts and eyewitness accounts, and volumes of urban myths.

To put it another way: New Atlantis was not a safe city, and the Warrens—and their mishmash of broken or failed translocations—were even less safe. It was the refuge of lost people. The Lowlands were even worse. They were where those lost people vanished. Things that couldn't walk the streets of New Atlantis had claimed the subterranean layers as their own.

The fact that Lady Jade may have built a fortress in or even near the Lowlands spoke volumes of her self-perceived ability to care for followers.

Brand was right—we were not prepared for a deep excursion. But any bit of intelligence we learned in the Warrens might help us pinpoint Max and Quinn's location.

The tunnel on the left opened into an aqueduct built from lime, sand, and water. Most of it was a crumbling wreck, which wasn't surprising, because I was pretty sure it had come from Rome. It was dry and dirty and hadn't seen water in decades.

It only lasted a short stretch, then ended in a rock wall that had been chiseled into a rough opening. By then, no cantrips were needed. There was light and motion ahead of us, and the sounds of dozens of people hawking wares or food.

"I can't march forward like a bodyguard," Brand murmured. "Act casual. Act like you belong. Act like you've been here before. Let me take point, and don't stomp around like fussy demigods unless I tell you to."

"Should I activate a Shield?" I asked.

Brand considered that but ended up shaking his head. "No magic. Except maybe your sabre, if you want to transmute it to hilt form."

"Good idea," I said. I'd returned it to wristguard form somewhere after the thirty-minute mark of eventless walking. I sent a spark of will-power into my wrist. The wristguard softened and stretched, slipping over my knuckles.

We climbed through the opening, Brand up front, me in the rear.

What I saw on the other side both matched and defied my expecta-tions. It was one thing to imagine creepy, another to stand in its smoky, polluted middle.

It was a church basement. Old, yellowed religious images were painted on the walls. The space had been built for children—and every-thing reflected that function. The doorknobs, a bank of lockers, a boys' bathroom with its walls removed—they were all sunk to a height that made sense for little hands and bodies.

The locals had turned the basement space, which was the size of a city block, into a food court. Rusted metal trash barrels burned whatever fuel was handy—mostly books and broken slabs of wood, some dried mush-rooms unique to the Atlantean underground. There was only one chimney-like chute overhead, and it did little except clear the worst of the smoke. The smell was horrendous—overpowering layers of roasted vermin, thin broth, spoiled vegetables and meat. One corner of the room was reserved for mismatched tables, some as basic as plywood on sawhorses.

Drug use was rampant. You could see it in the vacant expressions and listless movements of the people who shuffled from vendor to vendor, looking for a good deal. I'd heard there was a growing epidemic of use related to a new category of narcotics called the Agonies—I'd seen some of the effects aboveground, in a red-light district called the Green Docks.

One man at a table was dressed in nice new robes. I started in his direction, but then a roach crept from his hairline and sat on his eyebrow. He didn't blink once. Brand made a short sound to get my attention and guided us past.

In front of a booth made of cheap particle wood, with tiny, skinless rodent bodies hanging from a hook, we were challenged for the first time. Brand had expected it, and watched the large man close in on him with lidded eyes.

The man wore torn leather armor and had a bloodstained club at his side. "I like your knives," he said in a gravelly voice.

"I do too," Brand said.

"They'll cover your toll," the man said.

Brand kneed him in the balls. It was lightning quick; one second the man was standing, the next he was leaning forward, curled around his lap. Brand bent down, pinched the man's nostrils between two fingers, and twisted until the man began screaming from an entirely new pain.

"We square?" Brand asked.

"*Yes,*" the man panted.

"If you come back with friends, I'll put you all in body bags."

"We're square," the man squealed.

Brand tucked a twenty-dollar bill in the man's pocket after he flashed it in front of his eyes. The man's screams subsided to a whimper, and he hid his face from us.

We continued through the dingy room. I saw things that turned my stomach. One vendor was openly selling banned substances, including a hallucinogen called Votz, which was an extraordinarily disgusting combination of cheap cheese pizza and elven stomach acid. In a corner of the room, an emaciated girl gnawed on a double-A battery while staring out a window that had nothing but pebbled highway asphalt behind it.

When we reached the other end of our straight path across the market, Brand found us a corner amid the plywood tables. We huddled to talk.

"How can we help these people?" Addam wondered in a horrified whisper.

"Not the mission," Brand said. He reached out and tapped Addam on the back of his hand until Addam looked him in the eyes. "You are a good person, Addam. One of the best I know. But I don't need a good man watching my back right now—I need the son of Justice. Please?"

Addam swallowed and nodded.

Brand said something else, but I missed it, because I couldn't stop thinking about what Addam had said.

Why *couldn't* I help these people? If a seat on the Arcanum couldn't help these people, what the fuck could?

I'd learned more about the Agonies since the Green Docks. The application of them was horrific. One type of Agonies only manifested after the user sweated the active component. People would coat themselves in plaster of paris to keep the high locked in for days. But in the process, their skin accrued sores and mildew. Another type of Agonies localized the high in psoriasis. People would peel the dry patches of skin off their body to ingest the active component, leaving open wounds rapidly infected.

"I'm sorry," Addam said, bringing me back to the conversation. "I must at least try it my way first."

And with that, he stood up and walked three tables over to where a young woman sat. A girl, really—she couldn't have been more than sixteen. She was covered in scabs and scratch marks. Another type of Agonies, one I'd seen before. The high localized in one area of the skin, and you released it by scratching. Often the skin broke and became infected. The girl had kids' mittens on her hands—cheery and pink—as if she was making a token effort to stave off her own death.

I watched Addam touch a sigil at his belt. He murmured something to the girl, who, with a look of near disbelief, reached out an arm. Addam began to heal her wounds, stopping only when she protested the healing of a scratched area still ripe with narcotics. He began to talk to her while Brand sat there with his lips pressed into a tight line.

"Maybe," I said in a whisper to Brand. "Maybe Addam is our canary in the coal mine? Maybe we need to pay more attention to him?"

"A lot of people are paying attention to us right now. He's using a Healing we might need later, Rune."

"Let's give him some latitude. Maybe this helps. Maybe it doesn't. Maybe he'll learn something about how real life works, and maybe we will."

So we sat in silence until Addam came back.

And when he did, he had a name.

Addam had talked with the girl about local healers. In the course of the conversation, it became apparent most medicine was out of the reach of the average Warrens denizen. But there was one magic user living in the area whom she described as having powerful alchemical abilities. She said nearly everyone in this area of the Warrens was afraid of him. He'd been the focus of thieves and gangs before, but he'd repelled every attack with ridiculous ease.

It made sense that even an area like the Warrens would have a king perched on its moldering hill. It's possible she was exaggerating, but either way, anyone with a genuine amount of ability would live in the Warrens for only a short list of reasons. We would want to talk to this person.

The direction we cobbled together took us up a short stairway that ended in another dug tunnel. We passed through a surreal juxtaposition of translocation failures: a suburban ranch living room, a university lecture hall with stadium seats now turned into a tent city for squatters, a butcher's walk-in freezer. Much of the space was partitioned off into squatter hovels. Some had been turned into drug dens. We went the long way around the basement level of an abandoned high school because a carved sign on the wall indicated armed compound fighters.

Eventually we arrived at a dead end. A heavy wood door with metal struts sat in the middle of a wall of crumbled cement and dull red bricks.

I let my gaze shift into a deeper spectrum of perception, into the space where I was able to identify magic. The illusion in front of us was very, very good, but my own abilities were better. I was able to see it for what it was: the doorway now looked not like a door, but more the picture of a door Scotch taped onto the wall. It was a clever trap.

The area to the left of it was . . . smudged. Like an erased pencil sketch. That was the best way I could describe it.

I went up and knocked on that spot, and felt the real face of a door under my tingling fingers. Brand moved to a point over my left shoulder, and Addam to my right. I felt the chain of command pass to me through my bond with Brand; he would let me handle what came next.

It took two more knocks before the wall shimmered and the real door revealed itself. A man stood on the threshold. He was old and white, with thinning hair threaded through bone beads into an anemic ponytail. He was barefoot, and had thin toes with yellow, curling nails. He smelled like fresh incense and dried sweat.

"My goodness," he said. "You're not from around here, are you?"

"We'd like to speak with you," I said. "We'll compensate you generously for your time."

"Shouldn't you also promise me no harm? Most people insist they mean me no harm."

"People lie, and I expect you know how to protect yourself. I'll show my respect with funds."

And gods bless Addam, he pulled a wad of cash out of his pocket for a moment until the man noticed.

"And here I expected a droll morning," the man said in delight. "This is shaping up to be something interesting. Please, come in. Come in."

Past the door was a suite of rooms. Like everything else I'd seen in the

Warrens, it was a mix of exotic and decrepit. It had the cluttered, dingy look of a slum—but the floors were real marble, like a corner of a translocated ballroom, and the ceiling above was ragged with cavern stalactites. The stone ground was covered in years' worth of cigarette ash. The smell of brewed potions and mold was only alleviated by chai teabags hanging from pushpin tacks on the plaster walls.

"Please sit, sit, sit," the man said, shooing his hands at a sofa set behind an antique coffee table in bad repair. It was large enough for all three of us, but Brand remained standing in the doorway while Addam and I accepted the offer. As I sat down, my hand landed on some sharp, prickly items. I thought for a second they were shards of plastic, until realizing they were bits of chewed fingernail.

"I get the jitters and heal quickly," the man explained, which made me completely reevaluate my dislike of apple bitter. "That's a lot of nail to work through. Now." He clapped his hands. "I will make tea. It is custom."

"I'm sorry, but no," Brand said.

"Admirable restraint, young man," he replied. "If it makes you feel better, you can watch me pour the water, and I'll only use tea bags from a sealed box. I do love the taste of chai."

Brand shrugged as if he didn't care, but I also knew he had ways of testing anything we drank before we drank it. He shifted his perspective so he could closely watch the alchemist as he puttered over to an ad hoc kitchen built into a corner of the broken ballroom.

"Shall I introduce myself?" the man asked as he worked water from a sink well pump.

"We'd prefer to remain anonymous," I said.

"As you wish. I have nothing to hide, though. I'm the area's resident alchemist. You may call me Cornelius."

"There aren't many alchemists who can fend off armed raiding parties," I commented casually.

"Apparently you haven't met many good alchemists, then," he laughed.

He wore a simple, sleeveless wool shirt over a robe-like skirt, and I could see his ribcage shake with his humor.

"Have you lived down here long?" I asked.

"Long enough. I'm needed. The locals, poor dears, desperately require someone like me to help with the many environmental hazards."

"At a price," I said.

"At a price," he agreed affably. He slit open the plastic wrap from a box of tea, extracted four tea bags, and put them in chipped ceramic mugs. The water he poured had been put on a potbellied stove to boil.

"Perhaps you should tell me what information you seek," he said, leaning against a counter. "I would hate to talk money when I may not even have the knowledge."

"I'd be surprised if you didn't. You'd know if a new, large group moved into this area of the Warrens—or at least moved through it."

"Oh, many, many people move through it. The people who live here are transient. It's rare to see the same faces more than a week at a stretch."

"I imagine," I said, "that many people travel alone. I'm talking about a large number of folks from the Revelry moving through the territory."

"The *Revelry,* my goodness," Cornelius said. "That's Lord Fool. His compound is a half mile away, if not more."

"I don't believe his people are at that compound. They've found other patronage."

Cornelius made a deep *hmmm* sound but didn't reply. He buried his attention in the act of tending the water, and we remained quiet until it boiled. Just as he was about to pour the water in the mug, Brand said, "If I may?" and checked the mugs for any powder or residue, then nodded as the man poured boiling water on top of the tea bags. In a moment, the smell of spiced chai reached my nostrils.

Brand pulled a vial out of a pocket, repeated, "If I may?", and spritzed some in each mug. Nothing happened that seemed to alarm him.

"I come from Old Atlantis," Cornelius said. "The sharing of a beverage confers guest privileges. If you'll indulge me?"

Brand stepped back to his post by the door, but did accept the mug he was offered.

There was an overturned milk crate opposite the couch, which Cornelius perched on. He crossed a skinny leg over one knee and smiled at me. "The Revelry?" he prompted.

"Former members of the Revelry, if we're being accurate," I said. "A large number of them have passed through the area, haven't they?"

"Mmm-hmm," Cornelius said while sipping. Either because he liked the tea or agreed with my comment, I wasn't sure. He continued to stare at me until, slowly, I lifted the mug to my lip and took a small sip.

"You are my guest," Cornelius said formally. He repeated the same when Addam took a small sip, but had to wait an uncomfortable beat of moments until Brand complied as well. "There," he said at last. "We are all among friends. You are hunting members of the Revelry?"

"Absolutely not. We have reason to be concerned about their welfare. This is a matter that, if not resolved quickly, could bring the attention of the Arcanum into the Warrens."

"The Arcanum is already here," Cornelius said. "Let's not equivocate, shall we, Lord Sun? A bit of oil and dirt doesn't hide as much as you think."

I put the mug down on the table. "That makes it easier, I suppose. Yes: I am a vanguard of the Arcana. A great deal hinges on my report. If I can't learn what I need—as peacefully as possible—the full attention of the Arcanum will come to rest on your territory."

"My, I'd like to avoid *that*," he laughed. "That couldn't possibly end well. What, exactly, do you hope to learn here? Many of the folk in this area are clients, which places them under a healer's confidentiality. But I can see no reason not to confirm that there *have* been quite a few members of the Revelry tromping through. Nice lot. No problems."

"Rune," Addam said blearily, and collapsed over the arm of the chair.

Instinct took over. *Ambush.* I kicked the coffee table at Cornelius and jumped to my feet. A knife was in Brand's hand. Before either of us could do anything else, Cornelius lifted an arm and a blast of energy slammed us back into the wall. Fighting against the pressure, I turned my head left just in time to see Brand's eyeballs roll into his head. He sank to the ground.

Fire exploded along my arms. Cornelius, moving with superhuman speed, crossed the distance between us, grabbed my jaw, and slammed my head back into the wall. My concentration jarred and my fire faded, just as my brain began to fill with fireflies.

I clumsily swung my arm, trying to punch Cornelius. My hand sunk through whatever glamor masked his true face, because I felt something like scales slough off under my fingers. I drew my hand back and saw loose tatters of shiny dead skin under my nails.

"You will know me, child," Cornelius whispered as I began to lose consciousness. "For I am *her* vanguard."

I woke up tied to a hook from the ceiling. My shirt and pants were gone, leaving me in my underwear. Addam and Brand hung from hooks next to me. They were unconscious and half-naked as well.

My first thought was that it wasn't as mortifying as it could be, because my arms were above my head, stretching out my love handles.

I shifted weight, which made the chains squeal. "Sorry about that," I whispered to them quickly.

That was the point I realized I was heavily drugged.

My sigils had been stripped from me, along with my sabre. The chemicals made it impossible to concentrate, which made it nearly impossible to connect with the meanest of cantrips, let alone my Aspect.

Cornelius circled in front of me, a silver tea tray in his hands. On the tray was a wide variety of professional torture instruments. They were so exaggeratedly evil that he may have ordered the entire set from an online villain catalog.

"I call myself the Forerunner," he said. "Welcome to my little owl's nest. I've waited a long time to talk to you, Rune."

"I like that you're going to start with talking," I said. "Aren't you worried at all that Lord Tower and Lady Death know where I am?"

He picked up a clamp of some sort and breathed on it, buffing a spot. "No," he said.

He wasn't scared of me, and he should have been. There were a hundred different reasons that someone might not be scared of you—and dealing with people like that always required caution until you knew *why*. Cornelius might have protections I hadn't perceived; abilities I hadn't seen; or maybe just a garden-variety death wish that made him flitter and bat against open flames.

"Or you're a principality," I said, then realized I'd talked out loud.

Cornelius smiled at me. "How so?"

"I didn't feel a spell. Brand didn't find poisons. You didn't use a sigil. You're not scared of me. Plus, we've already possibly met one rogue principality today, so might as well make it two. Lady Jade's well-protected, isn't she?"

And then I thought maybe that was too much info to share? Brand really needed to wake up soon. Or maybe Addam? Addam was better at charming people.

Which made me remember I was drugged, because charm wasn't the tool we needed from the tool shed right now.

Or was it?

"Not many people get the drop on me," I said, and tried not to lay it on too thick.

He finished buffing another implement—this one looking like it was used to extract teeth or organs. "I'm much older than you, little Arcana. Do you really call her Lady Jade? I find that so funny. She mentioned that. It's . . . well, it's whimsy, isn't it? I almost forget to be offended on her behalf."

He picked up a knife, moved with astonishing speed, and suddenly the tip of the blade was at my throat. "Say her name."

"We don't know her name."

"Say. Her. Name."

I swallowed, and my Adam's apple was pricked. A trickle of blood ran over my collarbone. "She's Lady Time, isn't she? Whoever she is, she claimed the Hourglass Throne."

"She is the only daughter of the old Lord Time. She was born in an age of giants, escaped the fall of her court, and survived the grinding pressures of the timestream for *decades* and emerged into the *future*. She walks among us again and *she will be known*."

"Listen Foreskinner," Brand said, licking his dry lips.

"Forerunner," he yelled.

"Sure. If you're going to yammer, can I get more tea first?"

I knew that Brand was pulling Cornelius's attention onto him, and fuck that, I was not letting him die first. If—

"Rune, you said that out loud," Brand growled.

Both of them were staring at me. "I probably shouldn't be thinking about our plan," I said, "in case I say it out loud too."

Cornelius laughed and came over to me with the knife. "Oh, this will be so *fun* if you narrate the experience as it happens. It almost makes me want to use a sharper blade. This one is dull. Skin makes the strangest sound beneath it—like trying to saw through plastic wrap. You'll be too busy screaming to entertain me."

"I do not understand any of this," Addam said woozily. "What do you want?"

"I want many things," Cornelius said. "But I promised I would turn you over alive. Mostly alive. Such a lot of gray area in that."

"So she doesn't want us hurt badly . . . We can work with that," I said out loud.

"I will fucking come over there," Brand told me.

"Oh, you are a *treat*," Cornelius told me. "Maybe I'll begin with your men, so you can continue with your rambling."

"When did Lady Time take over a compound in the Lowlands?" Addam asked. The drugs had hit him hard and fast, but he also looked like he was coming out of it quicker than I was. I was able to understand that much—while biting down on my lip to keep from saying it out loud.

"You know about that," the Forerunner said.

"I do. We read Vadik's mind."

Cornelius froze, his hand paused over a long thin ice pick–like object.

"Does Vadik have a cool super-principality name too?" Brand asked.

"He is the Serpent. He guards his identity very closely. Does he live?"

"He ran," Brand said, drawing out the last word.

"He will be most vexed about that. I'd be careful, if I were you. Lady Time wants you alive, but he's known to react rather impulsively when angered. But, then again, it's all about to come into the open, isn't it? You poor little fools don't even know she's already on a topside march. All our time bent over battle plans are coming to fruition."

"We need to find out what that means," I said.

He laughed.

"No, seriously, we need to find out what that means and then kill you quickly. Shit! Drugs."

The Forerunner's fingers curled around the ice pick. He picked it up and went over to Brand. "I will learn everything you know about the Arcanum's efforts against Lady Time. You think you'll be able to resist. You've been *trained* to resist. But you've never been tortured by someone like me. I have practiced my artistry for centuries. I have survived wars, the Atlantean diaspora, even moments in the timestream. Much of my life disappointed me—which is why I take such satisfaction in carving a comfortable living from flesh these days."

"Take your best shot," Brand said.

The Forerunner laughed again, a high childlike sound. "I'll let you in on a little secret. You will survive the loss of a nail. And a finger. Even a hand. But the real moment you lose all hope? It's the eyes. Something happens when I puncture the second eyeball that just drains the life out of a person. Perhaps it's a moment that even their addled minds perceive as irrevocable."

He reached up with one hand, and his eyes began to glow.

"The drugs and magic will now stir to my bidding. They're sluggishly moving to the parts of your brain that control fear. Do you sense it yet, Companion? Do you feel the fear?"

"Fuh-fuh-fuh," Brand tried to stammer.

"Don't you want to hide?" he whispered. "You are so scared. You are so very, very scared. Wouldn't it feel good to scream and run and hide? Wouldn't it—"

Brand's eyes were wide, showing too much white. There was spittle on his lips. I felt horror flooding our bond, and thought about screaming even as I started doing exactly that.

And then Brand kicked up with his legs, drew back his heels, and slammed both feet into the Forerunner's face.

The principality fell backwards and hit his head on the table that held the torture instruments. Everything clattered to the ground. There was an audible popping sound, and a needle-thin spray of blood began to shoot out of the man's skull. It arced through the air with a soft pattering.

We all stared at it.

"That guy really, really didn't understand how you react when you're afraid," I said.

"He didn't, did he?" Brand said, somewhat astonished it had worked.

"Is he dead?" Addam asked.

"Give me a second to make sure," Brand said.

He flipped his whole body up like he was on gymnastic rings. He was able to get his hand close to the elastic waistband of his boxer briefs, which allowed him to pull out a small, thin nail file that had been woven into the lining.

Less than a minute later he dropped free of the ropes.

HALF HOUSE

It took the longest to free Addam. The Forerunner had removed Addam's metal hand and tied him to the hook with a complicated series of underarm knots.

The body on the ground never so much as twitched. The glamor did end, however, fading with the Forerunner's life essence. The illusion had covered an exceptionally old face with ruined, flaking skin. The man had not been entirely human—the skin flakes looked like reptile scales, still glittering on my finger from when I'd touched him earlier.

I'd love to say my metabolism had burned off the effects of the drug by then, but honestly, after we all spent a few minutes getting dressed, there was a stretch of minutes where Brand got mad at me because I kept trying to sit down. And my shoulder fucking *hurt* from being stretched above my head.

Right about the third time, he pulled a pill from a pocket and made me swallow it. I made a show of refusing until he told me it was caffeine. Then he said, "Here, bite down on this," and gave me a strip of leather. I did that, and a few minutes later realized he was just trying to shut me up while he searched the suite of rooms.

I spit the strap out. "Do you feel as weird as I do?" I asked Addam, who was sitting on the sofa in the main room.

"Do you promise you and Brand won't forget about me when you leave?" Addam said anxiously. "You'll take me with you?"

"Why . . . what? Why would you say that?"

"I've got a feeling in my gut. Like I'll be left behind."

"Of course we'd never leave you behind."

"But it would be so easy, because of that *we*," he said insistently, which made perfect sense to him, but worried me.

The drugs were making us paranoid and messing with our focus. So

I sat down and put my arms around him. I heard the weirdly comforting sounds of Brand ransacking drawers and cabinets, and just sank into the moment, especially when Addam sighed and rested his head against my chest.

The caffeine pill eventually ended the quiet moment. As the coffee-shakes hit the tips of my fingers, I untangled from Addam and stood up. "Brand?"

"Doesn't make sense," Brand shouted from another room.

"What doesn't?"

He appeared in an open doorway to a walk-in closet, once a pantry where ballroom linens were stored. "There aren't many herbs here. And not much alchemy equipment. If he really was an alchemist, where is the lab?"

"He's an alchemist," I said. "That drug, or spell or whatever it was, impaired my ability to call on my Aspect. I've never heard of anything so potent. Shit. Are we going to get in trouble for killing him? The Arcanum has these weird feelings about *institutional knowledge*."

"You're on the Arcanum, Rune," Addam said.

"That's right," I said in my *aha* voice.

"Would you try to hold a fucking thought in your head," Brand said. "We're heading back to the tunnel. We need backup, so we can figure out what he meant by Lady Time being on the march."

I considered that and saw the appeal. "Do you remember the way back to the market?"

"Of course I do," Brand said, peeved. Then he froze. He closed his eyes and I watched the pupils darting back and forth under the lids. He said, "Shit. Maybe I need a caffeine pill too."

Both of them ended up with a pill. We gathered our stuff and set out to find our way back to the surface.

Our next problem was immediately apparent. Addam and I were still having trouble with our concentration. Every light cantrip I tried to summon in the corridor outside the Forerunner's home just sputtered and exploded into fireworks.

We stood there in the darkness for a second. I heard Brand patting down his pockets to see if he had an extra flashlight so we could watch both the rear and front while we walked. That was good in theory, but I kept getting distracted and making bunny-ear shadows against the wall.

"Jesus Christ," Brand said, sitting down with his back to a wall. "This sucks. I want off this train."

"At least we got high a few weeks ago. So it's not so strange," I added, feeling my way to his side.

"Yes, Rune, I'm sure smoking twenty-year-old pot really built up our tolerance," Brand said. "This will surely be over in no time."

"Maybe we'll wait a minute until the stimulants really kick in?" I said.

Addam plunked down next to us. "I am useless. I cannot even make a light. I see now why you leave me behind so often."

"You are not useless," I said. "You're sweet and noble, and you got the information to find the alchemist just by being you."

Brand started laughing, but it was his *are you shitting me* laugh.

"Brandon," Addam said, and sniffed.

"Addam," Brand said, but couldn't stop laughing. "You have got him so *snowed*. It's like he can't see how sneaky you are."

"Addam isn't sneaky," I said.

"Oh, really?" Brand said. "Addam, did the girl tell you about Cornelius because you healed her?"

"I do not understand the question," he said stiffly.

"Because it seemed like you kept talking for a while after you started healing her. Kind of made me think you ended up using one of your other go-to methods."

"What go-to—" I started to protest, but Brand raised his voice, saying, "You either offered her money . . ."

"I—" Addam started to say.

"Or you used your dimples," Brand ended.

I actually heard Addam's mouth click shut.

"Sneaky," Brand repeated. "I see you, Saint Nicholas. Why the fuck do you think you're here? I'd walk into the Warrens anytime with you at my back. I'd walk into a firefight with it."

"Oh, you ended up making it sound sweet," I said.

"Thank you, I think," Addam said, but I heard the pleased note in the words.

"Are we ready to try this for real?" Brand asked.

"You blokes talk a lot," someone said. "Ain't a great idea down here."

Many things happened at once. We jumped to our feet. Brand turned on his flashlight. I swiped a finger over a sigil to release Fire. And Brand grabbed my arm and said, loudly, "Wait."

My eyes adjusted to the flashlight beam he swung at me. My arm was outstretched, and Brand was standing in front of me. Brand spoke first to the unseen figure behind him. "You—whoever you are, stand the fuck right there. And Rune, do you see how your hand is aimed right at my stomach? Does that seem like a good idea to you?"

I swallowed and sweat broke out along my forehead. Brand whisked the flashlight beam along my face. "What's wrong?" he demanded.

"I may have touched the wrong sigil," I said in a shaky voice.

"What sigil did you touch?"

"Exodus. And it . . . doesn't like to be held like this."

The light beam ducked to my hand, which showed rims of blood around my nail beds. Brand grabbed my wrist in an honest panic—maybe because we might both be about to die—aimed it at a stone wall behind us, and barked at me to release it. A surge of energy shot from my hand and tore the front off the Forerunner's home. The entire tunnel shook as stone thundered to the ground, caving in much of the translocated ballroom.

"Holy fuckballs!" someone cried behind us. The light beam swung on a young man's thin face. He put his hands up and said, "Not going anywhere!"

I tried to swipe clouds of dust out of my face, which, given the oil already covering it, made everything worse. Exodus was one of my strongest last-defense spells, an explosive magic I meditated over daily to strengthen. A year ago I'd brought down a cathedral—a *small* cathedral—which Brand still managed to bring up with alarming frequency.

"Who are you?" I asked, to change the subject. I stepped around Brand to look at the young man.

"Old Toby, sir."

"You're the youngest Old Toby I've ever met."

The scrawny young man shrugged. "My dad was called Young Toby on account of his da being Old Toby. But then my dad's da passed down the River before I was born, so I was the new Old Toby. Trying me best to grow into it."

"That man will give you a lot of money if you guide us back to the food market," I said, and pointed to Addam. Needs must when the devil drove. I'd feel bad about raiding his wallet later.

Addam gave Old Toby a wad of cash before Brand could stop him. We usually didn't pay off our sources until they'd done what we asked, or the dust had settled on all our collateral damage.

"Yes, sir, thank you, sir," Old Toby said in delight.

We dusted ourselves off, made sure we hadn't dropped anything, and followed the young man. Brand asked Addam to watch the rear with the flashlight so that he could walk abreast of our guide, who had a lantern that reeked of a caustic, homemade oil.

"You did for the Pill Man, ay?" Old Toby asked Brand.

Which was when I put another one of Quinn's predictions together. He'd talked about more than one pill guy, hadn't he? Godsdamnit. If I had to draw a metaphor of how this normally went, it would be spotting Quinn laughing his ass off in my rear-view mirror as I put the pieces together in hindsight.

"Is that going to be a problem?" Brand asked Old Toby.

"Not a bloody bit. Pompous ass, that one. Skint as all hell. Knew someone would come for him eventually."

"We didn't come here for him. We're looking for something else. There's more money in it, if you have the right information."

Old Toby turned a gimlet eye on Brand. "Ay?"

"You know Lord Fool and his people? The Revelry?"

"Ay," Old Toby repeated, but slower.

"Many of them have joined another group. There's an old woman in charge of it. They may be in a compound near the Lowlands—or on the edge of the Warrens?"

"That's the sort of secret people really don't like to talk about. Bad things have happened there over the years."

"I'm not asking you to lead us there, just confirm what we know."

Old Toby held up a hand and stopped walking. "Shh. The bit ahead is lousy with undead. Lemme handle it."

"What sort of undead?" I asked. Brand's flashlight beam slid across a long stretch of rock corridor broken up by alcoves on the left and right. I didn't remember walking through it before.

"Shh," Old Toby repeated, and pulled out something that resembled a gun from a steampunk comic. It had a huge bulb on the end. "Keep an eye on all the alcoves. If any are about, they'll drop to the ground as easy pickins."

He took a few steps in front of us, aimed the gun at the ceiling, and pulled the trigger. The flash reminded me of an old Polaroid camera, but a thousand times brighter. The entire hallway was lit up like day until I closed my eyes against it, seeing sunspots under my eyelids.

When I opened my eyes, the hallway was empty, and Old Toby was gone.

Brand ran a hand over his eyes, tired. Then he marched forward twenty feet, reached into one of the alcoves, and yanked Old Toby back into the hallway by the collar of his shirt.

"I'm sorry," Brand said. "Was this not like the fucking television show you watched? Did you think we'd just give up and let you escape during a commercial break? Give me that money."

"No, I can still tell you how to get back!" the young man begged. "I just don' wanna talk about that place in the Lowlands. Weird shit happens there."

"The lab," Addam said. "Toby—do you know where the alchemist kept his lab?"

The young man's small eyes darted among us. "Ay," he said. "You're probably after the warehouse that he and the other gentleman meet at. It ain't far. Just about six fuck-ups away."

"Six . . .?" I said.

"Fuck-ups. Wot we call the translectured rooms and buildings. 'Bout six of them between here and there. We can cut through market and take the tunnels."

"Let's go back to the market first," Brand said.

Old Toby led us out of the alcove hall, through a short series of hatches and man-made holes, and by then I was starting to recognize some of the sights we'd passed earlier. I even guessed we were about to enter the college lecture hall a minute before we entered it.

But now, all the makeshift rooms were dismantled. Earlier, residents had stretched tattered blankets among the stadium seats to make their own pseudo-privacy. All of that was gone now, leaving behind only trash and food wrappers.

Old Toby jumped on a chair back and skipped down the decline with amazing agility. He laughed over his shoulder, "And I wasn't tryin' to hide from you, you prats! I just wanted you to think that while I texted my cousins. There's more money in catchin' nosy folks like you than that pocket change you gave me."

Men in homemade armor began to pour through at least three other doorways: to the left, right, and straight ahead. Without missing a beat, Addam swiped a finger across a platinum disc slotted into his belt. A wash of Telekinetic energy shot from his hands in a stuttering wind.

"Concentration," he grunted, and then bit down on his lip and doubled down. A second blast of energy pushed the front wave of ambushers back.

Some lost their footing on the sloped floor and flipped over the lecture hall seats. Addam wasn't able to sustain a continuous burst with his fractured concentration, but he was able to pulse the energy to create a defensible space in front of us.

"This is our third fucking ambush today, and I am *done* with it," Brand snapped. "Put them down, Rune!"

"I . . ."

"They are straight-up bad guys," Brand said.

"Not living down here. Not if they're hungry. Not if we're the difference between them eating tonight and not." Maybe the caffeine pill was working, because that made actual sense. I added, "I'm not crossing that line. I'm not building a court on the other side of that line. Nonlethal tactics only."

Brand looked like he either wanted to tear his hair out, because he knew I was immovable on this, or shove me hard to prove that I could quite easily be moved if he wanted me to.

"Nonlethal," Brand snapped. "Push them back and I'll prepare an extraction route."

I started to touch a sigil, but Brand grabbed my hand. "Wait! You know which spell is in there?"

"Maybe not," I said honestly. "But can anything be worse than Exodus?"

"Good point," Brand said. "As always, thanks for being sure to fuck up the worst possible way on your first try."

I ran a finger across two sigils at random, and Fire and Shield pushed into my hands, a heat mirage segmented into fractal, pixelated light. I didn't often hold both spells in my hand at the same time, especially when drugged. Wondering what would happen if I put the two together, I wrapped my Fire in the Shield, stepped next to Addam, and pushed out a wall of energy.

Three rows of dry wooden chairs cracked and burst into flames. Men screamed and backed up. As the smoke pressed down on us, I decided maybe this wasn't as effective as I hoped. I ripped the magics apart, and reversed Fire to suck up the oxygen around the flames, smothering them.

My mind refused to let the idea go. Being high and struggling to focus made me both frantic and creative. I always anchored my Shield to a floor, wall, or ceiling. Why? Did I have to?

So I narrowed Shield into an invisible battering ram that covered a semi-circle of space at waist height, covered it in a slick skin of Fire, and rolled it forward above the wooden lecture hall chairs.

And it *worked.* The spell passed above the flammable kindling and smacked into the advancing wave of thieves. Half of them were tossed backwards; some started to scream and catch fire. At least five of them had to stop, drop, and roll.

Then the world began to shake.

"Oh, what the fuck now," Brand said, as dust and debris began to rain down from the ceiling.

A deeper sound than the rumbling filled the air. Like a god swinging a sledgehammer at rock. A piece of the ceiling above us cracked, and we backpedaled to avoid rock and tiles plummeting to the floor. Dust billowed, and Brand's flashlight beam turned into a solid cone of yellow, unable to penetrate the haze.

Things fell through the hole in the ceiling. A washing machine crashed into the ground in front of us. Streams of water began to trickle and spray. A lit camping stove sputtered flame and gruel. The arm of something that may have been a giant lizard plopped right in front of my toe.

Then a gust of wind flowed down, clearing the clouds of debris. Amidst it, the Tower floated, and landed before me.

Muted sunlight now fell in shafts from a massive hole. Corinne and Mayan descended on a Bone Hollows ghost steed, with Lady Death hovering behind them. Ciaran flew down last in a dramatic swirl of blue leather and white cape.

Lord Tower wore an ancient chainmail jerkin. A series of bronze links built into the armor glittered with the power of mass sigils. I'd read stories about the Tower's battle armor before, but had never, ever seen it in use.

He turned in a slow circle and stared at the ambushers, who were frozen in position with dropped jaws and whimpering injuries. They stared up at the skylight that hadn't been there before, now linking this room to the surface. I think I even saw people on floors above us peeking their heads over the rim.

"Brings a whole new meaning to *as the crow flies,* doesn't it?" Lady Death murmured at my side.

Before my friends could kill anyone, I cleared my dry throat and said—or maybe croaked, "This ends now. Lay down your weapons. Don't make us stop you, because we don't have much time, and there are few ways of ending things quickly that will allow you to walk home afterwards. Am I understood?"

A hand shot in the air from behind a row of seats. Old Toby peeked above the edge. He said, "Maybe we could still trade that information, yeah?"

"You stand in the presence of four Arcana, a scion of Atlantis, and three trained Companions," I told him. "There will be no trading. There is only our mercy. Where is the warehouse?"

"Warehouse?" Death said.

"*Four?*" the Tower murmured, which is when I realized I had called Ciaran an Arcana. If I didn't get my shit together, I was going to cause blow-back on my vow.

"Sorry, three," I said irritably. "I'm still maybe high, there's an army on the march, and some of these men have been burned. How about those of you with Healing get to work, while I talk with Old Toby."

"You are high?" Lord Tower asked.

"As fuck," I confirmed. "And there's a *whole* lot of caffeine in the mix, too."

The Tower touched one of the bronzed links on his suit of armor and released a mass sigil spell filled with Healing energy. He put his palm alongside my jaw and forced the magic into me. His personal brand of Healing wasn't my own refreshing sunburnt feeling; it was more like clear-cutting a forest with gasoline. I experienced three seconds of howling pain followed by a pounding yet lucid headache.

"Brand and Addam too," I said, wincing. "A rogue principality got the best of us before we killed him."

"Vadik?" Lady Death said sharply.

"No. A second one," I said, which made all the newcomers stare at me, because the idea of one rogue principality being loose on the island was unusual enough.

"Bad guys now, super-secret talk later," Brand hissed as Lord Tower razed the drug high from his brain.

We lost a few minutes to logistics and PR. The Tower gave me a look that, in his muted way, conveyed exasperation, but I got Ciaran and Addam to circulate along the burnt would-be attackers and heal their injuries. Mayan, Corinne, and Brand ordered them into a sorry clump, while I pulled Lord Tower and Lady Death into quick conversation.

I explained to them what had happened since Zurah and I had parted ways.

"He called himself the Forerunner?" Lady Death repeated. "That's a bit double-oh-seven, isn't it?"

"Vadik calls himself the Serpent. Unironically."

"I've sent three teams to secure the Amberson's holdings," Lord Tower said. "I would have gone myself but, not to put too fine a point on it, you usually stumble into the thick of things. I thought it best to find you first."

"Fair," Brand said, joining us.

"Luckily, you can hold your own," Death said. She touched the lapel of my leather jacket and said, "Nice wards, by the way."

I didn't tell her that Queenie usually handled my jacket's wards with homemade, and thus cheap, techniques. But they did keep me from getting too banged up.

"I want to find this warehouse. We're closing in on Lady Time," I said.

"We know she's taken over a secure space in the Lowlands. More importantly, we know she's on the *move*. So we need to look for those battle plans. We find Lady Time, we find our kids."

"You think these battle plans exist," Lord Tower said.

"The Forerunner made a quip about the time they spent over the battle plans. Lady Time is a relic, and Cornelius is a centennial. What are the chances they run around with iPads? I'm pretty sure they're stupid enough to have an actual battle map laying on a table somewhere. I want to look in this warehouse."

Lord Tower snapped a finger in the direction of Old Toby, who stood at the edge of the trapped crew with a hangdog look. The young man scurried over, tripping over some charred debris from the fire.

Lord Tower said, "This warehouse Lord Sun mentioned—"

"That one is Lord Sun?" he said, startled, pointing to me.

"This one is," I agreed, "and he's about to get very mad if you don't take him where he wants to go."

Old Toby led us through another kaleidoscope. A hallway flanked by church pews; a fast-food restaurant dismantled of everything except a clown statue; a bell tower resting on a forty-five-degree angle. We encountered no resistance, but heard many footsteps running away from us.

Eventually we climbed through a manmade tunnel opening and into the massive, person-sized barrel of a carnival's fun house. At the end of the red-and-white striped barrel was an invisible barrier that sizzled to my senses. Behind the barrier was a roll-up metal door.

"Just like the field around the rejuvenation center," the Tower breathed.

"We'll need to work together," I said. "We don't have time to lose body parts over this. Respectfully meant, Lord Tower."

"How long has the warehouse been protected?" Brand asked Old Toby.

"There's been some sort of shield that fries anyone who tries to muscle through it," Old Toby said. "But that's new. Few months maybe? But the old alchemist and his friend in the scaly mask have been coming here for years."

I exchanged a look with Lord Tower, who was already exchanging a look with Mayan. I don't know what that detail meant, but it meant something.

"I'm going to try something," Zurah said. She was at the rear of the group, leading the ghost steed. In the light of multiple cantrips I saw the fine, pinched lines around her eyes. Summoning the ethereal horses was a costly effort—she'd burned away months of her life force to do it.

"You did this for me again," I murmured as she passed.

"I'm keeping a tab," she promised.

At the mouth of the barrier, she mounted the steed and took a moment to touch a few sigils. I watched a Shield glisten around her body, lit with a deep blue hue that made me think she'd added Frost magic to it. With a loud *hah!,* she charged forward.

She and the ghost steed slipped through the barrier and ran right through the roll-up door on the other side.

Old Toby tugged on my sleeve and pulled me to the side. "Look, Lord Sun. Lord Sun, right?"

I stared at him.

"No harm meant. And here's some advice for free, since you did us a good turn. It's not just starry-eyed kids that lady's been gathering to her skirts. She's been down here for *months.* We shouldn't have been able to walk two fuck-ups without getting attacked—and we just walked six. It's because she's just about knocked off every local boss. That means all those boss's peoples are with her now, you follow? She's got an army that no one talks about."

I thought about what he'd said, then nodded my thanks.

Lady Death charged back through the door. "Dark on the other side—and huge," she said. "It's a warehouse for planes or ships, I think. I can get us past easily enough. Grab my hand," she said to me, and I tried to scramble onto the saddle behind her. It's not something I did often, and I'm not proud to admit Brand had to apply a swift push to my ass.

The ride into the warehouse took a second. I fell off the horse while Zurah *yee-hah*'d her way back to ferry the others across the force field. I was alone for all of twenty seconds before Brand was galloped in, and I spent all of it looking for a light switch or power source. From the echoes my footsteps made, the room was as cavernous as Zurah had said.

I was just about to manifest a light cantrip when Brand shouted, "I've found a bank of light switches. Throwing them now."

Overhead, rows of fluorescent lights snapped and began to warm to full illumination. Addam was—gracefully, of course—vaulting off the back of the ghost steed at that point. I spared Zurah a quick grin for her ferrying both of them over first, and she mouthed the word *Tower,* letting me know she'd be in the shit if she didn't bring him next.

That was as far as we got, because the lights fully powered on in that moment. The ghost steed came to a dead stop as Zurah stared, stupefied, at what was behind me.

"Rune?" I heard Brand said in a small voice.

I turned around slowly, and saw Half House.

The warehouse was at least ten stories high. Enormous. Larger than two or three city blocks. It must have held battleships or cruise liners in its day. Even with the lights on, I could barely see the other side of the building.

Not that I was tempted to look at anything else other than the replica of Half House which had been built in front of me.

It seemed to float in the air—an illusion starting with Brand's basement bedroom on the warehouse's cement floor. The rest of the levels rose above that, to my fourth-floor bedroom under its dormer roof. There was even a representation of our back yard—a huge platform of dirt and grass suspended on pillars so that it could abut the second level of the structure, which was Half House's ground level.

"I need to get the others," Zurah said in a subdued voice. "I would stay where you are. Please."

She raced back through the wall.

"Rune," Brand said again, just as uncertainly but now with urgency. "Over there."

He pointed to another structure past the model of Half House. Three wood and metal walls, with a fourth wall that looked like the exterior of a building. I whispered the words for a lens cantrip and put it to my eyes. Through it, I saw a bell motif worked into the stone. Past a window I saw the inside of a bedroom.

"Pac Bell," I said in a hoarse voice. "That was my bedroom at the Pac Bell."

"What is this?" Addam demanded.

Behind us, the Tower levitated off the back of the ghost steed and touched down beside me. The steed's clip-clops were already on the move.

He stared for such a long time that I forgot I was waiting for him to speak. The others were brought through, and everyone stood in silence until we were a complete unit.

"What in the gods' names am I looking at?" Corinne said. She walked past a stack of building material—huge pallets of cut wood, bags of concrete and nails—and approached the basement level of Half House. "There's a wall missing in the back," she called out.

Brand and I jogged over. Corinne was right—a doorway had been cut in the side of the basement apartment, where one had never been. It must have been used as an entrance.

I sent a light cantrip spinning into the darkness inside. Brand and I exchanged an unsettled look, and walked in. I heard Addam's footsteps behind us, followed by the others.

"Jesus," Brand whispered. "It's . . . this is . . . that's my same quilt." He went over to the foldout futon along the opposite wall. "But there's no stain from where you spilled the knife polish."

My nerves were crawling over each other in a confused scrum.

Brand went over to the counter where he kept a microwave and minifridge. He pawed through a pile of energy bar wrappers. "This is my brand. Are these . . . Did these come from our fucking *trash?*"

I grabbed the handrail of the spiral staircase and went up to the first floor. The entire structure didn't wobble and vibrate like the real staircase did, even when Lord Tower began to climb the steps after me. The first floor was so familiar that my stomach began to hurt. I stepped into the living room, but went no further.

"Quiet, Rune," Lord Tower whispered. "Clear your mind and stand within a quiet space."

He'd talked to me of quiet places before. He framed it in terms of moments when your concentration was paramount. What he never quite said was that it was the place we also went when we stood in a kill zone. Or when we were about to make one.

I took a deep breath and pointed at various things. "Same type of blanket. Of sofa. But look at the refrigerator in the kitchen. It has our weekly planner, but it's empty." I walked through the archway and opened the door to the fridge. There was a wine bottle and a milk carton. The wine bottle was empty, and the milk carton skittered back when I poked at it. "Trash," I said.

"Probably yours."

"Probably mine," I agreed.

"What did they do with this?" Brand demanded. He was climbing the spiral staircase, two steps at a time. Ciaran and Addam followed.

I had a thought. "Brand, check Max's room."

He continued up the stairs without missing a step. I heard his foot-steps above me—much too loudly. The floors weren't insulated.

"It looks . . ." Brand said, then trailed off indecisively. His voice gained more confidence. "Remember that bureau we got from the Sunken Mall? It's not here. This looks more like the guest room before it became Max's bedroom."

I went back to the stairs, climbed past the guest floor and past the third-floor sanctum, and stepped into my attic bedroom. It looked exactly as I remembered, right down to the old air conditioner hunched on the windowsill.

Ciaran had followed us. He swept a cold gaze across the room. I'm not sure I'd ever seen such a grave look on his face. "Rune, I'm assuming Addam knows nothing about the Majeure?"

"None," I said.

"Ask Brand to keep him downstairs. Corinne too. I'm going to try something."

"I heard," Brand said from the stairwell. "I'll keep . . . I'll keep everyone downstairs."

There was a rattled tone in his voice I rarely heard, and I would kill someone for putting it there. Someone would die for this. Someone would die for whatever I was about to learn.

Ciaran stepped into the middle of my bedroom and took a deep breath. He released it as a soft, low, long whistle, then shook his head. "Nothing. Not even when I look closely. Now with the Majeure."

I felt the warmth of his magic—a quicksilver rush of power tied to no sigil. Ciaran closed his eyes for two long minutes. Light spilled through his lashes.

He raised an arm and pointed at my bed.

The custom mattress filled an entire end of the room. The comforter was newer than mine, but the same colors. The same number of pillows. I walked over, grabbed fistfuls, and began to yank it apart. Sheets and pillows went one way, and, when I saw the mattress top was normal, I began to yank it from the box spring. The Tower and Ciaran were helping by then—there wasn't enough room for them to stand idly by.

It wasn't until I'd pulled the box spring away from the wall that I saw something unexpected. A thin strip of metal cleverly worked into the corner joints of the wall. It almost looked like a smudge or pencil mark at first glance.

The metal felt cold under my fingertip. I channeled a burst of willpower into it—

* * *

I stood in my bedroom.

The mattress was bare. The linens had been stripped and moved to Sun Estate. My dresser drawers were pulled out and empty. Through the open door I saw my tiny bathroom, dusty and abandoned as well.

My body—or whatever this astral equivalent of my body was—moved to the window. The blinds were open to the approaching evening. I could see the park behind our cul-de-sac filled with real, moving people.

I ripped my hand from the metal strip while my stomach burned with nausea and acid. "It's a fucking listening device," I whispered. "It's like an . . . antenna? A grounding ward for a clairvoyance spell? It's a fucking listening device. Did you see the room over there?" I wildly pointed in a direction that may not have been right. "That's my Pac Bell bedroom. There may be a listening device in the Pac Bell. I need . . . I need Brand. I need Brand."

I wasn't in my quiet place anymore. My chest hurt, like I wasn't getting enough oxygen. The next thing I knew Brand was there, and I was grabbing him, saying, "It's a listening device. These are all listening devices."

"I don't understand, I checked for bugs all the time, I still do, I promise, you know I do," he said in a rush. He gasped, and his dry throat clicked. "Oh, God, Rune, this is—this dates back. The guest bedroom. The *Pac Bell?* How . . . how fucking long has Lady Time . . .?"

"I don't think this is just about Lady Time anymore," I whispered. "The barrier around the warehouse is new. But they said the people who came here have met for years. Whatever this is, I think it may have been here before Lady Time arrived."

He pushed me away, just enough so I could watch his face. So I could see the understanding hit him. That this may have to do with the fall of my father's throne, and the men who held me, and what happened that night.

"We can't make conjectures," Lord Tower said. "Not yet. We must learn as much as we can, as quickly as we can."

I nodded.

A butterfly with wings of ice battered at the window. Lord Tower noticed it first, and went over to try to let it in. It was painted shut, so he ended up putting an elbow through a glass pane. The butterfly flew into the room and circled the Tower's head until he held out a hand. It landed and melted in his palm, while the Tower cocked his head and listened to an inaudible message.

"Ciaran," he said, his face shut down as tightly as I'd ever seen it. "Would you please join Lady Death by the Pac Bell replica."

Ciaran curtsied and left.

"I don't want to know, do I?" I asked Lord Tower.

"We will seal off this warehouse," he told me. "With our combined abilities, not even Lady Time will be able to breach our defenses. We will come back later and pull this abomination apart nail by nail."

"So Zurah found something other than battle plans," I said.

I turned and walked down the staircase with rubbery steps. Corinne and Mayan were on the third floor, in a bare replica of my sanctum. Addam waited on the first floor. My emotions were gathered in a threadbare net by that point, so I settled for just holding out my hand to him. He took it and, hand in hand, we walked down to the basement, into the warehouse, and over toward the Pac Bell room. Brand was walking behind me, so I stopped until he stepped to my side and the three of us could walk as a team.

Everyone else followed. The Tower gave me my lead, but I saw him let out a small breath when I stopped at the Pac Bell and went no further. Ciaran and Lady Death weren't to be seen, but I noticed a bobbing cantrip light around a massive partition in the warehouse ahead.

At the window—which would have faced a busy downtown street from the Tower's stone skyscraper—I spotted things that had long since faded from my everyday memory. A full-sized bed with a cherrywood frame. Matching bookshelves and a desk. A desk chair that Brand had rebuilt after I put it together with half the screws that came in the box.

"Do you think there's a strip of metal in there that would let you see into the Pac Bell right now?" I asked quietly.

"I suspect there might," the Tower said.

"What is this, Anton?" I asked.

He met my eyes. "We must stay our theories for now, Rune. These are perilous moments."

There was movement in my peripheral vision. Ciaran poked his head around the partition, saw us, and winced.

I let go of Addam's hand and walked over to Ciaran.

"No, Rune," he said.

"I think I know what's there."

"It's not the same as seeing it. Please. *Please,* my friend," he said gently, and put his hands on my shoulders. "Do not do this to yourself."

But Ciaran only had two arms to stop me, and, of course, Brand was already running past us, fiercely determined to take the injury before I could. I watched him crest the edge of the partition, see what was on the other side, and come to a wavering stop. A soft sound escaped his lips.

He yelled over his shoulder, "Rune, don't you come over here!"

I pried Ciaran's hands off my shoulder and walked toward my Companion.

"Rune, don't you . . . we don't need to do this now," Brand begged. "We don't . . ." His eyes began to glisten.

"It's the carriage house, isn't it?" I asked.

Brand nodded. He pressed his palms over his eyes and continued to nod.

"I need you to stay here," I said.

He ripped his hands away from his eyes and glared at me.

"Please?" I whispered. "Please do this for me?"

He pushed the words *that's low* through his lips, and I knew he didn't trust his voice not to break.

"You'll be right here," I said. "That always makes me strong."

I walked around him. The hanger on the other side of the partition was not as large as the main room, but no less massive for that. My eyes were drawn immediately to a replica of Sun Estate's beaten-down carriage house. The barn-like sliding doors were closed, and Lady Death stood by the frame. She shifted her weight as I approached, blocking my view of something.

For a second—just a second—I thought I saw Lady Time standing in the half shadows, a gloating smile on her face. The image vanished before I even blinked.

"Brother," Zurah said. "Why do this to yourself?"

But she lowered her head and stepped aside.

Behind her—nailed to the frame of the building—were two masks. A snake head and an owl head.

Two decades ago, a group of people who remain unidentified to this day invaded Sun Estate while its people slept. By the time they were done, everyone on the property was dead except Brand and I, including my father, who was nearly burned beyond recognition.

I was taken to the carriage house. Nine men in animal masks raped and tortured me for hours. Brand eventually came to his senses and saved me.

New Atlantis considers it an enduring mystery. It has dogged my every footstep, my every ambition, my every nightmare. In a rundown section of the city I even maintain a small apartment filled with secret research dedicated to learning more about *why* they did what they did.

Until recently, I'd only identified a single villain—Ashton Saint Gabriel. I'd killed him.

And now?

Two more. Two more names. One of whom still lived.

The masks were dusty and old and very, very authentic.

I felt the beginning of a panic attack stir. Only this time, the shouting that poured out of my mouth wasn't mine.

Brand had walked to my side and seen the masks. I watched the expression on his face as he recognized what they meant. What this entire warehouse meant. That whatever had begun the night Sun Estate fell had not ended—it had only become something different.

We had been spied on our entire adult life. In the sanctuary of our own home, *we had been watched.*

Brand screamed at the masks. His face was red, and the tendons on his neck stood out like steel cables. No words, just inchoate rage at the one thing that had hurt me he'd never been able to kill. Helpless fury at the one thing that had hurt us again and again and again.

"Brand," I said, and my eyes were blurry with tears. "Come here. Come here."

His screams were going hoarse. He was nearly staggering on his feet.

And then Addam came up behind him and wrapped his arms around Brand. He began to whisper words into his ear. When Brand stopped screaming, Addam lifted one arm, and I moved beneath it, so that the three of us were locked in an embrace.

Out of the corner of my eye, I watched my friends approach. They formed a semicircle around us, including Lady Death. They folded their hands over their chest and turned their backs, standing so close that they effectively formed a barrier between us and the world.

It was an old Atlantean custom among the closest of allies. It spoke of support and privacy and compassion. It was a deeply felt gesture from a group of people who'd all lived on the Atlantis homeland once upon a time.

After a small eternity, I pried away from Brand and Addam.

"I already guessed," I said in a cracked voice. "Vadik is stupid enough to call himself the Serpent. And Cornelius made a crack about an owl's nest. I . . . already guessed, I think, deep down."

"I am so sorry," Lady Death whispered. "I cannot imagine how this must feel."

We didn't have the luxury of breaking down now, though. Not for any longer than we already had. As Lord Tower had said, these were perilous moments.

Swallowing, I turned in a slow circle to see what other fun surprises the room might hold. The only thing within the reach of the overhead lights was a large table ringed by chairs. Behind it, flush against the wall, was something like an ancient computer. It was as large as a dining room hutch, and covered with glass tubes, bulbs, bronze dials, and heavy-handled switches.

Someone made a sound. When Ciaran saw he had my attention, he raised his hand. "I think I know what that contraption is," he said.

"Is it—" I bit off the words, because something else had grabbed my attention. "Holy shit. There really are battle plans!"

I ran over to the table. A map of downtown New Atlantis was stretched along the surface. Notes had been scrawled in the margin, but they all seem to be centered around . . .

"Farstryke," I said. "Of course. Why the fuck didn't I think about that? It's her ancestral home."

Farstryke Castle was one of the few buildings that the Arcana had attempted to translocate from the Atlantean homeland. Its lands had been considered a public trust since the dissolution of the Hourglass Throne centuries before. Something about the transference had gone bad, and Farstryke was largely known as one of the most haunted pieces of real estate on the island.

The Tower reached the table, a half step behind Brand. I glanced at him and said, "Did you suspect?"

"I did. But then again, I suspect a lot of things. Not only is it her ancestral home, but there are patches of null zone on the property—which she seems to use as a power source. So if she really is moving on Farstryke it is . . . not unideal."

"Ciaran, what is that?" I asked, nodding at the large device.

"It's a device created by the Hex Throne and widely used by other courts in the 1800s. Frightfully expensive, unspeakably ugly, but also rather secure for what it does."

"What does it do?" Addam asked. He put a hand on my arm, briefly, and squeezed.

"It facilitates communication between two fixed points," Ciaran explained.

"Activate it," I said.

"Rune, it would be wise—" Lord Tower began saying.

"Activate it," I repeated.

Ciaran bowed his head at me and moved to the device. He examined the panel for a moment, then pressed a button and turned one dial fully counterclockwise. Bulbs began to brighten to a dull red. Ciaran put his palm on a square panel and pushed. From inside the machine, I heard an electric current crackle to life.

We watched for a good thirty seconds, and the bulbs deepened to a dark green. A minute after that, a metal grill began to hiss.

A distorted voice said, "Cornelius? We agreed not to speak until your and Vadik's unfortunate arrangement with Lady Time has ended." The word *arrangement* was nearly spat.

Whomever this was, it wasn't Lady Time. And with everything else we'd just learned, I had to wonder if I was speaking with the person behind the unsanctioned raid on my father's throne. The person behind my torture.

"Something happened," I said, and hoped my voice was just as distorted on their end.

A pause. Then: "Tell me."

"The warehouse has been compromised."

"When? *By whom?* I swore to you if your *freelancing* with that woman jeopardized our own plans there would be consequences. I told you not to show her the monitoring station!"

"Lord Sun has identified us," I said.

The pause lasted longer this time. The voice said, much more calmly, "Who is this?"

"When you feel my boot on your throat, you'll know."

The grill sputtered. No. No, laughed. Whoever they were, they laughed, a synthesized crackle.

"Rune Sun," they said. "Even a blind pig finds a truffle now and then, doesn't it?"

"Especially if he has friends," Zurah said. "That makes all the difference, don't you think, Lord Tower?"

"I most certainly do, Lady Death," Lord Tower said, and the sclera of his eyes had gone black, a dangerous, dangerous hint that his Aspect was close to the surface.

"Don't I get named too? Include me!" Ciaran said. "After all, I knew the people who built machines like this. And once I take it apart, I promise . . . *I will find you.*"

The machine went dead. The bulbs blinked off, and the electrical hum dropped into silence.

There was no time to discuss what had happened, because Mayan stepped up to Lord Tower and said, "Are you all right? What's happening?"

The Tower gave his arm a frustrated look and, grudgingly, pulled up his chainmail sleeve. A welt was rising along the surface of his forearm, shaped like the seal of the Arcanum—a round circle filled with wavy River lines and connected spheres.

"Lord Judgment is using his staff of office," he said.

Mayan gave his scion a furious look, not unlike Brand would give me if he learned someone was mucking about with my skin.

Lord Tower touched the mark and said, "We're among friends, but speak guardedly."

A voice—distant and hard to hear, like the last word in a string of cavern echoes—said, "Former members of the Revelry are amassing on the city streets. We have people in place to track their movements."

"We believe her target is Farstryke Castle. And I feel confident we've confirmed that Lady Jade has, in fact, claimed the Hourglass Throne as Lady Time."

"Then we must deny her the chance to gain a greater foothold. The Arcanum moves now, in full force."

"Acknowledged," Lord Tower said.

The burn mark sank back into his skin. Lord Tower massaged the rash-like area briefly, and lowered the armor back into place.

He said, "We go to battle."

FARSTRYKE

Mayan and Corinne were given the ghost steed, and we cobbled together Flight spells for everyone else. Brand was chained to Addam through Telekinesis since he wouldn't have the ability to direct the movement of the flying magic laid on him.

Bursting into the swamp from the tunnel Lord Tower had drilled was glorious, despite my aversion to flying. As we flew above the mire, the clean air of early evening and the drizzle of a light rainstorm sluiced away my sweat and dirt. We crested as high as skyscrapers, pivoted in a wide arc, and shot toward Farstryke Castle.

It didn't last long, and I didn't swallow any bugs along the way, which about summed up what I wanted most from attempting to give gravity the finger.

We descended toward a five-story rooftop in the museum and theater district, a section of city about two streets wide. I landed first, hitting the flagstone terrace at a bad angle. I rolled to a jarring stop against a stone cherub, which tipped over and snapped its wing. I disentangled myself as the ghost steed plunged through the roof, dipped into the penthouse level below, and then emerged back topside with a jump.

Addam used Telekinesis to slow his landing. He and Brand touched down as gently as if they'd stepped off a curb.

Judgment and a group of Arcana were gathered around a pedestal by the northeast corner, a vantage point that overlooked both the theater district and the nearby blotch of darkness that was Farstryke. I walked over to them and saw, as I got closer, that the pedestal was a tree trunk that had sprouted from the soil of the rooftop garden. Leaves were still unfurling from wayward branches, linked by wispy bonds to Lady World.

"Where are we?" Lord Tower asked, striding past with Mayan at his side.

Lord Judgment gestured to a map of the city. "All activity is here, almost three blocks away, by the front gates of Farstryke. Those closest to the gates are well-armed criminals. Those further out—standing in the block between us and them—appear to be less organized followers. None of them have entered the grounds yet, possibly because of the dangers involved."

"Lady Time can't handle haunts?" I asked. "That doesn't seem right."

"We never acknowledged her throne," Lord Strength said, his lips curled in distaste as I named her. "She is not Time."

Lord Judgment ignored that. "Lady Time is not on site, which may be why they hesitate."

Lord Strength wasn't done interjecting. "We should move on them now. They pose no threat to us—a mix of Warrens trash and Revelry addicts."

Lady Death, leading her ghost steed, made a frustrated sound in the back of her throat. "Peace, brother. Many of them are as much hostages as supporters, whether they realize it or not."

"That may be so, but they stand in our way."

"No, Lady Death is right," I said. My Adam's apple bobbed as all the attention swung my way. "Those people down there follow Lady Time because we failed to give them someone else to follow. Hurting them will only make her stronger."

"This is not a referendum on the Arcanum—it is sedition," Lord Judgment said wearily. "For all we know, these people have murdered Lord Fool. We don't have the luxury of debating the issue right now, anyway. Our enemy is Time. We must make our way to her as quickly as possible once she arrives. We cannot underestimate the danger she poses. She hails from an era when magic was at its height and Arcana were vicious."

"As opposed to their modern puppy dog ways," Ciaran said cheerily.

Lord Tower's eyes flickered to him. "Lord Judgment, are you sure a forward assault is the best strategy? We already know she's a match for five of us—five of us firmly under her thumb at Lady Death's manse."

"Then we'll throw a dozen of us at her," Lord Judgment said. "We end this now, and we end this quickly."

"We should split into three prongs," Lady Justice said. "Two flanks and a forward advance. We can hold until she's spotted and focus on crowd control."

"Someone needs to clear the main street," I said. "Mobs can only work to her advantage. I'd like to take the forward prong." I could find a way to do that which didn't involve outright violence.

"We both will," Lord Tower said. He gave a quick glance around the table. His eyes lit on Zurah and Ciaran. "I'll keep my team intact. We've worked well together."

"Fine," Judgment said. "I'll take left flank with Chariot, World, and Hierophant. The Magician is already on the street there. The Moral Certainties can take right flank. Lady Priestess, perhaps you would join them?"

"Of course. Bethan is with my mounted forces by the Bluegaerd Theater. We'll circle forward through this alley here." She put her finger down on a lane.

As the others plotted their route, Addam touched my elbow and gestured aside. We went to the edge of the roof, where Brand stood alone. Below us, blazing theater marquees flashed through the drizzle. I could smell roasting cashews, and a busker was playing Cyndi Lauper acoustically, barely audible from our height.

The expression on Brand's face just about broke my heart. I could barely pull apart the currents of emotion flooding our bond.

"Brandon," Addam said, and put a hand on his shoulder. "I understand."

Brand kept staring off the roof. He said, "I didn't know we've been spied on our entire life. How could you understand that?"

Addam squeezed his hand until he got Brand's attention. When Brand glanced at him, finally, Addam said, "Because I protect him too."

Understanding passed between them. Brand allowed that to go on for all of three seconds before he shuddered and shook it off.

"We've got a fight ahead of us," he said. "I'm fine. Rune . . ."

"I'm fine too," I promised, which was a lie, but it was the lie I meant to tell him, which was a form of the truth, so all he'd feel through the bond was my conviction.

Brand nodded. He gestured to the streets below. "It'll all happen along this street. Procsal Avenue. Three block radius. There—" he pointed. "That's the corner of First Street, by the gates of Farstryke. Lady Time has her fighters there—the gang members she took over in the Warrens, I bet. Just up there, the corner of Second Street. She's put the Revelry followers in a group." His finger slowly slid away from us, toward the right. "The corner of Third and Procsal? Unaware scions sitting there like fucking bowling pins, right outside the theater. I don't think this woman does anything without a reason. This is a strategy."

"It is," Lord Tower agreed, stepping up to my side. "At least we can control things somewhat by taking the main street and clearing away Lord Fool's former followers."

"Hey," I said. "You know that stuff we just heard? About these people being traitors, or trash, or addicts? Those words came out of the mouths of people who should know better." The Tower remained silent, so I added, "I'm not going to be able to listen to much more of that before I get really, really loud."

"I know," the Tower said. "And perhaps I'm not inclined to stand in your way when that happens."

He signaled to someone over my shoulder. I knew it was Ciaran before I even looked, because his footsteps always sound like a choreographed dance move.

"Apologies for volunteering you," Lord Tower said.

"Wouldn't miss the fun for anything," Ciaran promised.

"I've always been most impressed with your stealth magics," Lord Tower said. "I would be grateful if you scouted our path down that street." He pointed. "We'll try to diffuse the crowd as we move toward Farstryke."

Ciaran touched two gems set in a cufflink. I felt the release of sigil spells, then Ciaran was rising above us. "I'll circle back in ten," he said.

"I can deputize you as an official representative of the Arcanum," Lord Tower offered. "You will speak with our voice."

"Maybe," Ciaran murmured, "it's time I do just that. Toodles!"

His body shimmered white and gray, then Invisibility hid him from sight. A whoosh of air announced his departure.

"What's the plan?" Death interrupted, approaching us with the rest of our party. Her ghost steed neighed and trotted through a massive clay urn.

"We take the straight approach," the Tower said. "Our main priority is to engage Lady Time as soon as she arrives. Until then, we'll attempt to clear the streets of obstacles."

"Or, put another way, we'll attempt to save average citizens from becoming collateral damage," Zurah corrected him. Firmly.

Lord Tower made a tired gesture with his hand, but at least it was one of acknowledgment.

"There!" Corinne shouted.

I followed her finger and saw a comet bearing down on us.

It came from the northwestern corner of the city. It wasn't until it was within a few blocks of our roof that I could see the form of a person within a nimbus of golden light. The fireball circled above, slowed its approach above the boulevard below, and came to a halt above the people gathered before Farstryke Castle.

The rooftop shook. I looked over my shoulder and saw that Lord Judgment had lifted his staff of office into the air. A sheen of amber fire rolled along its surface. "Bring that woman to the Iconsgison in chains, siblings and children," he called out. "For Atlantis and Atlanteans!"

Some of the more strident Arcana echoed the battle cry. I just looked at Brand and Addam. They were with me, and that was a source of infinite strength and infinite worry.

"I can lift us to street level," Addam told everyone. "No need to waste extra Flight spells."

"Do it," the Tower said.

Addam held out his metal hand, the fingers flexing with unnatural acuity. A spell released from one of the discs on his belt, and the buoyancy of Telekinesis rushed among us, a feathery current of magic. Addam tightened his hold on our group, and I felt myself tugged gently off my feet.

It was a skillful display of magic, and I felt so proud of Addam that my shell-shocked heart finally began to beat back against the surprises of the evening.

Everything became more real as we floated to street level. I could hear the scattered buzz of theatergoers who had abandoned their tickets to watch the strange events. I could smell food carts and car exhaust. We landed on the sidewalk between Second and Third Streets, by the two-story silver globe in front of the Museum of History. It was a true depiction, showing both Atlantis and the other hidden islands of the world.

"Oh, gods, there are children here," Addam said.

"What?" I looked until I saw what he saw. The scions behind us—the theatergoers—had children Anna's and Corbie's ages. None of them were moving toward the theaters—they were too engrossed with the spectacle of the protesting mob gathered at the other end of the street. "Why are there families out this late?"

"One of the new shows is a children's ballet," Corinne said. "Corbie asked to see it. This is not good, Rune."

"Mayan," Lord Tower said. "Please lock Operation Kansas to my command and alert all forces. And tell your team that I'm freeing the eagles."

Mayan gave his scion a grim nod, then stepped aside to speak on his phone.

"What is Operation Kansas?" I asked.

"Something I planned in advance with Lord Judgment," the Tower said. "First things first. We must—"

"Bear witness, Atlantis!"

Lady Time's voice—raspy but strident—rolled down the street. The consonants had the sizzling reverberation of an amplification cantrip.

The glowing woman rose above the head of her underground followers. Her magic illuminated the gates of Farstryke Castle, two blocks away, its rusted finials beneath her shining feet.

"Look at them! In their finery and jewels. Dripping with sigils— the legendary source of our power, a legacy meant for all of our society. If you get close enough, you'll smell the waste on them. The sheer gluttony of their petty magics. They use these sigils—Our sigils! Our tools of war and prosperity, our collective inheritance!— They use these sigils so that their fatty flesh smells like flowers. To keep the rain from their finery and hair. To keep the dirt of the city streets from scuffing the soles of their shoes. To make their lips and cheeks rosy, to hide the roundness of their well-fed bellies."

"Jesus fucking Christ," Brand whispered to me. "It's like she listened to one of your rants and wrote it down word for word."

"She doesn't mean any of it. This is all an act."

"I've returned to find that my people are refugees from Atlantis, now living on this mean scratch of land, tied to an infant republic of humans. I've returned to find the average man and woman of Atlantis—our backbone and source of strength—choking beneath the grip of the Arcanum's manicured nails. It is time for change. It is time for change!"

"Enough," Lord Tower said.

He strode out into the street, and the ebb of anxious conversations flared and died in his wake.

Lord Tower held out a hand and snapped his fingers. He used a clever cantrip spell at the last second to magnify the sound, which hit the city blocks like a crack of thunder. In the echo that followed he said, his own voice as booming as Lady Time's, *"This is the Tower of Atlantis. The woman who speaks is a charlatan and murderess. Your Arcanum moves amongst you—stand down and let us handle the threat."*

The last word was barely out of his mouth when a surge of power washed from Farstryke. I called on my willpower and saw the rippling barrier spread over the crowd gathered closest to Farstryke.

"Barrier," I said to Brand.

"Where's the edge of it?"

"One block up. Corner of Second Street."

"She's divided her forces into two groups," Addam said, confused. "The members of the Revelry are not within the barrier. They are exposed."

"No, she's kept the fighters by her side, and set cannon fodder before us," Lady Death corrected furiously. "Look at them. Castoffs from the Revelry. They barely have real weapons. This is a badly baited trap, Anton."

"Then we will attempt not to set it off," he said. "Corinne and Mayan: keep the scions from following. Drive them into the theaters. Connect with Judgment and find how close the Arcanum soldiers are—we need them for crowd control. Everyone else, with me."

We moved forward. My adrenaline level spiked, tunneling my vision. I saw Brand snapping the flanges of his dart-bow open. Addam grimly pulling his sword. Corinne pulling a razor-knuckled gauntlet over her fist.

I did not feel good about this.

Arcana were accustomed to solving situations by revealing who they were. *I* was accustomed to doing that. But that was the worst possible way to handle this situation, because who we were *was* the problem. I should have been more forceful on the roof. I should have pushed back harder on their dismissal of the mobs. Our attention was so focused on the woman with the match that we didn't see the gasoline spreading around our ankles.

And then, suddenly, there was no time to speak.

The ragged crowd of followers locked outside Lady Time's barrier had grouped together with homemade weapons—boards with nails driven into them, corroded hammers, chipped old swords. I was close enough to hear their anxious murmurs, close enough to smell their sweat and the musk of unwashed clothes.

Lord Tower brushed a hand across one of the links of his chainmail. Writhing blue energy began to swirl around his hands. But just as he began to hold his hand toward the crowd, Zurah shouted, *"Anton!"*

"A Stunning spell only," he said.

"Don't," I said. "She's right, don't. Don't do it. We need to try talking to them before—"

A block away, the windows of a building imploded. On the other side of it a fireball rose, its black smoke underbelly roiling. That was our right flank—the Moral Certainties team.

The followers saw it too, and the fear was stark on their face. They drew together but didn't lower their weapons.

Behind us, Corinne and Mayan were barking commands at the theater crowd, which only added to the tense smog of the moment. A food cart was untended, and the odor of burning popcorn filled the air. Mayan ran back to us while hooking a communication device over his ear. "Right flank is ambushed. Judgment is at the foot of the barrier on the left, and they're working to bring it down."

"Helpful but unnecessary," the Tower said. "She *wants* to engage. This delay is all part of her theatrics."

"Then we make a new plan," I said.

Lord Tower flicked his wrist, and the Stunning magic dispersed. "You have thirty seconds, Rune."

I licked my lips and thought what to say, so Brand helped by placing a hand in the small of my back and pushing me in front of them.

I recovered from the stumble with both arms outstretched. I kept them like that, palms held outwards, a sign of nonaggression. "Please," I said, raising my voice. "Please listen to me. I am Lord Sun. Many of you wear the colors of the Revelry. I've been to your home—I've seen the graves. We followed the route you walked into the Warrens. We saw what you lived through, and I must believe, I *must,* that you know in your hearts you're not being told the entire truth."

"She just wants her home!" one of them cried. "That's her home, isn't it? Can you deny that?"

"This is not about her home," I insisted. "You have not been stranded here, *on the other side of that barrier,* because she wants her home. This is a strategy. You are being used in the most vile way possible. This is an attack on our city."

A short wildfire of conversations spread among them. I heard the word *barrier*. I wasn't sure they could even see it or understand the significance, though.

Then the angry man yelled, "We don't have the same city you do. It's not *our* city! It never was! That's what she wants to change!"

"I saw the graves," I repeated. "The bodies at the Revelry. Did you know them? Were they your friends? Your family? What, exactly, did Lady Time want to change about *them?*"

That was when the moment fell apart.

Someone in the crowd threw a bottle with a lit rag stuffed into it.

The crowd pushed away from the person, surprised.

Blue energy burst around Lord Tower's hands.

I heard the whistle of a projectile and saw the dart-bow in Brand's hands.

And lastly, but most dramatically, a glistening, fractal wall of light sprang up between us and them. The Molotov cocktail exploded harmlessly in the air. Ciaran flew down from the sky, his hands still gloved with the Shield magic.

"We are not the enemy," Ciaran said.

"Ciaran," one of them said, and then, louder, "That's Ciaran."

"You know me," Ciaran said. "I've met some of you before. I have drunk your wine, and danced around your bonfires. And I swear to you, I am not the enemy. Nor is Rune Sun. He is trying to save you."

"They just shot someone!" one of them yelled back.

"That man wasn't one of you," Brand said loudly. His dart-bow was still pointed at the man he'd shot—or sedated, knowing Brand. It was the one who'd thrown the lit bottle. "Look at him. Dirty face, clean chest holster and new boots. He was planted in the crowd to stir violence. Tell me I'm wrong."

Overlapping words and shouts—some agreement, a lot of fear.

"Is Brandon wrong?" Ciaran asked them. "That man—the one in the tight pants, rolling on the ground—is he familiar to you? Do you trust him?"

"Doesn't mean anything," one of them said stubbornly. "We're only here to help her reclaim her home—which she is gonna *share* with us."

"She's lying," Ciaran said simply. "She's been lying all along. She's only using you to get power. She has no intention of honoring her promises."

And of course, another flaming bottle arced through the air, likely from another plant in the crowd, which got everyone riled and brought the conversation back to zero—even as Ciaran smothered the projectile in a small Shield.

"ENOUGH!" Lord Tower shouted, rising into the air. He looked down on the crowd before us and said, without amplification, "This delay is costly."

Ciaran waved a hand at Lord Tower and snapped his fingers. A sigil spell rippled from him, and then the Tower was falling. He jerked to a stop before hitting the ground—Addam, arm outstretched, had caught him in a Telekinetic grasp.

"Apologies, Dagger Throne," Ciaran said. "But I'm afraid your approach is costlier."

He turned to the crowd as his Aspect rose around him.

All magic in his presence began to shine like quicksilver—the barrier, the surge of Telekinesis, my sabre, the ghost steed. I heard the roar of a River as the color washed out of everything except my proud friend—his red lips and blue-green hair, his sodden white cape and his outfit's blue leather.

"It's time for proper names," Ciaran said. "It's long, long past time for proper names. The city owes you more than it's given. You deserve an advocate on the Arcanum. The moment—this moment, this vitally important moment—demands it. And I can provide that, can't I? You all know me. I've walked among you. What you don't know is that I am, as I have been for a very, very long time, the Magician of Atlantis. I am the true Hex Throne. And I ask you now to step from the path of this bloodbath that Time seeks to drown you in. When the dust of this conflict has settled, I swear, I will remain at your side. I swear this upon my name, and my name, and my name."

The force of the vow rang outwards.

Brand's eyes cut toward me.

"My gods," Lady Death whispered.

And Lord Tower's jaw dropped. His mouth was *agape*. As weapons clattered to the ground, the Tower rose to his feet, staring hard at Ciaran. Slowly, he lifted his hand, and made a visible demonstration of snuffing the magic that gloved his fist.

Lord Tower was about to say something else, but people cried out. The crowd's attention swung to our rear, where single-file lines of scions were pouring from the theaters and moving toward us. They were unnaturally silent, their faces slack of emotion.

"What are they doing?" someone called out, as another person said, "There are children there."

"Compulsion," Ciaran murmured. "This is one of her tricks."

Not far from the front of the approaching lines, I spotted Mayan and Corinne. Their weaponless hands hung limply at their sides. Their eyes were fixed on the shoulders of the people in front of them. My own anger flared—but it was a candlewick against Lord Tower's sudden fury.

He strode away from us, and I followed. None of the scions in the front rows even glanced at him. Lord Tower marched up to Mayan and put a hand in front of his chest. Mayan didn't resist or attack, and the people behind him—including Corinne—merely walked around.

Lord Tower put his hands behind Mayan's head and drew their foreheads together.

"*Mine,*" he hissed.

Mayan sucked in a deep breath and began coughing. "Mother fucking horsefire *shit!*" he gasped. "I couldn't . . ."

Brand grabbed Corinne by the arm and pulled her out of line. She didn't react; she just weakly tried to tug herself away.

"I was . . . there was a party. There's a party ahead. We're late for a party," Mayan said. He grimaced. "That's all I could think. She's leading us to Farstryke."

"She may be planning to feed the scions to the haunts," I guessed.

"She'll have to let the barrier down," Zurah added.

"We can't wait," I said. "The closer they get, the more we'll need to divide our efforts to protect them, fight her soldiers, and attack her."

"We need that barrier down," Brand said. "The Arcana need to hit her now and hit her hard."

"I can clear my friends from the streets," one of the Revelry members said. "And we can try to pull the children from the line." Some of his people had edged close behind him, close enough to hear. "Do it! Try to pull the children from the line! Something isn't right about this—help the children!"

"Two of us can get across now," Lady Death said. She reached up and put a hand on the ghost steed's glistening hide. I noticed, in shock, that her eyes were pinched in exhaustion. The steed was powered by her Majeure; she was pouring a constant stream of living energy into the ghost steed to keep it corporeal.

"Me," I said.

"Rune," Lord Tower said quietly. "Zurah and I should—"

"Me," I said again. "She has my people. My kids. I need to know if they're up there."

He sighed. "Rune and I will advance. No arguments, Brand," he added before Brand could even marshal a response. "There's only room for two. While Rune looks for your people, someone needs to distract Time and disrupt her influence on the crowd."

"Let the steed dissipate as soon as we're off it," I whispered to Zurah. She started to protest, but I raised my voice louder. "*Let the steed go.* You and Lord Tower brought a barrier like this down once—you can do it again, especially if Judgment is working on the problem, too."

She nodded.

I didn't have to worry about a clumsy mount. Lord Tower climbed up first and offered me a hand, and Addam helped lift me with Telekinesis.

I hoisted myself on the horse's ass and grabbed the Tower's chainmail waist for balance.

Lord Tower must have ridden one of the ghost steeds before. He galloped us through the barrier, jumped the curb, and phased into a building. Using that as cover, he cut a path parallel with the street. We rode through a bookstore, a card shop, a closed bakery. At the end of the string of shops, he jumped back through the wall, and slowed about one hundred yards from the gates of Farstryke.

Lady Time's forces had already engaged in battle. A contingent of guarda must have been either driving or moving within a block of Farstryke when the barrier rose. They were locked in a scrum with the Warrens gang members that Lady Time had recruited.

Lady Time herself floated above a dry fountain before the gates, over a small, open courtyard just off the sidewalk. In the corner of the paved square was a group of people.

I made out Vadik's scaled costume and Max's white-blond hair.

Everything began to narrow with the pinpoint focus of rage and urgency, because Vadik had been one of my torturers, and he was with the children. The man who had once tortured me stood with my children.

One of the guarda's green and amber patrol cars screeched down the street, aiming for Lady Time. Lady Time lifted her palm and lowered her head. The shining light around her flared, and the patrol car began to fall apart. The metal shell darkened and dissolved into flakes. The guarda officer inside clutched the now-rotting upholstery of his seat as sharp pieces of rust sliced his body open. He hit the asphalt at ninety miles an hour. What rolled to a stop in front of the old fountain was barely meat.

"Listen to me, Rune," the Tower said before I could start running toward Max. "I planted explosives in Farstryke days ago. I intend to destroy it once the barrier comes down. It will unbalance her, and we've seen before that her hold loosens when she rages. The Arcanum will hit her with everything when this happens. Hold nothing back. It is not certain we will get this chance again."

"I need to get the kids now," I said, while channeling willpower into my sabre hilt. A molten, garnet blade began to form.

"Do it quickly," he said. He put his hand on my shoulder, squeezed, and began to step backwards. He touched one of the sigils in his armor and faded from sight.

I began to run toward the stage as the damp air created sizzling wisps along my sabre blade. I crossed the street, and another car—a beat-up old Saturn—drove over a curb and smacked into a light pole. My brain was telling me that it looked a lot like my car, even as I saw Queenie's wide-eyed expression behind the steering wheel.

I ran toward it as four of the armed Warrens thugs advanced on the car. One of them spun around as I approached, and I cut his hand off, which fell to the ground with his dagger.

. The back door of my car exploded off its hinges. Diana Saint Nicholas climbed out. She grabbed a gang member in a Telekinetic hold and threw him into the side of a nearby building.

The remaining two thugs suddenly stiffened, dropped to the ground, and began to spasm. I was able to track the magic back to Layne, who had a box cutter in one hand. It looked—bizarrely—like they were wearing leg warmers on both arms. As I watched one of them soak up blood from a cut, I understood the purpose. Infection and blood powered their necromantic abilities.

Pushing wet hair out of my eyes, I stalked up to them. There were scorch marks on the hood of the car—not from the impact. It looks like they'd been trapped within the barrier and had tried to drive through it.

"The girl is missing, we had no choice," Diana said calmly before I could ask why the fuck they were there.

"Anna left behind a note saying she was going to 'save those dumb boys,'" Layne added anxiously. "We dropped Corbie off at the Pac Bell and came here."

"Then she may be near the gates with the others," I said. "Diana, *retreat*. Go there—try to get in that shop there." I pointed to a shuttered bodega on the nearest corner. "I'll get them there."

A car exploded about fifty yards away, sending a knot of guarda and gang members flying.

"Go!" I shouted and began to run for the small plaza in front of Far-stryke.

The fighting provided cover—I was almost sure I hadn't drawn Lady Time's interest yet. I ducked low as I ran, occasionally having to cut off arms and hands. The gang members were victims of Lady Time; I tried to spare their lives even while using quick and brutal methods to drop and disarm them.

I was close enough to the staging area that I would have been able to meet Max's eyes if he looked my way. Anna and Quinn were with him.

Above me, the barrier flickered into the visible light spectrum. Spreading tendrils of hoarfrost began to climb toward the apex. My friends were breaking through.

Lady Time lifted higher into the air, a small star of energy. She raised her arms toward the sky, and the clouds above the barrier began to blacken and churn—a storm in fast-forward. Weather magic. She was using *weather magic,* because of course this day needed to get worse.

The optical effect of rain hitting the barrier and smoking into steam was dramatic. A barrage of lightning—fiercer than any island storm I'd ever seen—began to strike the ground outside the force field. No Atlantean would fly in lightning, not without custom-built shields. She knew the barrier would fall and was stalling the approach of reinforcements.

I ran harder.

Ahead of me, one of the guards had grabbed Quinn by the collar of his shirt. Max jumped onto the guard's back, knocked him down, and began to punch him in the face. Vadik saw this and lifted into the air while forming a ball of fire in his hands.

I touched the Companion symbol on my belt, released a Shield spell, and clapped it around Vadik. In the air, Vadik jerked, his arms locked at his side. He fell hard to the concrete and cracked the pavement. I was close enough to hear him gasping for breath as my Shield tried to squeeze and shatter his own Shield.

Lady Time spun around and saw what was happening. She began to float toward the disturbance just as the barrier overhead shattered under the Arcanum's onslaught. A sheet of water fell down, and forks of lightning began to strike lampposts and buildings. I watched a gang member caught in a burning, magnesium flare. His smoking body landed in a wet gutter.

Eight stone birds screamed down from the clouds. Lord Tower had said, *I'm freeing the eagles.* These were the long-dormant gargoyles atop the Pac Bell building, one of the Tower's secret defenses.

As Lady Time battled with the constructs, I raced to where Vadik was still struggling to breathe under the force of my magic.

The children saw me. They saw the look on my face. They drew together, and Max was yelling at them to pull back.

I landed on Vadik's chest, straddling him. I released the Shield and let my sabre blade dissolve into fat sparks that burned through the hood of his snakelike leather.

As I put the hilt against one of his eyes, I felt cold metal under my fingers. An amulet had slipped from Vadik's concealed neckline. It was a gold sunburst—one of the sigils from my father's personal armory—sigils bound only to him that could have been seized during his defeat.

My magic faltered for a split second. Before I could steady my willpower, Vadik vanished, dropping me a few inches to the pavement.

I looked up just in time to see Lady Time floating toward me. The wreckage of the stone eagles was already scattered around the small square. She spread the fingers of her hand and made a slicing motion.

Telekinesis ground me into the courtyard tiles, while a spreading wave of energy sent everyone else flying. I watched the kids skid away down a sidewalk—jerking to a buffered halt as Diana Saint Nicholas caught them in a Telekinetic hold of her own.

"*You,*" Lady Time said to me. "I did warn you, didn't I? Now you'll see what comes next."

"I don't think he will," a voice said behind her.

Judgment, the leader of the Arcanum, dropped the magic that concealed his stealthy advance at the far side of the square, and pointed his staff of office at Lady Time. Whatever powered her levitation failed, and she hit the ground with a short, quickly muffled scream.

Lord Judgment swiped his staff—a powerful device that could focus and amplify his magic—in an upward arc. The mauled clouds above us began to break, showing weblike threads of moonlight.

Lady Time staggered to her feet and limped toward him. Lord Judgment aimed his staff at her again—and it detonated into burning splinters that made him cry out and cover his face.

He looked like he was about to shout something. I saw his lips moving at least. Then Lady Time reached him. She put one hand on the side of his neck and another on that same shoulder. Defense spells blistered her flesh and made her sleeve catch fire.

She tore Judgment in half. His head and shoulder went one way, and his split torso another.

While shaking the blood from her hands, she calmly patted out the fire on the cuff of her gown.

"You will not win," she said to me.

"We will," I promised, but my voice cracked in shock, in anger, in outrage.

She began to point to me—and Farstryke Castle exploded.

The Tower stood by the fountain, his mobile phone in his hand, his finger poised above a button.

For a long, long second, Lady Time froze and stared at the rising hellscape of flame and smoke. Her hands fell to her side in shock.

It was our moment to attack, and I didn't hesitate. Her grip on me had faded, so I raised my sabre at her and aimed for a headshot. At the same time, beads of mercury-like magic formed around the Tower's cocked arm.

Lady Time screamed.

Her power was in the sound. The ground underneath us buckled as an earthquake spread outwards in a blast radius. A crack of stone—the loudest sound I'd ever heard in my entire life—was followed by a falling building to my far right. A wall of dust and debris blew toward us like a nuclear cloud. Lady Time screamed again, and the dust reversed course and flowed backwards, toward my advancing allies. Toward *Brand.* I felt Brand coming toward me, an angry and inexorable force.

And again Lady Time screamed. It felt like my body was being pulled apart. Nothing should be that strong; nothing should have that much power.

On the other side of the square, the Tower had been knocked to his knees as well. Our eyes met across the shaking city.

He gritted his teeth, bowed his head, and called on his Aspect.

True night spread from him. It swallowed every source of light—the glow of a burning car, the flagging bolts of lightning, the electrical fires of the fallen building, Lady Time's glowing nimbus. It felt like the end of the world. It felt like the end of all creation. It was one of the most terrifying things I'd ever seen or felt, and all my emotion flatlined into a single feverish note of fear.

The Tower stood. He walked toward Lady Time, and the emptiness of the universe walked with him.

"You found . . ." Lady Time said, then coughed blood onto the ground beneath her. "You found the masks, didn't you?"

Lord Tower looked down at her.

"It upset you," she laughed. "I saw. Your pet is your weakness, just like that castle may have been mine."

She turned her head and looked straight at me. She winked a wrinkled eyelid, a grotesque parody of coyness.

The world broke apart into gray and white static, and I broke with it. The last thing I heard was Brand screaming my name, and strong arms grabbing me from behind.

Smell.

First was smell, a single sense from a body with no identity. I could smell wet grass and burning wood.

And that thought—*I could smell*—was a brick of consciousness. A piece of who I was. With it came touch. My fingers were grasping wet, muddy turf. Everything ached, including my eyes. They felt dried and gummed as I forced them open.

"Rune?" someone moaned.

I rolled to my left and saw Addam. Had he shouted at me? Or was it Brand? I couldn't feel Brand. *I couldn't feel Brand.* Was Brand . . .

Against the protest of sore muscles, I rolled to my other side, which revealed a new slice of lawn. There was a small building at the end of it. The grass was short and rough, the type you saw by shorelines. I rubbed my hands in my eyes, trying to clear my blurred vision.

Things came into focus after that, and I saw something that didn't exist. Not with fresh paint. Not without wood rot, not without missing shingles and a scabrous roof. It just wasn't possible—the carriage house had not looked like this in decades. It wasn't possible. It wasn't.

A man stood outside the building smoking a cigarette. He faced the ocean, his back to me.

The silhouetted tips of a hare mask rose above his head.

THE CARRIAGE HOUSE

The man in the hare mask goes back inside the carriage house.

"We need to be quiet, we need to be quiet," I tell Addam. It sounds like I say that all at once, but I don't. I repeat some words over and over, and there are whole spaces of white noise between syllables where I think I'm pausing, but I'm also shaking and scratching at Addam's hands and muffling screams in my palm.

I press into the ground not just for protection, but because I have the crazy idea I can dig a hole in the earth and hide in it. But the soil is hard; there is rock only a few inches below the surface.

Addam is saying something about bleeding, but I'm running, because I can't hide in the earth.

I run away from the carriage house. Away from whatever is inside. Away from this memory.

There is soft crying in the distance, even now failing to a dying gasp. There is the smell of burnt flesh on the wind.

I run up the slope and away.

"RUNE!"

Someone was gently shaking me as I came back to my senses. "Addam?" I mumbled.

"Yes," Addam said, and there were tears running down his face.

We were near the base of the mansion, off the path and near the forested fenceline. There was a body lying about twelve yards away just outside the reach of the guttering torches. Arrows stuck from its back.

Further along, around the bend in the mansion, I saw a low, inconstant orange light. They'd burned many of the bodies that night, including my father's.

"I don't," I said, but my voice was a croak. I cleared my throat. "I don't know what this is. This can't be real. We can't really be here."

"She is Lady Time," Addam whispered. "Are we so sure of that?"

"I can't . . . I can't feel Brand. I can't feel Brand. What happened? Do you remember what happened?"

For the first time, I really saw Addam. He had a long, reddening cut down one side of his face, the blood barely tacky. I made a sound of panicked concern and reached for a Healing sigil.

He touched my wrist gently. "It's fine. I healed our wounds while you were . . . indisposed."

I saw my hand. My fingertips and nailbeds were covered in dirt and throbbing with a bad sunburn. One nail had gone black, with purplish blood pooling underneath it.

"This isn't real," I said. "This can't be real."

"It feels real. We can hear things. We can *feel* things—we are not ghosts. Is this . . . Rune, this is the night your throne fell. Isn't it?"

"I can't be here Addam," I said, and hated the sharp, rising whine in my voice. "We can't be here."

Nearby were the glass doors, just off the largest patio. On the other side was the solarium from my childhood. There was a body splayed out on the table, and the tablecloth was soaked to scarlet.

The world shuddered around us. I couldn't begin to explain what the sensation felt like, other than the world shuddered around us.

"It is gone," Addam gasped. "Rune, look, the body just over there—it is..."

He trailed off.

I saw two things then. One, the body I'd seen dead on the ground was gone. And second, a young man I knew, a stable boy named Gregor, limped down the path and collapsed in the same exact spot. He had arrows sticking out of his back.

"Is this real or a . . . a simulation? Did it just rewind? Or . . . or loop back?" He put his hands on my shoulders and forced me to face him. "I must scout the area and look for a way out."

"No," I said, but louder. Because Addam must not see anything else. He must not be allowed to see anything else.

This new surge of panic mimicked rational thought, but there was nothing rational about it. "No, Addam! We need to get back. They need us in the fight. She killed *Judgment*. The Tower needs our help."

"I know, Rune. I will find a way out."

"Addam, no, please no. Stay here. Stay right here!"

"Rune—"

Any measure of control was slipping through my fingers. *He must not see anything else!*

"Don't," I said, and tears ran down my face. I could taste them on my lips, feel them dripping off my jawline. "I can't. I can't stand. This. Don't look. Don't look Addam, not if you love me, not if you want me in this world. I won't survive this if you walk away."

Addam stared at me with an expression I'd never seen on his face— whatever lay beyond shock. I think I'd just told him I'd kill myself, and I think he believed it.

"I won't," he whispered shakily. "I will not. I will stay here with you. I'm not going anywhere. It will be fine. We will be fine." He came over and hugged me.

He said things that may have been soothing. I didn't hug him back, because this couldn't be happening. This couldn't be happening.

Then Addam lifted his head away from me, staring at something over my shoulder. His next words were soft and fragile. He said, "I do not understand."

I pushed away from Addam and looked.

Brand had walked out a patio door, much further along the side of the mansion. He began making his way down the pathway. He barely glanced at the body of Gregor as he stepped over it. While his features were lost to the darkness, I knew he was young. Fifteen years old—he would have been barely fifteen years old.

Brand walked around a bend toward the carriage house, vanishing from sight.

"I do not understand," Addam finally said. "He was hurt. That is what you told me, yes? That night, Brand was wounded and unconscious, and with you. Then he woke up and saved you. What is—"

I tried to inhale but nothing reached my lungs.

Addam took a step toward the path. I don't even think he realized he was doing it.

Everything I loved was there, in my brain, like a photo slowly being leached of color, turning brittle, flaking away, scattering into irrevocable loss. There was no coming back from this. Addam was seeing this and it would trigger what I had always feared. People would find out. It would be the end of everything. It was the death of my world.

I was the boy crawling in the safe. I was the boy crawling in the safe.

"Breathe," Addam begged. He was at my side. I was on my knees? I think I'd fallen to my knees. Addam said, frantically, "Please breathe, Rune. What safe? What are you talking about?"

I cannot . . .

"Rune, you are with me, we are together. This is not real. Listen to me, Rune, I am here, we are together, we will be fine."

I cannot survive this twice. This is the death of my world.

Inside me was a power. The Majeure. I couldn't feel it, I'd never used it of my own conscious will, but I'd seen others use it and knew it was real.

I said to it: *Save us.*

The entire world lit up in X-ray shades. I could see the line where these captured minutes of horror ended, and something fierce and unlivable began. The timestream was there, its current not liquid and lazy, but roaring through the universe like a blowtorch flame.

There were paths to and from this place, and they had been walked before. The power inside me told me so.

I reached out a hand and—

* * *

On a roof.

We were on a roof.

There were small tables covered in heavy white cloth, and the settings were sterling silver. Some of the tables were occupied with people talking over drinks.

"Oh, excuse me, sir," a waiter said. His face had that startled look that humans adopted when they refused to admit that something magical had happened—such as two men suddenly appearing right next to them.

I moved in an unsteady circle and saw the Empire State Building. But it was all off—it didn't match my expectations. The city looked too much like New Atlantis, all stone and brick and marble.

And the people? They wore old-fashioned dresses that fell to their ankles, and bespoke suits with fussy vests and ties.

In the middle of the roof was a small building that might have housed the stairwell and elevator apparatus. Shade fell off one side, and the tables there were empty. I staggered in that direction so that I could get a corner to my back. Addam, just as shocked as I was, followed.

On the way I bumped into a weird sculpture of blown glass. It toppled off its stand and shattered on the ground. The horrified waiter came over, pretended he wasn't pissed at me, and shooed us away from the shards.

I reached my corner and pressed into the wall, glad for the solid protection against my back.

Trying to make sense of this, I watched the waiter go to an antique rotary phone, maybe to call for help. He flicked the receiver in frustration, then bustled through a door into the rooftop's stairwell.

Minor annoyances were beginning to break through my shock. My fingernails still pulsed with discomfort from Addam's healing. One of the nails was torn, and I wanted to tear a piece off with my teeth, but I couldn't, because they were coated in fucking apple bitter.

That made me think about Brand. I started crying.

Addam whispered more comforting words and hugged me.

I took advantage of those minutes to focus on my breathing. To lock memories back where they belonged in the basement of my brain. To remember that we were not safe. People I loved were not safe. Breaking down was a luxury that had too high a price tag. Plus, I'd more or less tossed an emotional shitstorm at Addam, and he deserved better.

"I'm okay," I breathed. I pushed away just enough to stare into his burgundy eyes, which also swam with tears.

"I'm okay," I lied again. "I just need to . . . focus. On this. Where are we?"

"New York," Addam said. "But not the present. And not . . . truly the past."

I wiped a hand across my eyes, but kept the other around his waist. "He . . . the waiter. He saw us. He reacted to us. Why did you say not *truly* the past?"

"The sun is strange."

I looked up. The overhang of the rooftop structure sliced the sun in half, but I understood what Addam was saying immediately. In the middle of an evenly blue sky—as perfect as a fresh brushstroke of paint—was a rectangular smudge of yellow. It didn't hurt to stare at it.

There was the bang of a door opening. The waiter stumbled back into view, clearly upset. He stared down at the broken sculpture, and then at everyone around him. Our eyes met and he came over, saying, "Sir, did you just walk up the stairs? Was there a . . . a . . . barricade there? When you came up?"

"What do you mean, a barricade?" Addam asked.

"It just . . . there's . . . it's like it just ends. The stairway. It just ends in a wall."

The world shuddered. The waiter disappeared from where he stood, and reappeared by a table of customers on the other side of the roof. He wrote down their order on a leather-bound pad.

"The sculpture is whole again," Addam whispered.

"It's a loop of time. It's like it's been cut out of reality. I saw that, when we . . . when we . . ."

The things on the other side of the basement door in my head began to pound and kick and grasp for freedom.

"When we left . . . Sun Estate, that loop of Sun Estate," I finished. "I saw where we were. It was a bubble of time, with clear barriers, separate, from whatever the fuck the timestream even is."

"And you took us here," Addam said. He didn't meet my eyes as he said this.

"I did," I said.

"You had a sigil spell conveniently stored to navigate the timestream," he added.

It was not a question that expected an answer. And it was not an answer I was allowed to give. Speaking of the Arcana Majeure was verboten. No one from Sun Estate, outside Brand and Anna, knew what it was or what it meant.

"You've seen me do impossible things before when I was upset," I said carefully. "It's like that, Addam. It's something Arcana can do. Is it okay if we don't talk about that?"

"What may we talk about? You mentioned a safe?"

I pushed away from the corner and detangled myself from Addam. Nearby was a railing heavily stylized with beautiful art deco stonework. I went to it, feeling the grain of the rock under my hands. So *real.* But the more I looked, the more I saw the absence of things you'd expect.

The city was there—this older version of New York. But where were the cars in the streets? Where were the people in the windows? Where was the sound of rush hour? What I saw was immaculate and detailed, and wholly devoid of habitation. Like a stage backdrop.

"The boy in the safe," I said when Addam stepped up to my side. "I suppose the boy in the safe is just something that haunts me. I saw it as a ghost on the *Declaration*—you remember, the first time we searched the battleship? It was horrible, and I think my brain turned it into a metaphor for terror."

"Not terror," Addam said. "Resignation. Defeat. Rune, were you so upset because of what you saw? Or because I saw it, too?"

I let a long minute stretch out.

"People," I said, and my voice broke.

I let another long minute stretch out. "People think I'm nuts to let Brand badger me the way he does. They don't understand. They can't. Too many of them don't have Companions or know what it means to have one. I can't read his mind, but I always know how he feels. I always know I'm the most important person in his world. I always know that his smartass comments are grounded in one single concern: me. That I'm okay. That I'm safe. Do you know what that means? When I can listen to what Brand says and know there's no real bite to the words?"

"I imagine you find him quite funny," Addam said quietly.

"He's a fucking riot. Sometimes it hurts trying not to laugh out loud. I never get tired hearing what he'll come up with. Through all the darkness. All the horrible times? I've had the most extraordinary life because he's in it."

Another minute began to stretch, but I broke it, and said, in a faltering voice, "I cannot lose him."

"Would it surprise you to know that I cannot bear the thought of losing Brandon either?" Addam asked, and his voice faltered too.

I clumsily moved my hand along the railing until I was touching Addam's own hand. We stood like that for a few long moments.

Finally I cleared my throat and said, "I promise, Addam, you didn't see what you think you saw. I know that I need to explain it. I know. But not now."

Addam curled his fingers around mine. "It shall be so, then."

"Maybe we can just focus on whatever the hell is happening to us? I'm good at that sort of stuff."

He squeezed the fingers, just enough to make my healed damage throb. "You are more than just good. You will unravel this puzzle and get us home."

I breathed in through my nose and slowly exhaled the tension, letting it whistle over my teeth.

"Let's call it a time loop," I said in a stronger voice. "Like a memory cut out of sequence and preserved in the timestream. I know Lady Time built that loop for me. She threatened as much in the Manse—she said something about building a hell just for me. And I could see the path she traveled to and from it. Just like I can tell she's been *here*. So this loop is important to her. It's not for me. We need to figure out what it meant to her."

"Are these . . . people?" Addam said, lowering his voice. "Are they real?"

"I don't think so. I think they're just echoes of who really existed in the loop when it was severed. Imprints. And even at that, they're limited. The waiter tried to go downstairs, but there was a barricade. A barrier. Let's say that's the edge of the time loop. The thing about loops in general is that everything in it follows the same path over and over. Right? I don't think they can see it—these ghosts. And they don't understand what's happening when you push them off their tracks."

"So we will look around," Addam said.

"We look around," I agreed. "Because I'm starting to wonder . . ." I looked up at the smudge of yellow that poorly aped our own sun. "I saw the timestream. It's vicious. It's not like a river, it's like a lava flow. I don't know how I'd survive in it for long. But we're surviving *here*, right? What if this is how Lady Time survived the timestream? Not just this, right here, but something *like* this?"

Addam studied me for a few seconds, and some of the grimness lifted from his half smile. "Hero," he murmured.

My cheeks heated, so I hid them by doing a quick turn to study the layout of the roof. "It would be a weird way to survive. Imagine if you even spent a day here. The entire world would just be a . . . what? Ten minute loop? Twenty?"

"No one is sitting there," Addam said. He pointed to a corner table near where we'd arrived. "It's warm and not in the shade, and no one has sat there—which means, quite possibly, no one *ever* sits there when the loop works as normal. If it were I, I would try to find spots like that."

"Smart, Saint Nicholas," I said.

We walked over to the other corner of the roof, past the waiter, who now seemed more surprised by our clothing than our sudden appearance. It had to be the 1940s or 1950s.

As we got closer to the empty table, I realized that Addam's instincts had been sound. Because this table was not like the others. There was only one place setting—the second lay shattered on the ground. The tablecloth was askew. I put a hand on the corner that was rumpled and felt indentations in the table. Grasping the edge of the cloth, I pulled it aside, and saw deep, senseless gouges in the wooden surface.

"It seems unnatural," Addam whispered. "Was this here when the loop started? Is it always here when the loop starts?"

"Imprints . . ." I murmured. "Imprints upon imprints. Use a record long enough, and you can wear new grooves in it. What if—"

I saw Vadik Amberson sitting on the other side of the roof half a second behind my own instincts, which already had me brushing a finger along my backup Fire spell. The magic hissed to life around my hands as I aimed my arm at him.

People around me saw this—saw a man with flames forming around his outstretched palm—and began to scream and push away from their tables.

And half a second after *that*, I realized that this was not my Vadik. This Vadik was young, and his face didn't have the unwrinkled agelessness that came after rejuvenation treatments.

I flicked my hand and banished the Fire.

"Good heavens, that's the new magic act from the Edison Hotel Arena!" Vadik said loudly to his dining companions—all young, all male, and none with the telltale glimmer of magical potential. Humans.

Vadik made his way over to me, telling people along the way that the "show was opening next summer."

"Is he an imprint too?" Addam said in a side whisper.

I didn't have time to answer. Vadik had reached us. He gave our clothes a quick, incredulous look, grabbed my shoulder, and roughly turned me so that we faced the street.

"What game is this?" he hissed. "Are you insane? I speak for a Greater House, and there will be consequences for this."

"I speak for the Arcanum," I said. "I *am* the consequence, little spirit."

He furrowed his eyebrows at this. It seemed to mean something to him, for just a moment, but then the trouble washed away into an unsettled confusion. "I do not understand."

The loop would be resetting soon, and I had an idea. "You are Vadik Amberson."

"Do we . . . Apologies, have we met?"

"Your father is the head of your household. You serve the Sun Throne." *My father.* For a second, my heart just ached. *My father is alive in this era.*

"You are in America for schooling?" I said, raising the lilt to a question.

"I do not understand," he said again, but with less attitude.

"What is special about this place?" I asked.

"New York? My family has always schooled in America. We—"

"Here. Right now. *Here.* What is special about this place?"

"Look here, who—"

Fuck it, I thought. I called on my Atlantean Aspect.

Flames rose off my sleeves. They licked harmlessly at my bangs, and singed the stone beneath my feet.

Perhaps it was the Aspect of the burning man—my father's Aspect. Perhaps I looked enough like my father in this day and age. But Vadik made the connection I wanted him to make, and sank to his knees.

Now people on the rooftop really started to scream. Addam stepped to the side to grab the waiter's hand before he could toss a pitcher of water in my direction.

"Vadik Amberson, *answer me!*" I roared.

"I don't understand what you want, my lord! My father lets the penthouse below, we can go there now and discuss—"

The world shuddered, and I snuffed my Aspect before the loop began again. I'd never tried to drop my Aspect so quickly, and I didn't like how it felt—like swallowing burning hot coffee in your brain.

"Follow my lead," I told Addam, wincing. "We need to move quickly."

I walked over to where young Vadik was seated, oblivious to me once again. He saw my approach in his periphery. A look of modest surprise became a lazy smile. Not the full-grown leer of his future self, but dickish enough.

He was about to say something inane, so I whispered in his ear, "I am an envoy of the Sun Throne. We will speak in your penthouse apartment now."

"What—" he began.

"I will not repeat myself," I added. I straightened up and began to walk to the stairwell door.

Vadik scrambled away from the tables, making abrupt apologies to his friends. He circled around me to take the lead and held the door open.

The stairs were spotlessly clean and smelled like beeswax. As Vadik moved down the steps—with anxious looks over his shoulder—I asked, "How long have you been sitting at that table?"

"An . . . hour? An hour, my lord. Can I ask—"

"No. Is anyone in your apartment right now?"

"No, my lord."

"Does Lady Time have a key?"

"Does—" the question so surprised him that he lost his footing and bumped into a wall. Addam had to grab his sleeve to keep him from slipping off the step.

"Did you say *time?*" he asked incredulously.

"Thyme. Like the herb. Hurry up, move," I said.

We rounded a midflight landing. Down another short flight of steps, a corridor branched from the stairwell. There was only one door, painted yellow and gilded in goldish metal.

The key lock on the door was broken, and it was partly ajar.

"That wasn't like that earlier," Vadik said. There was a sort of disorientation in his eyes not unlike drugs. "But it's been . . . It's been a long time? That's not right."

Addam made a point of brushing past me to enter the apartment first—which was just like Brand, and my heart ached again. I followed without concern for ambush, though, because I already had an idea what I'd see.

The penthouse had a small foyer that opened into a respectably sized living room. A small kitchen was set behind an island, and the door to a bedroom was open.

Every mirror in the apartment was smashed. Odder yet, the glass beneath each lay in a pile far too deep for a single mirror.

The bed was made.

The cupboards in the kitchen were open and empty.

There were deep gouges along one wall—burn marks, fingernail scratches, missing chunks of plaster.

"By the River," Vadik whispered.

"Was there food in those cabinets?" I asked him.

"Was there . . .? Yes. Yes, there was. Am I under some sort of attack?"

"Have you ever let a woman stay here?" I demanded.

"I have invited certain . . . female acquaintances over," he said. The confusion in his eyes deepened, and a flush was creeping from his neck.

"Tell me about the old, powerful woman," I said.

My raised voice startled him, and his eyes began to dart back and forth in genuine fear. "There . . . She was . . . I don't understand. I do not understand what is going on."

"Are you a principality, Vadik?"

He laughed crazily. "A principality? Me?"

"How long have you conspired against the Sun Throne?"

He lifted up his hands and backed away. "My lord, I swear, I have been loyal to my house and court. I do not understand what is happening!"

I made a sound of dismissal and exchanged a look with a curious Addam. "He won't have any useful information. He doesn't know yet."

"Know what?" Vadik cried.

"What you'll grow into. That you will betray your Arcana. That you will become a murderer and a rapist. That you will conspire against the Arcanum."

"Who are you?" he demanded. "What is this?"

"*This?* I'd be less concerned about this false present, and more concerned about your real self's future. Or lack thereof, as soon as I get back home."

He stared at me, and I stared back, and I watched something not unlike understanding pass between us. "Am . . ." he said, and licked his lips. "Am I real?"

"No," I said.

He turned and ran. I heard his footsteps hit the stairway, and from the sound he went downward. He'd hit the barrier soon enough—and hopefully busy himself with panic until the loop reset.

"What do you see, Rune?" Addam asked in a hushed voice.

"More of what you saw outside," I said, because he was the one who'd started my theory. "If you were stuck in a loop, you'd want to hunt down areas where you didn't need to constantly explain your presence. Let's say the loop is ten minutes—or even twice that. The boundaries of the loop extend down to this apartment, which Vadik wouldn't visit in the normal course of the loop without prompting." I pointed to the bed, the cabinets, the mirrors. "Shelter. Food and water. And that? The damage? That's repetition. Maybe that's what happens when you repeatedly carve a new imprint into an existing imprint."

"You think Lady Time took refuge here?"

"Until she broke it or ran out of resources," I said. "Until the loop was . . . exhausted? Of food at least."

"The questions you asked. Vadik does not know Lady Time at this point in his life."

"Yeah. But I don't understand the rest." I looked at Addam. "There were other paths in the timestream, leading to and from these loops. I could see them when I . . . did what I did. Took us here."

"Can you see any path that leads out of the timestream?" he asked.

"Not yet."

"So we follow another path."

The world shuddered, and the open door flickered to its original slightly ajar position.

"We follow another path," I agreed.

"Shit," I whispered, as my leg buckled under me and I dropped to the pavement.

My physical senses assaulted me. The grit of cobblestone. The smell of horse shit and straw. The air was heavy with a bitterly acrid smoke—like a car had belched exhaust right in my face.

Addam helped me off the street just as a horse and carriage barreled by, the horse giving an alarmed bray.

"I'm okay," I said—or at least I pushed the syllables out in a gasp. "Just need to get my breath."

Addam was turning in a cautious circle, absorbing whatever dangers might be around us. "This is the past, but something is amiss."

"Where?" I asked. "Where are we?"

"London, if I'm not mistaken. Like a page out of a Charles Dickens novel. It was harder to take us here, wasn't it?"

I waited until my breathing had evened out. "No. It's just tiring. I'm already feeling better though."

I stood straight and felt the bones in my back crack in relief. It took all of one glance, though, to understand why Addam was so tense. The busy street around us was touched with troubling details.

The sky was a patchwork of pixelated clouds against a single, deep blue, like a cheap computer graphic. The Victorian-era street looked almost real, but the people about it were milling in chaotic patterns—not flowing along sidewalks.

"This crowd is mafficking, innit?" a woman said, grabbing my arm. "Please, sir, if you're going inside, deliver this for me? My lady sent me t'do it, but I'd rather stay out here."

She shoved a calling card in my hand. The edges of it were threaded with colorful green floss. The young woman ran off, and I looked around to see that Addam had moved us to the steps of a graceful brownstone.

Across the road was a row of less pristine houses and a small boy in heavily patched clothing was standing on a wooden box, clutching a stack of papers in his arm. People were milling around the base, unusually attentive.

"His majesty's health is a'proving!" the child yelled. "He's taking walks in the garden! Court to be held at Saint . . . Saint James . . ." He edged away from a man who tried to grab at a paper. His voice jumped to a squeak. "On June 4th!" He started to sob. "I dunno what you want! What do you want?!"

"What is happening? What is wrong?" a man shouted, while a woman shrieked, "This is the work of the devil!"

Another man grabbed the boy by the collar of his jacket and swung him to the cobblestone with a thud. People began grabbing for the papers in a desperate mob.

A wave of magic washed past me, and Addam strode forward with his hand outstretched. The newsboy was jerked into the air Telekinetically and soared toward Addam, who snatched the boy in a two-handed grip and shoved him behind us.

The world shook. The boy and the mob vanished, as did the flossed calling card in my hand. We remained standing where we were—but everything else reappeared in different places. Across the street, the boy emerged from an alley, struggling under the weight of a bundle of news-print sheets.

"This loop is deteriorating," I said quietly.

Addam's jaw was like stone. I can't remember ever seeing such a hostile look on his face. "This is inhuman. This magic is obscene. Cruel and obscene. Whatever they are, these people, they *know* things are wrong."

"I know," I whispered. "We—"

"The world is ending!" a man shrieked across the street. He was ripping at the fussy tie around his neck. Dropping it on the ground, he grabbed a loose cobblestone from the ground and threw it into the window of a shop that said *Apothecary* in gold lettering. People began to climb into the shop and loot. One woman in particular—portly, with an underbite and a messy pile of black hair on her head—cackled at the despair around her.

"The timestream is filled with loops like this," I said. "I think we've guessed right. That these loops are expendable. That they become corrupted and break apart." Another piece of the puzzle drew my interest. "When we left the carriage house? And then the rooftop? I saw all these paths leading to and from other loops. Some were fainter than others. Maybe instead of following one of the brighter paths between loops, we follow one of the faintest ones?"

"Do you have the strength to do that? To do . . . whatever you're doing, to move us between loops?"

I heard the frustration in the words and realized, almost in surprise, that I was sick of keeping secrets from Addam.

The man had followed me into possible death. He was lost in the godsdamn timestream because of me. And here I was, acting coy about the very instrument that may save us.

"You deserve so much better than me," I sighed.

Addam saw the expression on my face and grew a bit alarmed. "Brand has spoken to me about this on many, many occasions. I am not allowed to speak about feelings while we're in danger."

I gave him a watery laugh and wiped my eyes. "Can you keep a secret, Addam?"

He dipped his chin.

"Do you remember when I broke apart Ashton's weather magic in the Westlands? Without using a sigil spell?"

Again, that nervous nod.

"It's an . . . ability. One unique to Arcana and principalities. One that *defines* a true Arcana and principality. It's called the Arcana Majeure. It means that I can use my own life's energy to power magic."

"Truly?" he said, almost a whisper. "This is real?"

"It is. And I never get back the energy that I use. It will cost both me and Brand. That's why the rejuvenation magic failed with Lady Time, Addam. She must have used the Arcana Majeure so often to survive the timestream that there is no youth to return to. It's that limitation—the drawback of the power—that makes it a secret, because it could be used against us. Brand knows, of course. And Anna, because she's used it too. But that's it, in our court. No one else."

"Thank you for trusting me with that knowledge," he said. "Though I must admit, it does not ease my mind. What is it costing you to bring us from one loop to another?"

"I don't know. That's why I think we need to be smart about where we go next. I'm going to follow the paths to the oldest point."

Addam shouted in pain. The world was spinning around me, and my mouth stung with acid—but I heard Addam's distress.

"—cave!" he was yelling. "Can you walk?"

I tried to speak, but bile just dripped from my lips. I let Addam drag me to my feet, and tried to move in concert with him.

The dirt path was the only thing remotely recognizable as even vaguely lifelike. I saw rain as sharp as razor blades, cutting slices on our exposed skin. A sky that churned with indigo thunderclouds. Chunks of earth—whole bites of rock and soil—spinning through the air like helium balloons. The air wasn't air, either—or at least the balance of oxygen and other compounds was off, so that every breath was laced with corrosion.

With a final grunt of effort, Addam threw us over a line of white stones, onto a dusty cavern floor. I felt my body pass through a powerful defensive shield. It was like a pane of glass holding the sheer insanity outside at bay.

"What by the River was that?" Addam cried.

"I have no fucking idea," I said with utter sincerity. "But what if this is what loops become? When they disintegrate enough? What if broken loops actually dissolve or return back to the timestream?" My brain throbbed with racing thoughts.

"Rune, you are speaking very quickly, and you are feverish. This is hurting you."

"I know," I said hoarsely. "Okay. We need to see where we are. I'm still hoping we learn something here."

"I will look around after I Heal us," Addam said. "You will sit down and rest. This Majeure you speak of? It's draining you. Let me do what I can."

There was a rocky ledge along the side of the cavern, which was lit up by a light cantrip that Addam had summoned.

After Addam Healed the cuts from the violent rain, I went over to a pile of leather and sacks that were messily laid on the ledge, and sat down. "Check the wardstones," I suggested. "Maybe you'll be able to tell who left them there? We can—oh, this is *a motherfucking body!*" I shouted and leapt up.

Addam grabbed me before I tripped. We both stared at the corpse on the ledge. Its skin was ancient and leathery, like an embalmed mummy. The fabric may have once been colorful velvet but had long since rotted to a threadbare gray.

"What is this?" Addam whispered.

Swallowing, I reached out to nudge the fabric around the corpse's neck. I had a sinking suspicion this might be the Lord Time who was known to have vanished in the timestream. If it was, he'd almost certainly have sigils or court symbols around his neck. But the neck was bare.

The skin on the corpse's lips split as they opened. *"Dominus Tempus sum."*

Addam and I both jerked back, and Addam even dropped an F-bomb.

A single desiccated eyelid opened as well. A bead of gelatinous fluid bubbled along a stretch of cracked skin.

"Dominus . . . Tempus . . . sum . . ."

"Is . . . he undead?" Addam whispered. "Is this a recarnate?"

"No," I said. I edged forward and touched the rawhide skin. I repeated, "No. There's a pulse. I think . . . he? I think he's been surviving in stasis. I've seen magic like this before."

"That is Latin," Addam said. "I studied it at Magnus—it was once a common language in Atlantis, much as English is now. I believe he said he is Lord Time."

"Appropinquo ad meam mortem. Prendas manum."

The words were growing fainter, the sound barely a breath through the ruined mouth.

"I am . . . approaching death? Take . . .? Take my hand?" Addam shook his head in frustration. "It has been quite a while."

"I'm going to touch his hand," I said. "There are ways of communicating by touch. Can you pull me away and break the connection if anything bad happens?"

The look on Addam's face was priceless, and even better, I could almost hear Brand speaking in my head. *By all fucking means, say IF.*

I blinked away the burn in my eyes and breathed until I felt steady again. There was a slight chance I'd begun to have a nervous breakdown, I thought. Wasn't it best that I acknowledged that? Would it have been worse if I didn't see that?

"Very well," Addam said. "But I do not like it."

I looked back at the corpse, with its sightless eyes and flaking, necrotic skin.

I touched his hand.

It was not a dialogue—just a string of ideas or facts that patiently unraveled into coherence. No single sentence that formed was made of just words. Whatever magic this was, it used my own mind to fill in the blanks. Meaning was conveyed by thoughts, feelings, shared human concepts.

He was barely sentient. He had a mind, and he had thoughts, but his state was closer to that of dreamlike than coherent. He was far past the point of recovery.

But even in his dreamlike state, he was responsive.

So I thought about me. My seal. My throne. I put the picture of a burning man in his head and remembered my vow. *I am Arcana. I am Arcanum. I am the Sun of Atlantis.*

And I asked him for his story.

At first, he was filled with braggadocio. He told me he was *{a golden crown}* – followed by an image of his crown sitting atop a mound of other crowns bent under his own crown's weight.

I pushed through that and forced thoughts of *family* at him.

He didn't know a word for daughter that I understood, but I saw a quick mental image of him kissing the top of a baby's head. I saw her grow to young adulthood in a *{a man puts his finger to his lips and whispers shhhh}* palace.

A secret palace?

The woman I called Lady Time was his daughter.

The cavern I was in? It was all that remained of a glorious citadel carved into and hidden in the side of a mountain in old Atlantis. Or rather, I saw the citadel as it appeared in a handful of minutes stolen and sealed into its own, separate world.

I think he meant a loop—he was describing the creation of a loop.

Entering loops properly took great preparation. I felt like a century passed as he conveyed the sense of that—many rituals required, many safeguards put in place.

When his court was destroyed, he'd fled into a *[a möbius strip, an endless shining strip—a loop?]* with his daughter. The lack of an *[a ship sinks an anchor into deep waters]* both weakened and trapped them. He expended all of his power simply to keep this decaying *[möbius strip]* alive. Without a *[a cast iron chain]* his abilities were *[an outgoing tide]*.

I barely grasped that.

He told me his daughter grew and left him. She had become great in power along the way: she was as a *{regal woman with a tall golden crown on her head}*. She found a way to breach the timestream, if not flee it. She formed *{two people laughing over a table, breaking bread}* across time, which she sought to turn into a *{that same image of a cast iron chain}*. Through these connections, she formed new loops, at the very least. She found a way to . . .

I had no parallel for the phrase or imagery he was trying to impart now. The best I could understand is that she found a way to survive among the dangers of the timestream.

Lord Time had been alone for decades of *{a minutes-long image of a small hourglass trickling to its last grain}*. Which I think I understood. From my perspective, Lord Time vanished into the timestream over a thousand years ago. His own objective experience would have been different, limited to the seconds and minutes of a mortal life.

It was growing harder and harder for him to exist, even while spending long stretches of time in a form of stasis.

He was ready to die.

He didn't believe he'd be able to wake up again, and his youth was lost.

His death would . . .

I didn't understand the image he imparted. In my head I saw a picture of the citadel, in full health, under a normal waking sky. Then I saw a picture of his withered body breathe one last time, and crumble into dust. And then I saw the citadel again, the real-world citadel, but there were tiny fault lines in it.

I stepped away from Lord Time, dropping his hand a little too quickly, because it hit the rock ledge with a tiny crack.

Lord Time's body shuddered with a dry cough. *"Cuique nostrum, ultimum granum harenae."*

"Did he speak to you?" Addam asked. "You were very quiet but did not appear to be in distress."

"Can I ramble for a second?" I asked. "Can you listen to me while I ramble?"

Addam simply stayed quiet and nodded.

"This loop—what we call a loop—came from old Atlantis. It was a slice of one of the palaces he lived in, or at least where he raised Lady Time in secret. Remember how Lord Tower only had information of male heirs? Wasn't it common in Old Atlantis to hide your real heirs, or foster them? For their safety?"

"It was," Addam said.

"So he did that. That's why we didn't know his real heir was a woman. And when he fled the fall of his court, he was desperate. He wasn't prepared. He wasn't *anchored*. So he couldn't get back out—it took all his strength just to keep alive.

"But this is where things get confusing. Or maybe it was confusing from the beginning. There's something I'm not understanding about entering the loop. He was very clear about needing rituals. And anchors. But there was also this recurring image of a metal chain."

"An anchor is attached to a metal chain," Addam suggested.

"I know, but the images were separate. That's important. I almost got the sense that the chain was a metaphor for a type of power. Or . . . a source of power?"

I knew a source of power like that, didn't I?

I'd lived my entire life at the end of a chain—willingly and happily.

"Brand," I breathed. "What if . . . what if I can find my way out by reaching for Brand?"

"It is a very good thought, Rune."

"We need to go back to where we started, though," I said.

Addam closed his eyes. "I'm so sorry."

I was too. But it was inevitable. My entire life, one way or the other, had been a narrowing gyre to that bloody carriage house.

* * *

We appeared in the loop just as the masked man walked back into the carriage house.

When I first arrived, I'd tried to dig a hole in the ground to escape. Even remembering that was painful—remembering that I fell apart so quickly, and that Addam witnessed it.

"I . . . need a second," I said.

Addam pulled me close, and we huddled together under the overhang of the nearby tree line. I pressed into the line of cologne he'd drawn across his jugular in another life. I inhaled sandalwood. And breathed.

"Rune . . ." Addam said after a while, his voice hushed. "Brand is coming. The . . . the Brand of this loop."

Was this what heart attacks felt like? This sharp ripping in the middle of my chest?

I turned in Addam's arms so that I could see what he saw.

Last time, we'd watched Brand leaving the mansion, stepping over the body of a stable hand. And now there he was, walking down the path that led to the carriage house. He was so crushingly young. He was so bloody *young.*

Brand stopped under the door's lintel. He stood there, straight backed, straight shouldered. Moments later, a man in a hound mask met him at the door.

The man put his hand on Brand's shoulder and gave him a friendly shake. He said something we couldn't hear and drew Brand into the building. The heavy door shut behind them.

Desperately, I watched Addam's face. As closely as I'd ever studied anyone's reaction before.

Addam stared hard at the door. "Oh, no," he finally whispered. "Oh, no. Oh, Rune. He's under a spell, isn't he? He's been compromised."

I covered my face and exhaled a pent-up cry into them.

"Does Brand know?" I heard Addam ask.

"Nothing. He remembers nothing. It's a . . . it's a geas—a mind control spell. And it's my fault."

I pulled my hands away, wiping my face as I did. "Will you come with me?" I asked. "There's a break in the forest over there. We can talk there without . . . this. Seeing this."

We walked. The tree line curved around a bend, opening into a small hidden copse.

I didn't hear sounds of dying or death. Couldn't see the carriage house. Couldn't even smell smoke riding the air. The grass was thick and springy, and for a few minutes—just a few minutes—I remembered the times that Brand and I had found a patch of shade and sprawled out. It was an odd and wholly unexpected memory of my childhood.

"Stop it," Brand said crossly, nine years old and full of temper.

I couldn't stop laughing. "But it was funny. Did you really think magic runes were named after me?"

For a second, his temper split into something vulnerable, because of course he'd thought that something big and real in the world could be named after me.

"I bet there will be fighting moves named after you some day," I said.

"I'm ready to make one up right now," he said, pissed again.

I swallowed. My hands felt wrong—I didn't know what to do with them. So I put them in my pockets and sat down, as Addam sat across from me.

"I don't think I can do this alone anymore," I said hoarsely. "It's not safe for anyone if I'm this vulnerable, and I have so much more to lose. So many people could get hurt because of me. And if I need someone else to know these secrets, then I pick you. Because I know you'll be there for me. And I want you there. I want you in my life from now on."

He reached up and brushed a lock of hair from my forehead.

"I'm not just saying this," I swore. "And this may not be the right time to say that. But I swear it's true—I pick you, Addam. I . . . I even bought a ring. I bought a ring for you."

"I know," he said.

I blinked at that for a while to make sure I heard right. "You know?"

"Yes, Hero. You hid it in my sock drawer."

"I did?"

Addam nodded, his fingers still in my hair.

"Does this mean I've been wearing your socks?" I asked.

"I do enjoy the way your mind works. But let's not talk of a ring now. You do not need my love, you need my strength. It is yours."

And he leaned in and kissed me. It was not a passionate kiss; both our lips were dehydrated and chapped.

"This isn't fair to you," I whispered.

"If you are picking me," Addam whispered back, "then I am picking you. We can trust each other."

And, oh, it stung. It stung that a moment like this would be ruined by what came next.

So I did what I always did when I couldn't avoid the truth—I tore the Band-Aid off and hoped I didn't take much skin with it.

"There are nine people in that carriage house with masks," I said. "And I can tell you who three of them are."

"Three," Addam repeated. "Vadik. Cornelius. You . . . already knew of another?"

"Ashton."

Addam jerked back from me.

"Ashton is in there," I said. "Or an echo of him, at least. He's wearing a cat mask."

"Ashton Saint Gabriel was one of your attackers," Addam said in a voice that began to shake.

"Do you know what happens next, Addam? After the shock wears off? You'll start dissecting everything you know and putting it in a new context. You'll feel guilt. You'll feel stupid. You'll probably try to hate yourself for bringing Ashton back into my life—which is wrong. You'll want to tear the memory of Ashton apart to see where it leads, to figure out what else you may not know. He'll stop being just the man who tried to kidnap and hurt you. He'll stop being just the person who was your business partner. He'll become so much more. Something between an obsession and a fear, maybe? I don't know if there's a word for it."

I took a ragged, hot breath. "Do you understand why I'm telling you this? This is the *least* of my secrets."

"I understand," he said after an emotional pause.

"No," I said. "You don't. You can't. Are you sure you want to know more?"

"I think you need me to be sure, which is the same as being sure. I will not, I cannot, walk away from this."

I lowered my head as I spoke, letting my hair hang in front of my eyes. The knife in my heart began to turn and turn and turn.

"I was . . . an asshole," I began.

Then I stopped and had to breathe for a bit, only the breaths were hot and damp and felt like tears.

"I was such an asshole when I was fifteen," I told him. "I was rich. Pampered. Spoiled. So many people loved or looked after me, and I took it all for granted."

"Brand gets mad when you speak like that," Addam said, leaning toward me and into my hair. "He says you are too hard on yourself."

I took a few more deep breaths.

I said, "I love you. I really, really love you, Addam. But I can't tell you this story if you insist on defending me. I am not the hero. Not then. I was not the good guy. I can't tell you this if you try to make me one."

He tightened his arms around me but said nothing.

"I," I said, and it was right in front of me.

How would I even put the truth into words?

"I . . . would sneak out. It was like a game. Could I get off the estate without Brand knowing? Or my father, or the household guards? I would sneak away to spend time with Geoffrey. Or to drink in the Bowers. Scions would go there at night to drink and get high. I usually was caught sneaking back home—but I was good at sneaking out. And . . ."

Oh, Brand.

"Brand," I said, my voice cracking. "I didn't know this. Not then. But he snuck out too and would try to find me. When . . . If he . . . If he knew I was gone? He would sneak off the estate to find me."

Brand. My Brand. My fifteen-year-old Companion on the city streets at night. Alone. *Alone.* Because of me.

"That's how they got him. They . . . I don't know who was behind it. I don't know who led that group. I don't know *why* they did what they did. I just know *how.* I know how they broke the Sun Throne. I know *how* it was done. Brand let them in."

Addam wanted to say something. Anything, I think. But he stayed quiet, his arms heavy around me.

"They took him one night," I said, and my voice broke, "when he was out looking for me. They put him under a geas. They found a way to peel back whatever emotion they wanted—loyalty, love, even our bond. They subverted a Companion bond. And in the place of these emotions there was only what they wanted. What they needed.

"Everyone wonders how the assailants could get past my father's wards. They wonder how my father was so easily attacked. He was dragged from his study—his sanctum, one of the seats of his power—and burned alive.

"But that? That was the easiest part to figure out, once I knew Brand was under a geas. They used him. They caught him, and fucked with his mind, and used him—because I didn't have his back. He was the most precious thing in my life and I left him to wander the city at night *alone.* And all he wanted to do was find me, because he was worried about me, because . . . he *missed* me. He wanted to be included."

I covered my face for a minute until I could breathe again.

"Brand knew how to let visitors past the wards. Everyone loved him. There's not a single person who wouldn't have gone with him, if he asked. Getting my father out of his tower would have been simple. All they needed to do was have Brand knock on his door. Maybe cut himself, and cry out for help? Or just say I was injured? My father wouldn't have expected an attack—he would have opened the door in a heartbeat.

"I'd snuck out that night. They caught me when I was reentering the house. I don't even remember much of that—just waking up in the carriage house. I can't . . . I can't open that door. What's to gain by opening that door? I don't gain anything by telling you my shoulder still hurts from when they took a pitchfork and pinned me to the wood frame of the sofa. Because. I was. Struggling. In the beginning. I can't . . ."

"No," Addam said, and I could tell by his voice that he'd started crying too.

"But I'll tell you this much. He saved me. *Brand saved me.* He always saves me."

"He fought the geas?" Addam whispered.

"He did. But only after . . . hours. Hours passed. And I was . . . close. To giving up. But they said if I did, they would cut Brand's throat. So I stayed alive, and they would hurt me, and heal me, and hurt me. And eventually that was worse than death. I just wanted it to end. I . . . In the end. It was too much. And I couldn't . . . I almost lost the world, and the world almost lost me. But I guess the universe wasn't satisfied with that, because . . . something . . . happened.

"I could feel it happening. I could feel it *when* it happened. The talla bond."

Addam sucked in a startled breath.

"You asked me once if Brand is my talla," I said in a shaky voice. "I didn't lie. I didn't. I don't know why, but when I woke up in the hospital, the talla bond was gone. I haven't felt it since. I think the geas corrupted it somehow. Broke it? I don't know. But for a few minutes, Brand was my talla, and that connection severed their hold on him. As soon as the men in the masks were occupied with something else—they would come and go, and gather in another room to talk—but—as soon as they weren't looking—Brand grabbed me and ran. He knew ways to get us off the property quickly, and he ran for help at a neighbor's door."

In the distance, someone screamed. Had I heard that before? When I first arrived? The idea sickened me. Constant torture, time and time again, an undiminished echo.

"Tell me what you're thinking, Addam," I begged.

And I heard the grief in his reply. "You had a talla bond. And you . . . lost it. You lost your talla. I think my heart is breaking. I cannot begin to imagine what it must feel like to know that. To bear that knowledge."

"I live with it because Brand is still here. And you're here now, too. I lost the talla bond too quickly to even understand what it meant. And maybe . . ."

No.

No maybe. No what if. No.

"What I have now is enough," I said firmly.

"And Brand remembers none of this. Which scares you. You worry he'll blame himself if you tell him," Addam said.

"Oh, Addam," I said, and it felt like I was swallowing glass. Like the words were literally scoring my throat. "There is no *if*. He can never know."

"But—"

"He'll kill himself," I said.

And there it was.

There it was.

If I had to sum up twenty years of near-constant fear that my secrets would be revealed, it was this simple, simple statement.

Brand would kill himself.

"He," I said, and fuck, more tears. "If he remembers? Letting the killers in? That alone will destroy him. I know him, Addam—I *know* him. The guilt will unmake him, and that's just the beginning of it, because he'll figure out soon enough that the geas could be repeated. Or maybe it's still there? That he could be compromised again. Brand has spent his life eliminating anything that threatens me. What do you think will happen once he considers himself the threat?"

"But . . ." Addam tried to argue. Helplessly. He didn't see the larger picture—how could you, unless you'd had decades to consider it from every vicious angle?

I tried to keep the panic out of my voice, but the rest pushed loose in a flood. "And that's even assuming he'd survive learning about the geas. A geas is built from magic and logic. It could have built-in commands to protect itself. If Brand becomes aware of it—if it's still there—it could just break his mind.

"And what if *other* people learned about this? If people know Brand was a link to what happened? Hell, if the *Arcanum* knew Brand was a link? They would fucking dissect him. They would break his mind apart.

"I'll lose him, Addam. If this gets out . . . if people figure it out? I will lose him. And I don't think I'd survive that. So all of this? Me keeping this secret for decades? *I am fighting for our godsdamn lives.*"

Addam slid around me until we were facing each other. When I didn't meet his gaze, he put his hands on my shoulders and squeezed gently. He said, "Tell me how to save him, because I will not lose him either. Do you understand? I have chosen my family. He is my family too. So tell me what we do next."

I searched myself for anger. Or conviction. Or anything, anything at all, that would drive me from this place.

Addam's grip tightened, the grip of his metal hand almost painful. "*Rune.* Do you remember what you told me in the Westlands? When I was too nervous to store magic during the siege at my family's compound? You said all emotion is fuel. Fear, joy, grief—it is emotion, and all emotion is the raw power behind our sigil magic. So *fight,* Rune. Fight now. Use this, use this strange Majeure of yours, and take us home so we may protect Brand, and the children, and those we love."

"I . . ."

"No. No thinking—just react. *How?* How do we leave here? I know you have a plan."

"I'm going to destroy the loop," I said. "Then use the Majeure to reach for Brand. I'm going to pull us to the exact moment we left, if I can."

"And you believe that will work?"

"I . . ." I closed my eyes, swallowed, opened them. "I keep picking apart one of the last things Lord Time said to me. I think he was showing me what happens when a loop breaks. I think . . . when they break down, they're connected again to the real world. Or a real *when*."

"Are you sure we'll appear when we need to? What if we return to this moment in our timeline?"

"Brand is my chain back to our own when."

"Then break this world and take us home," he said fiercely. "If Lady Time can do it, so can you. Whatever *chain* she used to bring herself to our time, it cannot possibly be as strong as the one that links you and Brandon! For gods' sake, Rune, he was your talla. *Brand was your talla!* They took that from you! They took it! Are they to pay?"

My Aspect rose.

Addam's face began to glow orange, and I saw flames through my eyes.

"Yes," I said.

"Then *take us home!* You know it can be done, so *do it.*"

I brought my arms around his neck, and fire spread along our clothes. It felt like armor, not pain, not damage.

Slowly, together, we rose to our feet. I saw the world around me—this perverse, stolen slice of my worst reality—and imagined it as a snow globe resting in my palm.

I flexed my fingers shut and reduced the globe to atoms.

Everything that was, is, and will be roared around us in an almighty storm, and I reached for my Companion.

I am standing in a hallway, looking at everything and nothing, until I remember how to breathe again. A lithe, brown-skinned fae with corn silk for hair is waiting outside a closed bathroom door.

I am in a rundown bar with a deer's head on the wall.

And I am in the Westlands, and Ashton has told me he wore the cat mask, and my vision is filled with black fireflies.

A woman's voice.

She says, "You must fight the current."

My chest is burning. Only it is cold, not heat. Lady Death is in front of me, and her palm, brimming with Frost magic, is pressed over my shirt. The fabric glitters with rapidly melting, crusty ice.

I am on my knees on a dirty cement floor in a sunken mall, and a metal pole is in my stomach.

"Even your instincts are stubborn. I said to fight this current, child!"

I say, dizzily, in a Westlands forest, "What just happened?" I look around, but don't see any danger. We aren't under attack. Were we? My stomach churns with nausea as Addam tells me it's snowing.

"You are hurtling through moments of déjà vu, through moments of shock, through times when you lost seconds and minutes. Fight that, child—reach for him. Reach for him *and where he* stands."

I absurdly wonder where my coffee is. When did I lose my coffee? I press my eyes shut, because the circles on the Tower's war room table are still blinking and there are so many of them. I—

"Do as I say!"

Brand watches me with worry across the war room table, and wishes he'd brought more than one cookie.

And oh, the waves are approaching New Atlantis, and they are the size of mountains. But Brand is there, and he gives them a look as if his annoyance could burn water.

I am on the floor of the Sun Estate courtroom—*my* courtroom. A shining liquid is eating through my Shield—Brand is there and he's yelling for a healing sigil.

There, I think. *There!*

"Yes," she says.

That happened just days ago. I'm close and I scream Brand's name. I scream his name, and I scream his name, and—

THE WESTLANDS

It took a few long seconds to realize I was on grass, not pavement. And I smelled pine trees and plants, not car exhaust or battle smoke.

In front of Addam and I was . . . a Westlands compound? No. *My* old Westlands compound—a residence I'd leased out for funds since the year I bought Half House. Why the hell had I appeared back there?

Across a huge lawn, I heard raised voices verging on screams. There were a lot of excited people, and I knew them all.

"Oh, shit," I whispered to Addam, and maybe exhaustion made my words slur a little. "Are we presumed dead?"

And then everyone was running at us, and no one was as fast as Brand. He crossed the length of an American football field in a dead sprint. A few yards shy—tears streaming down his face—he stopped and leaned over, hands on his thighs.

I started to speak and he said, in a congested voice, "Don't. Don't, it won't be as funny as you think, and I deserve a moment of fucking silence. Just nod. Is this you? Is this happening?"

I nodded.

He launched at me and put me in a full-body hug. Quinn slammed into Addam. Max slammed into me. And then things got confused as everyone else refused to pick a favorite, so we became one massive ball of arms and legs and sobs.

But at the heart of it was Brand and me. His forehead was against mine. I whispered, "We always come back."

"We always come back," he repeated. He craned his head to look at me. "You look like you're about to faint. Are you going to fucking faint? Right now?"

As I slid into unconsciousness, my family kept me standing.

* * *

I slept for a very long time.

Every now and then a rational thought scurried within arm's reach. I trapped the intruding idea like a small animal and told it to fuck off, then sank back into dreams.

Eventually the questions I had became more important than the answers I was ignoring. My eyelids opened, and I saw the same thing I remembered first in life: the face of my Companion.

Brand was asleep in a chair pulled up to my bed. I was in my old room at the Sun Compound in the Westlands, uncomfortably and implausibly and literally. There was even a *Wham!* poster on the bloody wall.

Brand opened his eyes and stared at me.

"The kids," I said. "Anna and Max and Quinn. They're back? All of them?"

As if bored, Brand said, "Yes, they're okay. Yes, we're in our old Westlands compound. Yes, we're all here, all safe, all together."

"Why are you talking like that?"

"Because you ask this every time you almost wake up."

"Oh," I said. "What if I'm really awake this time?"

"You always say that too."

"Well, what *haven't* I said that would convince you?"

Brand's sleepy gaze sharpened, and he sat up in the chair. "Rune?"

There was a hollowness to his cheeks that hadn't been there before. "I scared you," I said softly. "You look like shit."

"I look like shit? Me? Jesus fucking Christ, you look like the tree that Charlie Brown dragged home." He put a hand on my forearm and gently squeezed. For a moment—only a moment—his expression cracked open into something raw and hurt. He whispered, "Rune." Then his gruffness fell back into place and he withdrew to pull out his phone. "I need to text Addam. He's been freaking out too."

"How—" I cleared the dust from my throat. "How long?"

"You and Addam vanished for two days. And you just took another two-day nap."

"You let me sleep for two days? Why didn't someone heal me?"

"Rune, I swear to God, I am trying to be nice to you, but you need to not say stupid things. Heal you? Layne used their immolation magic. Addam has stored and used so many Healing spells that he's practically pissing sunburns. Ciaran used his magic, the Tower used his . . . Yes, we tried to heal you. You just needed time. Addam said you used the Majeure a lot."

"Oh, shit. Does the Tower know I told Addam about the Majeure?"

"He kind of figured it out when Addam wasn't asking questions on how you pulled a miracle out of your ass. He didn't get mad. He just wanted you to wake up."

"What—"

"No," Brand said. "Start small. New Atlantis doesn't exist, as far as you're concerned. We can debrief on that soon enough." He cracked open a bottle of water and poured a few inches into a glass.

My father's seal was on the glass. My seal? My seal now, but his old stemware.

I was able to take two sips before it felt like I'd start coughing. I nodded gratefully and sank back into the pillows.

"How can there still be a *Wham!* poster on the wall?" I asked.

"Because you've always had shitty taste in music."

"I object, and you know what I mean."

"Turns out," he said, "that the Tower was the one paying the lease. All this time. He was keeping the compound ready for when you needed it again. It . . . worked out. It worked out well. We needed a place to be together."

I opened my mouth and he glared, so I didn't ask why that was. I said, "What did Addam tell you? About where we were?"

"He told us about the loops. Which still sounds batfuck crazy. And he said Lady Time tried to trap you . . . then. Back then. But you destroyed it and found us and came back."

"I found *you*."

His cheeks got a little red as he shrugged. He hid his expression in his phone, typing a message.

I pulled myself up against the headboard, spotting more details in the room. A purple octopus with singed arms wrapped in old bandages sat on the nightstand. A sleeping bag was laid out on the carpet in the corner.

He always did that when I was in really awful shape. A sleeping bag always appeared near my room. And he looked every inch of two nights on a hard floor.

"The corner?" I said. "Last time I was this bad, you slept across the threshold so the door couldn't open without hitting you."

He lifted narrowed eyes.

"Did you use the bathroom at least? Or are there water bottles filled with pee in the closet?"

He held the narrowed gaze another second, then a small smile flitted across his lips. He shook his head, because he knew what I was doing. "I'm okay, Rune. I'm okay now."

Salt bit at my eyes. I blinked the tears away. "I think I need to be okay now, too. I need to find out what's happened. Is Lord Tower here?"

"Yeah. He and Ciaran spent the entire two days you were gone trying to find a way to bring you back, because he still doesn't understand how fucking stubborn you are about doing it all yourself."

The voice in the light. She'd called me stubborn.

I'd forgotten about that. About her. But that wasn't the first time it had happened, either, right?

That was not today's mystery, though. And it scared me more than a little to even *imagine* understanding what it meant.

"Is your brain going soft again?" Brand demanded, more concerned than angry.

"No. I'm awake."

"Can we talk about the fact that you didn't tell me Ciaran was an Arcana?"

"It was his secret to share. Are you mad?"

"Yes I'm mad. Do you know how rich the Hex Throne is? What if something happened to him before he put us in his will?"

I grinned, picked up his hand, squeezed it. My smile sobered. "I really need the debrief, Brand. I have to know what's happening."

"You need to get better," he said firmly.

"But she hasn't been stopped yet. Has she?"

Grim faced, Brand shook his head in a *no*.

"I know how to stop her," I said.

Brand swore into his palms and began growling.

"And I'm in the best position to do it," I added.

It took longer than I would have liked to get out of bed and dress. At least my clothes had been cleaned and aired—though I caught a whiff of London's industrial-age pollution on my leather jacket.

I couldn't point to any one part of my body that hurt; it was just a general feeling of marrow-deep exhaustion. Brand suggested three times that I give up and rest until I finally threw my shoes—with the annoying laces—at him.

Barefoot, I opened the bedroom door, and immediately faced a small child on the ground.

Corbie blinked at me, jumped up, and wrapped his tiny arms around my leg. Then he backed away and stared at the ground, while making occasional furtive glances at the room behind me.

"You really want that octopus back, don't you?" I asked.

He nodded so hard his teeth clicked.

"It did its job. I'm better now. He's all yours." I ruffled his hair as he ran by.

"The others are in the common room," Brand said. "Addam is waiting for us."

"Is there food?" I asked.

Brand opened the backpack he'd brought with him and snagged a plastic chip bag. Or at least it made reassuring crinkle sounds like a chip bag. But there was a picture of salted and dried seaweed on the front.

"You need vitamins," Brand said. "This shit will help you get better quick."

"Not when I break my leg searching every top cabinet for a packet of sugar," I said, and ignored his hand.

There were only two wings to the compound—living space was often kept modest in the Westlands, with the strongest design elements going toward perimeter wards that kept homes safe. Considering that, plus the fact that it had been over thirty years since I'd last been here, it was a good hiding spot if we needed one.

"Are we on the run?" I asked. "Are we hiding here?"

Brand said, "Eh," and tilted his hand back and forth.

We took a left, into an enclosed loggia that bridged the two wings. Heavy squares of canvas were folded on the ground next to uncovered furniture. The décor was sparse but striking. White paint, white plaster, and lots of crystals. My father had loved how light reflected off crystals.

"But . . . how long has the house been empty?" I asked. "Has someone made sure our defenses are all working?"

"I don't know," Brand said. "I try to make sure the windows are locked before I go to bed. Does that count?"

"Okay, you would have checked our defenses," I said. "Is Lady Death here? Is she okay? Damn, I forgot about Judgment. Judgment died . . ."

"She's fine, she's with the rest of the Arcanum, just hold your fucking horses. You've got a lot to hear. There's Addam."

Addam had opened a set of interior French doors at the end of the hallway. His eyes were only on me. And if I had to be honest, my eyes were only on him, because our experiences in the timestream raced to my attention.

Brand left my side and said something to Addam, who agreed with a nod. Brand closed the French doors behind him as he left.

Addam walked up to me—stopping just within arm's reach.

I didn't know what to say. And yet, that wasn't awkward. There were too many things to thank him for, so it all just got shuffled into staring at his face as he stared back at mine.

Finally he kissed my temple and said, "We will attend to sock drawers later."

He opened the doors, letting me pass first. The room on the other side was a modest-sized ballroom, but informally laid with warm wood floors, brick-red walls, and lots of plush sofas. My father had prized comfort in his common areas.

I had all of two seconds to see where everyone was standing. The Tower and Ciaran and Diana at a wooden table. Layne trying not to eavesdrop from an eavesdrop-able distance. Max and Quinn hunched over a leather journal. Queenie putting a bowl of pretzels on a sideboard. Anna on a chair with Corinne planted right behind her. That girl would have a shadow for *weeks*. Brand always did the same thing whenever I snuck—

My knees almost buckled as dark thoughts swept over me. The Band-Aid I ripped off wasn't going back on easily, and it'd taken more skin than I liked.

Then the two seconds ended, and I was swarmed with crying and laughing people rushing me, which helped push my shock away.

The reunion was short, and left me deposited on my own puffy sofa. Brand and Addam stood behind me, and the three of us faced the room.

Queenie was the only one who left—reluctantly, but someone needed to watch Corbie. I was a little surprised that Anna, Max, and Quinn were allowed to stay, but assumed they had information to offer.

"Aren't they punished?" I asked Brand and Addam. "Did I miss the punishment? Because Quinn has donut crumbs on his shirt."

"You should hear them out," Brand said. "But call them by their new job titles. Part-time Gardener Number One, Number Two, and Number Three. It's a six-month gig."

Quinn, immune to anything but silver linings, said, "I'm going to plant a butterfly garden."

"We should bring you up to speed," Lord Tower said.

Brand had mentioned that Lord Tower and Ciaran had worked two days straight to save Addam and I. I could tell by the dark, heavy bags still under his eyes. Not so much Ciaran, who'd used liberal dabs of concealer.

Lord Tower rose from his chair and said, "The children—", at the very same time that Diana rose from her chair, and said, louder, "I've prepared the details in a report, as any good seneschal would do for matters in her own court."

Lord Tower looked at the back of Diana's head. Diana didn't even flinch. And damn if he didn't give that a small, smiling nod of approval.

Diana continued, "The battle outside Farstryke ended shortly after you and Addam vanished. The barrier fell, and every Arcana present advanced. Lady Time took advantage of Lord Tower's immediate concern over you, and fled."

She continued. "The children were not harmed. They've been in our custody since the battle outside Farstryke, though there was an . . . incident at Magnus Academy. The children were escorted to Magnus to retrieve their things before being pulled from school, and Lady Time attacked. Ciaran saved their lives—and many others that day—but Magnus Academy was destroyed."

"I want to be homeschooled," Anna said immediately.

"Magnus?" I said in surprise. "Magnus was destroyed?"

Diana said, "Effectively. We believe Lady Time was specifically targeting our children. They returned with critical information that will help in whatever you decide to do." Diana, finally, turned and gave Lord Tower a patient look.

Lord Tower cleared his throat. "In the days since, Lady Time has launched a series of increasingly dangerous guerilla attacks. There's damage to the Convocation building. The subway lines were hit, and public transport is disrupted. The entire traffic grid has been compromised. There were separate attacks on the office holdings of the Dagger, Hex, and Chariot thrones—one building was destroyed in the small hours of the morning. And then, of course, the damage to Magnus Academy."

I heard a pained sound behind me. Addam. "She was definitely after the kids. That's why Brand relocated everyone to the Westlands. She must be aware that they learned far, far more in captivity than she realized. Their knowledge is dangerous to her."

"But she must know they would have told you anything important by now," I said. I looked over my shoulder at Addam. "Why would she continue to pursue them?"

"Lord Tower believes she thinks they wouldn't understand the gravity of what they learned. And to be honest, if it didn't match what you and I learned in the timestream, we may have missed it entirely."

A slow, grim smile spread across my face. "Tell me."

"We now understand the source of her extraordinary strength," Lord Tower said. "And if our suspicions are right, we've neutralized it, at least for the moment."

"The witch is running on fumes," Ciaran said. "It was all smoke and mirrors. We so easily believed that ancient Arcana were a different and stronger breed. It never even occurred to us that her strength came from the oldest of sources. She cheated."

"The chain," Addam said. "What we learned in the cavern? We think the chain was a necromantic ritual. She exponentially added to her ability by draining the lives of others."

"Disgusting," Layne said.

That sort of necromancy hadn't been permitted in settled memory. It wouldn't have even been allowed in Lady Time's natural era. Powerful Arcana abhorred any magic that leveled the playing field. They didn't need more power so much as they needed the teeming masses to be less powerful than them.

"We knew there was something important to her being moved into

Farstryke," Max said. "Something very expensive to build, and part of a ritual. And . . . she killed people. We know she killed people. We just didn't realize she'd killed them for this."

"I saved the boys," Anna said.

"You *found* us and got captured too," Max snapped back.

"How on earth did you find them?" I asked.

"Lady Time took our phones, but she didn't take these," Max said, and showed us a watch on his wrist. No—not a watch. It was a Magnus Academy communications device. It ran on internal servers, a closed network for school announcements and messaging.

"We have our units linked to find each other on campus," Max said. "Anna kept an eye on her unit until we passed close enough to the surface to transmit a signal. We didn't have one most of the time—we were in this bizarre underground compound in the Warrens. Nearly the Lowlands! But anyway, that's how she found us."

"I left a note!" Anna argued, when I opened my mouth to ask why, why, why she didn't tell one of us this. "And you were all in the Warrens already looking for them!"

"Enough," Corinne said, putting a firm hand on Anna's shoulder.

"The point," Diana said, "is that they came back with vital information on how Lady Time accrued such a reservoir of magic. Lord Tower, unknowingly, destroyed that equipment when he destroyed Farstryke Castle. Lady Time's recent change to guerilla tactics suggests this assumption is correct. Her source of power has been compromised. Why else these hit and run attacks?"

"What does the Arcanum think?" I asked.

"They're having the same discussions we've already had, now that we've passed them this new information," Ciaran said. "Many are gathered at the Magician's compound in the Westlands to prepare a battleplan."

Ciaran immediately grimaced and sighed. *"My* compound, I mean. *My* compound with *my* fancy defenses and *my* silverware and *my* horrific houndstooth drapes that should have come with the eyeballs of the official who chose them."

"Subways. Traffic. Office buildings." Gears came to life in my head. "She's isolating people. Targeting the symbols of scions? What reason did she give for destroying Magnus Academy? She wouldn't have told everyone the truth."

I saw a smile spread across the Tower's face. "Well spotted. Brand?"

Brand's cell phone edged into my eyesight. He'd queued up a video—Lady Time's green lipstick frozen in a deflated O.

I pressed the arrow.

"*—bring it down. All of it. Every symbol of their corrupt lives, their corrupt wallets, their corrupt compounds! We have burned their exclusive school. Pulled down their businesses. Buried their leader! The time has come to redistribute the fruits of what it means to be an Atlantean. Why do you have no sigils? Where is your protection? It lays ahead, for those who follow me!*"

The video ended, and I handed Brand the phone.

"It's all a lie," Quinn said quietly. "That's not how she thinks. She's using them. And they deserve better. A lot of her followers are just hungry. And scared."

"Do we have any idea where she is?" I asked. I looked straight at Quinn. "Do you? I mean . . ." I wiggled my fingers above my head.

Quinn shook his head *No.*

"She isn't underground anymore," Lord Tower said before I could ask what Quinn meant. "Mayan is running our intelligence operation from the Pac Bell. He's convinced she's hiding in the city. We can find no traces of her underground anymore."

"But her followers are everywhere," Ciaran said. "They have brought protests to the streets."

"Please tell me the Arcanum isn't moving against them," I said.

"There was some discussion about that," Lord Tower said, "but I persuaded the others that Lady Time's propaganda effectively counters this move. We must not appear to be the enemy she describes."

"That won't last long," I said. "Will it? They'll want to attack someone."

"The Arcanum meets tomorrow," Lord Tower said. "With your permission, they'll meet here, and decide on the next course of action."

"There's a *here* because of you. Thank you for that. For keeping this compound for us. I didn't realize my tab was as big as it was."

"There is no tab," he said, and Brand was not exactly able to cover up a snort with a fake cough.

"Rune must eat and rest as much as possible until then," Addam said.

"I'll go light the grills," Max offered. "Queenie has hamburgers and hot dogs."

My mouth filled with saliva so quickly I barely caught a string of drool. I gave Brand as pathetic a look as I could muster. He dug around his backpack, produced an actual small bag of chips, and tossed it into my lap.

"Food, and then you nap," he said severely.

"Who are you?" I asked.

He ignored me and ordered our new gardeners to go help Queenie.

We linked two picnic tables and a folding poker table on a lawn I barely remembered—tucked behind my father's old wing. The reality of the compound challenged my height-disadvantaged memory from when I was younger than ten.

My energy was flagging by the time the meal was over, but I did walk Layne over to a bare-branched shrub that I thought they'd like. It looked dead, but if you broke a branch it sprouted fluorescent blue flowers, their fat petals heavy with sap. The sap was used to heal light burns. Layne was delighted, so Brand stomped over and insisted Addam also point out every plant on the other side of our wards that had teeth and digestive systems.

The strangest thing was the dynamic between Addam and Quinn. I hadn't realized how thoroughly pissed Addam was at his brother. He barely gave Quinn a polite thank you when Quinn ran over with a plate of food, which got cooler with each nice thing Quinn tried to force on him between every bite.

Finally, Corbie provided accidental entertainment by eating a box of chocolate donuts when no one was looking. He got sick and ran around with his hand slapped over his mouth. Everyone shouted helpful, contradicting advice on where he could throw up, which led to the demise of the poker table. Corinne took him in for a nap, with Anna in firm tow.

"You need to sleep," Brand said, dropping into the chair next to me.

"I'm fine," I said.

"Not only are you out of breath, but what breath you do have smells like Doritos."

"This sucks," I sighed. "Can't I just get back into shape with a montage? Start a thirty second timer and connect your Bluetooth."

"Perhaps Brand is right," Addam said. "I'll walk you back to your room."

"Saint Nicholas," Brand said angrily.

"I will *deposit* him in his room," Addam amended. "Rune, please. Rest now while you can. Tomorrow will be long."

Which is how I got wrapped in a blanket and hustled off toward my bedroom. I acted grumpy about it, but as soon as we entered the loggia between buildings, I said, "We're going to make out a little, right?"

"Or talk for a moment?" Addam suggested back.

"That is not the multiple choice answer I'm going with."

He put his arm around my shoulder and squeezed. "Everyone was very worried as you slept. Lord Tower insisted the recovery was not unexpected, but . . . we were worried."

"Is it weird that being forced to take a nap makes me want to exercise?"

"Yes, Hero." Addam looked like he wanted to elaborate, but Anna ran up behind us.

"Where's Corinne?" I asked, which earned an immediate sour expression.

"I told her I'd stay inside. I wanted to talk to you." Usually she had no problem aiming her frown at me, but this time it sank to the floor.

"Am I about to get angry about something I already knew about, or is this a fresh source of sleeplessness?"

"Why don't I leave the two of you," Addam said. "Rune, we can talk later."

I watched him reverse his path through the house, a little sadly. I didn't really have the energy to fool around, but I was hoping he'd volunteer to be a pillow.

I opened the door to my room and ushered Anna in. "I can't help but notice you didn't answer my question," I said.

"Maybe you won't get angry," she said, walking past me with arms stoutly crossed over chest. "Maybe you'll be proud."

"No, I'm pretty sure there's going to be anger," I said. "You snuck off the estate and ran straight toward our enemy."

"Aunt Corinne already got mad at me about that. She's already said everything."

She jumped up on the desk to sit, and started kicking her legs. I took the bed, but stared at her, frankly, until the kicking stopped.

"She told you what you did was thoughtless, right?" I said. "And that you endangered others? That you divided attention during a dangerous moment when an enemy was moving against us?"

Anna let her hair fall over her eyes.

"But she probably didn't tell you that you shamed her. You truly shamed her, Anna. She's your Companion. You snuck away on her watch and humiliated her."

"I—"

I raised my voice, but not angrily. "Don't you know what that means to a Companion? How hard they are on themselves, when it comes to our safety? They deserve so much better. She deserves so much more from you."

One of her hands went up, vanishing beneath the curtain of black hair. She made a wiping motion over her eyes.

"Did you use the Majeure in front of Max or Quinn?" I asked her quietly.

Her head jerked into a nod.

"Did you explain what it was?"

"No," she said quickly, and finally met my eyes. "I promise. I told them it was just a trick I knew. And we were in trouble—or at least, it kept us from getting into trouble. And it helped get the information that Addam and Lord Tower were so interested in. I promise, Rune."

The mattress was feeling very soft beneath my ass, just as the weight of all this began to lay heavily on my shoulders. "I feel like I'm failing you," I said tiredly. "I don't know how to make you understand. Anna, why would you put yourself in so much danger? Why?"

"Because I want—" Her mouth pressed shut, and furious tears filled her eyes.

"You want what?"

"I want to be your heir."

"You *are* my heir."

"You just said that to protect me," she accused. "I want you to *want* me as your heir. I want to show you I can do it."

Every now and then, insight sounded like a click. Like a puzzle piece firmly laid into place. This time? It sounded like a head slap. "You think I need you to *be* an heir. Now? Already?"

"Yes, and look what happened!" she said. "I heard the Tower and Ciaran talking. They were wondering if I'd be Lady Sun."

That was when I realized how very, very badly I'd failed her.

All this time I thought she was resisting my exhortation to be young and happy, and she was the smarter one. She was worried what would happen if *I wasn't there.* Why hadn't that even occurred to me until now? What had the poor girl gone through, with me vanishing for two days, and her with the mantle of heir on her shoulders?

"I am so sorry," I whispered. "I should have prepared you better. I'll do better in the future, I promise, Annawan. But I'm not planning on leaving you anytime soon. And . . . do you have any idea how strong you are—how ridiculously strong?"

"But I'm not strong enough!"

"You will be. I promise. You are going to leave your footprints over this entire city someday. I'm not sure I've ever met anyone with your potential. But I don't need you to be that person *now*. I need you to be a teenager. This will never, ever happen again. Not ever, Anna. You'll be young again—you'll rejuvenate and live a long, long life. But you'll never, ever get to be *this* young again. I want you to enjoy this time in your life. I promise, someday, I'll need you. And when I do, I'll call on you."

"But what if—"

I held up a hand. "But I will also train you. Just in case. I won't fail you like this again. We're going to start spending a lot of time together, you and I. Deal?"

She wiped her nose on her sleeve and her shoulder slid into a shrug—but the tension had left her.

"I sent some videos to your phone," she mumbled.

"You need to stop taking pictures when Corbie hurts himself."

"No, *videos*. I recorded Lady Time when she was acting like an asshole. Quinn's right—she doesn't care for anyone except herself. She's using all those people from the Revelry, and the people who live in the underground. I was thinking maybe they need to see the videos."

I stared at her as the cogs in my brain spun. *Maybe indeed.*

"I'll look at them. But after I take a nap."

She jumped off the desk and bolted for the door.

"Hey!" I shouted after her.

She froze, turned, regarded me nervously.

"Thank you for wanting to be my heir," I said.

She stared at me, puzzling why I was thanking her. I held out my hand for a fist bump. She ran back over and hugged me.

"I knew you'd come back," she whispered. "I told them you'd come back. Maybe later . . . if it's okay . . . I can show you something?

My Aspect, it's . . . something. I mean, it turns into something. Is that okay?"

Her Aspect was already developing. I'd had glowing orange eyes into my thirties, and her Aspect was already developing form. Pride stuck in my throat like a lump. I could only nod.

She raced off.

I made very, very sure that Brand was asleep before I ventured out of my room, early the next morning.

He would not stop sending me back to bed to "take a nap." Before supper. After supper. When I wanted a midnight snack. It was like a godsdamn monkeypaw's wish.

Since my bedroom was on the first floor, I climbed out the window. It was very warm—the Westlands had settled on summer today. I didn't put on shoes, and dew-covered, bioluminescent weeds in the lawn outside the south wing lit up in response to my footsteps.

It was so beautiful. The sun felt perfect. It was heavy and gold, not long after dawn. My entire, tired body seemed to drag through it like syrup.

Not far from my room was a series of stone benches facing a small, sunken amphitheater. My father had always filled his court with creative types—for centuries we'd been the throne of artists. I'd vaguely appreciated that when I was younger, though looking back, as an adult, I wondered how much of his true face my father showed the world. There had been a reason he was best friends with Lord Tower.

A half hour later, Brand sat down on one side of me, and Max sat on the other.

"Sorry," Brand said. "I know I'm nagging a lot. Did you want to be alone?"

"No. You can stay. I miss my brothers."

Max seemed confused for a moment until he realized I meant him, and the smile that broke through the frown was worth a fortune. Brand grunted his lack of displeasure—and handed me a hot coffee.

So we sat and relaxed. Above us, in the wet morning air, a rainbow formed. It was the sort of thing that could only happen in the Westlands. The colors were as thick as crayon strokes. Even as we watched, a bird flew through it, emerging on the other side dripping in yellow and green.

Then whatever the colors were made of hardened, and the bird thunked in a dead drop to the amphitheater's basin.

"Fucking Westlands," Brand said.

I sipped coffee.

"Are you guys still mad at me?" Max asked.

I took the question seriously, because I knew the answer would mean a lot to him. "The way I see it, you didn't have much of a choice. Quinn did. Anna did. But you had to make a quick decision about whether to go with Quinn when he turned himself over to Lady Time, or stay behind."

"So I did good?" he said hopefully.

"If it were 1876, sure," Brand said. "Now there are fucking phones. You should have called us."

"Quinn can be pretty unstoppable when he wants to be," Max said. "That's not an excuse! I know. But . . . thanks. I tried to do what I thought was right."

"You don't get points for trying," Brand said. He leaned forward to look at Max. "You don't get points because you're willing to follow someone into the dark. You get points when you do it even knowing what's waiting for you. I'm pretty fucking proud of you."

Max started blinking quickly. "I'm going to see if I can clean the bird off." He got up quickly and went down the amphitheater steps.

"That was a nice thing to say," I murmured.

"It's true. He has good values. He'll have his hands full with those two, though."

I leaned against his shoulder. "I need to tell you my plan."

"You never tell me your plan in advance," he said.

"I need you to understand what's waiting in the dark this time."

ENDGAME, PART I

The Tower stood on the patio outside my father's study. My study. I watched him through a window as he evaluated an idea I'd just put before him.

Inside, Brand was trying to get me to eat more seaweed. I picked up the package and laid it firmly in the middle of the table as an offering for anyone else who liked chewing on salty Scotch tape.

"Fine," Brand said. "Convalescence is over. Please, go ahead and let the fucking world revolve around you again."

I couldn't help it. I gave him my smallest smile, because who was he kidding? It never stopped.

He tried to hide his own *you're-such-an-asshole* smile by pulling out his phone.

I leaned back in the chair and gave an upside down, backwards look at my father's stately desk, which took up the entire rear of the study. I reached out and plucked something off the edge of it. "Look," I said to Brand. "We own a snow globe of New Atlantis."

His eyes darted from his phone to my face, deciding whether to play. He could feel my emotion underneath it: *isn't-it-weird-to-be-back-here-this-is-all-ours.*

He snatched something off the bookshelf behind him. "Look," he said. "We own a small reproduction of a . . ." He squinted. "Old whaling boat, because apparently your dad liked memorializing the awful shit humans used to do."

"Can you believe we have this place back? We have a vacation home. And who do you keep on texting?"

He'd gone back to his phone. "I'm seeing if I have a signal. Addam should be here for this talk."

I was surprised because that didn't surprise me. They'd spent the days before I woke up shouldering all the decisions. There was a new partnership between them, and I liked it. It felt like the catch of a necklace you'd been struggling to click closed.

The patio door opened, and Lord Tower returned to the table. He left the door ajar, which was nice, because the breeze was warm and carried the scent of cut grass. Brand had found some old push mowers hidden behind the big riding mowers in the tool shed, and handed them off to Max and Quinn. Anna got handed hand pruners and sent to trim weeds from a thousand paving stones.

"So it'll work," I said.

"In theory," Lord Tower sighed. "It's not a new idea. It actually has a name, if you're old enough to have learned it. Arcana once called it the Quadrans Gambit. Lady Death used it herself to help end the Atlantean World War. The question is whether the situation is urgent enough for such measures now. I worry that you've let Lady Time into your head."

"That's my secret," I said. "My head hasn't been a very safe place to be for a long time now."

Brand rolled his eyes at that, a little angrily. And the Tower didn't seem satisfied with flippancy either. So, in a more sober tone, I added, "How many people died when Magnus Academy was destroyed? When Lord Chariot's office building came down? The subway attack? Every day we take to flush her out of hiding brings the potential for a new attack. We may win the war but lose the city. Or we may lose the support of the people we're supposed to be fighting for."

"It's as if someone taught you well," Lord Tower said wryly. He sighed and pushed away from the table again. "I think you should bring this before the Arcanum—or at least those of us meeting today. If you'll excuse me, I'm going to see if Ciaran and Mayan have arrived with the others."

As Lord Tower exited, I swung my worried gaze onto Brand, who was still staring at his phone screen. "What are you worried about, Brand?"

"Too much is coming down on your shoulders. Why can't the Tower do this? Or Lady Death, if she's used this Quadrans strategy before?"

"You know why. I'm in the best position. Do you think I can't do it?"

Now he raised his eyes, and he was pissed, because I was forcing him to defend me. "You know as well as I do that you're at your best when your back is to the fucking wall. Life has made pretty fucking sure of that. And look where we are. Rune, fucking wall. Fucking wall, Rune."

Thinking of necklaces had made me remember something. I pulled one off my head, undid the clasp, and let the sunburst sigil that Lord Judgment had bought me slide into my hands. Then I handed the dwarven steel chain to Brand. "Here. I don't need this for the sigil."

"Oh," Brand said, a little nonplussed. "Really?"

"Well, you hinted pretty strongly that someone could choke me out with it."

"Choke *someone else* with it," he said. "I said *someone else*. But . . . yeah. This is cool. No one makes chains like the dwarves. Thanks."

"I bought a ring for Addam," I blurted.

Brand's eyes flicked up to me. "Wait. You told him about the ring? You asked him?"

"What the hell," I said, genuinely aggrieved. "How did you know about it?"

"You paid for it with our joint credit card, you asshat."

Trying not to sound too guilty, I said, "I probably should have talked with you first."

"Why? You didn't think I knew you were heading in this direction? Rune, you're not even an open book. You more or less engrave your intentions on the wall with firebolts. Did you think I'd be mad?"

"Are you? Mad? Or anything?"

"Addam is giving up his court. He's giving up—everything. Everything he grew up with. He's entrusting us with his brother. His *kid.* He deserves better than to go around being introduced as your boyfriend. Being your husband or consort or whatever term you use will mean something to him, just the way that me being your Companion means something to me when I'm introduced."

I could only stare at him for a few seconds as the back of my eyes started to burn, maybe with some tears, maybe with some Aspect. "I don't give you nearly enough credit, do I?"

"If I had the money, I'd pre-order and chisel it on your fucking tombstone," he replied, but his lips twitched as he said it.

I wiped my nose discreetly and blinked out the patio doors, until the emotion subsided. "Are there any Companions coming today except for you and Mayan?" I asked.

"I don't know," he said. "Why?"

"Because I want you in the room. When the Arcana meet. Let Mayan know—it's nonnegotiable. Though . . . maybe not Corinne. It's not that I don't trust her, but we're going to be talking about the Majeure, and I may be in enough trouble that I confided in Addam. If he was wearing my ring already, it'd be different—they have rules about who can know. But I want you and Mayan in the room, because you deserve it. It's time things change."

"Like any of you have a choice about things changing," Brand snorted. "I can already see it. They're all acting officious arguing about attendance, and Ciaran is standing on the table tilting the chandelier so that the light hits him just right. Companions in the room will be the least of it."

Brand swung a look to the doorway a few seconds before I heard the approaching click of boot heels.

Zurah stopped, stared at me, and crossed the room at a swift stride. I stood up just in time to be engulfed in a tight, fierce hug.

"You did it," she whispered. "You came back. Remind me never to bet against you, little brother."

She put an affectionate hand on my cheek. Her fingers smelled like beeswax and honey.

"Now," she said. "What's this I hear about a plan? Because I'm moving into this compound until matters are well and done."

* * *

Someone had lugged extra chairs into the family room and pushed the sofas into a lopsided circle. Most Arcana who were on Nantucket soil were at the estate, excepting those maintaining order inside the city.

Lord Wheel remained in continental America, outside the barrier that protected us against the human pandemic. Lord Devil and Lady Moon remained likewise removed.

Lady Justice, Lord Strength, and Lord Hermit represented the Moral Certainties, while Lady Temperance and Lady World oversaw concerns in the city. We had Hierophant and Chariot, but not Priestess. Lord Tower and Lady Death were helping me as hosts.

And we also had two Magicians.

One of them was standing in an adjacent parlor by himself, looking at old photographs on a mantle. I was alone at that point—Brand had gone ahead into the family room to speak to Mayan. Even though I had only the barest of familiarity with the Magician—or whatever I was to call Warren Saint Anthony—I felt obligated to welcome him, despite the awkwardness.

"Did you know him well?" I asked politely, seeing that he held a photo of my father. It was taken not long before the Sun Throne fell.

"Everyone knew your father," the Magician murmured. "He insisted on it."

He put the frame down and turned to me. He was a handsome man— ridiculously square jaw and just the right kind of height, somewhere between imposing and looming. How had I never noticed before it was as if he'd come straight from central casting? Ciaran couldn't have picked a more convincing puppet.

"I wield the Majeure," he said abruptly, annoyed at whatever emotions he saw scrolling across my face. "I have the power to run a court, as Arcana or principality. It would be a mistake to underestimate me, Rune Sun."

"I try not to do that," I said. "And I don't want us to get off on the wrong foot. I know this is strange."

"Is it? Is it strange?" he said, only he wasn't really asking a question. "Because things felt quite normal and familiar until you came along. After all these centuries, I'm a bit surprised that *you* were the one to hound the secret from Ciaran."

"Me? Wait, what? This is my fault?"

"It won't be as easy as you think, installing Ciaran back into the court. Make no mistake, the Hex Throne will not easily respond to another's lead. You will not find it a steady alliance."

"Is that so?" Ciaran said from the doorway.

He wore a mustard-colored jumpsuit with a gold chain for a belt, and he sparked with the just-barely-visible glow of more than a dozen sigils. His bone necklace was intertwined with a string of pastel SweeTarts.

The Magician opened his mouth to speak, and Ciaran's eyes flared into liquid mercury. *"Attend me!"*

The Magician dropped to one knee.

"You are only my face and my voice, not my Will, and I will have you remember that," Ciaran said. "If—" He stopped and frowned. "What a strange sense of déjà vu."

"That's exactly what you said in Farstryke," I said. "Back when it was getting into your head? The day we found Addam. Huh."

"Good grief. I detest refried drama." He aimed a *tsk* at the Magician. "Well, that's you off the carpet. We'll continue our talk later."

Stiffly, with just a hint of angry, mottled skin at the neck of his tight cape, the Magician strode past us.

"It was the cleft in his chin that got him hired, wasn't it?" I whispered to Ciaran. "He looks like a movie politician."

"Don't be fooled," Ciaran sighed, glancing over his shoulder. "He has never been an easy ruse."

Then he rubbed his hands and clapped them together. "Enough of that. It is so very good to see you on your feet, Rune. I did try to spend some time with you—I have the most bawdy romance novel and thought you'd enjoy being read to while comatose. But Brand tried to stab me."

"He was worried."

"Yes, but just imagine if he picked up something more constructive, such as knitting. We'd be surrounded in socks and scarves instead of blood and Band-Aids."

There were things I needed to say to Ciaran, and this time seemed no worse than others. I went to the doors behind us and closed them. Ciaran raised an eyebrow and said, "Since you're not *that* type of fun, I find myself worried."

"I know what happened at Magnus," I said. "Brand and the others are trying to keep me from getting upset, but I've heard pieces of what happened when Magnus was destroyed. The kids were there, gathering their stuff before being moved into hiding. You saved their lives."

He opened his mouth to downplay it, so I held up a *wait* hand and said, "They might have died. Max, Quinn, and Anna may have *died* if you hadn't been there. I might have lost them. And they? They are such a big part of my world now."

Ciaran sniffed and fussed with the gold chain around his waist.

"It's important that I say this," I told him.

"It's not important, it's importune. I'm not doing this in my good eyeliner, Sun!"

I barreled over the objection. "I guess what I'm saying is that I kind of love you. You feel like family now. I hope you're all right with that. I really, really do. For gods' sake, I'm pretty sure Corbie gave you that SweeTart necklace, and that kid does *not* share candy."

Ciaran stayed quiet for a moment, and then raised his glassy eyes to me, within which swam sunshine. He'd always had mesmerizing eyes.

He lifted his hand to my cheek, not unlike Lady Death had just done. Only Ciaran smelled of clove and good tobacco.

"I am all right with that," he whispered. "Knowing your family is a rather extraordinary gift, I am finding."

"And when Brand talks about the kids calling you uncle now that you're rich, just know that he kind of loves you too."

"I do adore his practicality," Ciaran said. He gently dabbed his thumb at the corner of his eyes, careful not to smudge anything. "Now. You have guests. Let's have fun fucking up their stodgy worldview."

Lord Hermit stood at the focal point of the circle. He was the oldest of all gathered, and by ancient pact would be the one to assume rule in an interim capacity with Judgment gone. There would be politicking later, but for now, the seat was his.

"We will not open this meeting with the staff of office," he said. "The staff is lost, along with our brother, Pillan Judgment. We will honor his legacy at a later point, but for now, our city is under siege. We attempted to draw Lady Time's attention to the Westlands by removing many of us from New Atlantis, in hopes of picking our own battleground. We failed—her attacks in New Atlantis continue unabated. Why?"

"She doesn't know we're here," Lord Strength said immediately. "We were too damn subtle. We left too many of our forces behind."

Lord Tower gave this a thoroughly blank look, which meant he found the assertion lacking.

"Why would she come after us?" I asked. "She doesn't want to kill us. She wants to hurt us. She wants to punish us. Staying in the city and kicking down our buildings is exactly what she wants to do."

"I think Rune is right," said Lady Death. "We made bad assumptions because we didn't have good information."

"We continue to make bad assumptions because we overestimate her," Lord Strength said. "Her hit-and-run tactics are a response to her anger at seeing her ancestral home destroyed. Do not forget—she looks like an old woman, but she's still in her first cycle of life, and relies on brute force to solve her issues. She is emotionally a child. Our stratagems fail to take hold because we overestimate her capacity to even *comprehend* our plans."

"You've all been told about the ritualistic equipment that was destroyed when Farstryke exploded," the Tower said. He leaned back in his puffy sofa chair, somehow elegantly, and crossed one knee over the other. "If we are right, her anger isn't about the loss of Farstryke, it's about the loss of her seemingly limitless source of energy that said equipment provided."

"That does appear to track," Lord Chariot said reluctantly. "If we must rely on assumptions, at least that appears to be sound. We all saw her tactics change. From frontal assault to ambush tactics. If her source of power has been compromised, it could explain these hit-and-run attacks."

"Have we independently validated the truth about this . . . ritual she used?" Lord Magician said.

"There are records of it in the Hex Throne archives," Ciaran said. "I'm happy to show you."

"We need to talk about these two, as well," the Hierophant muttered. "Is Atlantis to have two Magicians?"

"That you should be so lucky," Ciaran said, as if he'd been complimented. "I do have some thoughts, however. Perhaps one of us can secure a Vegas residency."

"Let's focus on the matter before us," Lady Justice said. I'd watched her eyes flicker to the door every now and then, where Mayan and Brand had remained, and were now joined by Addam.

"Back to what Ciaran said earlier," Lord Strength said. "There are records? We truly know this equipment she used is real?"

"It's real," the Hermit said in a heavy voice. "Once upon a time, it was called siphoning. I may be the only person alive to know that, excepting our Empress, and make no mistake: the Arcanum at the time worked *very* hard to make sure that type of magic faded from living memory. It's a disgusting power—a form of cannibalism and slavery combined."

"So . . ." I said, and dragged out the word. "If we can agree that the ritual equipment was real, and we can agree that it was destroyed—then it means her source of magic really has been limited. She is vulnerable."

"Do we know if she can repair it? Or rebuild it?" the Chariot asked.

"From what I can gather—and I was, believe it or not, a young man when I last even discussed such things—it's not unlike imbued summoning circles," the Hermit explained. "The effort involved in creating the ritual and its devices is extremely difficult. How long does it take to create an imbued summoning circle? Years of work and dozens of magic users?"

"She is vulnerable," I said again.

"Except . . ." Lord Tower said, and drew out his own syllable. "We have no idea how much energy she'd already siphoned before the equipment was destroyed. We cannot assume she's acting as if her source of power has been eliminated. Only her ability to refill her power has been compromised. She's being cautious now, but that doesn't mean she's vulnerable."

I wasn't sure if he was lobbing me a softball or not, but I caught it. "Which is why a Quadrans Gambit might work."

Lord Strength slammed a hand on the arm of his chair. "Clear the room! Hermit, order the room cleared!"

"No," I said. I looked at the two Companions and Addam. "They stay. They all know about the Majeure."

"*Addam* does," Lady Justice asked sharply, just barely a question.

"Yes, it couldn't be helped, since it's how I pulled us both out of the timestream," I bit back. "He watched me use it—and he knows what it meant. It was unavoidable."

"And that's that?" Lord Strength demanded. "Do I get a say?"

I turned a flat expression on him. "Sure, but the problem is that you keep saying the wrong thing."

"Enough," Lord Hermit said. "This is a strategy meeting, and the Companions are elements of our strategy. They may stay. Rune Sun, do you know what you're proposing? You're proposing a Majeure battle with a woman who—if she truly retains any of the lives she's siphoned—may have a significant reservoir of energy left."

"Just like me," I said, and there, when you stripped away all the fancy words, was my plan. "I've only just *started* using the Majeure. I'll never need to rejuvenate to five years old. Or ten. Or even twenty. I have my *own* reservoir of energy."

"One you'll never regain," Lady Death said. She did not look happy with me. "It's not as easy as simply canceling out a year you have no desire to get back. It takes stamina to use, and your ability to draw on it can be depleted. You could cripple your use of it for months, maybe even years. Why make that sacrifice? There are other paths forward."

"Which paths save most of the city from burning? She won't stop what she's doing. Haven't you watched the broadcasts? It's not just a war we're fighting—it's propaganda and counterinsurgency. She's laying *all* of the deaths at our feet. At the very least, she's been reframing the narrative to suggest the lives lost don't matter because they are scions, while she protects everyone else."

The Hierophant sighed. "There's a reason you want to do this. What is it?"

"We all know she needs to be put down," I said. "I want to talk to her first. She knows . . ."

—and my brain gave me an immediate, Technicolor memory of the carriage house, and the masks, and—

I hesitated, thrown, not sure how to mention what needed to be mentioned. Brand saw my hesitation and stepped in, like he always did. I felt him moving to my chair. "Lady Time has somehow been able to identify and co-opt the resources used to kill Rune's father," Brand said. "It's conclusive. We don't think she's *allied* with all of the conspirators, but she knows some of them. The Sun Throne has every right to learn more."

"It's a brave move, young brother, and that's no lie," Lady Justice said slowly. "Truly. But if Lady Time is connected, even indirectly, with your father's murder, it may be a reason why you should *not* be the one to face her. Perhaps the wiser path is to wait, and flush her out, and fall upon her as a group."

"And the city burns," the Hermit said. "How quickly we forget the past, even those of us old enough to have lived it. Do none of you remember the March Strike?"

Well, *that* caused a reaction. I knew it from an old school lesson—I could literally see the heading in a textbook—but it was buried well in Atlantis's past.

"I'd rather the River's current not bring that one around again," Lady Justice sighed.

"The March Strike was put down," Lord Strength said. "That's the lesson of it."

"And we lost three Arcana in the uprising," the Hermit added. "It's foolhardy to be dismissive when it comes to the power our citizens hold—because they *do* have power. Lady Time is stirring unrest that could turn catastrophic. Lord Sun's plan may prevent that. It will cost little for us to support his Gambit."

"What do you need of us?" the Hierophant asked, though grudgingly, because he didn't like sharing his secrets and tools of war. I was half-tempted to lay claim to the tools of war he kept hidden in the Westlands.

"Find her," I said. "Find where she's hiding. Give me a target."

Ciaran and Lady Death stayed behind long enough to record some . . . I didn't know what to call them. Commercials? Interviews? Statements, maybe? Our own propaganda.

We used the recordings that Anna had snuck out of Lady Time's underground compound. They showed an entirely new side of Lady Time, and reminded me that, soon, I needed to find out what exactly had happened to those kids. It was enough for now that they were safe and healthy, but I know there were parts of the story they hadn't told me.

Using Lady Death, Ciaran, and me for filmed excerpts was intentional. Ciaran was a known trickster. Lady Death had publicly fought against the historic trappings of the Bone Hollows. I was young and untried, and more outsider than insider. We were a new face for an old institution, and the Tower gave us his implicit blessing by making himself scarce.

When we were done, Ciaran and Zurah headed back to the Magician's compound, just to pack up their things. Now that I was awake, we were going to plan our next move together.

Quinn, Anna, and Max were whispering—possibly colluding—in the corner of the living area. Addam, Brand, and I were debating whether it was too early for a beer. Lord Tower was gluing macaroni to a piece of construction paper on the outside patio with Corbie. I knew this because Brand had set up a live feed to record it.

Brand's phone buzzed. He glanced at the screen, answered, and put the phone on the table. "Mayan, you're on speak—"

"I can't reach Anton, I'm not getting a signal to his phone. Lock down your estate. Attacks have been launched at Half House and Pac Bell in the last few minutes—they may be trying to flush you out of hiding, if they don't know where you are."

I think the fact that Mayan used Lord Tower's first name had me moving quicker than anything else, because Mayan *always* called Lord Tower by his title around other people. Brand and Addam were already sprinting toward the patio door and—

And Quinn had started crying. That was the last thing I remembered before the explosion tore a hole in the wall: Quinn had started crying, a bewildered look on his face, as if he'd lived this moment before and didn't like the memory of it.

And then there was the explosion. I can't remember much of that.

I picked myself up from the hallway floor. I think I'd been flung into the hallway.

I staggered back and saw Addam and Brand on the ground—Addam had managed to bring up a Shield.

The children were huddled behind a table on its side. Max had flipped it over.

Through a jagged tear in the wall, I saw the Tower lying still on the flagstone patio, covered in the fading static of a dead Shield. Corbie was pressed under him. I saw his little body twitch—alive.

Hovering above the lawn was Vadik Amberson, and my rage became my instinct.

I flooded my body with willpower, feeling my connection to all my sigils, which I'd refreshed and refilled over the last day. I called on Fire and Shield and Telekinesis. The conjoined Companion symbols at my belt flooded my body with Speed bolstered by Endurance to protect my bones and muscles.

I moved.

The world was a blur of blue and green—sky and grass—as my body flew forward. I was already a dozen yards from the mansion before the shock of my displacement cracked the air in a sonic boom.

Vadik was wearing his Serpent costume—the scaled leathers hiding his face from me.

I swung a hand at him and lashed out with Telekinesis. The leather mask was ripped off Vadik's head. He yelped in surprise a second before throwing up a Shield—and not a small one. I felt his spell releasing from a mass sigil, like a train roaring inches past my face.

"You're not my match," I told him. "You're just not."

"Maybe, but I'm not stupid enough to face you alone. She *really* wants you dead," Vadik said.

He didn't move, and Brand was shouting in the background, but I'd already put two and two together. There was movement along the perimeter of the estate—pockets of movement in the foliage, where Vadik had somehow managed to tear holes in the estate wards.

As the mercenaries fired, I saw missiles come at me, just lines of fiery exhaust trails.

"Barrier!" the Tower said, and there he was, stepping to my side. He threw out his arms as midnight bled from his eyes and blood snaked from a cut on his forehead.

I linked my Shield to Lord Tower's. The missiles struck with a searing explosion. Lord Tower twisted his hand, and the Shield wrapped around the detonation, creating a sphere of sunlike fury. Lord Tower whipped his hand toward the tree line and the sphere hurtled back to the mercenaries, who exited my attention as quickly as they'd entered it.

More magic flowed from the Tower. A hand of rock rumbled from the earth and grabbed Vadik by the waist. Lord Tower held up another hand, and Vadik's Shield turned dark and cracked in a hiss of released power. The principality was slammed against the lawn with a force I could feel in my ankles.

I strode forward as Vadik coughed up blood. He said, "I yield. I've got to admit—that bastard wasn't supposed to get up. And wait until you hear what I have to say next."

"He's stalling, it's a tactic," Lord Tower said immediately from behind me.

That's when Brand started shouting again. I heard Anna scream.

Lord Tower gestured, and more stone covered Vadik, dragging him beneath the soil.

"Take the front, and I'll flank from behind," the Tower said. He shot off the ground and arced through the air toward the far side of the compound.

I called on my Speed, and ripped through the air toward the patio. Flagstones cracked beneath me as I came to a stop.

There were at least a dozen mercenaries in the living space, and I saw Corinne fighting more through the adjacent hallway as she battled her way to Anna. Max had a thin stream of fire swirling around his hand. Quinn had produced a Shield.

Brand had already put four men down, and Addam slammed another into the wall with Telekinesis. Not a single one of the mercenaries used magic. The Tower's words came back to me. *It's a tactic.*

Where was Lady Time?

I heard a scared sound and saw that Corbie was hiding in the bushes just off the patio. His eyes were wide and white, his face covered in dirt smudges. A mercenary heard the sound at the same time I did, saw it was a child, and raced to grab Corbie.

I threw willpower into my Telekinesis, reached out with an invisible hand, and crushed the man's trachea with a wet snap.

I ran over and swung Corbie up onto my hip, while touching a sigil and releasing a fresh, new Shield.

"They're down!" Brand shouted as he pushed his last assailant off his knife.

"Down!" Corinne shouted from the hallway. "I think there's more at the entrance—I hear fighting."

"It's the Tower," I said. "Corinne, find Layne, find Diana, find Queenie—I'll watch Anna for you. Addam, back her up. Quinn, maintain your Shield around Max and Anna, that's an order."

I didn't have to tell Brand where to be, because he wouldn't have accepted any order except the one he followed—he came to my side. I lowered the Shield as he held out his arm and took Corbie from me.

"Vadik?" Brand said.

"He yielded, but he's also a liar," I said. "Corbie, are you hurt?"

Corbie, in Brand's arm, had made himself as small as possible. I saw the shiny mop of hair shake *no* against Brand's shoulder.

"Let's put him in Quinn's Shield," I said, climbing through the hole in the wall and entering the living room. Brand passed me, walking in their direction.

"We need to move them to an interior room and secure the perimeter," Brand said. "Doesn't the compound have a crawl space? Maybe we can—"

Gunfire peppered the room. No—not guns—rocks. Small bits of stone shrapnel as Vadik exploded from beneath the patio and threw the force of his arrival at us. Multiple Shields sprang up or were flung between us and the rocks. Vadik stepped into the living room. He was bleeding from the nose, eyes, and ears.

Quinn's Shield overloaded and failed. A rock hit Anna and blood droplets sprayed the wall behind her from a nasty slice on her temple.

The outline of massive wings made of fire appeared above her. They stretched wide with a sound not unlike thunder. Corbie saw this monster forming above him and began screaming his confused head off. And I felt magic in that scream—a trembling rush of confused, directionless magic.

A roar came from outside as shimmering white light flooded through the hole in the wall. The roar repeated—a fluted, trumpeting sound—and a six-foot lance of bone and keratin pierced the plaster and impaled Vadik from behind. Vadik had barely a second to form an O of shock with his lips, then the horn jerked upwards. A window shattered and more wall crumbled as he vanished into the outside air, flung over the back of a four-ton unicorn.

I'd beat myself up for this later—not understanding what it might mean for a creature to spend tens of thousands of years as the familiar of an ifrit.

Flynn was not happy. His horn pierced the wall again as he tried to tear his way into the living room and find Corbie.

"Corbie, tell Flynn you're safe!" I shouted. "Tell him you're all right!"

"It's okay Flynn! It's Anna, she scared me!" Corbie shouted.

Flynn trumpeted his anger again and tore a drapery rod from the wall, which spiraled through the air and cracked a mirror on the opposing wall.

"Corbitant Dawncreek, tell Flynn you are okay!" I yelled.

"I'm okay Flynn, I'm okay!" Corbie piped up.

The horn withdrew from the tear in the wall. I heard heavy footsteps, and an eye the size of a teacup saucer peered in at us.

"What the almighty fuck just happened," Brand said, joining my side as I rushed toward the opening.

"Flynn has bonded to Corbie as a familiar," I said. "Where did Vadik land?"

Brand pointed to a crumpled body on the lawn.

I wanted to put Vadik down, but couldn't leave the others behind until—

The Tower walked into the room. Layne, Diana, Queenie, and Corinne were behind him, and Addam had the rear.

"Clear," Lord Tower said. "Lady Time?"

"I haven't spotted her yet," I said. "Mayan called just before it happened. He said there are attacks at Half House and the Pac Bell. He thinks she's trying to flush me out."

"But not Sun Estate?" he said.

I started to answer and stopped, because that was a question that made a lot of sense. "Did Mayan have a team watching Sun Estate? Maybe they attacked there and he doesn't know?"

"Of course he would know," Lord Tower said. He shook his head. "Later. Let's deal with the principality."

He, Brand, and I climbed through holes in the wall and tried to edge as unobtrusively as possible around the prehistoric rhinoceros. Flynn was standing on a flattened resin picnic table, making confused lowing noises.

"This?" Lord Tower said.

"Corbie's familiar," I replied, just for the quick pleasure of seeing Lord Tower's raised eyebrows.

We reached Vadik a moment later, stopping a healthy distance from his prone wreck. Vadik turned his head to watch us approach, but his arms were twisted in impossible positions. I couldn't be sure, but it also looked as if his spine was severed. The hole in his abdomen was a mess of failed Healing and fresh blood, with the pink, telltale glimmer of intestine.

His leather outfit had been torn open, revealing what lay beneath.

Vadik Amberson was covered in sigils. *Covered.* He wore a custom-built chest rig to hold them in leather slots. I couldn't even count them in a single glance. Sigils and mass sigils alike—and most of them? Most of them were forged into golden sunbursts.

"Our sigils," I said in a hoarse whisper. "My father's sigils. Those . . . *those are mine!*"

Vadik laughed spit-bubbles of blood.

"Now this makes sense," Lord Tower said in disgust. "I was wondering why you hadn't engaged in a Majeure battle. Are you even a real principality? Or just a cheap imitation of one? Anyone can cover themselves in mass sigils and pretend to be a god."

"I bled the Tower," Vadik coughed in satisfaction. "Didn't I? I claimed Lord Sun's tools of war, didn't I?" His eyes rolled to me. "And I know what it's like to have you broken and bleeding and *begging* beneath me."

Brand did not waste time with a dialogue flourish. He walked over while pulling a knife from his harness. As Vadik took a breath to say something, Brand felt Vadik's ribcage with one hand, found the right spot, and slid his knife in. He used his palm on the pommel to drive it home like a stake.

There was hard breathing and spasming, but what Brand walked away from was a dying thing, and he refused it the attention it no longer deserved.

"Claim them," Lord Tower said to me. "This is your legacy."

I stared at the sunburst sigils. An entire *arsenal* of them. I said, "By conquest, I claim these sigils as my own. Their will is now my will."

Power snaked through me, dozens of needlepoint connections, linking me to the devices.

I was about to say something, and that was when I saw the Tower's calm expression break into alarm. I realized he was reacting to something I hadn't seen yet—and even as I realized this, I saw a crystalline bolt of light streaking toward us.

Lord Tower stepped in front of Brand and me.

The magic hit his right shoulder and ate a hole in it. Flesh seared and dissolved as the wound spread. Within that hole I saw a portal forming, and through that portal I saw eternity. I saw the timestream widening and pulling Lord Tower into it.

He had one hand thrown forward, a last-ditch attempt to Shield; and he was looking over his shoulder to make sure I was ready to fight whatever came next. He saw me, and I saw him, and the emotion in that gaze was bigger than any single word could ever describe.

I watched the life go out of his dark eyes.

The portal anchored to his body expanded and flashed shut, too quick to follow. Lord Tower vanished in a roar of primal energy.

Standing on the lawn, just a few yards away, was Lady Time.

ENDGAME, PART 2

"Damn your eyes, but you're a slippery little eel," she said to me. "I just can't seem to knock you down, can I?"

"I don't . . ." Shock muddled my brain. I didn't want to understand what had happened. I couldn't understand why she was speaking about anything else but the Tower's disappearance.

"There's a prophecy about you," she went on. "It has a lot of people worried. Personally, I think you'd be underwhelmed if you knew. It doesn't even make much sense. But nevertheless, this I know, and this I see: if I cannot defeat you, I will never have New Atlantis. And yet, there you remain, scurrying away every time I slam my heel."

On the ground by me, a phone began to ring. It was the Tower's. I could see the screen. Could see Mayan's name. He would have felt . . .

"Bring the Tower back," I said hoarsely.

"Your Tower? Why would I do that?" she laughed. "For any matter, *how* could I? There's nothing to bring back, child."

Something was building inside me. An emotion filled with broken bits of rage and fury and trauma. The part of my brain that liked to hurt people who hurt me lit up like a power grid.

"Bring him back!" I roared.

She simply smiled at me.

My eyes burst into flame. Fire raced down my arms, and my hands filled with globes of light too bright to look at.

I said, "I met your father."

Her smile froze.

"I know more about your powers than you think," I added.

"Then by all means, attack my Shield. Have at it, boy."

She was surrounded in a Shield, that was true. I could see the dome around her—that near-impervious Shield that had started this chain of events weeks ago.

But that was the entire point of a Quadrans Gambit, wasn't it?

There was no limit to our power, if you were willing to pay the cost.

Break her Shield, I told the Majeure, and gave it as much of my life as it needed.

The power—that willful, nearly sentient power—reared to do my bidding. Magic raced from me in a blast radius. The crack of Lady Time's Shield was so loud the earth trembled beneath us.

Lady Time fell to one knee. A look of shock spread across her face. That frailty was a myth. I knew it even before her shock turned into a hungry expression.

"My turn," she said.

She lifted her arm—and her mouth formed a moue of confusion as black vapor began to rise off it. I could see the darkness bleed from her skin in slick, shiny beads, and trail off as smoke.

"It's disgusting," Layne said, and in the corner of my eye I saw them stumble off the patio with Addam behind them. "You are *disgusting.* It clings to you like rotting tissue . . . it's disgusting and wrong and *you aren't allowed it.*"

Lady Time understood what was happening quicker than I did. Layne was a necromancer—and Lady Time had used necromancy to steal power from others. Layne, somehow, knew how to release or reclaim it.

Lady Time swatted the air with a hand just as Addam raised a Shield to protect him and Layne. The Telekinetic blow hit with a sizzling sound. In fury, Lady Time slashed her arm again and again and again—each blow striking Addam's Shield explosively until it began to darken and break.

Rings of ghostly chainmail began to form on his chest, sparking into existence link by rapidly forming link. I could feel my own magic reach out for his—a connection with Addam I hadn't felt in a long time, not since the days I first met him.

I could feel the magic of the Westlands around me—I could feel the power of Addam and Anna, and the furiously approaching, skyborne power of two others not far away. The bonds between all of us were as real as steel bands, and their magic became my magic became our magic.

My Aspect grew.

Evolved.

Everything became a furnace haze. Sheets of white fire soared upwards as I became the living heart of a pillar of flame.

I heard a sound behind me and saw Brand drop to all fours and press his eyes into his palms. I couldn't see much else—everything beyond Lady Time and I was a boiled streak of fusion.

"I know your tools of ritual are destroyed," I said, and my voice sounded sibilant, like flame racing along a seam of coal. "You will not be allowed time to replace them. This ends now."

Beyond the rushing haze of flame I saw two figures land at my side.

A ten-foot-tall woman with frost-rimmed skin and pale blue hair.

Ciaran, his eyes burning with living magic, giving all spells around him a mercury shine.

And to my right, from the patio, strode a knight in chainmail. By his side was Anna. A growing dragon made of fire rose above her head, beating wings that cracked thunder.

Torrents of barely visible Majeure magic whipped from Ciaran and Zurah, quickly countered by arcs of the same power from Lady Time. She didn't even flinch under their assault.

I could feel magic building around Anna and shouted, before she could use the Majeure, "Addam, make Anna stand down! Make her stand down now!"

All I could do was hope Addam would handle it, because it was my turn to join the fight. My magic lashed forward and struck Lady Time, who immediately countered it with a third stream of her own power.

I felt the constant, draining tug as we battled her stolen energy. This was what a Majeure battle meant—tit for tat, second for second, waiting until your foe blinked or stumbled or flashed an exposed stretch of gut.

Fuck seconds. I threw a *year* of my life at her.

The opaque, almost iridescent magic mixed with my Aspect and flared into blinding white. Lady Time screamed and was blown backwards. She slashed her arm and righted herself with a quick, inelegant bit of Telekinesis, and flung up a Shield. Her astonished look lasted a full second before she turned and vanished.

We had her on the run.

But the Tower, the Tower, the Tower—

"I need to go after him," I said. The pillar of flame above me vanished, but continued to swirl over my hands and jacket. "I can do it, I can open a portal. I have to try!"

Lady Time had done it. She'd anchored a portal inside Lord Tower and pulled him through. So it could be done. I could . . .

I imagined shaking the timestream like a tin can and making the Tower fall out. And magic was metaphor. This was my life, my Majeure, my power. I could make it so.

Holding my clasped hands in front of me, I poured willpower into the space between them, and tried to stretch open a portal. A glimmer of the timestream appeared.

I gave it minutes, days, weeks, *months.* I spread my fingers and pulled them apart, and a cat's cradle formed between them. I could see the timestream's distant, raging flow.

My body started to shut down. People were shouting, but my failing hearing couldn't make sense of the words.

I fed what felt like another year of my life into the Majeure just to will my lungs into taking another breath.

More. I could pour *more* energy into this. If—

A fist slammed into my left eye. I stumbled back a half step, and Brand punched me again. He held nothing back, and the flames rising off my face made his knuckles blister, which should never happen if I was in my right senses.

He was sobbing.

"Don't you do it, don't you dare!" he cried. "Don't you do it Rune!"

My Aspect died. Brand saw that, stumbled, fell to his knee. I dropped beside him, horrified. "I have to find him, Brand. I can find him."

"You can't," he said.

"Rune, please!" Addam begged. "You saw what I saw. We have lost him."

"But *we* survived," I said desperately. "You and I survived. He could have—"

"We were thrown into a time loop. He was thrown into the timestream. We traveled through it, we saw how deadly it was," Addam said.

"But he could have—"

"Brother," Lady Death said in a ragged, grieving voice. "Someone has died here. I can feel it as surely as my pulse. Do you hear me? Someone died here."

"But . . . hearts can be restarted," I tried to argue. "What if—"

"The Tower and I spent days researching the timestream, trying to find a way to save you," Ciaran said. "If there was an easy way in, we would have found it. If there was a difficult way in, we would have taken it. But we do not know this magic, Rune. You do not know this magic. I am so sorry."

"But . . ." I watched Brand's face. Saw his broken expression. "Oh, no. Oh, no. No, no, no, no. No, Brand, no."

Brand got to his feet clumsily and came to me. He grabbed my face and forced my eyes on his. "Not that either. I don't want that Rune either. Do you hear me? Grieve later. Fight now. Because she does not get away, Rune. *She does not get away with this.*"

"I'm going after her," I whispered. "I'll use whatever power it takes. I need you to be okay with this."

He knew what I meant. That this wasn't the sort of fight where I could take him with me—and yet, he would bear the indelible cost of it.

"She doesn't get away," he said.

"Keep everyone safe."

I let go of him and began to back away. I looked at Addam—and my family, people I'd come to love. "Oh, gods. Oh, gods, someone needs to call Mayan."

"I'll do it," Corinne said from the patio. She'd grabbed Anna before Addam could, apparently—her hands were hooked on Anna's shoulders to keep her from joining us.

"Ciaran and I—" Zurah started to say.

"No," I said. "This isn't your Gambit. Yours especially—you can't afford it. Stay here and watch them. Please."

She shook her head angrily and squeezed her eyes into a glare to keep from tearing up. She came over and hugged me, and whispered in my ear, "You can use the Majeure as a source of energy when you start flagging."

I stepped away from them.

"Be careful what you ask for," Zurah added hurriedly. "Be very precise. Do not ask to find her—ask to follow her trail. It makes an enormous difference. But go before the trail fades—it's been minutes already."

Addam stepped to one side of me and Brand the other. They walked me away from the others. We crossed over the patch of grass where Lady Time had teleported. It was blackened and crisp, and broke into pieces beneath my feet.

"You will return to us, Rune," Addam said.

"You better have your fucking phone on you," Brand said.

I just looked at them, back and forth, until it was a memory I'd always have. Nodding, I turned and strode deeper into the lawn.

Maybe it was the magic. Maybe the Majeure was already heightening my senses. But even with them at my back, I knew exactly where Brand was standing—as I always did.

But I could feel Addam, too. I could feel Addam.

Shelving that thought, I called on the Majeure. I imagined my life as kindling. Seconds, minutes, days, weeks, *months*—I imagined feeding months of my life into the hissing grill of the magic.

Follow her trail, I told it.

There was a deafening sound, and a curtain of light ripped across the lawn, showing me a street. Lady Time was kneeling on the sidewalk, a hand pressed to her side.

I stepped through the portal, onto the grit of unswept asphalt. The air lingered with the smell of cold, burnt plastic. We were in front of the remains of Farstryke

Signs of our street fight were everywhere. The fact that so much damage hadn't been cleared yet led to sobering conclusions on the state of New Atlantis.

"You've hurt my city," I told her.

She straightened to her feet, still holding her side.

"It was a stupid move, trying to play the role of their savior," I said. "They would have all hated you once they saw the video clips my kids recorded of you."

Her surprise—and displeasure—was only a flicker across her thin lips. "Your verb tenses are interesting," she said. "But I've already abandoned those plans. I must. You gave too much away in the Westlands, child. You'll understand that soon enough."

She vanished.

Follow her trail, I told the Majeure, and stepped through the rippling portal the moment it stabilized.

We were now in an underground cavern—a truly titanic underground cavern. The wall of a building covered the face of the side opposite me. Lady Time was already walking toward the ten-foot-high front door when she noticed my portal.

"The next time you run," I said, "I'll burn you."

She was having more trouble controlling her irritation now. "Do you not understand that I've won? I'm simply on a new path. You know about the ritual, and the ritual equipment. Bravo, little Arcana. So now I abandon the city and rebuild. When I return, I promise, you will not see the blow before it lands."

"Or maybe there is no path left. Maybe you're just going to die."

She vanished—but I was getting better at spotting the rise of the magic before it actually manifested. I told the Majeure to follow her, and stepped into the warehouse that housed the simulacrums of Half House, Sun Estate, and the Pac Bell. Lady Time was running across the cement floor, past the Pac Bell, toward the partition that hid the false carriage house from view.

My stomach was threatening to heave, so I used the Majeure to eat a little of my own life force. Energy surged through my limbs.

I threw two years of my life at her while asking the Majeure to infuse it with Fire.

She swore at me in old Atlantean as she countered the Majeure attack, but her forearms were raw and blistering in the aftermath. She grunted and threw her own massive burst of energy at me—a feint, because she was preparing to jump away again.

I countered her attack and told the Majeure to take us both to the place I was picturing in my head.

The drain was immense—and it wasn't nearly as easy as stepping through a portal. We were both whisked across the island and dumped in unceremonious, nauseous heaps on a yellowing lawn by a swimming hole.

Lady Time furiously threw up a Shield. She'd already healed her arms, though her sleeves were browned and tattered. "Don't think for a second I won't throw everything I have at you."

"I don't think you have much left. I've got a good twenty-five years that I won't need again."

"Little snakes that spill all their venom in a single bite don't last long," she said.

She tried to Teleport, but I told the Majeure to block it. Months of life bled from me along with the magic. She tried to throw up another Shield—and I blocked it again, and then threw a wave of magic at her that I imagined as teeth—as sharp, serrated teeth.

She screamed as blood blossomed on her dress, and threw an insane amount of magic at the world. A ring of fire rose around me, and Lady Time vanished. She had expended even more energy to hide her trail to me, too.

I froze the flames, which cracked and collapsed into shards of ice.

I didn't need that trail, though, did I?

At my command, a portal formed before me, showing the warehouse. I did not walk through it. I just listened until I heard the pound of her footsteps in the distance.

I had a guess, and like any good guess, it was swarmed by a bunch of clues I'd already missed.

Take me home, I told the Majeure, and the dim image of the warehouse floor rippled into a new dark image: the Sun Estate carriage house, set against the deep purple ocean sky.

I stepped through the portal, onto my own grass lawn. My stomach convulsed. I barely dropped to all fours before throwing up.

Using the Majeure, I fed months of life back into me, deconstructed into raw, healing fuel. I rose light-headed to my feet and walked toward the carriage house.

The barnlike doors were weak and rotted. It took barely a second's energy to flick a finger and send its pieces spinning off into the night.

It should have hurt, what I saw as I walked into the building. The memories should have come at me with knives bared.

There was a lot of dark, spoiled leather and exposed wooden beams. Moldering straw was everywhere, and a fungal smell had long since covered the old scent of grease and animals.

I knew there was a daybed in the back room, with bad lighting and narrow walls.

There would be a sofa behind the partition in the room ahead of me. It would have hard wooden edges under meager cushioning.

The roof was vaulted like a cathedral, crisscrossed with water stains and spiderwebs. The spiderwebs had been there before, too. I remember staring at them.

Lady Time's heavy, pained pants came from the back room. On my way to it—as dust and dirt crunched under my boots—I passed a spark of magic. Mounted to the wall outside the door was a bent carpenter nail that radiated the magic of a sigil.

Its fastening had weakened over time. It took little to dislodge it into my palm. I almost laughed, because just like that, I had an eleventh sigil. Technically many more—I was just swimming in them now, wasn't I?

Lady Time was pressed into the corner of the back room. Half of her chest was covered in bright, glistening blood.

"I do believe my arm is barely attached," she gasped and laughed. "You followed me."

I should have figured it out sooner. Those simulacrums allowed Vadik and the Forerunner to spy on me. Why wouldn't they work in reverse? There was a connection between the false and real buildings.

And why not use that connection for travel, too?

I knew there'd been a reason she'd been running for the fake carriage house when we teleported to the warehouse. And I'd also remembered that brief, was-it-real sighting of her when I'd first been in the room.

Past that, when she'd sent forces to places I'd lived before to flush me out—Half House, the Westlands Compound, the Pac Bell—there'd been no attack on Sun Estate. She'd known we weren't there.

"You were teleporting to your bolt holes," I said. "Not into them—but near them. That's the sort of paranoia my Companion could get behind."

She chuckled, coughed up blood, wiped her mouth. "You are buckling a century of work. Do you know there were entire decades where I could only see and hear events outside the timestream—a virtual ghost existing only in the eyesight of my worshippers?"

"They aren't worshippers. They never were."

"Perhaps you're right. It's always a mistake to gamble when you don't know the odds. I badly underestimated you. You're rather quite good with our little power, aren't you? Somewhat of a natural."

I didn't say anything.

She coughed again and smiled. "I know you. I've watched you. You've made do with less your entire adult life. I know what that's like. I spent *my* adult life trying to survive and escape a never-ending series of moments in the timestream."

"Do you expect this to work?" I said. "Making a play for sympathy?"

"If you kill me, you lose the secret of unending power. Your people have lost the art of sigil making. You've lost the art of siphoning rituals. I can give you that source of energy."

"Maybe I'll just kill you and pry the secrets from your followers," I said. I watched her mouth open—and then slowly close.

I'd caught it, though. She was the only one who knew how to recreate the siphoning equipment—and she realized too late I had no intention of letting that secret survive this moment either.

She started to pull on her Majeure.

I didn't even need to use my own life to respond. This was my home. This was my court. The four mass sigils recently planted at cardinal points on the estate, and filled with Defense magic, were tied to me.

My willpower mixed with the earth and formed a connection between me and the mass sigils. I released their stored spell in a floor-rumbling flood, then drew their deadly magic to me while using the Majeure to build a thick Shield.

I let the Defense spell loose.

The carriage house exploded in pieces barely longer than a matchstick. In the settling smoke and debris, the two of us stared at each other from behind our Shields. Lady Time had been forced to one knee, but was attempting to use her remaining Majeure to rebuild her body. Her movements became spasmodic but strong, and she faced me on two feet.

"He was my *father*," I said, my voice raw and hoarse. "In every way that counts, he was my *father*. He made me into this man. *And you took him.*"

She attacked at the same time I did.

Our magic screamed across the distance between us. We hurled months and years at each other, compressed in blooms of incandescent magic. In desperation, she tried to destroy the estate, to distract me while she fled. I contained her magic. She tried to poison the soil, to light the mansion on fire, to boil the nearby ocean—and I turned the toxin to water, calmed the waves, doused the flames.

She grew weaker and smaller until, for a small forever, we were reduced to just the raw loss of month after month of whatever mortal time we had left—until she had nothing remaining.

I almost fell over, the end was so abrupt.

Lady Time's skin was withered leather. Her dress hung off skeletal shoulders. I drew magic from my exhaustion and set the heap ablaze.

For a minute I stared at the pieces of the carriage house. Small fires were dying on the grass, and the shifting smoke began to blow out to sea. The bent carpenter nail was heavy in my hand, so I put it into a pocket.

There was no reason to waste any more magic. None. The idea of wasting more than I'd already expended was criminal. And yet . . .

Ask them if they'll come to me, I told the Majeure.

My knees began to buckle as a portal ripped open nearby. Brand and Addam came running through.

I closed my eyes while they did whatever one did as they tried to figure out what the hell had happened. They'd see the body. The destruction. The lack of further threat.

"Hey," I said, and cracked an eye to look at Brand. "You punched me."

"I sure did," he said, while raking his eyes up and down my body for signs of damage.

"Can I hit you back?" I asked.

"I sure fucking hope so, if I ever try to do something as stupid as you were doing," he said.

I laughed, because I really did find Brand funny, and it was better than crying over what we'd lost.

And I also liked that Addam knew enough to see through the jokes. He stepped to one side, while Brand stepped to the other, and said, "You rest now, Hero. You rest."

THE RIVER

The River Room is a quiet place.

Sitting on a pier, just above the waterline under the stewardship of the Bone Hollows, it is made of three windowless marble walls. There is no wall facing the water: that is the point of the River House.

There is a breeze today, and every wave is tipped in white foam. Outside the building, in the open, rows of angled benches fan out. No one sits precisely next to each other, and there is little talking, even among friends and loved ones. Each is alone in their thoughts, thinking what they will say when it is their turn to walk into the building and speak to the River.

Inside the River Room it is an old custom to speak of secrets shared and secrets unshared. Some of the island's deepest magics protect the sanctity of those final conversations between two souls and the water's tide.

At the head of the seating arrangement outside the building is a single, ornate chair. It is reserved for the Empress, and make no mistake, people will glance at it more than once. If anything would bring her back to the island, surely it would be this—the wake of the Tower of Atlantis.

Inside the River House, Corinne Dawncreek paces along the marble lip that divides the edge of the room from the waves that slap against the pier. She shakes her head and begins to laugh.

I thought I would have trouble with this. What secrets do I have with you? And now I'm trying to decide what *not* to say.

I am . . . There is this . . . guilt. There is so much guilt. I think of you, and I feel guilt.

I held Mayan at arm's length after Kevan died. I accepted only the barest minimum of help, though he offered more, because Mayan is a good man and one of my oldest friends. But I refused. Because of you. Because I saw you as another Hanged Man. I didn't want my children near your court, and now I'm not sure I can forgive myself for that.

You finished raising Rune, and he is good and protective. You were capable of that. And if I'd accepted help sooner, my kids wouldn't have lived in poverty. Layne may never have fallen into the Hanged Man's path. Layne might not have nightmares, and I know they do, I know they still do, and it breaks me.

Corinne stops. Gives a small smile.

Hey. I said they.

Max sits on the edge of the drop, dangling his feet toward the water.

So . . . Okay. The thing is, Rune and Brand aren't exactly secretive about passwords. I mean, they fight all the time about Rune writing new passwords on yellow Post-Its that he sticks right on the monitor. So, sure, I read their emails. I know that's bad, but it's sort of court stuff too, and I help where I can.

Anyway, that's how I know they're looking for my uncle.

They've been working with private investigators for months and months. If they send someone to Antarctica, they'll literally have hired investigators on every continent—and I read one email where they're trying to find contacts at the international bases there.

And I also know it was your people that provided that report. You were helping Rune. I haven't said anything, because they don't want me to know, and I'm still getting used to how that makes me feel. Not many people have ever looked after me like that. I want to do the right thing for them, even if it's keeping my mouth shut and letting them take care of things.

Max pauses. He puts a hand over his heart, where his first sigil rests. He amends what he said by adding:

For now.

* * *

Quinn finishes reciting twenty-three important secrets he'd jotted down on a page of lined notebook paper. He will destroy it later, once he adds a few notes to his new Prophecy Journal.

I know it's a lot to take in. Maybe none of it will happen, but . . . but so many times, there's the Devil and the Moon, and Juror Waylan, and Lord Wheel, and . . . and gods, the Storm. And Tavis! Tavis almost always happens, and I miss him so much. There are so many different ways this *all* can happen, but it does happen *most* of the time, in one color shirt or another.

I haven't told Addam yet what happened underground. With Lady Time. Well, we told him a lot, but not about . . . what she did. What Lady Time did to me. How she took my Sight away.

I can't see futures anymore. I can barely see *my* future a few seconds before it's even about to happen. That's why I've been taking so many notes lately—because I think some of this stuff needs to be remembered.

But in the meantime? I guess I'm . . . normal?

I never can remember what that's supposed to be like, though. I never saw it happen before.

And I know this whole talking thing is supposed to be about secrets, but I want to say that I love you. I really love you, Lord Tower. You were the first person Addam took me to visit. He bundled me in a backpack and took me to see you, and asked if you wanted to be my godparent. Addam loved you, and I do, too, because you always made me feel important. You told me I had a rare gift, and that the city was stronger because of it. I'll never forget that.

I hope wherever you are right now, it's warm, and you can hear what we're saying.

I will look after him.

Lady Death speaks finally, after a long pause.

Of course I will. Even more so now that I know him. I'll finish what you started. I'll step into your very, very large shoes.

But that's not a secret, is it.

I suppose I never mentioned that Amelia and I were . . . close. For a certain period of time. Your daughter made very clear that her business is not your business, and yet . . . It's too bad that you and she did not speak more. You are more alike than you ever admitted to each other.

Lady Death closes her eyes. Smiles.

Who am I kidding? Of course you knew about us. That would be just like you. And if so, I'd like to think you must have approved, given our ongoing friendship.

Sleep well, my friend. Until the current brings us back together.

Lord Magician—the one with blue hair—floats cross-legged above the marble floor.

Pay attention, Anton. There was never quite time to share this truth with you before.

You wore too much black silk. Olive and taupe would have been beautiful against your complexion. Also, since you insisted on going everywhere barefoot, you needed a better pedicurist.

Ciaran pauses as a weary expression settles on his face.

Oh, you bastard. You magnificent bastard. I was just starting to have fun with you.

Brand stays inside the River House longer than anyone. He needs it, to still the noise in his head, finding the one secret to share.

Okay. So, look. I'm grateful you never told Rune what I said. About being in love with you. Which I'm not anymore—let's be clear about that? I don't doodle your fucking name in my diary or anything.

But things were confusing back then. Rune and I were almost done with that ten-year deal. We were planning on moving out on our own. It was scary, and you were safe, and . . . and whatever. I was young and stupid and said what I said.

You let me down gently, but . . . but you could be really petty sometimes. It drove me nuts, thinking you'd say something someday. I could see you dropping what I said like a bomb to make a point to Rune.

But you didn't, did you? I worried about that, and now I don't have to. And that's the sort of weird and complicated feeling that I'd stab if I could.

And, hey, since we're sharing secrets, I can tell you where Addam is right now.

Brand points behind him, to his four o'clock position, without hesitation.

I feel him. It was the same way it felt with Rune, back when our bond was still growing. I don't know what the fuck that's about. This is the sort of weird shit that always happens around Rune. It's like he puts personal ads in *Weird Shit* magazine.

Brand trails off and needs another few minutes to speak again.

I'm seeing that time differently now. All the time, I mean, since I lived at the Pac Bell. You always let me snap at you like an equal. You let me say shit to your face that no one else got away with. And that's not a tiny thing. I know that. I know that. And maybe sometimes, when I thought you were testing me, you were actually . . . I don't know. Testing Rune's development of the Majeure? Being fucking playful? Maybe you were kinder to me than I realized, because of what I said. That time. And maybe you would have been a shit boyfriend, but you were a half-decent dad."

He closes his eyes and adds, hoarsely:

And I'm going to make you a promise that you once made to Rune. He told me about it—when he and Addam went into the Westlands after Rurik. He got you to promise that you'd watch over me after so that, if the worst happened, I didn't—I didn't follow him.

I'll watch over Mayan. I promise you. I'll watch over Mayan.

I stayed until it was just me, Mayan, and Brand. We sent everyone else back to Sun Estate, because there were things to be said.

Mayan has always been one of the tallest men I've known. He stood a few feet from us, waiting, his gaze pinned on a spot in the far distance.

"Here," Brand said. Then he held out a knife—hilt first.

Mayan blinked in surprise and took it.

"It's a gift," Brand muttered.

"Thank you. Brand, would you mind if I spoke with Rune for a moment? Please?"

"Sure. I'll be at the car. But you need to stay with us tonight."

Mayan opened his mouth, and Brand more or less rose on his toes so that he could glare straight into Mayan's eyes.

"I will stay at Sun Estate tonight," Mayan sighed.

Brand turned and left. I may have blinked at him in surprise, myself. "I think he just gave you his favorite knife," I said. "I'm not sure why though."

"It's a weapon he uses to protect you," Mayan said quietly. "It means many things." He smiled and shook his head. "He also left when I asked. How long do you think I'll be able to milk that?"

"Six days. Don't shoot for seven—trust me, it'll backfire."

Mayan continued to look down at the expensive weapon he was holding—vulcanized coal, inlaid with obsidian and coral. "Brand has more potential than he's willing to admit. That's a problem, Rune. You'll need to deal with it at some point."

"I know," I said, and honestly, I did. We all would have growing pains as the Sun Court grew—and Brand's role in it was one of the most important decisions I had to make, because he wouldn't make the right decision on his own.

Mayan slowly moved his gaze to my eyes. "You wanted to talk."

"I noticed you didn't go inside to mourn him," I said.

He said nothing.

"Are you?" I asked. "Mourning him?"

The stare that Mayan and I exchanged was profound. I'm not sure he'd ever seen me so clearly before in a given moment, nor I him.

He said, cautiously, "I felt him when he entered the timestream. I felt his pain. His surprise. And then I felt nothing."

"I'd accept that, normally, only the thing is . . ."

"The thing is, he's the motherfucking Tower," Mayan finished.

"If every moment of time exists all at once, then why not pull him from the timestream at the moment he entered?" I pointed to the River House. "They want me to walk into that building and talk to the water? No. No, I'll do that when there's a body."

"They'll think we're crazy to look for him," Mayan said. "I will have to fight hard, and quietly, to use Dagger Throne resources. We'll need to talk soon about that."

I held out my hand. Mayan shook it.

Once Mayan and Rune leave, the waterfront is quiet. Orange and red rays of sun bounce off the water and turn the marble of the River House into a dusky pink.

A woman has waited to speak for a long time, unseen by all around her.

When she is ready, she rises from her chair and walks into the building. She speaks as she slowly approaches the water's edge.

I can't be like this for much longer, so I'll speak quickly. Though . . . are you even there to listen? I gave you what chances I could. At the very least, you're clearly not *here*, and that's a frustration.

I relied on you to help him. The boy is stubborn and reckless, and will be the death of me. You helped keep him from biting off more than he could chew.

But this is about secrets, isn't it? Forgive me. I have so many to share that they thicken the tongue.

I'm not entirely upset you're gone. I suppose I can admit that. You were a useful ally, and you managed the boy—unknowingly on my behalf, but you managed him. And yet, you were not pliable. You were never pliable. That means that you'd never be a very comfortable endgame weapon.

And I have a strong suspicion that an endgame has begun.

EPILOG

The Tower's wake happened two weeks after the events in the Westlands, which was just as well, since I spent half that time in bed. The use of the Majeure had burned through whatever reserve energy I had or was capable of replenishing. Those days were just a blur of sleep, protein, and Corbie sneaking stuffed animals onto and off my bed.

There was no way of knowing how much of my and Brand's life energy I'd used. Ten years? Twenty? I was almost certain I hadn't eaten more than thirty-seven years, since the effects of that would have been immediately apparent.

Lord Fool had been found. As suspected, he'd been taken prisoner by Lady Time—though the rest of his captivity was a bit of a question mark. He'd somehow wound up working happily in Lady Time's kitchen, manning the oil fryer. He'd been returned to the Revelry, but, for reasons he declined to share, he showed little interest in reclaiming his lost followers. That was a problem very much in need of a solution.

The Ambersons—those who'd survived Vadik's leadership of it—were losing their status as a named house. The Arcanum was currently investigating to see whether Vadik had been aided by his remaining family. At the very least, they would be stripped of all stolen sigils or artifacts from Sun Estate. If their culpability ran deeper, the house would be dissolved and all its assets absorbed into Sun Estate. I could have asked for harsher sanctions—I was encouraged to, actually—but the idea of punishing a once-valued ally for the actions of a single asshole grated on me.

There were signs that Warren Saint Anthony—the False Magician—was resisting his loss of power. For the moment, he continued to sit on the Arcanum. Whether he'd segue into a leadership position within the Hex Throne, or begin to operate as an independent principality, was unknown.

Ciaran was playing his cards close to his vest. I suspect he wasn't entirely anxious to become the operational head of a court that was just as much a corporation.

My armory had grown bigger with the absorption of sigils that Vadik had stolen from my father. Well, honestly, my armory was *created* by it. What that meant, I wasn't sure. It was a resource over twenty years outside my current experiences. Its return could not have come at a better time, since I was now responsible for the sigil use of others, too.

During my recovery, I read through Lord Tower and Ciaran's research on the timestream from when they were trying to rescue Addam and me. I understood now that I could have killed myself trying to find Lord Tower. I could have killed myself and Brand.

There was a particular metaphor that helped me understand the sheer task ahead of me.

Time isn't a physical stretch of space—but if it was, imagining the sheer size of it is almost impossible. Consider everything that was—New Atlantis, the Northern Hemisphere, the solar system, the Milky Way . . . *Everything.* All of it.

Now multiply that times every second that has ever existed. Because every second in the timestream is as big as all that space. And the next second? It's as if it contained its own unique copy of all that space. Finding Lord Tower without knowing where he was in the timestream was just not possible. I would have aged to a hundred before I could even comprehend the vastness of the task.

There would be another way to approach the issue. Someday. And I would find it.

I told Zurah and Ciaran about my rent-controlled apartment in LeperCon.

The days when I secretly gathered information on the fall of my father's court were behind me. I saw that now. There were too many people in my life to keep it a secret—and I would not gamble Brand that way. Not anymore. While much of that night would remain a secret between

Addam and I, we were far past the point where I could pretend that forces weren't moving against me.

So Zurah and Ciaran helped me box up the apartment and transfer the investigation to the now-empty Half House. Ciaran didn't complain about the physical labor once. In point of fact, he came dressed in farm overalls with the name *Wayne* sewn into the breast pocket.

"And Brand knows nothing about this?" Zurah said in amazement.

We'd just finished moving the boxes into the sanctum, and I'd already created a clear wall space for nine squares drawn in permanent marker. There were now three filled squares. A clipping of Ashton's face. A photo of Vadik taken by one of the coronation's photographers. And a pencil sketch of the Forerunner that Addam had drawn for me.

"I told him about the apartment before the pandemic hit. He never saw it, though."

"Will he now?" she asked.

"I promised him I'd involve him. Soon. Things are moving so fast. A few years ago, I was living off macaroni and cheese. Now my fingerprints are on the fall of three courts."

"Technically you re-destroyed the Hourglass Throne," Ciaran said. "Not sure if that counts." He made a sharp sound of delight and removed a lava lamp from the box he was unpacking.

"Fine," I sighed, giving it to him with a gesture. "Don't tell Quinn. It was a set of two, and he got the first, but Corbie snuck it out to Flynn's paddock, and Flynn ate it."

"I do adore both the seventies and your domestic woes," he said. Brushing off the knees of his overalls, he straightened. "I'm going to walk off the house again and look for eavesdroppers one last time, and let you two talk."

He tapped his way up the spiral staircase. We'd torn Half House apart no less than four times to make sure all the magical listening devices were destroyed.

I broke the short silence by saying, "So. A frost giant, huh?"

She threw back her head and let loose a roaring laugh. "So says the pillar of fire. I expected phoenix wings, at least."

"Yeah, but what about Anna? That dragon? Points."

"Points," she agreed. "For all three of those children. Layne went toe-to-toe with Lady Time. The other has a familiar. Those children are very lucky to have you to train them."

My smile faded, just a bit. "I want them safe. More than anything. I just hope I can be what they need me to be."

Zurah left the box she was unpacking and walked across the sanctum floor. She put a hand on my arm. "You have resources you have never had before. Even without Lord Tower."

"I have enemies I never had before, too."

"No," she said firmly. "That is not true. You have always had enemies. You see their rustle in the foliage now only because you are scaring them. Do not forget that."

I nodded and looked out the window. I'd missed the view of our back yard; it was good for soul-gazing.

After a pause, I said, "I like you."

"I like you too, little brother." Her phone buzzed, and she brought it before her. "Ah. The sandwiches I ordered have arrived. Find our erstwhile Lord Magician and meet me in the kitchen."

As she went downstairs, I went up, where Ciaran was walking the perimeter of my empty, old bedroom.

"Not a smidge remains," he announced. "I only wish we could have traced a connection beyond that which lay between here and the Warrens warehouse. Perhaps we'll learn more from the devices there."

"Thanks for helping me deactivate them."

He waved off my gratitude. "I'm glad you've decided to keep this house. It's quaint. I'm always impressed when people build on the bones of their past rather than the ashes of it. It makes for a solid foundation."

"Can I ask you a question?"

"You are so sweet with your warnings," he said,

"Why did you return to the Hex Throne?"

He gave me an elegant shrug. "It's not as if I never felt responsible for it. There are people who depend on it—very smart people who do very smart things, and who make the court an insane amount of money. They deserve safety and protection. And whenever that was jeopardized, it bothered me. Such as when I learned Ashton had found a way to sneak into my Westlands compound. Impudent little shit."

"That was a while ago. Why now? Why reveal yourself now?"

"For many reasons." He gave me a bit of side-eye, the sunlight in his eyes flashing across his thick lashes. "But if you're fishing for how many times your name winds up in my autobiography, then yes, I did this for you, too. I can't begin to understand the current you are caught in, Rune Sun. But you need friends at your side. I am now in a better position to help."

I began to say something soppy and awkward, so he raised a nail and waved it at me. "It's not without its rewards. I get beat up often around you. I get blown off my feet, knocked unconscious, batted into walls . . . I'm really not a good fighter."

"You pulled the Tower out of the sky," I reminded him.

"Yes-yes, true, but that's somewhat the point. When you're as powerful as I am, you gain a fondness for anything that leaves bruises. I see interesting days ahead, Youngest."

"Youngest?" I said.

"Too many people call you little brother. Did I hear someone mention food?"

"Yes. Let's go grab some and talk about prophecy."

This wasn't a fade-to-black moment. I could feel his sharp, curious gaze on my back as he followed me down the stairs. Then I wondered which part of my back he was looking at, but when I glanced over my shoulder, he was buffing his nails on his overalls.

As Ciaran moved into the tiny kitchen with Lady Death, I texted the Hermit, saying, "Can we talk?" Then I ran for the chicken salad before I ended up with tuna.

Before I even had time to choose my bag of chips, my phone was beeping back at me. It read: "Now is fine." There was a brief surge of magic which no one caught except me, because I was waiting for it. Fool-me-twice and all that.

I said, loudly, "Are you on my sofa again?"

"I was invited this time," Lord Hermit said from the other room.

I walked back through the archway with my sandwich, half of which I put on a plate in front of him. "I'm not sharing my chips," I said. "You have to earn that sort of love."

He pushed back his brown cowl and tucked his sandaled feet beneath him. "Unnecessary. And I was expecting your call. I suspect it's about the prophecy."

I'd never really studied the Hermit before. Not only was he the oldest Arcana currently serving on the Arcanum, he *looked* it. I'd never wondered before why he maintained a late-middle-age rejuvenation. For the first time I considered that perhaps he, too, could not regenerate younger.

"Does he do that often?" Lord Hermit said to the others.

"It's like he's eyeballing the fattest chicken in the coop, isn't it?" Ciaran said.

"Look," I told everyone. "Yes, I want to know about this prophecy. And don't worry, my expectations are low. Do I save the world? Do I turn evil? If I turn evil, do I have a really cool and scary title?"

Lord Hermit's smile didn't exactly reach his eyes, and I began to wonder if I did want to know the answer to the question.

"Zurah, Ciaran, please give us a moment. If Rune wants to discuss this with you afterwards, I will not stop him. But I believe it must be his informed choice."

Lady Death and Ciaran exchanged a look not unlike any two super-powered beings who could hear through concrete might exchange. They stepped out on the porch and let the screen door slam shut, which sent a fresh wave of pollen into the kitchen.

"I wonder yet if you realize this seat could be yours," the Hermit said to me.

"You better be talking about the sofa."

He shrugged. "I lead the Arcanum by law for the interregnum. We must find a long-term leader. Perhaps it's time for a new voice."

"Ah, okay. No. I vote for you. All for you. Do you have something you want me to sign?"

"Perhaps it's best, Rune Sun, if you don't joke with me. Your humor can be misleading."

I put my sandwich down on the coffee table and took a seat in the only armchair. My armchair. I couldn't remember why we hadn't moved it to Sun Estate yet, but I was glad we hadn't.

When I was settled, I said, "I'm not ready for that, Lord Hermit. I'm just not. I support you in this role for now. You are wise, and apolitical, and I respect that."

The Hermit grinned at me. *"For now,"* he repeated.

I may have colored a little. "I'll always try to be honest at where I stand."

Now he laughed. "Oh, you most certainly will not. You are the trickiest Arcana to come along in generations, and don't think I don't know it. But that's well enough. If you end up playing games with me, I'll likely deserve it. You have a rather consistent moral compass, Rune Sun."

He folded his hands in his lap and added, "Very well. Leadership issues aside, you wanted to speak."

"I did. About a couple things. I want to return the battleship to America, for instance."

"Indeed," he murmured. "You wish them to know *why* we have it?"

"Oh, gods no. Not even a little. But we can come up with a story that makes sense. The ship should be with them. And those sailors should be laid to rest in family plots. Is that the sort of thing I need to run by the Arcanum?"

"It is, but as you were awarded the ship in a formal raid, your decision will carry weight."

"Okay. And also, yes, I'd like to know this prophecy."

He turned bushy, salt-and-pepper eyebrows at me.

After a long, long pause, he spoke. "In the days before Atlantis revealed itself to the human world, what did humans believe they knew of Atlantis? In the most general terms?"

"Well . . . nothing. That was the whole point of being secret. They thought we were tied into—"

"Atlantis, Rune. What did humans think they knew of *Atlantis?*"

"Oh. That it was a myth. That we were an ancient civilization that sank in the ocean."

"It was never a myth, Rune," the Hermit said. "It's always been a prophecy."

I said nothing. I thought of saying something, and then immediately forgot what I was going to say, because . . . What?

"That is a secret known only to certain members of the Arcanum," he said. "But it's been corroborated time and time again by some of our most powerful seers. And it also ties into another prophecy that, some twenty years ago, gained new perspective. *When the Sun rises again; Shadows will burn; Hidden enemies will stir; Atlantis will sink beneath the waves.*"

"Twenty years," I mumbled. "When Sun Estate fell?"

"For the first time in its history. Ever. Do you realize how unusual that is? For a court to last this long without ever once faltering, even for a generation?" He leaned forward and fixed me with a stare. "What does the prophecy mean to you, Lord Sun?"

"What it's always meant," I said. And the numbness gave way to . . . anger? Exasperation? When has my life ever been different? "I've got a fight ahead of me."

Anger.

Yes. I felt *anger.* Did I really need an ancient prophecy to point out my obvious? That people had been after me since I was a teenager?

"There is something else," I said. "I'm not leading the Sun Throne."

The Hermit blinked. "Excuse me?"

"At the coronation, Lord Tower told me it was time to name my court, and I said the expected thing. But screw that. My father led the Sun

Throne. I may be the Sun, but what I'm starting is something new. And I do things differently. The people around me are different."

The Hermit slowly smiled at me. "And what do you run, Rune? What do you sit at the head of?"

The back door slammed open—which wasn't easy to do. "You may want to come outside," Lady Death called in.

The Hermit and I exchanged a surprised look. I was halfway across the kitchen before he unfolded from the couch.

Zurah and Ciaran were on the porch, staring above the backyard. Spirits—blue-skinned, indigo-veined air spirits called Apsaras—flitted among tree branches; swooped along the eaves of Half House; pirouetted in the empty flowerbox of Queenie's empty little cottage. One of them even landed on the railing near me, to stare at the now-flowering vine I'd summoned into being once upon a time.

Apsaras—sky dancers—appeared rarely and often alarmingly during critical turning points. Usually you could drive yourself nuts interpreting their timing.

"And I ask again," the Hermit murmured behind me. "What do you lead, Rune Sun?"

"The Misfit Throne," I said. "I am Lord Sun of the Misfit Throne."

And all that led to today: a barbecue. Because we were Atlantean and we celebrated our victories, no matter how Pyrrhic, no matter how great the losses. The survivors needed that.

As people ran about the estate finishing chores before we fired up the grills, I was told Lady Justice was being escorted to the patio for an unexpected visit.

When I went out there, Addam had beat me. He was facing the ocean, giving me a chance to sneak up and goose him. My hand was half an inch from his ass when I backpedaled because holy *shit* that was not Addam.

Christian Saint Nicholas sensed my stumble. He turned and smiled, and gave me a quick bow. "Lord Sun."

He had a thicker Russian accent than Addam or Lady Justice. He was as tall as Addam, with the same sandy hair and burgundy eyes. Unlike Addam, he had a widow's peak and vampire-pretty hair. At his side, in a custom-made sheath, was a legendary weapon of the Crusader Throne—a telescoping naginata with a mass sigil embedded in the actual blade. When fully extended, the polearm became a devastating battlefield tool. Addam had told me once that Christian stored a Defense spell in the mass sigil, meant to protect family in an emergency. He said in all likelihood that meant enclosing Quinn or Addam in a sealed bubble, because Christian treated anyone under the age of one hundred with rabid overprotection.

"Christian," I said. "I didn't know you were coming. Can I get you a refreshment?"

He didn't have time to answer, because Addam was escorting Lady Justice onto the patio. Christian and he must not have greeted each other yet, because they did this weird little dance where Addam acted mature and professional, and Christian rolled his eyes and slapped him into a bear hug.

Lady Justice and I took a seat at one of the patio tables, while the brothers stood. I used the hem of my T-shirt to wipe at the pollen, but that only smeared yellow everywhere.

"A financial agreement," Lady Justice said, putting a folder in front of her. "It will be a starting point, at least, as we navigate the separation of my sons and sister from the Crusader Throne."

I looked over to see that Addam and Christian were involved in some sort of staring contest, silently communicating a range of emotions that would make Brand and I proud.

"We can talk about that later," I said. "Today is all about burgers and beer. You both will stay for dinner, won't you?"

"There are other matters to discuss first," she said. "I wanted to wait until you'd recovered from your use of the Majeure before we addressed it."

She set that before me like a landmine. I know she did. But she hadn't been raised by Lord Tower.

"This means you've manifested the Majeure," I told Christian.

"Christian!" Addam said, conflicted between staying quiet and being genuinely happy, especially now that he knew what that meant.

"Because I think your mother is making a point by saying this in front of you and Addam," I continued firmly.

"You have put Addam at risk," she said. "Do you understand that, Rune? I know your court is more . . . accessible than most. That you share intelligence among each other. But scions far stronger and less well-connected than Addam have been silenced for knowing about the Arcana Majeure."

"That's enough, Mother," Addam said.

"Let her speak," Christian told him, gently but firmly. "You are a new court. Do not turn away advice."

"There were years where I would have greatly appreciated advice from other members of the Arcanum," I said quietly, and waited until Lady Justice flickered her eyes away from mine.

It was time to nip this in the bud. "How long have I been a house, Lady Justice?"

"That would be rhetorical," she replied.

"Actually, no. Six months? Nine? And in that time I cut the Hanged Man's throat, and became a millionaire overnight. And now I've put Vadik Amberson in the ground, and regained control of a significant portion of my father's armory. All within nine months. You may need to get used to the idea of me not being poor. Give it time and I may not even be poorer than you."

I didn't get the full effect of her shifting eyes behind her sunglasses, but the small smile said enough.

"And I know the rules regarding the Majeure," I added. "You are permitted to confide in consorts and Companions. I had every right to tell Brand—and Addam? Addam will have my ring. I—"

I bit that off with an exasperated huff of breath. "Godsdamnit," I said. "Why do I keep bringing this up at the worst possible time? Addam, I'm sorry, I promise, this is so damn important to me, I don't mean to shout it out like this. I'll make it up to you, I really will, but—I mean—will you marry me?"

"I will marry you, Hero," he said.

"There," I said, and slapped the table. "Addam has every right to know about the Majeure."

Lady Justice dipped her chin. "We're done here, then. Make no mistake: my wedding gift will be lavish, so that I may prove a point."

She rose, went to Addam, and kissed him on his cheek. "Perhaps I will stay for your burger party. Though I was hoping . . . if he was around . . . perhaps I could visit with Quinn?"

Addam blinked for a second in surprise, and then blinked a bit more because his eyes got wet.

He left the patio briefly to escort Lady Justice and Christian inside, where Diana was waiting at a discreet distance to find out what was happening. She took over from there. I stood by the table and waited for Addam to come back. I pretended to be wiping pollen stains from my shirt, but mainly was twisting and bunching the fabric in my hands to settle my nerves.

When he was back, he didn't stop until his hands had slid around my waist.

"You always did hate the word boyfriend," he said.

"You know I meant this, right?" I said. And maybe my voice broke a little. "I just . . . I want to do this. And I want people to *see* this. I need everyone to understand that you're not just joining the court—you've agreed to assume a powerful place within it. So it really is a marriage, right? Even if there weren't a ring, it would be like a marriage. But I want a ring. Because I'm not sure how a guy like me ever got a chance with a guy like you—but I did, and I do, and I'm not letting you go."

I'd pushed back enough so that Addam could stare at me. And that's all he did—he stared at me, burgundy eyes swimming with tears.

"I used to always dream of fighting," I said. "In my actual dreams.

There's always fighting. But now I dream of you, too. I dream of you, Addam Saint Nicholas. Will you marry me?"

"I will marry you, Rune Saint John."

"I love you," I said.

"I love you, too," he said back.

Not all decisions swarmed with Apsaras. Not every important moment was backed by orchestra music, or fireworks, or a crowd of allies and loved ones.

Sometimes the most important moments in life end in something as simple as the smile that my fiancé and I exchanged.

After a forced nap at the direction of Brand, I woke to the smell of burgers grilling.

I lingered in front of my bedroom mirror. I'd spent an uncomfortable amount of time doing that lately, trying to see if my use of the Majeure had aged me at all. It shouldn't have—that's not how it worked—but I was obsessed with the lines around my eyes. Brand had finally taken pains to loudly remind me of *every fucking summer you lost your sunglasses and forgot to replace them.*

"You've done that for *minutes,*" Anna said in exasperation at the door. "Do you need a comb or something?"

I bit down on my smile. Anna had been shadowing most of my moves ever since I woke up from my second Majeure coma. She didn't say why, but I think she knew I was hurting. In her own way, she was trying to protect me.

"Come on, let's eat," I said, and we trekked through the mansion to the main floor.

Everyone had flipped over the news that Addam and I were formally engaged. The barbecue became a party. If that wasn't enough, there was an honest-to-gods engagement banner hanging from the chandelier above the main hall. Diana was offering helpful instructions to Queenie, who was on the top of a ladder, tying the last cord into place.

"You just had that lying around?" I asked Diana.

"I am prepared for many eventualities," she said.

"You don't have one for, like, my death or anything, do you?"

Diana gave me a quick look and said, "Crimson silk with gold lettering. Very tasteful."

I was ninety-two percent sure she was joking.

"Don't forget you have court hours tomorrow," she added. "There are already thirty-six names on the docket."

"Names? Of what?"

"Of people," she said. There was a second—just a second—where Diana stared hard at me, and I played dumb. "Apparently, members of the Revelry are looking for a new home, and our young people made an impression on them during their captivity."

"Can I rule them?" Anna asked. "For practice?"

"I am not prepared to have this discussion," I said. "I don't even know if I want cheese on my hamburger yet. No, I'm going in that room. It'll be quiet in there."

I went into the solarium, which adjoined the patio where food was being set up. It was not quiet. I managed to walk in at the exact second that Quinn snuck up behind Max's armchair and rubbed a ferret in his hair.

"What the actual fuck!" Max shouted, which sent a wide-eyed Corbie scrambling into another room.

Quinn let loose a flood of words. "I'm sorry Max, you're my best friend, but there's this prophecy, and I'm trying to change it. So now you won't be my arch-nemesis and rub a ferret in my hair!"

"You bought a ferret just for that? Oh hell, it smells!"

"His name is Remus," I said loudly. "I need to tell Lady Death I accidentally stole him. He's a mouse hunter. I'm finding another room."

So I walked through the open archway into the ballroom, where Corbie was rifling through his toy box for the swear jar. He'd staked that corner of the wide marble space as his own—though at some point we'd likely need to consider building an actual ballroom again.

On the mantel of a walk-in fireplace was a new framed photo. Lord Tower had Corbie on his hip, and both of them faced away from the camera. There were perfectly defined tiny chocolate handprints on the back of the Tower's blue silk shirt.

Corbie didn't know he could summon Flynn yet. I'm not even sure he could do it outside truly emotional circumstances. We needed to handle that carefully. I'd decided we'd start bringing Corbie inside the enclosure. Flynn would never hurt him, and being close to Corbie might lessen the need to see each other and prevent accidental summonings—and it had been one hell of an expensive headache getting Flynn back to the city from the Westlands. As soon as Corbie was old enough, we'd hire adept summoners to train him.

It would be expensive, and worth every cent of it, because when you had a gift like that you should do more than learn how to contain it. I learned that the hard way with Quinn. You should learn how to celebrate it—it was a rare and special thing.

Corinne came bustling into the ballroom just as Corbie found his swear jar. She chased him back into the solarium, and then came over to me with a cup of lemonade.

Outside, the stereo began blasting Soup Dragon's "I'm Free."

"I heard you were up," she said. "Nice nap?"

"Stop it. This is getting old. I wasn't careful what I wished for."

"You've earned the right to recuperate."

"There's too much to do. Actually, I wanted to talk to you about that."

Her face slid into that blank Companion neutrality.

"I have sigils now," I said. "I have a court. And we need weapons. We need so many more weapons than we have. I can't be unprepared anymore—not with the Tower gone. Godsdamn, Corinne, I need help even *managing* my sigils now. This is an entirely new level of resources. I can finally store spells in advance, and be able to respond sooner to emergencies."

Many would go into the protection of Sun Estate—into everything tied to its operation and defense. And Max. Quinn and Addam and Diana still had a lot of their own, but they were a factor as well.

Corinne slowly smiled. "Do you remember what Kevan did for you? For your father?"

"He worked in the magical research area."

"Yes. The area in charge of your father's tools of war. Are you asking me to be your quartermaster?"

"I totally am. Begging, even."

"Then I would like to do it—*aggressively.* Starting tomorrow. I want to turn the Amberson House upside down to find what else Vadik stole from you."

And now I smiled, because I'd made a good decision.

She continued, though, her excitement obvious. "A research division, at the start of your court, would be a long-term investment. I can look up Kevan's old contacts. And the type of magical research we do can be geared around you—what you need now, what's important to your day-to-day activities. And gods, Rune, the biggest magical research entity on the island is the Hex Throne, and with Ciaran maybe taking it over? It's just smart. He could do a lot for us, and maybe we could even do something to help him. He'll face challenges."

Maybe I'd even made a great decision.

There was a crash of glass, the sound of feet hitting the ground, and someone shouted, "Don't let him run outside!"

Corinne sighed and hustled toward the solarium.

I had about half a second of solitude before Layne leaned through a hallway door. "Is she gone?" they whispered. "Can we talk?"

From the way Layne nervously entered, I knew what was coming. I just did. I'd known this was coming for weeks. It felt a little like I was about to get punched in the heart.

"Of course," I said. "Is everything all right?"

"Yes. It is. It really is. But . . . Ciaran is on his way over. I want to ask him something big."

I said, subdued, "You want to apprentice with him."

Layne's face faltered between scared and happy. "I'm that age. And he knows magic—he can help me train my magic. And . . . I mean, he . . . he's helping me with . . ."

I held out my hand. Layne's seesawing expression settled into simple gratitude. They ran over and hugged me. Afterwards I took their hand and tugged us over to two chairs by the archway.

"He helps you with your nightmares," I said.

"He does."

They look like they wanted to explain what that meant, but they didn't need to. I understood. "I get it," I said. "People want to see the bright, shiny exterior. It makes them feel safe, thinking you've moved beyond the bad stuff. But what's inside? No. That doesn't go away that easily. Darkness hides. If Ciaran is helping you with that, I approve. If he can train your immolation magic, I approve."

"Then why do you look so sad?" Layne whispered. "And your eyes are glowing."

I closed my eyes against my Aspect. "I'm sad because I failed you."

"You haven't!"

"I really have," I said.

"I just . . . I want what Anna has with you," Layne said. "I think I can have that with Ciaran."

I heard the bounce of plastic and splash of liquid. I opened my eyes to see Corinne frozen in the archway with a horrified look on her face.

"Auntie, it's okay, it's okay," Layne said hurriedly, standing up. They didn't go to Corinne, just danced a bit in place, not sure what to say next.

"No," Corinne said.

"I'm old enough to get apprenticed. I'm *past* the age where a lot of kids get apprenticed. I—"

"No, please, no Laynie," Corinne said. Tears spilled over her lashes.

"Listen, please, you know Ciaran. You know he'll be good to me."

"I know you're fond of him—"

"Not like that. Never like that. I trust him. I trust him with whatever I want my life to be. That makes sense, right? I just want to *be* someone someday."

"Layne Dawncreek, you faced Lady Time," Corinne said sharply. "You made her *run*. You're already someone." She swallowed and wiped at her cheeks. "This is important to you."

"So important," Layne whispered.

I kissed Layne on the cheek.

I kissed Corinne on the cheek.

Leaving them with my blessing, I walked back into the solarium, where everyone was gathered in a quiet, eavesdropping crowd.

Staring at Max, Quinn, and Anna, I said, "You better not go anywhere ever."

"Hell no," Max said. "Quinn and I are going to freeload for years."

"We really will," Quinn said.

Anna shrugged and said, "I'm waiting to inherit."

"Plus, Addam said you said that we're rich now," Quinn added. "Why leave?"

"I want a raise," Max said.

Brand lightly slapped the back of his head. "All of you go outside. Set the table. Let's eat."

He managed to herd everyone outside except for Anna, who stubbornly wanted to stay by my side.

"Fine," Brand said. "Watch him, and tell me if he gets tired."

Anna slowly put a potato chip in her mouth and munched on it. She said, "Snitches get stitches."

Brand left. Anna stayed with me. I was beginning to feel a new bout of tiredness dragging on my limbs, damn Brand, but tried to hide it. This is what it was like: stretches of normalcy suddenly crippled by bone-deep weariness.

So I went over to one of the puffy, mismatched sofas we'd liberated from a used furniture store. Anna sat next to me and said nothing. She was good like that—it reminded me so much of Brand. Or, to give credit where credit was due, Corinne.

"We're not really rich, you know," I said.

She gave me a fixed stare that was her version of an eye roll.

"What I'm saying, is that we're not rich, but we do have access to funds that we didn't before. I've been meaning to ask you something, but I'm worried it may upset you."

"Is it about giving me an allowance but not Max?"

I smiled. "It's about your scar. I wanted to know if you'd like to talk with specialists about it."

Her hand shot to the curtain of hair that she tended to drape over the left side of her face. She stopped just short and balled her hand into a fist—and then, slowly, relaxed.

I think she surprised even herself by saying, "No."

"No?"

"No. It makes people nervous. That's an advantage, right?"

Oh, gods was she like a Companion. Smiling at her, I reached into my pocket and rummaged around, eventually pulling out the silver dove brooch I'd bought in the Arcanum bunker.

"Hold out your hand," I said.

With wide eyes, she complied. "I can feel it," she whispered.

I laid the sigil on her palm, then covered it with my own hand. I said, "This sigil is now your sigil. Its will is now your will, Annawan Dawncreek."

I felt her hand jerk as the sigil connected with her. Her one visible eye glimmered with tears. She closed her fingers around the sigil and brought it to her chest.

"They'll tear it off me in a battle," she mumbled.

"It's not for field work. It's for practice. Don't worry—you'll have your battle tools one day."

She bowed over the sigil for a second. I heard her breathing steady and she said, "Everyone's hugging you all the time lately. You must be sick of it."

"Not really."

She jumped at me, her thin arms squeezing in a ferocious embrace. It lasted for barely a second before she was up and off, running out to the patio to hide her emotion.

I sat there by myself for only a little while longer, because the sounds of my family outside—for just that moment—was everything.

I climbed a tower in a storm. Lightning set the world afire in strobe-like gunfire.

I was not scared of the storm, or the darkness. But I was terrified of the climb.

I looked up and saw an infinity of slowly decreasing handholds, and the horror in my chest felt like death.

I woke up with a start, heart in my throat. I smelled burning cloth and looked down to see a crisp brown handprint on the bottom sheet of my bedding.

And that scared me more than anything. I had to sit still for a full minute until I stopped shaking.

I'd been having nightmares lately—not the normal dreams, just moments where the simplest things were a source of formless terror. It wasn't prophecy. There was no metaphysical shakiness about it. It was just a nightmare.

It wouldn't take a psychiatrist to tell me I'd been fending off too much trauma lately. There would be an accounting.

The red numbers on my bedside clock told me that everyone else was still likely awake. I'd begged off earlier when the exhaustion hit particularly hard. Now, I whispered quietly through my bond *I'm okay I'm fine I'm okay* so that Brand wouldn't come charging upstairs to punch my bad dreams.

I wasn't ready to be around people again. I pulled on sweatpants and a T-shirt, and my last pair of clean white socks. (My socks, now that I knew which sock drawer was mine.) I was just finishing when a tiny knock sounded on the bottom pane of the door. So I opened it and looked out, then looked down, and saw a stuffed red and black animal being held up toward my face.

"You're up late," I told Corbie.

"I got a video," he said, and held up his phone with another hand. "And Liege Ladybug wanted to stay with you."

We ended up going back into my room and crawling on the mattress. Corbie had taken to using his new phone to capture candid family moments, including nose picking, butt scratching, and sneeze wiping.

This, it turned out, wasn't one of those videos. My breath caught as I saw a paused clip showing the Tower's face.

"Oh," I whispered. "I know what this is."

During the last equinox celebration, Lord Tower had babysat the kids. That wasn't the shocking thing. Of *course* I asked him to watch the kids while the adults went out for the evening—who better to protect my estate in my brief absence? No, the shocking thing was that Corbie had somehow maneuvered the Tower into accepting an invitation to his neighborhood school to be Corbie's show and tell.

The Tower had point blank refused to let anyone else show up at school that day, but I'd heard the event was recorded.

My heart hurt. Oh, did my heart hurt as I reached out and pressed play.

"But where's your tower?" one of the kids was asking.

"It's a metaphor, young one," Lord Tower said. "It stands for the fortitude of Atlantean institutions."

"Is it made of stone?" another kid asked.

"Yes," the Tower said with a smile.

"Can you make my freckles disappear?" another kid said. "My oldest brother knows how to make freckles disappear."

The Tower bowed his head for a good three seconds, and then giggling started to break out across the room. Until the phone camera panned back to the audience, I didn't realize he'd cast a mass glamor to give every child different colored, polka-dot-sized freckles.

("Mine were purple," Corbie said.)

"How old are you?" someone else shouted.

The Tower's lips curled slightly. "How old do I look?"

Kids started shouting everything from eighteen to six million.

"I am old," he said. "Older than New Atlantis."

"That's old," a somber kid in the front row agreed.

"Do you really know Corbie?" another demanded suspiciously. "Corbie DAWNCREEK?"

"I do indeed."

"Corbie is weird," the kid concluded.

"Is he?" the Tower murmured, and even on video I saw the shadows swirling in his eyes. "Perhaps you'd all do well to be just as weird. After all, Corbitant Dawncreek is kin to an Arcana, and summoned me here. And I came."

Well, that silenced them for a few seconds, except for an unfazed Corbie, who took advantage of the gap in talk to say, "Rune said he lived in the Pac Man."

"Do you mean the Pac Bell?"

The camera panned on Corbie's broad shrug.

"The Pac Bell is my home," Lord Tower said. "Rune came to live with me when he was about ten years older than you, my young friend. Both him and Brand. Do you all know who Brand is?"

There was a clamor at that, and I'm almost positive at least three children actually screamed.

"Do you have a job?" someone asked.

"I do," he said. "I've had many of them. It's been my great privilege to look after the city, and find our footing again in this strange new world we've created with the humans. Just as now it's my great privilege to make room for a new generation of caretakers."

"Do you have a Dad?" yelled a girl in pigtails—whose name was Elsie, and whom Corbie had already asked to marry at least twice.

The Tower smiled at her. "Not for a very long time."

"Are YOU a dad?" someone else shouted.

He quieted over his answer for a moment, and then said, "Yes. I have children of my own. I've fostered others. I'm a godfather. It was never quite one of my gifts, but I did get it right with the last two." He paused and smiled at the room around him, then settled his eyes on Corbie. *"They appear to be giving me grandchildren at the very least."*

The video ended.

I felt a sob clawing up my throat, its fingernails taking flesh with it. But that was as much grief as I allowed myself, because there was a wide-eyed six-year-old staring at me. I wanted to keep my shit together for him. For all of these new people in my life. It was only a matter of time before I asked Corinne if any of them would want to take my name.

Corbie said, in a wavering voice, "He saved me."

"He did. That makes you special, you know. In Old Atlantis, being saved by a hero was a type of blessing."

Corbie puzzled over that. "Like when I sneeze?"

I hugged him and said, "Why don't you go see your Aunt Corinne? I bet she wants to put you to bed."

In the darkness, I made my way to the steep stairway in the northwest wing, up to the turret roof.

I wasn't alone for long—even before I heard his steps on the ladder, I could feel him approaching. It was how I always knew I'd finally woken from a nightmare, or when grim thoughts were finally lifting—I felt the approach of my Companion.

I opened my eyes against the struggles in my brain—and Brand was watching me. He sat down, and we stared through the darkness toward the invisible ocean surge.

"I'm okay," I told him. "Corbie had this video . . ."

Brand groaned. "He's been running around showing people. It's like sniper fire." And that was the first time I noticed his own eyes were red and swollen.

The words crashed out of me. "He's gone. Wherever he is, I can't reach him, and it's like he's gone, and I don't know if I'm enough," I said hoarsely.

"I don't know if I'm strong enough to protect us, even with allies."

Brand said nothing for a moment, thinking that through. He said, "When shit goes wrong on the estate—when something breaks, or people are fighting, or there's a construction decision—do you know where they go?"

I turned my head to look at him. "Yes. You. That's a fucking awful pep talk."

He continued without pause. "But when something goes really wrong? When there's a demon walking down a street, or an avalanche headed our way, do you know who people run toward? You. They run to you, Rune. Because you have, you do, you always *will* be able to handle the serious shit. I'll never bet against you."

I said, "Yesterday. You bet against me *yesterday.* Max had to pay you five dollars because I didn't do that tenth pull-up."

He blew a raspberry at me, and then said, "We're going to be fine."

"Are we?" I asked. "We just learned the people who broke my father's court are still . . . here. Waiting. Will they come for us now that the Tower is gone? I'm not enough, Brand. I'm not enough to protect us."

"Goddamnit, Rune, look at everyone in our life. Look at all the people we've brought into it—the people we protect now, and fight for. They aren't stick figures in a diorama, they're our family. They move and react. And that is the good thing about family—this is the payoff. It's not always about *you* taking care of *them.* They take care of you, too. So fuck whatever problem is headed our way. There's one of it, and a dozen of us, and it doesn't stand a chance."

I warmed myself in his words, calmed by the strength they offered.

Eventually I cleared my throat and said, "Everyone still awake?"

"Eh," he said. "There was some drama. Layne tickled Corbie, and Flynn popped into the ballroom. Corinne and Diana are trying to figure how to get him out."

I gave Brand an incredulous look.

"I'm guessing we'll have more moments like this to look forward to?" he asked.

"Until Corbie's trained, yes."

I expected Brand to start swearing, but instead a slow, sharp smile appeared on his face.

He said, "Our boy is going to *rule* that fucking playground."

"By the way. What did you do to terrify Corbie's class?"

"Meh," he said. "The first time I dropped him off at school, I tried to be funny and spoke in a Yoda voice, only they didn't know who Yoda was, and also, maybe, it sounded a little bit more like Darth Vader now that I think about it."

"I'm going to need you to be like this forever."

"And by the way," he said, "Diana also cornered me over the Revelry applicants. About how surprising and convenient it is, getting the pick of Lord Fool's best."

"Hmm," I said.

"Because you acted all surprised," he added. When I didn't reply, he said, "It's possible she's figured out that you're a manipulative little shit, and also that she approves."

"One might also use the phrase *freakishly brilliant at seizing an unexpected opportunity.*" Lady Time was a monster, but she wasn't wrong about one thing: ready-made bodies of supporters came in handy.

"One might," Brand acknowledged, "but it's pretty fucking unlikely I'll ever say that out loud."

At that point, Addam came out. He was juggling a plate filled with cookies, and Brand slid over to make room between him and me. I'm not sure when we decided that Addam sat in the middle, but it felt like a thing now.

"Kids in bed?" Brand asked.

Addam pulled a face. "I heard Max whisper something urgently about locating grass seed so that *they* never find out, and then they all disappeared. I do not want to know if I am *they*. So I have escaped, here, to you."

Brand pulled a small black box out of his pocket and thumbed open its lid. Inside was a gold ring with two overlapping motifs engraved on it:

a sun and a scale. Brand said, "Will you still agree to marry my dumbass scion, who still hasn't put this on your finger, even though everyone already knows about the proposal and there's a fucking banner hanging in the main hall?"

Addam stuck out his ring finger. Brand slipped it on, and we all stared. Then Addam began to say, "It is very—"

"Nope, no, nope," Brand interrupted. "I heard Russia in that, and you only get that Russian when you're pissed or emotional. We will not be crying anymore tonight. Got it? Welcome to the family, now give a stout nod."

"It is very beautiful," Addam said, and snuck a sniffly breath while nodding.

"So I guess Diana gets to plan a wedding," Brand said, while holding a not it finger alongside his nose.

"I was thinking either that, or maybe we elope in America?" I said, while covertly wiping at my own eyes.

Well, that had them both turning to stare at me. So I added, "I've got a battleship to return, and we need a vacation."

ACKNOWLEDGMENTS

I could go on forever. My apologies in advance for everyone I miss.

I dedicated this book to my writing group, but a special shout-out to Michelle, Justyna, and Vivi for beta reading. That involved countless hours of exceptionally detailed work to help me get across the finish line. I appreciate you all so much.

For Ben and Keith of TGG Podcast for their talent and support and my first official HOURGLASS review. To David Slayton for the wonderful blurb (and for the gift of reading his masterful urban fantasy). To Julie Czerneda, a friend and godlike sci-fi writer; and Patricia A. Jackson, teacher and author (read her urban fantasy debut!). To Meredith Moon for the life-saving web and IT support.

In a breathless shout: To Bruce for the stunning blanket. Steph (@electricpurple9) for the idea of using the chicken church, and also for finding blueprints of Beacon Towers! (I literally have the floorplans of a mansion demolished in the 1920s, to preserve the accuracy of where Brand drags Rune when they go room to room.) To Charlie for customizing the Beacon Towers blueprints. To Neya for contract advice. To Krista for a million and one things. To Mary for helping establish a TTS merchandise store. Thank you Dkauffman, @hearts530 (Sam!), @orbynit, Perry. To @aildreda and @raenbowpunk for helping name Lady Death. To Luga and God of Mugs and @Quass for Wiki work. To @atavaniel for Lady Priestess's name and Lady Moon's name. To @flarpfreak for Lady World's name. To SheLion-Who-Misses-Remus for helping name Remus, and Vic Grey for naming Flynn. To @PirateTrisha for Lady Justice's first name and diminutive. To @egglorru for the kakodaimōn naming. To @electricpurple9 for Cornelius's name. To @KahviPro for Christian's Naginata. To One of the Many Brians, Jake Shandy, Menonorc and Matty (for Liege Ladybug, too!), Kop, Oblivionsdream, MJ, Reece, Glasspunk, Alix, Rox, Natasha, Alex, Cole,

Kathy Shin, Fiona, Frost Dragon, Kelsi, Thurmond, the author T. Frohock, and so, so, so many others. To be continued for six more novels... One of the things I love best about this series is sharing the world-building with longtime readers. I want people to be a part of this city.

To Lachlan Criptid for sensitivity reading on disability issues, advising on Bethan, and helping pave the way for Tavis. To Dr. E. Del Chrol, Chair of Humanities, Marshall University, @kingamongknight, and Katie Rask for Latin translations. (And Katie for her friendship!). To 8/11/20, the day I found out readers had appropriated a typo as their own war cry. (Helltdcctdcdctyc is when Brand gives up swearing at Rune and just bangs his head against a keyboard.) To Michele Zorrilla, who works at Insomniac Games, and asked me if Rune will appear in Spider-Man undies. (Huge applause to that game for its wide suite of accessibility options.) To Meghan Elizondo for helping navigate GR issues and restore lost pages.

Many thanks to the staff at Pyr—Ashley, Marianna, Hailey, Jennifer, and others. Thank you to Kim Yau at Echo Lake Entertainment, for media rights. To conference buddies Shawn and Arin; and Multiverse, ConCarolina, WriteHive, WorldCon. To the massively talented cover artist, Micah Epstein. I would not have completed this first trilogy without you. And to Audible for all its support, and especially its amazing, amazing, amazing narrator, Josh Hurley. To Flyleaf, Quail Ridge, Glad Day, and all the amazing booksellers out there who tirelessly support and champion new authors.

To my friend and superstar agent, the phenomenal Sara Megibow of kt literary. To my amazing editor, Rene Sears, who didn't blink ONCE when I first told her I wanted to publish a nine-book series. To my family, both near and far. I love you all. And my friends—especially the ones who refuse to let me hide for long (Love you Lance). To all the artists, writers, singers, poets who found inspiration in these stories and shared them back with me. I am constantly in awe of your talent. To the Discord crowd, especially folks like Pei and Sia and all the moderators (you'll get a book dedication someday too) – for your kindness, empathy, advice, and unflagging support. To Brink Literacy Project for letting me be a part of the Tarot Literary Deck—and letting me choose the Sun card! To Open Eye Café (and Michelle, Jack, Brady, Heather and others) for the picnic table and friendship. To Rainbow Crate (a marvelous book subscription service) for the constant support and amazing giveaways. To Matt, Jessica, Raisa, and all my colleagues who put up with my vanishing to conferences. To Miss Hubbard, the first teacher who recognized and rewarded me for writing, and cemented a lifelong passion.

And to you. Literally, yes, you. You right there. Thanks for joining me on this ride.

ABOUT THE AUTHOR

K.D. lives and writes in North Carolina, but has spent time in Massachusetts, Maine, Colorado, New Hampshire, Montana, and Washington State. (Common theme until NC: Snow. So, so much snow. And now? Heat. So, so much heat.) Mercifully short careers in food service, interactive television, corporate banking, retail management, and bariatric furniture have led to a much less short career in higher education. *The Last Sun* and *The Hanged Man* are the first two novels in his debut series, The Tarot Sequence. K.D. is represented by Sara Megibow at kt literary, and Kim Yau at Echo Lake Entertainment for media rights. Please visit kd-edwards. com for a glossary, content warnings, and lots of free stories.